HER MONSTER

Who rises for you?

M. A. ROSA

HER MONSTER

Copyright © 2020 M. A. Rosa

For information contact:

M. A. Rosa

http://www.marosabooks.net

Book and Cover design by M. A. Rosa

ISBN: 9798657505962

First Edition: July 2020

10 9 8 7 6 5 4 3 2 1

Dedicated to those who suffer my work.

CHAPTER 1

Knight in shining trench coat

I DESERVED TO ESCAPE. But white townhouses guarding a gloomy London street disagreed and bounced back my cries for help. When I scurried during my fight to survive, my echoed shrieks heralded a brief life's end. My life. The sky agreed with determined pursuers, as splattered raindrops on the urban filth created the street's slippery sheen. Stay or flee; death hunted me. A guttural growl behind me sunk my hopelessness deeper. The claustrophobic night further closed around me, and demonic howls mimicking my moans grew closer.

I lunged at the black street, my fists clenched tight, and screamed into the nothing, "I'd rather die than go back!"

My mistakes began as soon as I disappeared from a society gala. The second mistake? I never considered how a formal gown and stilettos might affect a dash for freedom. A shuffle on teetering five-inch heels produced wobbled steps and an awkward run-walk. White knuckles clenched the jade dress, but no matter how fast I scurried, they kept pace. I used to laugh at horror movies when a stumbling mummy always caught up to a running person. I no longer laugh.

A blackened alley garbled my name, "Sarah. Sarah." When shadows stilled and obeyed the spooky call, my tiny neck hairs tickled an alarm. Before my shocked eyes, several tipped trashcans came to life and expanded as they breathed. A red telephone booth's door slightly opened as it inhaled. As the street's ominous shapes lumped heavier, a buzzing streetlight snapped off. I stood in stuffy darkness—with them.

I glanced for a better escape route, but cracked asphalt snagged a thin gold heel. Mistake number two bit me in the butt, or should I say my ankle? Agony bloomed up my leg, and my knees crumpled to the slimy roadway. Disjointed laughter drowned a sharp cry when I struck the pavement. My bodyweight skittered tender palms across the broken road, and gravel embedded deep in my delicate skin. Wine-colored nail fragments suspended in midair and raindrops paused before they hit the ground. From the darkness, someone cast a Limit-Motion spell. The maniacal person twisted my senses and altered how I perceived reality. Fanatical tormentors dragged out the inevitable. I refused to quit.

Again, I slammed into the filthy ground, and painful pebbles under my knees tore at delicate silk. I bit my tongue, a copper taste filled my mouth, and they laughed. Desperate despair demented a determined youthful woman, turning her into a cowardly animal. More nails splintered as I grappled pothole rocks.

Across a shoulder, I expected to see someone paused half-way through a death blow. I gritted and searched the gloom but found nothing. As they enjoyed a bit of sport, my distressed whimpers tumbled into frustrated sobs. Fearful demonic cackles and suspended time sagged my head and torso above a puddle. Bloody knuckles broke the water's surface as a rainbow oil slick swirled and oozed between my icy fingers. A red curl fell from a rhinestone clasp and fanned in the oily muck. Sick ideas about death and a rotten meat stench pulled my gut into my ribs when canapes ate earlier threatened to join hair and dirty water.

I clutched my wet abdomen, and past a bare shoulder, a phantom breeze brushed my skin. Sounds decomposed, and shadows froze, a thick fog blanket rolling across the shiny black road. The dense silence hurt fired senses more than dry heave scrunched muscles when someone or something joined us. Who or what paused the worst evil ever known?

Brisk movement again flashed, but before I could sit on my haunches to investigate, I became weightless. Fearful eyes bulged even wider when a man lifted me, and a trapped squeal discharged.

"Are you daft? Save yourself!" But the obscured stranger never answered. "Did you hear me?" When the questions met more silence, I pounded the man's damp coat lapels. Either pure terror or my hidden enemies froze a would-be-savior. A blown newspaper caught against his leg while he scanned the thick gloom. When he touched an outer thigh, my muscles contracted as I tracked his pointed stare. When he found them a short distance away, murky phantoms recoiled. I posed another logical question, "Who are you?"

The foolish man again ignored me as we stood paralyzed in the dense fog. Drizzle and profound silence drenched us, but the soundless vacuum and suspended time flickered. The spell snapped the same moment a shoe slipped off afoot. Between the dangled foot and the pavement, an expensive heel dropped in slow-motion until near the ground. Then it tumbled normally when someone released their Slow-Motion hex. I exhaled brief hope.

A male voice boomed behind the tall stranger, "Sire!" Broad shoulders blocked my view, so I never saw who foolishly joined us. Muscular arms tightened around me.

From a shoulder, an even tone spoke to the new voice, "Our ride, please Dmitri."

Six elongated black forms cackled a disjointed chant. "Try as you may—take her away—rue day." More shadows separated from their inanimate objects. The flat gray Victorian townhomes, minus their shadows, looked one dimensional as abnormal silhouettes called the broken darkness. Void-like blobs slithered along the gutters towards my shapeless tormentors, condensing into faceless humanoids.

The fearless man realigned his chin against the bizarre scene as I buried amongst soft overcoat pleats. "We're so dead."

A faint Eastern European accent enriched his rich baritone voice as he said, "Miss, thank you for your concern. Alas, if you hope to live past tonight, please consider your silence."

The man's words slinked humanoid shadows closer. I drew no comfort from his firm grasp, confident tone, and ridiculous courage. When the rot intensified, my vision darkened as I swallowed rising vomit. Tires squealed, men murmured, and acrid rubber stung my nose as I tucked into merciful unconsciousness.

4

* * *

A shiver from a million spiders crawled along my flesh as I jerked awake, and a leftover, trapped scream died in my dry mouth. I awoke to find my neck bent at an unusual angle and against a solid, cool surface. Weak arms and a painful ankle prevented sitting upright, and fresh nausea rolled my stomach when I tried. I groaned. But my face only partly lifted from the dark glass as fingers splayed against a black car window and streaked the breath condensation. No longer tormented by my family's trademark rotten meat odor, I drew comfort from a new leather scent. When mages cast spells, non-humans smell the telltale aroma a mile away.

Blurred vision supplied a quick assessment as I sensed no imminent paranormal threats. But the tires screeched, and an engine growled as I rode in my savior's car. I struggled to uncurl in the tilted vehicle but produced a squeak. When the automobile straightened, I gripped the quilted seats, and a palm smashed against sleek door paneling. Again, and again, the swerving car's gravitational pulls ping-ponged me in the cabin. A strong need to know if we escaped clutched my hand to the rear headrest as I peered from the back window. Busy London streets swapped for the A1 North's moderate traffic, but the oversized SUV still bobbed and weaved around slower honking vehicles. Why did he drive without headlights?

The passenger side reflection cast from blue dashboard lights snared my attention. Two glittering rhinestone clips dripped red ringlets plastered to my skin. Black meandering rivers from mascara, flushed cheeks, and scarlet lipstick smudges created a hooker-like appearance who enjoyed a three-day cocaine binge. A soaked and torn dress chattered my teeth, but the rescuer read my mind. A brown glove twisted a rear console knob, and before I thanked him, ribcage muscles scrunched under achy bones. A twisted gut felt impossibly full, and a scratched hand flew to contorted lips.

"Miss do refrain from retching in my auto, as my driver detests cleaning up bile," the voice from the road purred beside me.

The mysterious driver's head trained on the wet pavement. Annoyance clipped a similar accent, "Sire, since when am I the chauffeur? The thanks I get for giving Sprat the night off."

If we rode together, who drove? Tense knuckles flew off the cocoa-colored seat, and my fingers splayed at the curious passenger. "Ignis."

A white pinprick light grew golf-ball-sized, and the weak yellow glow illuminated the backseat. My magic big time broke a cardinal rule, never to expose humans to sorcery, but a mad dash inside a stranger's car excused the irresponsibility. The hazy glimmer revealed my confident hero sat in the dimness. I breathed relief, and the tiny glow grew brighter.

The man stared transfixed at an invisible landscape whizzing past a black window, and a leather glove curled under his chin. The other hand rested between us on the middle armrest. A tasteful overcoat, Burberry scarf, platinum cufflinks, and a chauffeured SUV broadcasted comfortable wealth.

"Hey. Thanks for—"

The silent man leaned closer to his door like he avoided a sick person. "A mage. Of course, you are a bloody mage." The hand between us snatched to his lap.

"Excuse me?" But before I brightened the light and extracted my disappointed savior from the shadows, a fresh ankle throb broke the weak spell. The pain crumpled thin concentration and extinguished the faint orb at my shaking fingertips. How did the guy stay so during the street's spooky events or when a stranger practiced magic? Humans categorized witches as Halloween fodder or new age fanatics, and disbelieved magic existed.

The motorist's silhouette spoke, "You ended a card game to rescued one of those?"

Despite constant jerks around other cars, my rescuer persisted a calm taciturn behavior. Did high-speed adrenaline chases and magic in his rear seat happen often? "Who are you guys? Thanks for the assist but can you just pull—"

"Do they still give chase?" said the knight in shining trench coat, his jaw catching the blue dashboard lights.

Energy weakened, and my trembled fingertips oozed a delicate glow instead of a radiating beam. "Sir?"

The driver shifted his head upward, and after he paused, "Cannot tell, Sire."

"Ignis!" The tiny light changed from dull yellow to a brighter white.

The rear passenger cracked towards me, and I swallowed. "Extinguish the sphere this instant."

When the mysterious stranger leaned closer, I illuminated my savior's face and identity from obscurity. A realistic SGI horror movie monster flashed ruby-colored eyes, drilling into my blue ones. Other headlights caught the aberrant pupils, and crimson became empty silver. Imagine a blind dog's eyes but on a human. But no man sat with me. After I figured out who he was, I wanted a time-reversal or amnesia spell. That night, a different sheen forever slicked reality. A gasped recoil extinguished the magical light as I slapped freckled cheeks when I scrunched into the farthest corner. My family's uncertain doom swapped for a monster's torture. "You—you are a—a—"

"A what pray tell, Miss?"

"—a—a—" Atrocious eyes erased every word loaded on my snappy tongue, as I traveled with the most unholy befoulment of God's greatest creation.

The driver oozed, "Well, I know what she is, a stuttering dolt."

The human shell housing a monster inside, plucked off a glove one finger at a time. Once the leather freed, a bare hand extended towards a cringed shoulder. "Quite enough, Dmitri. Let me introduce myself, witch, I am Count Vasile Dimitrov, former chancellor to the Immortal Nation—" The introduction endangered my future breaths more than the ones my family risked in London.

"Prod—Prodig—"

"At your service, Miss." The scourge acted like greeting a mage fell beneath some perverse dignity.

When the car pulled off the A1 other cars disappeared as merciful dimness hid the abomination's eyes and allowed me two words. "—A prodigium!"

The driver growled.

"You—are—are—prodigium." I named the arrogant lord's brand of horror.

The singular form of prodigia was prodigium, the Latin word for monster or omen. The evil ghouls inspired worldwide imaginations humans wrongly called them shrtiga, strigoi, or vampire. But the freaky creatures sucked worse things than blood. I never met one of the cursed few but managed to score a lift with their old leader. And why say, the former chancellor of the Immortal Nation like the foul thing lost an undead election? Who knew the nasties even had a government. I shuddered.

"We risked our lives to rescue some retarded witch?"

"Now, now. Those statements are—what is the term—"

"Politically incorrect, Sire?"

"Precisely, m'boy."

"Lemme out!" When damaged nails tore at the door panel, my sick captor chuckled.

"I shan't risk my life and pull over."

"You didn't care that they were going to kill me, did you? You just wanted my bones!"

"Though mage and immortal battle each other in this infernal war, I perish the thought of eating one of you."

"I agree, Sire. And I lost them."

Again, a gloved hand rested between us on the divider. "Most excellent, thank you, Dmitri. As usual, you served me well." The armrest's long fingers strummed in time with my thrashing heart as he counted my last moments.

"I forgot how mortals unfear death. But die once, and you would dread it. Therefore, why prefer death to a ride with a cursed being like myself?"

I ignored the terseness. Broken nails intensified their claw for a door handle, but when icy metal met a shaky touch, a sound clicked. A new destiny and doors locked in place because I lacked potent magic to pick the locks.

"Let her jump."

"Ignis."

"Stop obstructing my driver's view at once. I do prefer to reach home before the—"

"—sun rises soon, Sire." Sunlight killed prods and their watered-down fictional counterparts, and that night the star took its sweet time to rise.

"You state the obvious." What aggravated the snide lord more, the driver, me, or the situation?

A horn blared, and a compact car swerved off the road to clear the way. "You never mentioned why you rescued that—that—" For emphasis, headlights snapped on the second, 'that.'

"I'm curious why they wanted her dead and use the information to my advantage."

"But, Sire—"

An expensive lambskin glove tapped a headrest. "And I also desire a silent ride." The mouthy human driver acted afraid of Count-Chancellor-Whatever because he shut his mouth.

During a few mute moments, my mind raced over options. If I unlocked the car doors and survived a jump, my relatives finished what they started. But if I rode with the bone-breaking monster, I became his next victim. Hopelessness plastered a flushed wet cheek against the cold window. A pulsing laser buzzed in my ringing ears as dark pinpricks collected around darkening vision.

The car's dizzy pulls, sharp ankle pain, and the hateful prodigium, sunk me into blissful blackness.

Chapter 2

Undead pot calling the mage kettle

AN ANKLE THROB DISTURBED my blank nothingness, and a swollen eyelid cracked open. A confused ogle swept the room to search for revealing clues to my whereabouts. An antique clock ticked in time with the fire snapped logs. When pain zapped a stiff leg, noisy air sucked through my gritted teeth. Agony cramped my muscles and prevented movement when I took a chance to analyze the strange surroundings. Unlike home's lavender candles and sleek modern furnishings, I sniffed moldy books, years of smoky fires, and laid on a giant bed adorned by heavy mahogany posts. An ornate hearth cradled modest flames that flushed fissured lips, and eighteenth-century antiques illustrated an owner's old-fashioned tastes. Whose house was it?

When the brass doorknob rattled, I panicked and feigned sleep. Through a cracked eyelid, I saw a hunched senior woman positioned a silver tray on a small table. The platter presented several plastic water bottles and one sparkled glass. She smoothed a white apron before she gave me a knobby-kneed curtsey. "Outta a long while, you were. Cleaned you up and gave you me own nightgown, I did." I lifted an oversized lacy sleeve.

"Thank—thank—"

"Seeings how his lordship ain't—" the Scottish sounding North Hartlepool thickening her words.

"—you."

"—never brought home a proper lady before. Got a name, milady?" She neared the bed on a mothball and a mint-scented cloud twitched my nose.

"Name?" Split lips and a dry mouth gummed my question.

"Poor wee mite forgot her name. Don't fret, milady I'll—"

"Where am—?"

"—take care of ya, don't fret your pretty head, your ladyship."

"Sarah," my dry throat rasped.

She cupped an ear, and her bun wobbled when she asked, "You said?"

Pleasant dreams had nice grans and gentleman rescuers who chased away diabolical monsters. I prayed everything was a nightmare and not a new reality. "My name is—S—Sarah."

"Do ya have a last name, lass?"

"Wardwell." When I sat upright, a grimace twisted my chapped lips, sinking me back into the pillows.

She recoiled from the bed. "What'd you say?"

"Sarah, Sarah Wardwell."

"Wardwell? A bloody hag here in his lordship's house?" The terrible dream continued, and my new reality, a nightmare.

Beyond the bedroom door's shadow rumbled Count Vasile's lux baritone voice. "Smith, she happens to be my guest—for now." When ghoulish ruby pupils bristled from the gloomy hallway, I remembered the wild ride's horrors. The familiar sternness tangled fresh tense dismay through my aching limbs. I knew why the servant cared for me and the reason he didn't eat my bones. The prod emulated the rich gentry, who gathered grouse at country estates for hunts when he cloistered for a version of his own sport.

She spun and faced the door, "Milord, I don't—"

Diabolical menace forced through his clenched jaw. "Smith, you overstepped the mark." I squirmed me deeper in bed, and the senior woman's yellow teeth clamped shut. She huffed and grumbled past the shadowed creature when she left the room.

A polished oxford shoe stepped into the soft light when I released a plugged nose. "One does become accustomed to her stink."

The yellowish lamplight accentuated the tall creature's smooth olive-skinned face. And for the first time, I got a proper look at him. A well-sculpted brow, square jaw, and pronounced cheekbones belonged to a young European man but formed a monster's face. Like me, he looked close to eighteen-years-old, but I wondered about his actual age. An expensive tailored jacket fit the average man's build and boasted broad shoulders. I sucked at guessing people's heaviness, so I estimated he weighed two hundred pounds. Chocolate locks waved centimeters above a starched white collar, firelight mixing orange highlights in with warm hues. An absent tie and Hermes belt completed the appearance of a trendy, but a wealthy gentleman. I hated to admit it, but the ghoul was hot.

The dapper statuesque thing clasped hands at his waist while we studied each other. An uneasy silence split when I drew a long-forgotten breath and picked at chipped maroon nails. An upright, silent panther stalked deeper into the room each time I shivered or moved. The thing passed by the bed, and his stare never left mine. He continued the hunt. Between good looks, gestures, and an ever-growing fear for my life, wide eyes barely peeked over the clutched duvet.

With a practiced dancer's grace, Monster Boy perched on a delicate chair, his stiff back off the chair. A slow, deliberate movement crossed long legs when the young creature's wrist flick released a jacket button. A brisk touch swished the fabric aside. Then his fisted hand rested on a hip. An open palm settled on a knee, and a large ring tapped. Lips pursed to peruse a future buffet. The stuffy hubris alone would strain anyone's nerves, but the oozing predatory air deepened terror levels. Each tap, tap, tap, delivered those evil fangs closer to my intact bones, so I held the fresh-scented duvet tight against my chin.

After pregnant moments, the beast purred, "Did I hear correctly. you are Sarah Wardwell?"

"Ye—yeah? What's the big deal, and why did my name flip her out?"

"Lord."

"Huh?"

"You will do well to address me as—Lord."

"Oh, um—yes—lord—um lordship—majesty—"

"I must advise caution because further mendacity tosses you to those foul things that still hunt you." The taps stopped when King Thing rested his finger against his nose and studied the rug.

"Mend—mendacity?"

Blood-red pupils drilled my eyes, not the floor. "Lies, Miss Wardwell. Lies."

I craved a scornful enemy's attention, and the odd emotion tightened my chest. I just wanted to return Hell's creature into a sexy savior. A ring's giant centered ruby tossed crimson sparks and drew a petrified stare.

"But I'm telling the truth. I am Sarah Wardwell," my declaration laced with insolence. Mother once said my pride and stubbornness marked an inevitable downfall.

"Over fifty years, that coven bore no children because the rival Sutton clan cursed your lot with infertility."

I swallowed past my tongue stuck against a dry throat, lips begging for the water bottle on the bedside table. "How'd you—you kn—know?"

A smug look told me, he appreciated how his words stammered mine. "But who am I to complain about one less mage to eradicate. And to answer your question, I know everything." An old clock's subtle tick marked seconds while I planned a response, but finding one proved difficult. The guy with a clear serial killer vibe acted like a young medieval king, wise beyond years and spoiled by riches.

"Miss Wardwell, you were saying—"

"Yeah, the Sutton's did that, but my mom broke the curse. She concocted some deal with the devil to have me."

"Do you infer, your mother and Satan collaborated so that she might welp a child, and you are she?"

"Crazy, right? She was pretty desperate, I guess."

He flicked a finger off a lip. "Go on."

"And after I was born, they locked me up and hid my existence. End of story."

"I dare say, the entire story sounds very, V. C. Andrews, Flowers in the Attic."

"Why do you have flowers up there?" The tapping loon ate bones for breakfast and needed a gardener for his attic. What was next, tell me about the cows in the music room?

"Not my attic, but the book?"

"Huh?"

A finger tapped once. "Never mind but do go on."

"Um yeah, where was I? Did she give me something for pain, I feel kinda fuzzy."

"After you were born—"

"Right, that. I turned sixteen, and Grandfather revealed some dumb prophecy about my birth."

"A prophecy?"

"Pretty lame, huh?"

"Prognostications are nonexistent," he smirked into a fist.

"Prognos—Progos—"

He sighed, "Omens, Miss Wardwell. Omens." Long fingers again tapped, but his entire body remained rigid.

I pulled at the silky, white sheets and wrestled a cheeky reply or smart explanation, but I chose to summarize my life's meager details. "When Mother broke the infertility curse, Grandfather said some omen's timer started."

"And what exactly does this omen entail?"

"Oh, yeah! Some God grants a doppelganger born of Satan's path or something and gets immeasurable powers and abilities great enough to lead covens worldwide. Ya know, typical junk."

"And you have this substantial magic?" chest and shoulders wiggling. The jerk thought I lied and got the sense he bobbed me around for a laugh. Well, if he stayed on my bad side past me getting superpowers, I would nuke his butt.

"Hardly. I have to pass some divine test first."

"Miss Wardwell."

"Yeah?"

"Do you expect me to believe the future mage Queen Regent recuperates before me, in my home?"

"Um, I guess—"

"The very woman who lacked sufficient magical skills to evade her pursuers or flee my auto?"

I mangled sheets into twisted knots. "Well, they think I am."

An even liquid timbre deepened. "The druids lived the last time anyone commanded all mages, and I am fantastic with the history given my age."

"I know it sounds stupid, but I'm honest."

"Convince me."

"Con—convince you?"

Stammers and mixed-up words restarted my story. I explained how several years ago, my grandfather pulled out an ancient grimoire and confirmed the legend before the entire coven. Mother never acted surprised, while everyone agreed with the fantastic tale. The movie Rosemary's Baby sprang to life in my house. "I'm a savior or something like that."

"Or Antichrist."

"That's the undead pot call the mage kettle black." How dare someone my age act like my father? Oh yeah. He was super old.

Eyes snapped as he barked, "Miss Ward—"

I cut him off before his words ended me. "Look, I'm no satanic offspring."

Plump lips pursed millimeters while he considered my jumbled story. God, I hated drugs. "And your parents knew when you were born?"

"That I was not an Antichrist? Sure, I guess."

"I will rephrase my easy question." I blinked, itching to fly across the bed and rumple his perfect suit and perfect hair while sitting in his— "...correlate you to the prediction?"

"Huh?"

"When did your parents draw the connection between you and the omen?"

"Oh, that. Pardon, I feel a little woozy. During Mum's conception ritual, Satan told her."

"I hear doubt."

"Because I never listened, and would you trust them?"

"Not even with my dead dog. And your father?"

"Your pet died!? No wonder you're so—"

"Focus, Miss Wardwell. Your Father—"

When I spoke, words clacked, and my mouth made sticky noises. I wanted water in the worst way. "Didn't know him because he committed suicide when I was a baby."

"Tragedy."

"A mercy. You'd kill yourself too if married to Mother."

"I would end my very own immortality if married to any witch."

"Um, I—"

"No, no. I unrequired a response. Now, tell me about the time you discovered your purpose."

I gulped tears, and a cool touched a hot cheek. "Um, sad, I guess."

"And why was that?"

"Because I thought they hid me away my entire life to protect me. But—hey, are you gonna grill me all night? My head kinda hurts."

He ignored my complaint and continued to press the interrogation. "They hid you to prevent rival mages from stealing their prize."

"Yep. Pretty much. Sucks, huh? Oh! And I found out yesterday why they refused to train my magic abilities." If I harvested hard-won sympathy from the unfeeling monster, I might live.

"And why is that, Miss Wardwell?" Men in my family acted like stiff snobs, but that git took the cake. The next time he looked at his shoe tassels, I would rip the—

"—Miss Wardwell?"

"They kept me weak and untrained to stay their prisoner longer." The infected silence begged for a vaccine, so I filled it with rambled words. "And Satan warned Mother, I would someday kill her, so she let the servants raised me." I swiped a peek at the stony face and detected no pity or a slight crack in the icy veneer.

"Are you quite certain?" Life's crunching grains fled a proverbial timer and piled higher as time ran out. No evil green witch rubbed an hourglass, but a finger tapping red-eyed freak.

"Um yeah, I guess," unsure which statements killed me or minutes to live. "Do you know what time it is?"

"Yes, I do. Continue, please."

"Yes, um—Lord. When the ritual got closer, everyone got amped up. But who cares about the stupid powers? I just wanted to get the hell away from there."

"Why so?"

I puffed hair from my face as frustration tugged an eye roll. "Because it sucked watching other kid mages, then adults walk past your flat living normal lives."

"So, why the sudden desire to leave?"

"Because in two months, I flip some magical somersaults to become the queen."

"In two—"

His wit buzzed circles around my fuzzy mind, but I remembered an important detail. "Oh!"

"Yes?"

"What drug did you guys give me? I forgot what I was going to say."

The gorgeous statue squinted at manicured fingers draped across a knee and then snarled, "Alas, I now comprehend why simple questions confuse you."

"It's the drugs, bub. And you do?"

"Smith gave you a mild sedative, and I believe the medicament is called Ketamine. I gather you had no formal schooling?"

The belittling appraisal robbed a perched quip. "You guys gave me an elephant tranquilizer? Sheesh. And how you know about my education?"

"The Wardwells are very wealthy, and their offspring always attended the best schools, but I hear no boarding school accent, and your grammar is atrocious. And you lack any grace—"

He was a teenager in an old fart's clothing, and the monster wished me dead. "And you have no manners, even for a—"

"Therefore, I shall endeavor to avoid tough words."

"You—lucky I can't cast daylight spells."

He chuckled. "Oh, am I? You are lucky that I find you useful. Very well, let us continue. So, you fled your home," he said as a hand extended at my bed.

Okay, Monster Turd, checkmate. Mum was right. My mouth would be my downfall. "Yeah, I left."

"But you are worth more alive than dead, so why kill you?" The heartfelt story's frosty analysis from a coldhearted undead thing shriveled me further into the plush bed. Under the covers, knotted knuckles dammed hot tears.

"They have always hated me. And they planned to steal my powers once they took my place at the ritual." More information might delay the inevitable massacre. How badly did breaking bones hurt? Based on the number of drugs they pumped me up with while I slept, I would feel nothing.

"How—sad." The word 'sad' lacked a hint of empathy but bore a speck of hope.

I perked up, and my shoulders lifted. "Right?"

"Right about what, Miss Wardwell?"

"About—about—you lost me."

"I am sure I did. I will have to ensure Smith reads the prescription directions so that she might properly dose my next guest."

"Sorry."

"Yes, you are. Did jealousy or greed motivate them?"

"You switch topics faster than your driver changes lanes. I am so confused."

An ineptitude to keep pace lowered the jerk's brow, so he spoke slower to prove a nasty point. "Did jealousy motivate your murder?"

Under a judgmental glower, my petulance surfaced, but I think I resisted an eyeroll. My memory fuzzed. "I dunno, Mum's mental and claims I stole her destiny."

"A fact?"

A sting from a fissured lip tore my thoughts from the plastic water bottle as he flipped a finger in the air to end my embarrassing drivel. Expensive black loafers squeaked across the bedroom, the blanket dropped from my quivered chin, and I admired the perfect male's posture. The crackling fire and a far-off dripping pipe in the aged walls sang to the anxious manor. A crack in the fireplace wafted dusky wood smoke to my nose. He lifted the plastic and twisted off the cap, and after he poured delicious water into a crystal glass, passed me the drink. He seemed careful to touch a mage, sure to break out an Ebola epidemic in his house. Pretty stupid when the guy lived forev—

"What were you saying?"

"If closeted your entire life, how did you manage to flee?" Monster Jerk's pinched features eased a bit.

I held up a finger while I gulped the snatched the water, but my throat still burned. After a small choke, I willed false courage and continued the tale. I told him how after nagging Mother, she allowed me to attend a big gala if I promised to give up my birthright.

"But your escape failed when I found you—"

"Well, duh. They cast a tracking spell to stop me from running. Everyone knew the minute my feet left the building." Count Stuffy's red wine pupils drew me into bottomless predator traps, and the palmed glass became cumbersome. I slid the water onto the bedside table. The skillful wordplay planted me right where he wanted me. Exposed.

Inches above the painful ankle, his massive ring clanked the bedpost multiple times, and the thudding wood reminded me of a stake driving through his black, miserable heart. "So, Miss Wardwell, if uncontrolled by them, they ensured they took away anyone else's chance to manipulate you?"

"Call me, Sarah."

"Quite, Miss Wardwell, but wanting you dead seems illogical."

I blurted, "And I killed Mum." I jabbed further under the blanket. If he regarded me evil enough to slay my mother, he might consider me a threat worth leaving alone.

The clanking stopped one eyebrow shot into his dark hairline and bit his lower lip for a second. "You did?"

"Yeah! Who cares about them, anyway?"

"You don't?"

More bought time meant another jailbreak from a new paranormal prison, so thought fast. "Look, I'll make a deal."

"I avoid deals with mages. Miss Wardwell."

"It's Sarah, and you might like this one."

"I doubt—"

"Protect me, and I'll be your weapon for your stupid little war." I plucked at the sheets and avoided his hard stare as I mentally chanted, 'Please don't kill me. Please don't kill me.'

"Our war, Miss Wardwell. Our war."

"Yeah, sure. I'll be your weapon. But I didn't start it, so don't expect me to fight and get my hands bloody."

Lips thinned, "You will not fight, but as my weapon, wielded from my hand."

"Oh, I—I—"

"You find me so easy to manipulate, little witch?" he questioned, crossing his arms.

"Wait. What?" Damn, he caught on fast.

Arms still crossed, Lord Horror wheeled on his heel to leave, and a tailored jacket flared at the sides. "Until I decide upon your fate, the housekeeper shall see to your needs."

"But wait!"

"Stay in your room. It is much safer whilst living among Hell's creatures." Graceful strides left behind a rich spiced masculine scent as the door shut, a lock clicked, and my held breath released. The stupid prophecy kept marrow inside my bones one more day, or should I say night? The prison swap banged an already throbbing head against the headboard. All I ever craved was a regular life, doing normal things with normal people. But if I wanted to change my life's direction and purpose, I needed to win a few maniacal head games. But to beat an undead master, I required the patient spider's perseverance. During the day, things destroyed fresh webs. But at night, determined spiders spun new silk to catch insects. Mages boasted remarkable talents for fantastic web weaving.

abilities and lessened any escape chances. The weak

yielded green -fireplace flames, frozen tea, and b'

against the window. No curse, chant, or scr'

rippled glass overlooking dewy fields. Th'

locked.

If only a typical family plan'

concerned because a mortal ene'

motivations, they would co'

prod to steal their future

a black mood, and li'

She broug'

clothes. I w'

two of m'

as ar'

h'

TWO LONG WEEKS PASSED until I stepped outside the lavish bedroom. Each dreary day from the room's single window, I watched the clouds hide sunrises and sunsets. The contempt the household showed towards me worsened sick loneliness. Though I feared the ruthless monster's return, I hated the enormous suffocating room. But he never came to eat my bones or further interrogate me even when I screamed for hours. The prod forgot about me or decided to lock me away forever.

Every spell I tried fizzled. I only succeeded in ridiculous parlor tricks because my family declined to train my raw magic

attempts

gs peppered

m cracked the

oedroom remained

a rescue from loved and

y might kill me. Regardless of

. The coven would never allow a

ueen. The churned thoughts worsened

ng conditions forbad a cheery disposition.

a small meal each day and never any clean

e the same borrowed nightgown big enough to fit

inside. I reeked even though using the bathroom sink

underwear washing machine. One cloudy afternoon, the

undredth failed spell wedged the door lock tighter and more

frustrated anger ignited. I screeched, wrenched up an iron poker high in the air, then waved the long black wand before I smashed it against the wall. When the delicate wallpaper ripped, I smiled for the first time in weeks. And the window was next.

The Victorian brass doorknob clicked as I lowered the iron to gape at the gold clock beside the bed. But the hour ticked too soon for the crappy daily meal. A mint mothball scent preceded the detested housekeeper before she entered the room. Impossible to despise anyone more than the dead-but-not-dead warden, the crone teetered close.

"What do you want? Where's the food?"

When she spied the damaged wall, she howled, "You spiteful, hag!"

"I'm the hag!?"

The bun-wobbling senior scowled over crossed arms, "His lordship wants you."

"He wants me, wants me, or wants to see me?"

"Now, you foul thing."

"Well, the prog can sod off." I raised my chin higher and hugged myself. I turned from the wrinkled maid to scowled at a window. I later intended to break after she left. Unbearable pain erupted at my hair's base when the old biddy dragged me backward several stumbled steps. "What the—"

"Keep him waitin', and he'll eat me bones too!"

"I'm fine with that."

I followed while I rubbed my tender scalp. As we traipsed through a cherry paneled hallway, dead aristocrat paintings watched my procession towards certain doom, and the paint swirls glared at the stomped footsteps. I wagered Mr. Creature-Serial-Killer hung the trophy portraits of people he ate. The gloomy hall, lit by elegant lights, ended at closed double doors. A resentful tour guide snarled and crooked a thumb at the brass doorknob before she left.

Before I touched the carved brass, a familiar voice rumbled beyond the mahogany woodgrain. "Enter." Lips thinned and posture set as I entered the lair, but ill-prepared me for what I saw.

Masculine furnishings and impressive old-world wealth fashioned a cozy den. The room's full bookshelves yawned high to tall ceilings. Gold brocade wallpaper accented blue velvet drapes closed over the floor to ceiling windows. Grandfather owned one rare Chippendale chair, but the room boasted two million dollars' worth of precious antiques. A fire roared inside a Tudor-style fireplace, wide enough to fit three men. The flame's flickered shadows danced across the fearsome prodigium's face, who worked behind a large oak desk.

"Hi."

"The door."

"Right."

Silence.

The chancellor, wearing a light green dress shirt rolled at the elbows, twirled a pen while his eyes scanned a paper pile. When my stare traveled from his hairy arms to disheveled hair, a vivid flashback popped into mind. I remembered running my fingers through the gorgeous locks, yet I never did such a thing. The baffling vision disintegrated when two commanding fingers lifted from his desk to sweep towards a chair, eyes unshifted from his work.

He grumbled after my jaw dropped, and my feet ignored me, "Sit, Miss Wardwell." The fountain pen scratched one more thing before placed exactly two inches perpendicular with a leather journal, stressing the beast's regard for complete control. The journal snapped shut after the young-old man stood and then rounded his desk. When he stood twelve feet away, arms crossed, and for several minutes he analyzed my complete body.

I gulped as a fiery blush spread fire across my pale chest. "Didn't your mother teach you is rude to stare?"

"The Tsarina taught me many things, but I see yours failed to teach decency. Not a modicum of modesty—"

"Excuse me?"

"—or do all witches admonish decency?"

"I—I—" Where was a good comeback when I needed one?

"Do you protested staying with this vulgar display?"

"I—I'm not vulgar, Mr. Simeon."

He sighed, "Dear simpleton, might I remind you to address me as Lord, Chancellor, or Count?"

"Yeah, whatever—"

The jailer ignored the cynicism, a hand breezing through the air. "I hate to think witches so—vile and filthy," a posh British RP accent and Eastern European lilt melding.

"And I hate thinking prods can think at all."

The monster bent at his waist and snarled, "Mind your spiteful tongue, witch."

I jumped, faked a cough, then inspected the red oriental rug. When I squinted at my bare feet, horror unhinged my mouth. Firelight created a near-transparent nightgown, so my arms whipped across my small breasts. I hugged myself so tight that my hands touched each other behind my back when the judge peered down his nose. To draw attention from my near nakedness, I ratted out the maid. "She gave me no clean clothes or any decent food for that matter."

"She has no call to cook and, therefore, quite out of practice."

"Oh." Under his stony stare, I squared my torso to hide my vulnerability, but a wobbling sore ankle betrayed me.

The monster's neck cracked sideways before polished loafers closed the distance between us. The brute planned to stuff me in the fireplace after he crunched my bones one by one, or so I thought. I stepped backward, and pain dislodged a whimper. The silent monster swept eyes over a forgotten, stuffed animal, not a person. I squealed when again, muscular arms cradled my slight frame. The closeness to the monstrosity and a spicy cedar and amber sent, frazzled my awareness. Though clean-shaven, I noticed dark hair follicles under his skin. Prodigia grew stubble and needed to shave? But did he have soft skin, and what happened if I kissed that pulsing neck artery? I encircled the monster's upper shoulders, and wondered what happened if I rested my face against his collarbone and if my nose touched his warm skin, and just maybe—

"—then we talk—"

The rich voice snapped me from misplaced musings, "Huh?"

He set me upon a high-backed chair facing the fire. Deft fingers lifted my bruised ankle, the enormous ring's metal warm against clammy flesh. The malicious brute became a wealthy gentleman attending a guest as he cradled a calf to slide a footstool underneath the leg. I unknowingly fastened apt interest to his classic profile, but another gentle touch sharpened my wandering focus. The young undead creature played with his food and withheld any concerned care. I hated myself for swooning at the beast. I hated his hatred, and my entire soul hated him too.

"Your story justifies the unfortunate stench."

"Gee, thanks. So, what did you want?"

But he answered my question with a question. "Shall we address Smith's neglect?" When he strolled towards the fireplace and tugged a dangling silk cord, petulant eyes rolled at his back. I pictured obedient servants deep in the manor's belly who scrambled to obey the summon. In minutes, a hunched-over Smith reported, so I assumed he interrupted her eavesdropping.

The brocade armchair I sat on formed a wall to peek from and gauge the housekeeper's punishment. Two curling fingers demanded the ancient Yorkshire woman step closer. She obeyed with half-steps and a bowed head.

Her torso slumped when she conceded, "Yes, milord?"

The count loomed three paces before the guilty employee. "Mrs. Smith. Would you be so kind as to explain why you neglected my guest?" Trickled menace exacted precise words.

The crone stepped away from her master and wrung dry palms. "Your lordship, she brings nowt but death to this house! Just looking out fer ya is all."

A ghoul, from a Shakespearean actor, tapped an iambic pentameter-counting finger against a thigh. A delayed response increased cruel tension before he dictated our fates, so I ducked behind the chair's back and flashed her a smile.

"Whilst I appreciate your keen regard, you overstep the mark."

"Sir—"

He smartly spun around like struck by an idea, and called, "Miss Wardwell!"

"Wha—huh? I mean, yes? Yes, Lord?"

"Care to rid the world of a useless human?"

"Do I want to rid—"

"No, milord, please!" A long arm fired from his side and clamped her mouth shut. Mrs. Smith's tears slicked her pale wrinkles and his white fingers. Terrified attention flicked between us. A wild-eyed count's torso twisted to look at me, but a hand stayed glued against a panicked face. Internally I cheered.

"Where are my manners? How shall we dispatch her, Miss Wardwell?"

"Dispatch—"

"As my guest, I shall give you the honors of deciding her death."

"Honors?"

"'Tis only proper."

I blinked when something came over me. "Yeah, thanks for the mind games, but how's it my job to control your staff?" My nails dug tender palms so hard, and for days crescent-shaped marks stung.

"Yes, twas vulgar of me, and you are quite right."

"So, it's wrong to kill her?"

"No, her expiration is acceptable, but I erred asking you to discipline my employees whilst performing their duties."

"It's okay to murder her and make me decide how she dies, but running your household is wrong?"

"You catch on quickly, Miss Wardwell."

"Wait, you said duties—do you mean mistreating me was her job?" The pair wrinkled my forehead. What a bunch of monsters.

"She afforded me a chance to separate truth from lies and learn of your mother's fate." Crap, he found out about Mum. I shrunk. Soon, mage blood darkened the pricey carpet.

"You know you mother lives, Miss Wardwell."

"Yeah, I—"

"Tell me, are you a cold-blooded murderess or a compulsive liar, as you lack the intelligence for both."

"I—you—"

"And might I add, one with poor diction."

My arms dropped my torso, and my chin popped forward. "Yeah, well, you—you—talk old as dirt."

I knew why the monster locked me up and refrained from eating me. The jerk safely gauged any occult powers I might have, verified my implausible story, and studied how I acted around mistreated humans, topped with cheap entertainment. Under the cunning killer's gaze and truth's heat, fury blazed my freckled cheeks.

"Now, now, limit the theatrics, or you will make poor ole Dmitri jealous."

"It's rude to play with your food, ya know."

"And I find lying to someone who extends help quite rude. Pray tell Miss, what other lies did you tell?"

"What's with this Miss Wardwell crap, call me Sarah. And I only lied about Mum."

"Doubtful, Miss Wardwell. Doubtful." A controlled tone showed my life faded by the second.

I pressed ahead with nothing to lose. "It's true, I swear. I'll stick to the deal if—"

"And which deal would that be?" The smirking ass baited me, and God how I hated each repeated each word.

"For God's sake, to be your damn weapon!" I muttered, "Pompous ass." An open palm cooled a cheek heated from the hot fireplace and fresh degradation. Why was the old maid so quiet?

"You will do well to check your temper."

"Fine."

A flipped hand lifted from a hip. "But please do not misinterpret the displeasure in your behavior as a declination of your terms."

The big words again. "I'm confused."

"Of course, you are." The smug bastard turned on a heel. "May we return to Mrs. Smith's actions?" The smile bounced wicked light towards his creepy eyes.

"Do we have to?" When did planning a murder becomes a suitable topic?

He scorned my discomfort when he sing-songed, "Time for a younger model, do you agree? Shall I crack open a femur for tonight's feast, or show mercy and slit her throat?"

"Slit her—"

"Brilliant option, by Jove!"

"Option—"

"Glad we agreed about one detail. Care to have a go, Miss Wardwell?"

The warped words spun my head and moaned, "A go?"

"Yes, yes, I do see your concern. Tis an enormous task for those lacking the proper skills, so do you prefer to position a decanter whilst I harvest her marrow?"

"The decant—"

"Brilliant choice! Tis like we are of one mind."

"I'm gonna be sick."

The count ignored my moan while he inspected the dismayed woman. The terrified maid shook against an apron and wobbled her tight bun. "Shall we begin?" The insane host echoed his thoughts, not mine.

"Wait, hold on—"

"Be a darling Smith and fetch Miss Wardwell the decanter from the parlor."

"You're bloody mad!"

Smith's mouth twisted and gasped, and shoulders convulsed. Worried she was about to kick off as I watched, I swiped hair from my face for a better view. Smith erupted a cackle, not a plead for mercy. My jaw dropped. She waved an arthritic waggle at the blinking lord. The constant hip taps ended.

"Shut up, Mrs. Smith, he's going to kill you!"

The maid shot me one withered glare before she turned on the sneering count and growled, "Harvest me bones, milord?"

King of Mean snarled back, "Mrs. Smith—"

"Blimey, ya bloody daft, lad?"

He crossed his arms and pinched his features. "Mrs. Smith—"

"Don't ya go Mrs. Smithing me. Can't keep a decent cook, let alone find me replacement!"

The jailer's forehead smoothed, tone more tongue-in-cheek, "Now, now, Mrs. Smith."

"Oh, bugger off your high-n-mightyship!"

The old lunatic had a real go at the ghoul! I whipped back and forth between the stunning characters from a mental asylum movie scene. More of my hair poked further from the chair.

"But Mrs. Smith, it shan't hurt when—"

A plump fist shook under his nose as she crazily grinned, "Don't Mrs. Smith me! Come near me, lad, and I'll box yer ears."

A genuine smile released snarled lips, and his crinkled eyes belonged on a youthful prankster, not a dastardly villain. Some evil prod turned a poor teenager into a monster before he had a real human life.

"But you spoil my game!" He pouted the unusual attempt at banter. A tickled boy replaced a cold-blooded freak and weathered a loved grandmother's rebuke.

She huffed, spun on a heel, and left without a proper dismissal. The employee grumbled beyond the dark hallway's depth, "Drain me bones, he says! Drain me bones! Like to see the lad bloody try!" Hearty cackles echoed past the slammed den doors.

He scratched the back of his head. "Now." Contrasting emotions churned inside the complex creature. How odd that prods suffered madness, but other illnesses left them whole. Could insanity kill the monster is a virus could not? King Manipulator's sheepish grin ended after seconds, and Count Simeon reclaimed his role as an undead serial killer.

He purred, "Miss Wardwell?" Iced goosebumps crossed my flushed skin when a hard stare traveled my length to review his word's effects.

I squeaked, "Yeah?"

"Never harm her," with a low, flat tone.

"Um, never intended—"

"Never intended—milord."

"Yes, your, your lord, milord, lordship—lord."

The creature slapped a leg as his rigid posture relaxed. "Excellent. Tonight, we dine, so make yourself—" A glower raked my transparent nightdress. "—presentable." The taciturn timbre and hard analysis congealed blood into sludge.

"Um—Sure, but what do I wear?"

"Pester someone else. Uneducated blight."

Another squeak, "But, how do I find my room—"

He roared, "Leave." The gorgeous creature spun on a heel and strutted to his desk. The eavesdropping maid opened the den's door.

I whispered, "Jerk."

We marched down the same hall, but she led me to a different, cleaner bedroom. Inside a different opulent space, my dirty skin itched when I spied jeans and a tee across a vast bed. The wish for a clean body and the weight of recent mind games occupied my thoughts, not the room's stylish décor. The erratic encounter blazed fresh anger while I ripped away soiled clothing. When I considered how the parasite flaunted my puppet status for fun, I wanted to punch the bathroom mirror.

I turned on the shower. Blissful hot spray-soaked my dirty body and trickled among the French soaps against the blue marble tiles. A luscious gardenia soap eased tense shoulders. Someone boasted impeccable taste. Couldn't be Mrs. Smith or the count. I snapped at the lingered housekeeper. "I see clean clothes. You guys have shops way out here?" I arrived at new imprisonment unconscious, so I guessed at our country location.

A cackle reached the bathroom. "No. From his lordship's last meal." A plastic bottle and my jaw both dropped. I clambered to collect expensive soap as she called, "Bathe, ya filthy hag. If he hates you now, go ahcad an' keep him waiting."

Stolen moments in the humid heat relaxed my rigid body. In no rush to encounter the undead ghoul, I took my time to get ready. As I slipped on the slightly baggy jeans, I thought about how he exposed a lack of skill. Despite the odd dinner invite and playful banter with the calculating maid, he sucked at pretending to be a human. Nasty, manipulative traits ran too strong through his dead veins. I rested against a wet scrolled tile and considered my personal weakness. Recent conversations showed my drastic inexperience and how my fault allowed the monster's easy wins. If my thoughtless nature and immature behavior persisted, I might save my life but forever stay someone's pawn or prisoner. I prepared to confront the creature after I ate the first decent meal in weeks.

CHAPTER 4

Clean up aisle 13

AS WE MOVED ALONG THE dim hall, Mrs. Smith prattled, "Last week's meals didn't have much clothing. Rotten bodies stains are hard to remove." The ghoulish image fluttered a palm to my stomach, and a corpse wearing my borrowed jeans curled my toes inside too-large sneakers. Thank God I wore my own underwear. Somewhere deep in a dark cellar, a bloated and naked carcass lay on other putrid corpses.

"After dinner, you can send the clothes back to the Prodigium Goodwill. He's just gonna kill me." A smoker's throat rattled a raspy cackle.

The macabre tour concluded when the hall maze ended at two massive closed doors. She threw open the thick paneled wood and revealed a pretentious dining space. An enormous lily centerpiece's floral aroma mingled with delicious food smells. I blinked inside the lighter room as my stomach growled. Eating live bone required fine china? Next, I learned they slept in beds while they stayed away from coffins. I turned at the warp of nature, who masqueraded as a posh gentleman entertaining a guest. Another strange scene hurt my head. I strove for a less feeble vibe, so I left hammered temples alone.

Count Simeon reigned at the head of a table large enough to seat twenty people. Beside him sat a handsome effeminate man, and they huddled in hushed tones. Two soldier-like servants, wearing starched black and white livery, reported on each side of a buffet. Though King Monster and his guest stood an executed a gentlemanly greeting, my shock left well-cultivated manners at the door. And why should I act graciously towards such that thing? Even I kept standards.

The blond company contradicted the other's brooding appearance. He resembled a tan Roman sun god. Both males wore smart black dinner jackets and swirled foamy pink highball glasses. I walked closer after the count gestured at the empty chair beside him. When I took the first step, the other man's telltale red pupils announced his true nature. My saliva curdled as my nervous gut slammed to the floor. I contended with not one, but two immortal aberrations. I prayed their personalities differed. If the new prod mimicked our host's behavior, I mentally promised to stick a fork in my eye. The night refused to end.

From a drink's gold rim, the casual companion dissected my appearance. "Finally. You indulged in female companionship."

"I hardly classify—"

Plucked eyebrows shot into his hairline. "Wait, is that *Anna*? Annalyse? Anna, is that *you*?" He sounded like the count's driver. The motorist slammed a drink. I jumped then whimpered as the excited sun god rushed past a chair. The furniture wobbled on two legs. Once he rounded the long table and reached my rigid side, he snatched a limp hand. The warm, undead skin shuddered my taut muscles. "Anna?" I yanked away when puzzled blood-colored eyes slashed across my face.

"Who's—"

"She is not Annalyse." The host's throat cleared before he smoothed, "My poor manners. May I introduce Prince Dmitri." The smooth introduction elevated the room's pressure even higher. How many bad meetings required scalding water buckets and cleanser to scrub biohazard off the walls? If blacklight wielding cops stormed in, how many telltale purple splatters of cleaned blood might materialize? For the moment, I avoided the most crucial question. Why was a prince a count's driver?

The prince dropped a poisonous snake, not my hand. He bowed at the waist as a long-forgotten salutation rolled bejeweled fingers down his chest. "My mistake. Your pleasure, I'm sure." Like his mate, the guy sounded like a total prig.

"Yeah, hi."

"And Prince Dmitri, this is the one and only, Miss Wardwell."

The shocked driver locked his focus on me. "Why exactly does this bone bag resemble our Anna?"

"I'm in the room, ya know."

The rude count smirked while he talked over my head. "Steady on, man."

"What did you do, Sire?"

"She is a Wardwell witch."

I snarled an upper lip then barked, "Mage, not witch." They locked heated stares on each other, deaf to my correction.

"Wardwell? Then why smell and look like my sister? One second we, *wait*—"

"I told you to brace yourself, lad."

"Tell me this is *not* the witch from—" Hell's golden boy sounded worse than a hateful schoolboy when he stepped back.

Count Monster sighed at Prince Obnoxious before he panned a hand at the table. "Please sit while I explain."

The prince's nose wrinkled. "I see six issues."

"Of course, you do," the host groaned.

"First, she's Annalise's copy. The next five involve you playing house with this *mage*." The spoiled snot drew out the word 'mage' as his neck extended towards me.

The count admonished, "Dmitri—"

"—bloody daft, a witch here with us—"

The razor-sharp tone more forceful, "Prince Dmitri—"

The spiteful gold monster twirled from me and regarded the master prodigium. "What in the colossal hell, Vas!" The former chancellor sighed and straightened his dinnerware, like above but entertaining the theatrics.

"Both of you sit. Tis not a request." When the driver glared at the prod politician for a second too long. No longer pleasant, the count growled, ""Dmitri if I must speak one more—"

44

"That *thing* can pull out her own seat." The angry noble flipped shoulder-length hair, glittered rings catching the crystal chandelier light. Absent the host's perfect grace, Dmitri flopped onto a chair, legs spread wide apart. Two sets of blood pupils fixed on me as Count Simeon pulled out a seat for me, and a platter carrying servant moved. Crackling electricity bobbed about the room, ready to pop.

Everyone took a seat, and then the count rang a silver bell. The clang sprang a gulping boyish-man into action. The human, no older than me, filled one of three wine glasses with sparkling gold liquid. Another blank-faced servant lowered a platter topped with juicy poultry near an elbow. I selected several meat chunks and returned the tongs to the balanced tray. Menservants swapped places and presented steamed veg. Once they served me, the white-gloved men placed plates of pale pink marrow before the prods. The small china rested on the crisp white tablecloth simultaneously. The count flicked a finger over his shoulder, and the robots resumed places at the odd buffet.

One-half of the glossy top scrumptious food trays spread delicious aromas, and the other half glittered heaping platters of bone marrow. Me on one side, undead animals lurching on the other. Despite their best manners, fancy attire, and opulent elegance, nothing appeared normal. If prods integrated into public society, humans, disgusted by prod eating habits, would never give them separate bathrooms and eateries.

While the count touched the glass before him, I bit into the succulent poultry. Yummy juices pooled on the bone china. My gut rumbled. Despite the royal's earlier proclamation, Smith knew how to cook.

As we all ate, Count Simeon said, "Dmitri, I must impart some astonishing news."

The driver pouted, "More? Be still my beating heart."

Head Monster ignored the pantomime and recounted every part of my story. After he finished, Prince Dmitri banged on about my idiotic presence at the secluded manor. The man-child continued to spew hatred until his boss lifted a palm. The arrogant driver's mouth snapped shut. The Prince knew his place. What atrocities or blackmail controlled such vile creatures?

Trademark defiance flared when I butted in, "So how bad did you screw up, going from royalty to a chauffeur for someone younger and less well-placed?"

Prince Dmitri's chair capsized when he jumped to his feet. "I will tear—" Servant exchanged quick glances as a fork clattered an expensive plate. Under strained legs, my feet arched, ready to bolt.

"Crap—"

"Enough maledictions."

Prince Driver blinked after he abandoned plans for a fatal strike. A footman restored the toppled seat, removed the spilled drink, and served a fresh glass. White gloves tipped a red filled decanter, and a crimson film slid down the crystal. Although the tense dinner resumed, I lost my appetite.

"She falls underneath my protection while her family still hunts for her."

The prince moaned, "Of course, she does."

"I am? Since when?"

"And safely, might I add." The stern count bore eyes down on the peevish prod's pout.

The glum prince swirled a golden salad fork while he glared at the utensil. He quietly added, "Because she looks like Annalyse?"

Again, the name. Who was this woman, and why so important to the heathens? I thought it wise to keep my questions to myself and followed through with the smart determination.

"I will protect her—we will defend her. The witch is Anna reincarnated.

"By Jove, you are *absolutely* smashed."

The prince and I tried to wrap brains around the idea I was his dead wife, reborn. Marriage to a prod, including the sexy one on the right, turned my stomach. As he fleshed out more of my miserable life's details, my forehead lowered. I hid my building tears. Count Nasty made my life sounded more pathetic than when I told it. The smiling creature tipped backward, chuffed he wedged a disgraced enemy into an impossible position. Eating a cruel sadist's food before an undead brat near tears frazzled my nerves. Between a mistaken identity for someone's dead wife and the humiliation, the air's energy zapped as someone peed on an electric fence.

A programmed footman lowered a meal tray near my elbow, and for a moment, I marveled at their calm demeanor around the red-eyed ghouls. I bet the creatures stared into the men's eyes and compelled them to meet every disgusting need silently. Later, I discovered the marrow-suckers relied on money power to force human compliance because compulsion powers came from movies.

"But why keep her here, sire Perhaps the caves—"

The royal monster smoothed a handsome chin and explained, "After she presented herself as my weapon, what choice did I have but to spare her life."

"But, you're no longer the chancellor tasked to fight the war."

"Well, in a manner—"

"Do you—*Wait*—Do you plan to use her to win the—"

I dared, "Win what?"

"For now, my reasons are my own, but may I depend upon your loyalty?" The smug way he refrained from blinking was pretty cool, but why ask? But what I witnessed; Boss Monster always got what he wanted.

The surprised prince vented hysterical laughter. "You inquire about loyalty whilst keeping company with that *thing*."

"I can count on your support?"

The prince rubbed his head and sighed, "Never fear dear brother, never fear. I'll stay to heal the burns from the fire you playhouse with."

The count's forehead dropped, and the taps stopped. "I must caution about the possible danger—"

"I'd soon experience death again than be disloyal, Sire."

Later I learned how much and why the prods feared death. A million questions popped into mind. In any sane society, a prince outranked a count. But in the prodigia world, a prince sat below even a former immortal chancellor.

"Thank you, Prince Dmitri."

"But—" When Prince Dmitri chimed, for the undead life of him unable to keep his mouth shut, the servants and I wanted to groan. "Don't ask me to be nice to the witch."

"Not a witch!" But I breathed a different air.

Our host snarled, "Mind your tongue, boy! Respect Anna's memory—"

I grumbled, "A teenager disciplining an adult, not bizarre at all."

The pompous monster arms crossed and stared through me like the wall behind owed him money. "Can't be, Anna."

Again, the woman's name. I hoped the resemblance bought me more time to plan another escape. "Whoever Annalyse—" Before I finished the legitimate question, my captor's hands slammed the table and everyone, to include the tableware, jumped.

In record time, the formally dressed aberration stood at my side. Before I questioned him further or sprinted towards the door, he fisted hair at the base of my skull. After one angry twist form the furious prod, I involuntarily wrenched halfway to my feet. A strained neck bent at an awkward angle, discharged a weak whimper. The tight grasp forced me to absorb monstrous rage. The brilliant whites of his eyes offset crimson pupils that flashed pent-up resentment. If the hard fist twisted a fraction, my spine snapped. Jagged nails dredged into the silk tablecloth, and nobody breathed.

He thundered, "No witch will ever speak her name in my presence. *Ever.*" A hinted fang teased under a snarled upper lip when tense trembling muscles erased any smart reply. The servants never blinked, yet they seldom did.

"Ye—yes, sir. My lord. Your lordship—"

Stiff fingers coiled tighter to stressed complete control. "I will toss you into the night, and to the very same evil cruelty forced upon my Anna."

"Hell Vas, I'll open the door myself." The magpie got on my last nerves, albeit ignorant of our relationship's future drastic paces.

Screw the cruel Prodigia Mental Mind Olympics. I was over it. "My evil people? What about those you murder for food?" Monstrous eyes darted left and right several times as he mentally reviewed the best way to kill me. At least if I died, I cost him an expensive tablecloth.

"Rip her throat out, Vas. Here, servant boy." He thrust his highball glass. "Fetch me her blood when you see it."

The monster's flared nostrils smoothed, but the painful hair grasp further cranked my neck to the side. Only my toes touched the floor. "We are civilized and obey strict laws forbidding such things because manipulative witches murder enough for both species."

"Say the king of manipul—"

When he released my hair shoved my head once, I crashed to the marble floor. I yelped when a chair leg cut into my stomach as the impervious footmen kept ice sculpture postures. Fat tears trailed my colorless cheeks when his pinched features scoured over me. Why did he let me live? Hateful trances broke when a grandfather clock clanged.

I rose on weak limbs humiliated, and a sluggish clap rang from the table. The count snapped his jacket downward and dusted off a forearm. "Bravo! And brava! Jolly good show chap. Shall we salvage the evening, she bores me."

When the head monster flinched at me, I cringed. "Remove yourself at once. And exhibit respect deserving of a prince. If not for him, your bones would disintegrate in my mouth as we speak."

"My life—"

"*Out!*" The crushing roar vibrated air thick from poultry smelling tension.

The childish prince's chest quaked, then the jerk flashed me a grin before he kicked expensive Italian loafers onto the table. Frail dishes skittered across the wrinkled tablecloth. "Bye, witch."

Tears clouded my vision, and at that moment, I almost crawled over the plates to claw out his smug eyes. For weeks later, the chancellor's red anger haunted my restless sleep, and many mornings, a silver animal stare from deep bedroom shadows woke me screaming.

CHAPTER 5

One-way trip to Disaster Town

A TINY CLOCK AND BOREDOM ticked in time. Each minuscule needle jerk sunk fresh loneliness into my throbbing temples and inflicted a depression rivaling Sylvia Plath. Tired twilight sucked away the sun's remnants as I propped a drowsy cheek against the bedroom window's icy glass to catch the day's last glimpse. I fought to sleep during the day if monsters roamed the halls at night. The terrible waking hours, coupled with yesterday's dramatic dinner, took a toll. The cool glass tingled my forehead pounding from the daily horror story fate forced me to live.

Fried sausage, fresh tomatoes, and a smoky fire blended into one aroma, but the English breakfast lay forgotten on a silver tray.

I only ate twice that week when Mrs. Smith forgot to bring an appetite with the food. The evening began differently when the housekeeper returned to clean my room when she carried an armful of books. I moped while she straightened bedcovers. Shaky breath fogged the glass. An invisible digit traced circles in the condensation. I went for it. "Who's Annalyse?" The dire threat against saying the name required an explanation and willful disobedience.

She collected the tray of untouched food. "His Lordship's wife?"

I peeled away from the window. "Wait. Can that thing love? You're telling me a woman married that that thing?" The loyal servant shot me a withered expression. Before another question formed, a slight movement from the twilight's drifting fog snagged my attention.

I searched the gray-green fields encased in drippy fog. Several pheasants beat their wings against the air when they launched into the gloomy twilight. The castle's terrible king rode a black warhorse from behind the bricked stables into the wet grasses. He reigned in the impatient horse and glanced directly at my third-story window. Did he hear me utter the forbidden name? I jumped back into the shadows and jammed hands under my armpits.

When the haunted glare found me past the dim shadows, I tingled everywhere. Unable to look away, I became desperate moth drawn to the wrong darkness and who avoided light. An undefined gravity pulled me into a detested thing, then fluttered headfirst into the prod's complex flames. Every day, while I laid in bed, tossing and turning, a former life bombarded me. I felt someone else's memories. When the dead wife's ghost left me alone, nightmares shifted, then ran screaming from scornful blood-colored eyes. Each remembrance tossed emotions closer to an unwanted fatal free-fall for a hateful ghoul who considered me an inanimate object. The glib monster galloped whipped the horse's head towards the open countryside then raced from view. After my shaky breaths relaxed, I twirled on the nosey maid prattling about the room.

Smith wielded an iron poker to stab the smoldered logs, unaware of our wordless exchange. After the oblivious older woman straightened and rested a fist against her lower back, she confessed more details about the strange Anna. Lucky for me, she had no problem blabbing her mouth.

I learned Count Dimitriov married three hundred years ago, but enemy mages hunted down his human wife a few years later. And the following described events chilled me to my bones. The occultists forced Anna to perish multiple times, trying to whittle her spirit to nothing, hell-bent on preventing her reincarnation. I wait a moment then discovered the reason but understood why the undead widower clung to blind hatred. Evil people, my people, inflicted his centuries-long grief, and his precious Anna returned to life in a mage's body. My body. But did her death relate to no longer holding office? I stymied new feelings. Sympathy for the devil won a one-way trip to Disaster Town. But while under his so-called protection, more of my people's evilness exposed and the resulting misery.

She broke strained thoughts. "Here, read about her. In this," she offered and thumbed through a book she placed on a mahogany dresser. Then she closed the door and left me alone. I plucked the dusty gray volume, sneezed, and limped to the overstuffed chair close to the warm fire. Lips thinned when I read the nonfiction title, *Bulgarian Supernatural Myths and Legends*. But I counted on the yellowed letters to either ease boredom or put me to sleep. The spine spewed tiny sparkled particles at my nose when I cracked the stiff binder.

Historians struggled to uncover facts about Chancellor Simeon's wife. A few folktales offered some information about the Grand Duchess. One tale suggested the royal's murder resulted from a war between the prodigia and mage. However, such folktales never mention the paranormal war's cause. Stories also described the rage of her grieving husband. After her murder, Chancellor Simeon disappears from mention. Other folktales mention an unpopular successor—

Boring sentences listed more deeds of long-dead individuals, but no further mention of my jailer. A tired mind fluttered around swallowed facts. The creature's wife was reborn to a species who not only murdered her but strove to eradicate the monster's kind. My presence in Chancellor Simeon's safe-house flaunted my ancestors' terrible acts in his face and his inability to save her. My audible heartbeats echoed down the hall to his dean and refreshed an unfeeling immortal's sentimental pain. Unexpected tears blurred the printed lines on my lap. A snapped log lullaby slipped a yawn.

The sun fell beyond little white dots of sheep that accented the fuzzy green pastoral hills. Clusters of trees yawned in the twilight breeze. Scattered lightning bugs rejoiced in the rising gloaming and wheeled a cheery rhythmic dance as they blended into the faint stars. A familiar countryside, filled with wet oat perfumes and brilliant wildflowers, tingled me with delight. My husband propped his lazy chin on my head while he handled the warhorse's reins. The gait rolled our touching bodies. Contentment hummed when a calloused grip flexed over my thigh. When I peered past a shoulder, Vasile's mischievous grin caught my smile. How odd, he never smiled.

He long lost humanity's vestiges. Each year after a human becomes immortal, mortal coils fade away. As people age, one loses hair and wrinkles. An aging prodigia loses human traits, and because my husband was so old, I cherished the rare smile.

Though my brother and I admired the immortals, I prayed my carefree brother stayed mortal. I loved Vasile and found most prodigia affable, but Husband's father terrified Dmitri and me. Whenever Vasile's maker looked at me, I swore he picked apart my secret identity and my soul. Only Dmitri understood what I was, but I knew who I was. The dream and horse swung forward, and then the scene switched before I dwelt further in Anna's head. Or was it mine?

When she felt the night's joy, so did I. I never breathed fresh country air before, so profound giddiness urged happy, fast feet through the dewy fields. Court life required me to live at night, so I wanted to explore until the tranquil farmland faded into blackness.

"Stop the horse." When the animal eased, I slid off. The intention to sprint as fast as possible to feel the twilight breeze rush past my skin turned bare feet loose. I ignored the annoying call at my back.

Seductive dirt under my toes propelled faster legs. Tall wheat tickled my waist. Excited arms extended wide and grazed the tops when I raced. Grasshoppers and birds alike scrambled away from my giggles. A magical lightning bug cloud lifted high above and danced with the brightening celestial objects. When mellifluous trees drew closer, I slowed.

How silly that the locals feared the forest, and never dared to walk among the craggy trees. I quite liked them. Then again, the dark drew me like no other shade. Country mothers weaved frightening tales to frighten children about the terrible things that inhabited the woodland. But I knew the truth. The fabled monsters secretly lived among them, and parents had no clue when they tucked children into warm beds. When I the dark treeline dreaded by the locals, my running slowed, and my racing heart leaped faster. I gasped, "No! Can't be." A real monster waited for me.

I turned and searched for the horse on the hill, but a pregnant twilight obscured the animal. I tripped and fell. I bit my lower lip and whipped my head towards the tree wall while I forced more fresh air into burning lungs. I jumped up and kept moving, as there would be hell to pay at the bottom of the hill where the monster waited amongst black shadows. No ordinary monster waited for me, but an aggravated Vasile.

The immortal plied supernatural speed and beat me to the treeline. He propped against a tree trunk, and a thinned mouth bobbed a lengthy piece of grass. Husband detested it when I dashed off. "You know about the mage dangers, my sweet lady."

A few feet in front of him, I rested my palms on kneecaps to catch my breath. Upward, I craned my best smile. "Nothing could ever happen with you here."

"Anna—"

"And you cheated!"

"I simply—"

"You never let me win, Husband."

When he pushed off the tree, a tiny smile tugged the rugged face. "Leave the subject where it is." He scooped me into a mind-scrambling embrace, then buried my nose where his neck met a collar bone and breathed deep. When Vasile set me down, a grasshopper entangled in his long dark curls. I flicked the insect away. Only one person ever dared touch the immortal, me. The first time I grabbed the count's hand, I swore all Transylvania gasped.

"What is my punishment, Your Imperial Highness?"

"This." He laid me in the lover's bed created by fragrant vegetation. An athletic frame hovered above my heaving chest, winded from running and desires. A lengthy hardness against an arched hip ached our minds. Did Anna's lust tickle my senses, or did I feel my own wants? Was there a difference? I raised my jawbone to the night sky and exposed a vulnerable neck. He growled. Our mouth lingered an inch apart. Breath cascaded along tingled skin. Eager nails sank into triangulated triceps. A jeweled finger traced a line from my chin to the bottom of my breastbone. The moon entered its highest apex when carnal delights tangled our limbs.

When lips lifted, "Your heart hurts my ears."

"Eavesdropping is rude."

"These old ears will hear your heartbeat across canyons of time." The dream's bad VCR tape flickered out of tune. Vasile's speech sounded dissonant. I tried to clear the fuzzy vision and enjoy the reprieve from a vengeful hatred. I think my subconscious somersaulted from sharing Anna's intense feelings and muddled the confusing dream.

When I concentrated on the odd feelings, a murmur tickled. *"Join us, Anna."*

"And do what? I'm Sarah." I craved things other than talk.

But before we went further, the vision bubbled and shifted. The dark's peace splintered. Grasses stilled. The crickets silenced rubbing legs. Trees stifled secret sharing leaves. A familiar, ominous mood bulged frightened eyeballs. Rotten flesh thickened the air. We froze, including the night. Fear far from sexual longing dug my sharp nails into Husband's bareback. Vasile's predator glower penetrated the gloom, but before questioning him, a tremendous force yanked me out from under his heavy body. A gut-wrenched scream pierced the empty night.

Large wings thumped a chilled breeze against ears and skin. The downdraft blew long red hair in my vision. A gray winged demon with soulless black eyes suspended Anna and me fifty feet high. The animated stone gargoyle's screech drowned out mutual screams. Granite talons dripped an oily goo down strained limbs and pierced painfully outstretched arms. The blueish-black substance and fresh blood mingled.

A diabolical statue hovered me above the frail-looking Vasile. I glimpsed abnormal mortal panic from hidden mages working a gargoyle spell and trickled time to a crawl. Deviant enemies manipulated seconds to force memorizing my true love's terrified face for many lifetimes to come. A feminine voice part mine and half of someone else's, mewled, "Catch me if I fall!" The nightmare's 8mm film bubbled and then melted off the mental projector. High-pitched screams and the gargoyle's feral shrieks melded into one sound. Nothingness darkened the terrible scene and dissolved the fantastic dream.

"I'll find—"

The nightmare felt like hours, but Mrs. Smith said I only yelled for fifteen minutes. Sweaty limbs bludgeoned the housekeeper as she labored to wake me. Tears dripped off my nose and chin. I shook so hard teeth rattled. Wheezing breaths hitched. An overused throat burned. Who was I, Anna or Sarah?

A creak snapped my head. At the door stood an eighteenth-century husband, no modern monster darkened the entry. "Vas!" The peculiar relief flooded fresh endorphins. Ugly dreams and reality merged into one murky mess. I pulled against the maid.

A shaved chin elevated at the older woman who restrained a hysterical lunatic. Paranormal ears heard my terrified screams miles away. The unexpected sound drew him into the house from a distant field. Muddy riding boots sullied expensive rugs when the count expected mayhem. The lord prepared to battle mages or interrupted the prince from murdering me.

Vasile clenched teeth and gloved fists. "Dear God, she's gone quite mad! Control her at this once!" The deep, accented voice broke the maid's slim shoulder grasp, and adrenaline-fueled arms pushed past the chunky woman. I hurled myself at a monster who wanted me and my entire occult species dead. I didn't crash into soft waiting arms, but hard outstretched hands. No muscle budged. Creaking leather gloves creaked protested.

"Just a dream, milord! Me thinks."

I strained against an iron grip to hug a distant neck, vexed at his rigid posture. A cry erupted when I clung to the image and love of a husband never mine. The fairytale faded under reality's truthful hard glare. An eighteenth-century lord morphed into a modern English gentleman. But then the man turned into a snarling undead creature who refused to move past the doorway to let me closer. He gawked at a wild-haired opponent far from being his wife. I looked down at my grass covered feet.

"Come, lass, just a dream." The maid patted my stiff shoulder blades.

I tore from restraining fingers. "Oh, my God." The dream's haze cleared and the recollection of how I threw myself at him. Stinging bile burned my throat when weak arms dropped. I backed away, but the oversized nightgown hem entangled my clean feet. I stumbled but somehow remained standing. I think the maid's hands caught my back.

"Catch me if I fall. Catch me if I fall." I shook a messy head and put more distance between us.

Vasile's controlled voice strained, "The very last words Annalyse screamed to me. What hex is this, witch?"

"I said that aloud? I—don't—"

"Why those words?" A clenched jaw spat hate when he leaned closer. I cowered near the bed.

"Now, now, milord. Just a dream. Just a dream."

"Get that thing under control, or I will."

Smith cooed, "Poor wee mite traveled hell's length if her story's true. Come, lass." She pulled the bed's covers over my trembled legs.

A shameful look darted between the pair. "But I am Anna?" An unreadable shadow flicked crossed the controlled prod's expression. Weak, baffled, and ashamed, I crawled deeper underneath the blanket. Knees curled into a fetal position. The clucking maid tucked warm blankets around my shivered shoulders.

"I ordered you to never speak that name." Why watch from the door and avoid storming inside to wreak havoc?

"Oh. I'm Sarah. Yes, that's right. Sarah." The prod's stony vibe remained fastened on me. I folded knuckled fists into my bony breastbone.

"Yes, lass, you're Sarah."

"But I want to be Anna. I want Anna back."

A dead woman's feelings compounded mine, and the two sentiments melded into one messy emotion. Did he consider me a disposable weapon, enemy DNA, or a woman deserving rare pity? A wintery ocean painting, of a cold sunrise and blown sands, captured my bleary focus.

He lifted an inch off the door frame to track my concentration. "My favorite piece."

"Pretty. I've seen that place."

"She painted it."

"She did?"

"Yes. Anna painted the seaside she wanted us to visit so I would forever remember."

"Did you?"

"Did we go?"

"No. Did you forget?"

"No. Never."

I knew why the masterful art hid in a rear bedroom. The colorful muted oil swirls whispered hints of two lost souls I understood.

"What happened?"

"Why we never went?"

"No, the dream."

"Perhaps you suffered her last visions."

Knobby knees pressed into my chest. as I shivered so hard, my bones hurt. "I'm so sorry."

"For what, pray tell?" The soft question posed no malice, so another free tear released.

I cracked, "Everything."

"Why?" He sounded mystified, far from snide.

"I'm both the murderer and the victim. Since we met, Ann— sorry for saying her name. Her memories and every care haunt my sleep." I curled tighter.

"Cold, Miss Wardwell?" empathetic face blank.

A shadow fell over the bed. "Not temperature related. Something else makes me cold."

The mattress dipped. I rolled over. A confused immortal perched on a narrow section of the bed. "You suffer her death. Death is unbelievably cold." I heard him murmur to someone at the door, but tearing my eyes away felt monumental. He half-turned without breaking eye contact. "She is fine. If they infected Miss Wardwell's dream, they might be close."

"Do you recall the other words you called to me the night you died?"

I nodded and whispered, "I'll find you."

The absent bedroom lights made seeing his elegant facial features hard, so a brave hand materialized from under the covers and stretched to touch a careworn face lit by the window's early moon. Soft, not angry fingers grasped my cold hand inches from his face. He whispered, "Don't."

Tender kindness tucked my needful hand underneath the duvet. A blurred dark flash and air movement disappeared the monster, a heartbreak left in his wake. I flexed empty fingers and then touched the dented blanket still warm from his body.

I rolled over, faced the painting and stared a long while. Eventually, I whispered to the memory of Vasile and Anna, "Don't go."

I think from the door's black shadow, pain murmured back, "I must." But maybe I imagined his voice while I suffered another dream.

I remember the lonely decision made while I stared through the empty dark at the cold painting, and how old I felt. I decided to yank back those crippling emotions at all costs, or my precarious life forever shackled to someone else's plan. For a while, a lifelong hunger for independence and a normal life outweighed any gross feelings for a disgusting monster. At least, that is what I convinced myself that night. But first, I determined to block a dead woman's memories.

CHAPTER 6

Vinny Prod the mob boss

THE EVENING'S NIGHTMARE WEIGHED me and the entire house in heavy weariness. A tiny clock's tick further oppressed the atmosphere while time's stagnant existence ran in short supply. Bored after I picked at poached eggs and toast, I jiggled the brass doorknob. When the cold metal rattled freely, I lost no time to jam legs threw jeans. Once dressed, I poked my head into the windowless hallway. Hardwood floors creaked under tired steps, but the frothing prodigia and their nosey employees tolerated the noise. If the prods resembled fictional vampires, the late afternoon sun guaranteed they hung from basement rafters.

Down the vast hall, bright daylight spilled onto the gloomy dark wood. In moments, warm golden light spread across bare feet. I peeked into the open door. Overstuffed furniture crowded a gorgeous space begged me to explore. Full bookcases and colorful flower-filled vases decorated a yellow solarium. The room I stepped inside starkly contrasted the somber manor. Soft white lilies and brilliant red roses bent their heads to conspire with each other between the glass. I waved through a luxurious sunbeam. The rare English sun broke a tired smile. I pushed hair behind an ear took two more slow steps.

"Cool!"

An expensive black Bosendorfer grand piano glistened under the sun's happy rays. Careful trepidation dropped as I wandered across the clean floor to the seductive instrument. A gentle clink of the ivory keys and its enormous black belly tinkled a note. I wished I could play when I slid across the slick bench.

I angled my legs towards the keys and the rippled window bank. Funny how time-warped glass but kept an immortal calm. I surveyed the peaceful hills' deeper country colors. The stretching virgin land copied the west coast moors. Giant dark cedars hugged the manor and hid colorful peacocks that echoed their spooky yearnings for something strange and foreign. When the comfortable room's colors took a soft greenish-yellow sheen, a willing mind drifted to the avoided nightmare. I chinned my hand and mulled Annalise's fantasies while the elusive sun dipped lower.

Of all recollections, my brain plucked out how I and my supernatural warden wrapped our limbs in the grass. When a raging pulse amplified a finger smeared the polished black instrument. The last sunrays stripped sparkles from the glass panels. On cue, a throat cleared behind me. A soft smile crashed. I jerked. Hands slammed on the glossy bench to prevent falling. A cherry flush betrayed intimate personal musing.

"Don't you just love this room?" A disheveled Prince Dmitri yawned while propped against the door jamb. Messy golden hair suggested moments earlier, Prince Driver languished inside a coffin or on a bed. A smooth bare chest and droopy blue silk pajama pants exposed lazy ease. He clutched a coppery red liquid-filled highball glass. Blood closely related to bone marrow, so prods often drank the biohazard like fine wine.

"I guess," feet planted ready to fly.

The awkward moment fashioned a scrutinized look and then a playful grin. "Anna inspired the decor." The prince's hair billowed behind him when he strode towards me. If screams brought the count miles away, could a yell wake him?

"I'm going. Sorry."

"No. You will stay."

I twisted and writhed as I decided between fight or flight, scream, or whimper. Long male legs swung around the bench. When the prince faced the piano, he placed the offensive drink on top of the shiny instrument. The foul copper smelling contents lurched my stomach. At least he drank someone else's blood and left mine alone. If I scooted over one more centimeter, I fell on the floor. He slumped. The half-awake prince used exaggerated piano-playing motions. Oblivious or inconsiderate about any discomfort, he began another leisurely evening among countless others.

"Quite the affair last night."

"How—how'd you—"

"Know?"

"Um, yeah."

A wink stressed happy chords that sprang from bedecked fingers. "Because I am in league with a devil named Mrs. Smith."

"She told—"

"Now, now, no need to flay her. I do prefer clean chambers."

"You heard?"

"My dear, the entire countryside heard the screaming."

"Crap. Sorry."

"And I must praise you for his rare mood." While he joked, the keys tinkled music under fast fingers.

"Mood?"

He fashioned a conspiratorial wink. "He's got the morbs."

"The morbs?" I wondered if I would repeat words all night.

"Yes! Sits at his desk brooding more than usual."

"He does?" cheeks flushing.

"Well played, Miss Wardwell. Well played." Fingertips danced across closer keys. I only half sat on the bench. The prince poised a crooked finger near a shoulder, and my jerk scored his chuckle. When flashing fingers returned to the keys, he tapped an upbeat song that combined ragtime with Debussy. "No female ever cast him in such a foul mood." The boyish imp pretended he conspired with an old friend, not a deplorable mage. Speechless and glad he no longer preferred me dead, I picked a jagged nail. The prince's new attitude mashed concerned eyebrows and lips pursed. Last night affected more than just me.

"Your Highness, I'm—"

"If we are to be friends, you must call me Dmitri."

"Okay then, Dmitri, I kinda climbed over him." My chest blazed after the vivid scene recall.

"No, you never!" Flying fingers stopped playing and tucked under his chin while he batted eyelids.

"I mean it. I was all over him."

The golden creature chuckled, and gaudy rings waggled near his breast. The fiend at dinner, who preferred to crack my fragile bones, vied for my friendship. Hips squirmed. A naïve youthful woman and a formidable beast sat at a piano pretended to be friends, not enemies locked in a deadly game. Despite a lack of needed companions, I still distrusted him. The sudden attitude shift masked a hidden agenda, more typical prodigium characteristics.

"Please ma petite, kill my boredom with more details."

"Nope. Never happening."

He grabbed the offensive drink, finished the clotted liquid, then rolled out more cheery chords. "Please?" He flashed a winning smile. "I'd pay my last pound to see anyone terrify Vas."

"The stiff prig once had a mommy who named him, Vas?" Cold concern iced strained nerves when I stepped out of bounds. I gulped, but the withered stare only lasted a second after he waved.

"Short for Vasile." I rubbed my neck. I only considered him a prod, my kidnapper, the count, or my favorite, jerk.

"The next time you unhinge the miserable devil? Ring me, as I must watch." Dmitri leaned closer. The wish to crack the brother-in-law's stoicism brightened us.

"Okay, um Dmitri, I'll ring on one condition."

He perked a plucked eyebrow. "A deal with a mage? Done."

"Can you tell me more about him?" I wanted to discover similarities between my jailer's history and recent nightmares.

Dmitri's fingers lifted off the ivories. He enthusiastically smiled, ready to indulge my dangerous curiosity. My excited companion launched into a spirited tale, and his jaunty arpeggio became theme music. I placed an elbow on the vibrating instrument.

"His maker is named, The Father—"

"Wait, The Father?" I lived a lousy prodigium movie featuring Vinny Prod, the mob boss, and his not-so-Goodfellow. A stern glare squashed any wisecrack when he signaled guessed my thoughts.

"I shall explain. The first immortal created our illustrious Count Dimitrov around 925 AD. He then charged Vas with training our army—"

"You guys have an army?" chin and hand separating at the information.

"Only the finest! Our military service holds great prestige."

Art and life mismatched. Humans wrote about monsters inspired by the prodigia. But the fictional vampires differed from their living inspiration. Victorian vampire books presented solitary monsters resembling blood-sucking Antichrists. Then modern vampire fiction further twisted the legends. Authors humanized the make-believe bloodsuckers. Proof of the incorrect parallel tinkered Mozart beside me.

I snarked, "So, let me guess, Mister Perfect always listened to his Dad and a rule follower."

"In a manner."

"Lame. Let me back up. The prod political movement isn't a myth?" I sailed the slur, but he continued.

"Hardly, Poppet." examining the ceiling while he recalled long-past glory days.

The proud prod bragged. Six elected assemblymen, one chancellor, and a well-defined court system formed the curious institution. The government executed crafted laws promoting cultural progress. The state resembled the British parliament. Unlike our Queen, the chancellor stayed politically active. The monsters wanted to become something more than bone-feigning atrocities. But as Americans say, one can put lipstick on a pig, but it's still a pig.

"Vas doesn't believe me. His people adore, love, and dread him with equal measure."

"They adore, not adored him?" my nose wrinkling.

Chords slowed, and his tone lowered, "A quintessential legend, our Vas." A crescendo emphasized the compliment.

"He's a politician and a soldier?"

"How else could he rule such a motley clan?" He acted like I was daft. "As a seasoned warrior intimate with the freed power effects, he avoided becoming a paranoid leader."

"Humans and mages only wished for such luck."

"I couldn't agree more."

"So, what's his leadership secret?"

The golden god shrugged. "Backbreaking work and war heroics. Vas never felt the need to tread across people's backs to keep control—"

"No way!"

A pinky tapped my nose-tip. "Immortals will only obey greater power. Healthy fear goes a long way with my kind."

The recent friend described matchless strength, fearlessness, and intelligence. That is until he met Anna. Load more of Dmitri's dramatic music. He recounted how a fiery redhead knocked men's knees, captured mortal and immortal hearts. She enchanted Vasile, as the archetypal bad boy, above all others. Dmitri's face softened when he confessed Vasile gifted immortality the day after they discovered Anna's body. "We changed forever after she left us. She never wanted this life for me."

I itched to touch his arm. "Why they fear him so much?"

"Sweet girl, if you witnessed the atrocities exacted to mold our kind."

"Atrocities?"

"Acts terrible enough to make Vlad the Impaler cry for his Mum."

"Wow."

"Wow is right, Poppet."

"But you don't act scared."

"Oh, I am. But I hide it. He has lines even I dare not cross. And if I do cross them, I hide those well too."

"Well, he scares me." He winked while music filled a comfortable lapse in talk. "Oh, you never said how you guys changed."

"So, I didn't. The first change was our address. Rotting in a capital surrounded her memories, and an absent father ate at his mind."

"You guys came here?"

"Reluctantly. But despite living in this hell hole," he bemoaned as an arm swept at the windows. "His principles stay fastened to his life's work and people. The Nation always came first until she died."

A quiet whistle sailed. "Like how?"

"The poor sod couldn't believe he failed to save Anna. What complicated matters, his maker abandoned him just preceding his hour of need. So, I followed a broken man."

"So sad." Again, I swallowed wrongful pity.

"Vas's heart blackened and lost the lust for life and war. He once lived as a tight violin string, played nightly by duty, honor, and passion. But now idle, he sags untuned. He fills nights not with running the Immortal Nation but brooding over newspapers or infrequent card playing. So, you see, dear Poppet, he needs someone to play him."

When I touched his arm, he startled. The music stopped. As I remembered our respective identities, I withdrew. "I'm sorry, I didn't—talking about her—"

The wild mane stroked the musical keys. "For centuries, she laid buried in our minds while inside a faraway grave, which is until he rescued you."

Painful long-distance memories turned his lips. But he continued his woeful tale. The Immortal Nation entered a constitutional crisis. Vasile's departure forced the council to find his replacement. The state architect, The Father, never predicted nor prepared for such an event. Nobody, not even his creator, expected the prized creature to abandon his official duties. "When Victor took office, the damn idiot conducted a proxy trial. He strong-armed the council and convicted Vasile for dereliction of duty and treason."

"They did what?"

"Shocking, right? To add insult to injury, under penalty of death, the government forbade contact with Vas."

"Are you serious!? Harsh."

Prince Driver beamed at my words, then somberly said, "The prig wants Vas to return for sentencing a traitor! Our Vas!" Disbelief rang an octave higher.

"You broke the law. You're here—"

He blinked several times at the most moronic thing ever uttered. "Where else would I be?"

I grinned and played along. "True."

"Back to my favorite topic. Me. You asked how I changed."

"Sure." If the prod believed I cared, he might divulge more useful information.

"I sacrificed time at court and many lovers for a team position."

"He has a team?"

"Yes. Me, myself, and I." I slapped my mouth when a half-giggle leaked. The likable prod improved damp spirits. "One simply does not comprehend what country life does to one's vim and vigor—"

"Then, why?"

"Loyalty. Besides, who wants to appease a shyster who shames my creator's legacy?" A somber frown eased into a brilliant smile, and a crooked pinky extended. I scratched my neck.

"Huh?"

"Pinky swear, you will fetch me posthaste if you again try to hug the poor sod. And go for a snog!"

I lengthened his name. "Dah—meet—tree!" I hid the repeated fantasy of losing my virginity to his brother behind a mollified expression. I thought, 'Thanks, Anna.'

My new friend wiggled the extended pinky. We linked our fingers. "Wake the lug, for all our sakes. We need him back in action." Surprisingly, I liked the colorful marrow-sucker.

"Deal." My eyes rolled, and teeth flashed while I shook my head no.

"Not so horrid, for a novice mage that is."

"Not so horrid for a pro—an immortal."

We chatted for an hour then I circled the original topic. "So, you think I can fix him?" Most women relish licking a quintessential bad boy's wounds. Based on prodigistic hot looks, I'd lick more than emotional injuries.

"Fix him? You? Preposterous."

"Oh."

"I must warn you. Be careful if you wish to win his trust and keep your bones intact. He detests being handled and holds no regard for mortals, human, or mage." He looked past a shoulder once then whispered, "Vas once drugged a one of your kind to keep them alive while devouring bones one by one."

My eyes popped wide when I flipped the chitchat. "Did you ever marry?"

A key clanked, and laughter echoed the room. "A warrior's life offered time for suitors, not husbands. Time to make myself presentable." Eyebrows waggled. He left as fast as he materialized.

The glass having congealed blood drops lingered on the piano, proof Dmitri shared time with me. A single long blond hair decorated warm keys. The possibility I made a new friend renewed hope and eased eternal loneliness until the next nightmare.

CHAPTER 7

Sweeny Todd and Dracula at dinner

IMMORTAL HOSTS REQUESTED 'the honor' of my presence at a little soirée' thrown for a shipping mogul. Mrs. Smith informed me that the count often entertained to preserve the human disguise, but I neutral to the real reason. I focused on how to extract freedom from an iron grasp. When the stiff butler guided me to the parlor, an odd question replaced the concern for liberty. Before the night's end, who became the meal, and who got their scalped yanked?

When we passed a mirror, I halted to examine the pale blue silk gown that hugged my curves and hid thigh lumps. I twisted and admired the draped fabric that made my pitiful cleavage look slamming. The latest fashion implied King Prod spared no expense, or Smith chose the best dress from a body pile. One might consider my attire perfect for an American prom. Coiled hair strayed select curls formed an elegant style. I patted styled ringlets. 'That's a bit o' me there. Let him drool.' No matter the events, I coveted two goals. I wanted more information about a new foreign world and determine how gleaned facts help plan an escape.

I tensed when the senior butler opened the door and stood aside. Martini clutching humans and prodigia sat scattered around the fancy parlor. Quiet talk and pleasant expressions suggested benign pleasantries. How many commonalities did the prods share with their odd guests? When I strolled inside, not a muscle moved, and four males from two species rose from chairs. Women love to own the room they walk into, but not me. I gulped down nerves.

The royal creatures looked dapper as they wore black ties and formal jackets. But bizarre colored pupils pulled a double-take. The pair wore contacts and turned brilliant reds into muddy brown pools. I tried not to appear shocked, as the humans fastened their interest to me. A ruddy-faced human near sixty elbowed a thinner, younger twin, assumed to be his son. An overdressed green sequenced wife, stuffed a chair, cleared her throat, and an icy smirk shifted coral lips.

I squeaked, "Good evening."

A new friend's megawatt smile glided towards me. When Prince Driver reached me, he grasped my hand, bowed from the waist, while the other hand lodged behind his back. An actual prince received a guest, so I ducked my head, tucked one ankle behind the other, and crouched a knee. Even Queen Liz might appreciate my perfect curtsy. After he clasped my fingers, he kissed my skin. The old-world mannerisms usually fired up my nerves, but that night I felt like a princess, not a dumb queen.

A winking Dmitri released me then rounded on the family. "May I present, Miss Jacqueline Hutchings." The alias baffled me, but I flashed an enthusiastic smile. The crowd murmured greetings.

A servant appeared at my elbow, and his white-glove balanced a fancy martini tray. I plucked a blue-green drink and waited for someone to say something about underage drinking. Not receiving a reprimand, I considered warning humans to run for their lives. Thankfully, the alcoholic drink dissolved the stupid vision, right after I lightly choked on the strong alcohol.

But the gallant young noble's polished demeanor and dapper appearance started more preposterous daydreams. I replayed the night I suffered the life-changing nightmare. In a fantasy, I reached for his cheek when he sat on my bed. A liquid voice washed a quickened pulse. I almost snapped the pinched the martini glass's thin stem when I imagined adhering to the classic gentleman's soft black jacket, fabric scratching my exposed breastbone. As I touched my flushed chest, I preferred to swallow every drink on the servant's tray. I cleared my throat, and Dmitri winked. He knew. I swapped a drained glass for a full one on the waiter's platter.

"Dimitri, am I correct saying, your nephew controls your companies?"

"You speak correctly."

"A rather bold trust."

"He is the business genius in the family. A natural-born leader, our Vasile. He keeps me around to fill in the difficult bits."

I choked on my cocktail. The monsters explained the difference in age and reverse pecking order. The family bought the clarification.

But the man's puffery was no match for the count's fresh dynamism. Confidence from centuries-old supremacy dominated the room's vibe. "I can assure you the arrangement will go smoothly." The old guy quieted, never expected the dominance and self-assurance from a young man. The strong personality only inflicted more of my ridiculous longing or refreshed Anna's love. My nervous stomach catapulted lurched butterflies. I yearned for the pure hatred spurred when he pulled my hair, not the—

"—don't you think Miss Hutchings? Miss Hutch—"

"Oh, me?" I blinked. Did the count notice my not so secret interest?

When I snapped out of my daze, the thin son, struggled to talk with me. So, I lowered my face and pretended to listen while I fastened discrete attention to the dapper chancellor. But someone noticed the coy tactic. The prince smiled while he raised a champagne flute as dull brown eyes darted between his master and me. When the chatty son leaned closer, a smirking Dmitri rolled his eyes while he faked drinking alcohol. I showed him my back and mentally cursed the scoundrel.

Anthony buzzed, "Don't you think, Miss Wardwell?"
"Huh?"

Dmitri breezed in my direction, positioned lips close to my ear as his chin directed towards the count. "We shall talk later, my pet.

I groaned, "Great." If my new friend noticed my direct stare at the hot host, did Count Dmitriov?

The son clapped Count Dmitriov's shoulder. "I take it you are an Eaton man. We must be the same age, but I never saw you there last year."

The chancellor bore the familiarity well because he refrained from ripping out a throat. "I grew up on the continent."

Anthony looked over the former leader. "Ah, yes. Right. Father says he'll invest in your little project. Jolly news, well done, you." Dmitri and I shared a glance. If the idiot only knew who he addressed. Something told me he would find out. The meal likened to the worse high school party ever. The talk, renegade daydreams, and swirled bravado spun tumbled thoughts. A hand steadied me.

Ahead of battling egos, a butler raised his chin and announced, "Dinner is served, Your Lordship." Dmitri and I loudly breathed.

The prodigium leader set a full glass on a servant's platter then swept an elbow at the sullen mother. Per protocol, the young count's arm presented to the senior female so they might first enter the dining room. She batted eyelids when the boyish charms affected her disposition. I transfixed interest on the pair when I placed the martini on the offered tray. The glass almost missed as the annoying son adhered to my side. An elbow raised to a stiff side. "—think, shall we?"

I jerked. "Oh! I—" A thin heel caught against the carpet. A tiny skip prevented a tumble angled me closer to our regal host. When I stared upward at an impassive face, my hem swooshed against a creased pant leg. Heat popped orange freckles across my pale, freckled chest. An unblinking Count Simeon gazed down his nose at my short figure. The mother peered past his arm to question the delay. I uttered an apology then turned to a yammering Anthony. Before I strayed from the tall male, silky fingertips brushed along my lower back. A man's secreted caress, not a monster's, erupted telltale goosebumps. Did he accidentally touch me or send a signal? Did anyone see the exchange? If I waited long enough, time would unravel the suspenseful evening's truths.

Dmitri popped from nowhere and whispered ice buckets into an ear. "Blink, Poppet. Blink." I blinked then jerked at the grinning blond snarling.

We drifted from the salon into the proper dining room. I wished to admire the extravagant setting, but Anthony vied for my attention. Unable to interrupt the steady chatter, the rude idiot left my side and rushed past the prods. Though born British upper-class, the half-American ignored handwritten place cards to pull out a chair for me next to him. "Miss Hutchings, do me the honor?"

The chancellor shook his head when he pulled out the plastic mother's seat. She tolerated the son's rudeness, or years of Botox froze facial muscles. Nobody had their hair yanked, but the evening presented perverse entertainment.

While the prods pretended to eat regular food, they slid discrete stares at the yammering insect seat on my right. Why did the son intrigue the monsters? Curiosity killed cats, but enough dead things already sat around the tablet. I ignored Anthony's chatter and enjoyed my soup's savory aroma.

"Do I detect an Essex accent?"

I paused my spoon a centimeter from the orange bisque. "Excuse me?"

"From London? Let me guess—"

Dmitri interrupted. "Yes, my ward is from London." I prevented a giggle and gripped a fork tighter when I heard the antiquated explanation. Dmitri shot daggers into my skull. Not uttering a single word, he reminded me I sat at a dangerous formal dinner, not around a children's table.

"How long will you stay?

"How long—"

"I ask because Father is throwing a charity event next weekend." A spoon clattered into a bowl when he leaned towards me and asked, "Say you'll be my date?" Count Simeon and Anthony's mother froze spoons in midair. The possibility of a date with the thin man sent a short nail into my mouth. When my neck tingled, I flew a nervous look at the brooding leader. He raised fingers off the table when Dmitri's lips parted to respond to me. While the silent guests waited for an answer, dark-colored contacts bore into the side of my head. An anxious pulse quickened in the room's anxiety quicksand.

"It's rather sudden."

My movements mimicked the watching control master. A careful thumb and index finger placed my spoon beside a full soup bowl. An urge to taunt the hosts niggled a wild impulse. If the young chancellor's masked jealousy, playing with fire might be fun. "I'd love to go."

Anthony's mum sniffed at my fake excitement. The new money American considered her station high enough to judge my fitness for her son. She tried hard to fit into the British upper-class and never hit the mark. The father, head buried in food, ignored the snobbish exchange. Tension tightened between players, some ignorant about the genuine conflict.

Dmitri's knuckles turned white around a thin glass stem. Dmitri waved away a manservant. "Sorry to disappoint my dear. We have our little soiree."

Score a point for the driver. "Right. I forgot. Sorry, Uncle it sounded fun." The mother and to monsters released a long-held breath. I smiled.

Anthony misinterpreted my smile. "Next time then!"

Talk at the table ebbed and flowed like the delicious gourmet courses. The nobles exploited expert conversational skills split between their guests. Murmured chatter about freight operations lulled boredom. Twice, I shoved Anthony's wandering hand off my thigh. Pencil Neck stroked an arm when not touching my leg. I checked blue-veined translucent skin after a nauseating caress left nausea in its wake. I preferred the troll's hair pull than the weasel's inappropriate touch.

The host pushed his chair after white-gloves removed the dessert plates. A deep baritone rang like a meditation bowl through my chest. "Shall we go through?"

The father chuckled and murmured to Dmitri, "You do let the boy run things."

Rather than listen to dull business-speak or engage in small talk with the icy mother, I longed to swap stuffy air for fresh garden delights. I executed debutante poise and offered a smooth excuse for why I left the party. 'Mister Dmitriov' pressed his lips and said, "I shall ring for Smith."

"No need. I know the way." While they hid their monstrous nature, a chase through the estate became impossible. As I twisted a doorknob, I wondered why the diabolical warden demanded I attend the fake dinner. Did the chancellor assess my behavior during a ruse in advance of awarding me a place on Team Prodigia? They supplied more cheap mortal entertainment inside a horror terrarium. New stilettos skittered onto the patio off the enormous hallway.

When I slipped outside, a mini devil on a shoulder urged me to run, but an angel argued against it. I would die before clearing the field, and even if I reached the road, my family waited. As an untrained mage and my family's target on my back, I sought refuge with the undead. If I wished to fight mages and prodigia head-on, I needed to buy more time to gain genuine powers. Thankfully, Dmitri mentioned the count actively searched for an occult instructor ahead of the next full moon. The opportunity arrived at the right moment because freedom became a precious commodity.

I scanned the landscape, but troubles refused to fade. A vast Tudor garden, adorned by an enormous fountain, threaded under a beautiful silver moon. Scattered torches back-lit the impressive water cascade and its millions of bright beads across an inky sky. Gardenia and green ivy whispered comfort against the brick manor as stiff shoulders sagged. A sculpted granite railing sparkled mica particles in the weak moonlight. A late summer breeze swayed hair ringlets and manicured grass.

Peaceful air and many consumed wine glasses later, I slipped into a complacent daze. As I enjoyed the stolen moment, I seized an opportunity to think about recent events and search for a helpful clue to plan a better escape. But thoughts drifted to my tormentor's broad shoulders and sexy bravado while a soothing breeze rocked my pensive body.

I unnoticed creaking leather shoes behind me. Stinky garlic and brandy swirled warmly past my bare skin, prickling tiny neck hairs. Prodigia breath smelled like copper and death. I jerked then turned on a heel. "Anthony."

The skinny guy narrowed the space between our bodies. Delicate silk snagged against the rough balustrade when he trapped me between blazed body heat and stone. I arched back. A sane person would push or bark at the forward sod, but I traveled the passive-aggressive route, a Brit to the very end. "I thought you left. Isn't your car waiting?"

"No."

A worried gaze whipped to the open French doors as I raced over feasible options. If I abandoned promised magical instructions and fled, the ensuing drama attracted those who hunted me. But chaos supplied a perfect opportunity to slip away. I swallowed impatience and the crappy idea.

"Surely your parents look for you. Your mother is not a fan." I arched further when the stinky mouth neared mine. The high-fashion dress's pulled fabric smashed breasts flat against my chest.

He licked spittle off narrow lips. "And leave without a kiss?" Another hip squirm quickened his breath. A hand slid along a chilled arm. I almost vomited inside the goon's jacket's breast pocket.

"Um, yeah. No."

"Why fight it?" A thin finger traced a freckled shoulder's curve.

I abandoned polite control and worries about attention-grabbing theatrics. "Excuse me?" When I pushed the narrow torso, Anthony stopped the caress when he slammed the railing behind me. My noodle arms and his iron grasp on the stone prevented me from fleeing, the half-American arching my torso.

When I again pressed as hard as possible against his heaved chest, and the words curdled my blood. "You were the one flirting with me. I'm just giving you what you asked for."

A heart thundered against a flushed chest. How many other women endured that sick statement? I slapped a slick face, but the strike hammered in lust, not common sense. Joy crinkled the feckless man's beady green eyes. A palm slicked along my ribcage. I groaned, not from pleasure but futility. Social ignorance and the low-cut dress sent the wrong signals. To this day, I struggle with how he helped himself to my body.

Needle Nose clamped the back of my neck and drew our faces closer. He had seconds before I kneed his groin. I pounded lapels, "Got off, or they'll kill you!"

The sexual predator's pant increased. "They're busy. It's just us." Why prods checked him while they feigned eating made perfect sense, they watched the human, not from jealousy, but sensing another predator wandered their territory and circled the count's next meal. The monsters recognized visible signs I missed.

Painful wideness watered freaked eyes. "Get your damn paws off me." Sweat beaded over my back when he snatched my skinny wrists and yanked me closer. Alabaster flesh under tight fingers curdled white. Thin high heels wobbled, and a still tender ankle complained.

Surrounding energy rippled as I barked another demand. Death stalked neared. The air thickened. A more menacing predator moved in the balcony's shadows. Chills crawled crosswise across my chilled skin. Then something significant blocked the porch lights. A darkness fell over Anthony and me. Young King Monster's head appeared above Antony's. Manicured fingertips snaked over the ignorant male's shoulder. The massive ring that symbolized a secret monster government caught the moonlight, and red flecks danced on the human's cheek. Anthony's brow wrinkled.

Distress changed to relief. "Better run, pal." Odd-colored pupils raked across his private property to inventory my condition.

Pencil Neck's nostrils flared. "What the bloody—"

A side sneer exposed a glinted fang when a squeezed vice grip popped Anthony's shoulder. My assailant released my pained wrists before he turned halfway to challenge the mysterious attacker. The immortal clamped down on the insect even tighter. He immobilized the sputtering bug. Again, the strange savior peered past the pissed person and inspected my body. "I heard your heart. Please forgive the unfortunate delay."

I rubbed blood back into tender wrists. "It's okay." Moments prior, a naïve fool who trapped me became entangled within another's immovable clutches.

Lips flew spittle and thinned to the point they disappeared. "Unhand me!"

"Mr. Buckley—" He over-pronounced 'mister,' and dragged out the name.

"Who in the hell do you think—"

The young count leered closer to the junior and spoke past gritted teeth, "Apologize to Miss Hutchings at once." Fangs peekaboo under plump lips.

Mentally I cheered, 'Say hello to my not so little friend.'

"Stupid Euro-trash. Let me go." The poor sod didn't recognize an unfair fight.

"Sir, please don't cause a scene over me. We could attract my family's attention if they are near." Bone-lust clouded him because the monster squeezed the assailant's shoulder tighter. The wimpy boy squealed powerless to escape.

"This pup needs a manners lesson."

"The slut begged for it. Let go."

A hiss tugged beautiful lips and bone-drilling tools exposed. The cream-colored fangs appeared two inches long and extended a centimeter past a lower lip. And the posh creature reverted to a natural state as death's messenger. Our mouths snapped shut as eyes popped wide. Unlike Anthony, I sidestepped the inevitable bloodshed. The first dinner at the manor's taught me, prods controlled their teeth, but the next physical change I learned about quivered my spine. Tiny dark capillaries webbed upward from a buttoned collar, across his face, and into his hairline. A few larger black arteries throbbed under a blazed expression. In seconds, smooth olive skin became dusky. Features that belonged to a boy-band popstar melted into a demon's visage. An audible gulp bobbed my larynx, and nails ground the railing against my lower back.

Windmill limbs flailed when he battled the world's strongest immortal. "What the fu—" Hell's creature squeezed both clavicles, and the sick crunch brought knuckles to my mouth. The sexual predator's shoulders collapsed into sharp angles. Anthony's crotch darkened, and a tangy odor hit. A hand fixed to my twisted lips traded for a nose pinch. A wounded deer bleated an alarm under a beast's snarls. I fastened to the gore. My heart quivered faster than hummingbird wings as I watched the prod's death instruments sink gum deep into my assailant's neck.

I ignored the Blood splatters that decorated the expensive dress, glued to the horror scene like a movie fanatic. Shrill human screams drowned mangled skin as it ripped and the pumping biohazard that splashed everywhere. The sloshed red liquid even muted the fountain gurgles. An iron odor replaced the pungent urine and gardenia perfume while the prodigium ripped flesh to reach succulent vertebrae. Anthony's little girl shrieks stopped. Imagine listening to a person grate their teeth into concrete. That is the noise I heard mixed with crunched bone. Lungs hissed pink foamy air where an Adam's apple once bobbed. The creature groaned while he sucked éclair's cream, not marrow.

Long fingers flexed against his victim's biceps when Anthony's mother arrived, screams on full blast. The trees, stables, then the manor bounced shrill cries. "So much for not attracting attention." The panicked mother skittered past the doors on a gold kitten heel, and loyal Dmitri followed.

The earsplitting woman stopped feet in front of the engorged prod as the dinning monster lifted from his human buffet to snarl. A few ripped tendons attached Antony's skull at an odd angle, and white rubbery arteries protruded from mangled hamburger meat. A chunk of bone fell from the half-severed head as one last heartbeat weakly oozed the final pint of blood.

"Smelled the mess. I came as soon as possible." The tantalizing scene changed Dmitri's golden visage, and dark veins webbed across his skin.

A huffed father joined the little party. "M'boy!" He skittered over an inky crimson pool. Wild waved arms prevented a slip.

Dmitri groaned, "Here we are."

The monster chucked aside the corpse like a young medieval king tossing a chicken bone. Fangs popped when they retracted. An enraged expression dissipated the spooky gray-blue capillaries but looked every bit the vengeful demon spawn. Blood and flesh bits coated the creature's face.

"My boy is—"

The count checked manicured hands before he finished, "—a sexual predator."

"And dead by the looks." Leave it to Dmitri to pipe up.

"Quite."

The prince cupped his mouth and boomed above the frenzied screams, "Told you he was trouble."

The chubby father yanked back the hysterical wife when he clawed the screaming woman's abundant waist. If I drew their attention, things could get uglier, so I bit my lip and hands folded across my Jackson Pollock dress. I glared at the crumpled body while the couple begged for mercy. A thickened burgundy puddle expanded closer to new designer heels. A terrible conclusion struck, so I hurried away. Living blood recalled new copper pennies, but dead blood reminded me of musty lead pipes.

"Sire, you know how I hate seconds. Might I have the parents—" The parent's screams drowned Dmitri's voice as he pointed to the hysterical pair. He looked at Count Dimitriov, pantomimed eating a caveman's bone, then shrugged his shoulders.

Count Dimitrov met the friend's amused expression above the panicked couple. A fist lifted at his shoulder, then twisted. The ever-obedient Dmitri obeyed the silent command. The blond gripped each parent by the neck when they clung together, and fragile necks snapped after a smart twist. A chiropractor appointment went wrong.

The body count grew when Dmitri lifted Anthony's corpse then tossed it on the corpse pile. Anthony gave the mother one last color treatment when his blood seeped into her gray hair and then touched the father's clouded eyes. The awkward drape of the son's corpse over his parents ripped the few attached flesh threads and the head detached. A sick thud rolled a frozen scream a few feet across the porch. But the prince again sprang to action and punted a soda can, not a skull, back to the heap.

The prince clicked his tongue and tapped a foot while he questioned, "Let me guess. He mauled Witchy-Poo?"

"Yes. And I arrived just in time. The poor girl intended to weather the advances in case mages are nearby."

"You noticed?"

Dmitri shot me a glance. "Well done, her."

The English gentlemen rounded the bloody mess, hands clutched behind their backs to survey the grisly scene. "Anger never causes you to kill. Anger holds no calculations—"

The count's head lifted and paused the quick inspection. "Don't be daft, boy," he barked as a pocket square snapped from his stained jacket.

"—something more than property abuse upset you, Sire."

"Dmitri—"

The prince's playfulness smoothed. "Right then."

I tried to figure out what Dmitri's statement meant, and the real reason the count kill Anthony. The chancellor heard my inner debate and sensed my focused stare because I received his side-long glance. An excited heart skipped a few more beats.

But the grinning prince ignored the chancellor's stern caution, fist-pumped, then clapped count's shoulder hard. "The great Count Simeon has returned!" A sharp slap reverberated off the blood coated brick building. The whack, capable of launching a sizeable man off their feet, stirred the leader a few inches. Wrongful familiarity evoked a glower. Dmitri's lowered arms then smiled.

The dominant boss snapped a dinner jacket waist. "Are you quite finished? Or shall I add you to the pile?" The silk pocket square wiped his chin's leftover blood smears.

"Sorry, Sire."

The elegant creature stepped away when the blood pool stretched closer to polished shoes. "Clean every trace."

The defeated prince shrugged, "Always cleaning messes—"

"Dmitri, you sail perilously close to the window of your death—" from under a dropped brow, he exaggerated the warning's last two consonants. Then a look, capable of freezing Hell's lava pits, sealed Dmitri's mouth.

"Yes, Sire."

An angry count spun after several steps towards the house when he remembered me. After he flicked a dime-sized flesh off a lapel, an evil James Bond stalked across the stained balcony. The master intended to execute the only witness. I swallowed past a closed throat and hugged myself.

"Are you quite alright, Miss Wardwell?" his tone and face softer.

My arms crossed, uncrossed, and crossed again while I glanced at three corpses then nodded, "Y—yes, sir." Dmitri's mistake taught me to extend Vasile's required respect.

The punctual housekeeper strolled through red splattered French doors and huffed, "Heard the screaming' from the kitchen. Staff's scared half to—jumping Jesus Christ and a table of hungry saints! More work for me, aye laddies?"

Count Simeon ignored the angry maid as he stepped over the dead father's legs while he bent an arm forty-five degrees. The elbow pointed toward me. "You suffered enough impropriety for one evening, so shall I escort you to your rooms?"

My attention flew to a brow furrowed Dmitri as he studied the bodies, too preoccupied to help. "I did?"

"Now, mind your shoes, Miss Wardwell."

"Shoes?"

When I coiled a hand in fine warm wool, my nervous fingers flexed. We left the congealed biohazard pools. New lightheadedness and a racing pulse refused to calm when I walked close to the demon king, not the actual events. The other two clustered around the fresh corpses, and hushed tones chatted. I never asked if Mrs. Smith repurposed the family's clothing.

"I must again apologize for my guest. After a thousand years, behaviors from the Lowers never ceases to amaze me."

"The, the Lowers?"

He perked a brow while we cleared the doors. "Lower creatures. Humans, if you must."

"Oh."

"You disagree?"

"To what?" I sounded meek and confused.

"Humans as the lower species, of course." He rattled on, "Your kind considers them as minions. And mine as take away bags."

"You're pulling my leg, right?"

"No need to pull legs when I tugged a neck, my dear."

I gulped. "I never saw them as lowers."

Merriment danced. "A pragmatist! Miss Wardwell! What a rare and delightful quality," as feet devoured the hallway.

"Praga-who?"

"Just think, two species hovers between men and Gods. We are the Highers."

"Us?" The elitist ideology creeped me out.

"Our people are equals. Quite the difficult concept I'll have you know, but alas there it is."

"We are?"

"Thankfully, Dr. Linnaeus named all three sapien species but only cataloged the one. Affable chap. More than happy to hold his pen and mouth quiet."

"Who?"

"Ah, yes, your poor education." He aimed a far-off gleam at the ceiling as he strolled, and I scurried. More than hurried legs worked to keep pace. "He termed witches as—"

"Mages."

"Very well—mages." As he touched a soiled collar, "Dr. Linnaeus's assistant penned our two species as, Magicae sapiens and Prodigium sapien."

"I didn't know—"

"He never published the names. I had the research stolen, then had his assistant's body dumped in a canal."

"I bet you did. So, immortals and human governments both controlled secrets.

"I guess—"

"Have you ever thought why the Highers permit the lowers to run the proverbial zoo?"

"That'd pass us complicit with humankind's atrocities, right? Thanks to men, we can pass as angels." He pursed lips when he contemplated my assumption.

We walked through the hallway maze while I puzzled at the happy chatting. The fresh bone flushed my walking companion with Anthony-like exuberance. The pleasant monster clacked heels when we arrived at my bedroom and then grasped my fingers curled under his arm. While he gripped my hand, then opened the door, wide-eyes I considered his touch. He wedged a free hand behind his waist and bowed above our grasp. "I bid you goodnight, Miss Wardwell."

"Goo—" Proof of my paranormal escort included a blurred streak, a hair tickling my neck, spiced cologne, and a pounding heart. I twitched empty suspended fingers. The ludicrous evening raised more questions than answers. How thoroughly did prodigia laws suppress their monstrous instincts? And why the lighter mood?

CHAPTER 8

Nailed the undead right on the head

I DRIFTED INTO THE SUNROOM, not seeking the prince's company but find undisturbed peace while I tried self-education. I loathed books but hated to sound ignorant more. Many dull nights, I poured over dusty volumes. A new routine included countless hours studying, countless daydreams, and copious cups of tea. I grimaced at the detested novel, forced to read thanks to no television, bored with my window reflection.

A thick book supplied dust, not a distraction from replaying the dinner's heart-pounding conclusion, over and over. I tried to wrap my mind around a human who assaulted me, not Team Evil

Undead. The dinner melded two gruesome plays, 'Sweeney Todd' and 'Dracula,' into one hot mess. I analyzed each vivid moment until a throat cleared behind me.

"Y—yeah—I mean, yes?"

"Milady, His Lordship requests your presence." The unmovable snappy butler wore a black suit and fastened his hands behind his straight back. I rose then dropped the boring book to a damask armchair.

"Someone left their coffin early. Requested or required?"

"A distinction milady?"

"Point taken."

At the den's entry, the white-gloved employee twisted a gold knob and stood aside. He announced, "Miss Wardwell, milord." Why the introduction when his master smelled me the second, I left the solarium?

"Thank you, Williams. Tea, please."

"Very good, milord." The aged guy executed a smart nod before he closed the door and sealed me inside the den with him.

The ancient lord, sleeves rolled up, wrote something at the familiar desk. A rumpled dress shirt and missing tie implied he labored on something important. Neat paper piles, a stack of maroon booklets, and large ledgers occupied most of the massive desk. For an unemployed former politician, he worked a lot.

The quiet pen scratch and soft fire snaps reminded me. No housemaid hovered, and we were alone. Would he act as pleasant as when he walked me to my room? I played with my shirt collar. The count twice curled two crooked fingers, not glancing from his papers. The spider commanded his prey to move further into his web. When I obeyed, a gulp hurt my esophagus.

Eyes signaled me to sit on a familiar chair near the crackling flames. "Please sit. I am nearly finished. If cold, ring the bell and someone will put a log on the fire."

Fireplaces burned inside every room during muggy summers. Thick surrounding cedars kept the manor unseasonably cold, and the house required heated all year. The monsters suffered from chilly temperatures, or the fires fashioned another human illusion to relax their prey. A shared vulnerability between beast and man blurred reality. But King Monster long ago lost any claim to humanity, no matter how he acted.

Curious about the tea invitation and each day lessened worries about becoming their next meal, I gave up a caution for another foolish adventure. After he pushed work aside, he claimed a matched chair then joined me. Count Simeon's legs crossed, and hands rested on armrests. He always gracefully calculated every minute detail of each purposeful movement and word. My favorite pastime became watching the sophisticated monster. I wanted to think the previous night's circumstances and our goodbye put us on better terms, but I remembered what happened the last time I stood in the room. Did he use me for cheap entertainment?

I stumbled for words to break the itchy silence. "We don't address you as 'your grace' and call you 'lord' like an earl. It's a lower rank. I thought European counts were like our dukes."

"Very astute. When a human, I was a Grand Duke."

"Sheesh, a mouthful."

"Quite. Arriving in England, in whatever year," as he winced at the high ceiling to picture an obscure date. "I settled upon an earl's title."

"Very Count of Monte Cristo."

Eyebrows shot up, and a soft smile shifted his plump lips. "Terrific book."

"I watched the movie," shrugging.

"The mov—"

I cut his chance to belittle me. "So, you didn't like being called, your royal highness?"

"Though a chancellor is like a king, a lord's title is far less ostentatious, don't you agree?"

A grin tickled my lips. "A chancellor outranks a prince? That explains why Dmitri bows to you. Kinda cool."

Chuffed from the barb, he smirked. Mrs. Smith was right about the frightful mood swings and nailed the undead right on the head. "If I insisted on Grand Duke, one would address me as—"

"—Imperial Highness." I watched enough Masterpiece Classic Theater understand formalities.

Pleasure worked to infect the passive expression. "Correct, Miss Wardwell." He paused before he lyrically grilled, "Sarah—may I call you Sarah?"

"Um, Sarah?" My spoken name buzzed my thoughts, but the master expected the reaction, and at last familiar wordplay began. "Yeah, sure. Um, when you are home—the other prodigia call you—"

He flicked a wrist. "We prefer immortals." His tone oozed ego when he explained, "During matters of state, one addresses me as, Your Imperial Highness while other occasions, I am referred to as Sire." A leg re-crossed, and another wave rejected the details as unimportant, but I knew better.

"Matters of state. Holy cow."

"Holy—?" My euphemisms and poor vocabulary offended the eighteen-year-old trapped in a thousand-year-old mind.

I teased him further. "You ain't familiar with the term?" But the butler interrupted before he admonished me, carrying a silver service. A welcome black tea scent and biscuits squirmed excited hips. After Williams set down the polished tray, I half-rose from my chair before the count flashed me a palm. The polite host stood from his pseudo-throne.

"That will be all."

"Very good milord."

"You don't have to play Mum."

"The least I can do given your experience at a guest's hands." He poured a dainty teacup balanced on a coordinated saucer, added two sugar lumps, then splashed some cream. How did he know how I took my tea, and what other habits did he memorize? I shivered.

When he refrained from pouring himself a cup, I nearly blurted something idiotic about the tragedy when forever denied a proper brew. Unlike the ill-mannered prince, he curbed the desire to drink blood in my presence. Once he returned to a chair, he propped on an elbow, and an index finger alighted against a shaved chin. It felt like he read my mind and dared my comment. Instead, I sipped the godly liquid.

It felt good to have a normal conversation with the guy, so I continued to chat if he acted sociably. "So, what's the ring for?"

Pride studied the family crest-looking jewel. "The Chancellor's ring?"

"Yeah."

"Yes?"

"Yes."

"An old life's light tower. My maker bestowed the seal, therefore only he shall remove it."

"Oh. But Dmitri was one too?"

"My warriors wear smaller versions. But yes, like mine, reminds them of who and what they protect." I drank. He stared.

Finishing my cup, "I see."

He flipped the subject like his unstable moods. "I wanted to extend my sincerest apologies for last night. Such wild guests and temper displays are rarities, not the norm."

"Wow, how do I rate?"

"Your peerage title?" Modern slang guaranteed me a small verbal sparring victory.

"What I mean is, when did I become a mage who deserved an apology?" If I baited him enough, our fireside chat might go down the wrong path. I analyzed his closed body language for anger hints, but the control master looked unbothered. My tight diaphragm relaxed while inside I kicked myself in the butt.

"A guest's comfort matters because I receive so few. Besides, I prefer civility between us." He over annunciated the 't' in the word, civility, and drew the 's' in 'us.'

I placed the teacup on a varnished Victorian end table. "So, I've been havin' a bit of a think. We've gotta deal?" Why did I goad the bastard?

"Do we have a deal?" He phrased constant corrections to remind me about undereducated ignorance.

"Yeah, do we gotta deal?"

He pinched his nose bridge and waved. "Restate this so-called deal, so we are both on the same grammatically correct page."

But two could play Evil Monster's game. "If you keep me safe and don't eat me, I'll join Team Prod."

"—crack your bon—I have not cracked anyone's bones since—Miss Wardwell, how uncivilized do you think we are?" He acted like Speaker Bercow admonishing a junior minister at Prime Minister's Questions. I suppressed a torrent of giggles.

"Don't catch me out! You're the one who ate human." My gut burst unchecked laughter. When the rapid blinks increased, I talked past the wrist at my mouth and went in for the kill. "So, you don't keep in your cellar dead bodies from old meals?"

"Bodies—" He reared his chin. Score one for Team Sarah.

After I found a slim edge, I rattled, "Smith said my clothes came from last week's meal. You have a rotten pile of naked corpses in your basement. The woman who owned last night's blue dress—was she as hot as me?"

The host's neck realigned, and his forehead smoothed. For a few seconds, the backs of his finger covered his mouth then responded, "She was having a go at you—"

"A go—?"

"—a bit of sport."

"Yeah, I know what it means."

"You do?"

"Yeah."

"Yes?"

"Yeah!"

Delighted eyes sparkled myriads of reds. "And sorry to disappoint, no corpses pile in my cellar, only fine wine and expensive coffins."

"Fine wine and—" A giggle tumbled, "Now who's having a go?"

The maid's admonishment again swapped a monster for the young man. "Quite."

"Then what do you eat?"

"When our labs created synthetic marrow, we outlawed direct feeds."

"Wait. What?"

"Twas necessary to preserve our anonymity. You see, secrecy allows the Lowers to keep control, and important after the witch persecutions."

"If you can grow marrow, just kill off the other two species and be done with it."

He cleared his throat. "Yes, well—"

"If you made the laws and are stuck here, break them. I won't tell you."

He perched a finger underneath his chin, legs re-crossing. "Though no longer chancellor, I am law-bound and lead by example, not an office."

"It doesn't explain Anthony as your after-dinner mint."

He inspected his manicure. "A lapse in better judgment and temper. Nobody toys with my weapons."

"Your weapon—"

"Especially a vile human. We are the Highers."

"So said every dictator." When my companion's mouth opened, I rushed, "What happens to me as your weapon?"

A business-like monster reappeared and swapped placed with the chatty guy. "Shall we craft the details of our little arrangement as we go?"

"I don't think—"

"—in the meantime, I afford you a guest's privileges."

"Guest privileges? Club Prodigia has perks?"

"Alas, you may not leave the grounds, for your protection, of course."

"Of course."

Hands tapped once against his knees. "Most excellent," speaking like my Grandfather.

"So—basically behave or go to my room and wear the same clothes for weeks?"

The barb knocked a new slow rhythm on his armrest as the atmosphere and burning logs snapped louder. "Sorry, shouldn't poke the bear."

"Poke the—"

"You know—"

"No matter. Our arrangement flushes nicely, Miss Wardwell."

"Sarah, remember?"

"Mmm, Quite."

I tilted my head at the door then asked, "Can I go?"

"May you go?"

"Yeah, sure. Can I go now?"

"A few more queries, if you will permit me the time, Sarah." My name purred gave him whatever he wanted, so why ask?

"I gotta choice?"

"No."

"For the record, you suck as a man."

"I am still blessed by minor miracles."

"So, what's your question, Count?"

"Your family neglected all forms of learning. You unused powers to escape because you have none."

"Still waiting for the question, Count Simeon." Did I want to jump up and kiss him or slap the hell out of his serene face? Maybe slamming his tapping fingers in a desk—

"Vasile, please call me Vasile."

"Huh?" I needed to improve my listening skills.

"Vasile."

"Okay, Vasile." The name became a heavy chunk on my tongue.

"Your schooling?"

"Oh, yeah. Our library's books taught me basic occult knowledge, but all mages are born with some abilities."

"Like?"

"Sensing energy, seeing auras, you know the usual stuff."

"Such a pity," clicking his tongue.

"You lost me again."

"The lonely existence you had."

"Have," correcting his verb tense.

"Yes, yes, of course."

I thought it best to bob him around and maximize the sympathy party. "So, can I get a telly?"

"Can you a—telly?"

"Jesus," puffing hair off my face. "Never mind."

"Why did you run?"

Another infamous trap wrinkled my forehead. "Remember— my mother's plan? To rob my powers and kill me?" A cupped gesture flexed towards his chest twice. "When I learned other occult kids had a life outside magical walls, I left."

When I worded the solitary existence, I looked to say anything else. Thankfully, the meager fire pulled attention away from me. "More tea, Sarah?"

"Oh, um, yeah."

"Yes?"

For a change, I felt defiant, not miserable. "Yeah."

He strode to the silver service, and elegant poise poured my tea. Without a single rattle, he brought me the delicate cup. When reaching for the gold-rimmed china, I touched him underneath the saucer, and my eyes met a deadpan glare. One cannot imagine the bleak fear when a monster stares right through your soul. Our touch lingered a second too long under the tiny plate, the moment supplying more thinking fodder for later. When he snapped away, I squirmed against the matching throne.

"May I inquire about any further nightmares?" as he sat.

An earlier life's memories assailed me every time I slept, but before I memorized details, the dream scattered to waking hours. I only remembered Anna's feelings, which compounded mine. "Nope. Not one."

He smirked like he knew I lied. I later discovered the prods had no compulsion powers, and the maid spied on me and reported my every fart. I shuddered while he questioned, "Care to particularize the one dream?"

"Nope."

"No."

"Nope."

"Pity, it drove you straight into my arms." The jerk's grin sent a hangnail in my teeth to prevent storming out. The need for more information to plan a better escape rooted me in place.

"Just snowy mountains, green fields, sheep, and thick trees."

"Sounds like my home, Transylvania."

"Shocker."

"Alas, you fail to explain the cause of your screams heard for miles."

Best to avoid the embarrassing talk, "No irony there, you from Transylvania. You read Dracula?"

"Dracula? Terrible middlebrow drivel. I read penny dreadfuls written much better."

"Classic literature is junk fiction? Harsh." When he shrugged, I continued, "So, is Dmitri from there too?" I smile, happy to avoid my nightmare.

"It does not shock me to hear you and the Prince on intimate terms. I caught the connection last night." So, he was watching me. "Limited immortal years has not fully shed all his human tendencies. Compassion still weakens the boy."

"Shed humanity?" Why did those words sound familiar?

"Yes. The longer the immortal, the more monstrous we become to mortals. Those mortal fragments provide more patience than what I care to possess."

"And more likable too."

"But the heart of an immortal beats stronger each day, as he yearned to slay you as I do."

"Do and not did?" Chancellor Grammar never misspoke, so I clarified the verb tenses to clear my neck from the guillotine he held above me.

He left the question alone and launched into Dmitri's story. The Prince and adopted sister hailed from parts near Transylvania.

One Christmas blizzard, the count wore a mortal noble disguise when he met the siblings at midnight mass. "My hat blew—"

"—off your head and I—I mean, Anna chased it down the road.

"She brought it back."

"Yeah."

"Yes."

"Yes."

"An eventual fondness for the spirited prince developed over time, but Annalyse—" voice trailing. Love and longing arched his aura higher as it sparked green turned a rich gold.

"I see why you adopted him. He's okay, for a prod."

"If we are to be friends, I detest the slur, Sarah."

"Oh, I didn't think—"

The massive ruby jewel caught his attention when the fire's glow cast red specks on delicate wallpaper. He waved off the fence and confessed, "Everyone loves the boy. Fancies himself a playwright more than the fine warrior he is. But most of all—"

"—your keeper."

"He prattles." I grinned while he waggled a finger. "Alas, any who cast my Good Time Charlie inconsequential, including myself, does so at their own misery. We both do adore duplicity. Therefore, he hides his bravery and intelligence very well."

"He does?"

"Quite so. The chap sets the most exquisite traps." I widened my dropped jaw. What trap did the prince set when he played the piano for me? "Besides, status as my heir is not for the weak."

"You lost me."

"Then, I shall do my best to find you." I gulped, "As my only living descendant, he wields a tremendous prestige capable of corrupting anyone weaker."

"Well, it worked because I see him as an Oscar Wilde, not Spartacus."

The comparison bore his half-chuckle. "Please do not say that to him and feed an already inflated ego."

I grinned. "Right?"

"I am always right. Did your family allow many suitors?" The tiny head tilt suggested he waited for a sign he successfully rattled me.

As I became accustomed to rapid mood and topic shifts, the ploy only half-bothered me. Wavy carrot-colored hair fell across my chest when I turned the tables. "Suitors?"

Crimson regard roamed the air above my head. "The modern term is—"

"—boyfriends?" Despite a palm across my mouth, a giggle slipped. "I was locked up, remember?"

"Yes, yes. I quite forgot."

I chuckled, "Liar. But someday, I'll have a bunch." When he scratched dark wavy curls and his brow knitted, I laughed.

"Your laugh charms and disarms, Sarah, and confess you cast me under your spell." Liquid words oozed an unexpected flirtation, intimate air closing around us.

"I guess I'll try to laugh more?" God, I sounded lame, so I again steered the talk from the brink of insanity. "That night you kidnapped me—"

"Saved you?"

"Sure, pal. How did you know I needed help? I don't act grateful and all, but I am."

"Quite by accident. While enjoyed a rare night of cards and cigars at a gentleman's club, I distinguished your familiar heartbeat and feminine bouquet. Rather overwhelmed my senses."

"Overwhelmed?" How long would we go on repeating each other's words?

"Constantly." The play with verb tense bobbed my esophagus. "Imagine my surprise to find savage dogs hunting my wife's carbon copy."

"Imagine."

"And one simply cannot stand for such effrontery."

"I guess?" After hushed seconds, the control freak's hands rested across his knees then stood.

"Very good. You may leave." Count Dimitrov dismissed me.

CHAPTER 9

Objects are closer than they appear

MY BEDROOM'S DECORATIVE ceiling and intricate crown moldings presented minor distractions. The swirled white wood glistened in the afternoon sun. Damn, I woke early. If only I owned a tablet or TV, my mind would stop reliving wrong fascinations. The jailor's weird teatime supplied another mental movie to repeat. Our time together fostered more concerns than answers and deepened entrapped feelings. Besides, I could not deny the lousy free-fall at the jerk. So, who was the real magic dealer? Screw the rite because before under his magnetic spell any further, and I needed to refocus my failing efforts and escape. Each night as a hunting coven neared, the master warped more of my fragile willpower to his sticky agenda.

Besides weak powers, another problem presented. If I trained or worked my raw occult skills, the energy shifts exposed my unexpected locale to any searching mages. It's hard to find a single human among billions. But magically finding a fellow mage came easier when one tracks disruptions from magic vibrations. I ground my teeth. I wished a family searched because a mortal enemy kidnapped their beloved child. But a foul need for their own supernatural weapon spurred their pursuit. I preferred typical relatives, unsure if other occult families acted like mine. Then again, no man could free me from him.

If the evil got too close, the prods would kill me to save themselves and after delivering my body like a bad pizza. Death laced every scenario. But one tiny detail supplied much-needed assurance. For now, the creepy similarity to the dead countess provided a temporary safety, but no shelter from a terrible temper.

What would it be like to be a human and not me? I imagined driving a car, buying groceries, then meet friends for a pint. Mentally, I wandered shops and a cute guy offering to carry my many bags. If I ever wanted such freedom, I needed a say about my destiny and an end to lasting loneliness. I refused to be anyone's weapon, plaything, or power tool, but strive for a better existence. But first, I had to survive. And I deserved better, even if fate disagreed.

A greedy thirst for independence combined with emotional pain darkened an already bleak mood. If I wanted to alter my life, I needed to stop drooling over a monster and leave. The freefall attraction for that perverse creature only fueled half-hearted plans.

Did Anna's memories inflict the wrong hunger? No matter where the fantasies came from, I loved a dream more than a narrow-minded ghoul. I cherished my human illusion.

I slapped the covers, growled, sprang from bed, then wrenched the wardrobe open. The clothing choice and life's crappy direction popped a hasty plan into mind. I hurled the cabinet shut. The paintings on the wall rattled their disapproval. The doorknob jangled. I smoothed my demeanor before Mrs. Smith marched in with the late afternoon breakfast. I displayed boredom. Another monotonous night sprawled before me.

"Up early." After she fixed the bed then left, I shoved the tray aside.

I jammed on clean clothes before the maid spied from some peephole. Inside a jean pocket, I tucked twenty quid stuffed in a bra before the gala. I growled under my voice, "I quit!" I walked off the job and gave up the weapon title.

I counted on everyone buying my complacent act. If Smith sensed I planned to run, she would zoom straight to her master. So, I maintained my daily routine and wandered to the solarium while I hoped my pounding heart undisturbed the monsters. A white piano key clinked under a tense finger. Thoughts drifted to the many nights spent in the bright room, the Prince my source of fun. Weak resolve to run faltered when I faced losing a friend because no childhood friends prevented good judgment when making allies.

A bullied staff received Mrs. Smith's shouted reprimand, and the yell bounced into the yellow sunroom. I tiptoed to the enormous antique windows. When steps pounded away from the far wall, I confirmed someone watched me all the time. A squeaky window hinge winced my eyes. Rippled glass panels glittered magnificent greens and yellows after pushed into the late afternoon sun. Heated roses and gardenias replaced smells of old fires and books.

Daytime weaved a seductive illusion of safety across the Earth where creatures lived unharmed, and horrors never existed. But I knew better. Soon, the sun sunk to its Yorkshire bed, and confined night masters returned to reclaim their property. I squatted on the window ledge for a moment then dove towards freedom or another bad idea. I landed a foot past the thorny rose bushes, and my injured ankle barked. I crouched and whipped my head around, but nobody saw me fly out of the building. Free from prying eyes, I focused on the yellow-green English fields.

The treeline teased an eternity away, so I propelled sneakers as fast as possible and ignored my angry leg. After jogging for what felt like miles, I reached a paved road. My chest heaved while I placed hands on my knees to scour the grand residence I left behind, now an insignificant speck. No ghouls or their vengeful servants chased me. A hand wiped my sweating brow, then fanned my shirt several times. While I caught my breath, odd remorse tickled, and the unwanted feelings fed fresh doubts. I bit my bottom lip, and shoes turned from the lane. I winced my eyes shut but still saw Dmitri's laughing face and Vasile playing off aggravation from our banter. I stepped towards the small dot on the horizon. A prized free life neared my control, but the prods pulled me back. My feet touched the grass again. I circled an emotional event horizon like light nearing a black hole. If I stayed, his gravitational pull locked me into an unmovable path to the point of no return. My soul fell into a certain empty hole, and once sucked inside, their dark world would shred me into nothing, like starlight forever lost to the observable universe.

I squared and returned to the road. "Right, then." The narrow roadway wound through poplars had waist-high stone walls piled on each side, and in the distance, a car crested a hill. "Oh, God!" I grinned, bounced eager feet, then waved excited arms. The compact auto meandered the country drive and then sputtered to the roadside before me. Different from the gala escape, things went better. But one's fortune can shift as often as the planet swallows a sunset, and had I know how my bad my situation would change, I would have begged for a return ride to the prison.

The ruddy-faced man twisted calloused meaty hands on a steering wheel and adjusted his tweed driver's cap when I asked for a lift. "My car's broken, and a worker at the estate is fixing it."

"What poor luck, Miss."

"Truly. Mum is at the hospital, and I need to get back to London." He readjusted his hat and then agreed to give me a ride. I squealed, leaped around the car, and climbed into the cramped two-seater.

During the drive, the farmer cheered about the rare sunny weather. Warm summer sunshine created his happiness, but I faked my cheerfulness while nervously clinging to the seat. Every few seconds, I cracked a sideways look at the passenger side mirror. I prayed the glass lied, and objects were no closer than they appeared. But no careening Range Rover chased us.

"How far the drive?"

"Oh, a wee fifteen minutes, lass." To calculate the time needed to board a train, I subtracted minutes until sunset from the travel time. If my luck stayed the same, I had an hour to spare. I hissed an exhale and clenched fists on the seat tighter.

When we reached the charming depot, I rushed my thanks then dashed towards a kiosk. The British find quick goodbyes awkward, but not me that evening. But the momentum crashed to a halt. I never bought a ticket before. The poster with the printed schedule and ATM-looking machine confused me, and after my dismayed frown, an attendant materialized to helped me.

"Where are ya going?"

"The next train anywhere."

"Course. It's Sunday, so the trains don't come as often."

"It's Sunday? How much is the fare?"

"Lucky for you its super off-peak rates. The next one is headed to Cambridge and only twenty quid."

"Brilliant! My lucky day, it seems."

The machine spat a white card with orange stripes on the front and a grayish-brown strip on the back. But the stamped time delay totaled over an hour, and that meant waiting for ten minutes after sunset. Did Vasile have supernatural speeds fast enough to reach me in that narrow window? I would soon find out.

I shoved the paper in a rear pocket. "Thanks." Who sat on the only cracked concrete bench? I waited. I watched.

My knees bounced like a crack addict experiencing withdrawals. But I waited for a train or death, not drugs. I tore inconspicuous gazes into each dark blue alleyway and examined worrying shadows. A black raven squawked overhead on a nearby pole. The ugly bird's beak twitched as five others joined it. A single crow created a loud racket, but more than one crow turned into a noisy murder. I froze my bouncing knees. I held my breath. The sun fell behind a hill. Mages worked the eyes of crows to see long distances. I twisted at the obnoxious birds, and their synchronized head twitching earned my middle finger.

The platform vibrated under jiggling feet. Calves poised for a mad dash into the train, which took forever to grow larger. I bounced on a yellow line designed to coral passengers away from the electrified tracks. A whoosh blew messy hair in my face as the blue carriages whizzed past and halted on squealing wheels. I hopped on the balls of my feet. Electric doors dinged before whirring open. I did it. I really pulled it off. A single person got off.

Just as I plunged inside the gray and red interior, someone or something grabbed a bicep. I inhaled an alluring male scent through clenched teeth because I knew who awarded fresh bruises. I glowered at his matched fury and tried to yank my arm to wrench free.

He hissed, "Quiet and followed if you care to live." The backward jerk massacred any smart retort, and the angry count towed me farther into a dark alley connecting the platforms.

"Let go!" When he tugged my stiff limb, I stiffened my legs and jerked back in return. Tucked deep in the shadows away from invasive stares, he slammed me against blue cinder blocks and pinned me. The same demonic growls heard the night he kidnapped me echoed down the alley. Goosebumps shuddered my bones and rattled clenched teeth. Panic widened my terrified eyes.

But a smooth touch on a cheek quieted a certain scream. He placed the other splayed hand against the structure beside my shoulder. The gesture and when his body mass smothered mine, and wiggly squirms stopped. Hell's growls and the hissed train silenced. Breaths evened. A blown piece of litter froze. My assailant tucked me inside a suspended time where a breathless young woman and a hot guy hid, not predestined enemies. The passageway's shadows secreted a hunted mage who mentally begged a violent prodigium for her first kiss. Warm breath cascaded around a chilled earlobe when he rumbled, "Try a cloaking spell. She must see sweethearts if we are to survive."

"Huh?"

More urgent, "Sarah, I am vulnerable. They will slay me in seconds."

Slay?"

"If I leave to save myself, you'll die."

"Die?" I blinked.

"Yes, Sarah. Die. Concentrate."

"No, wait. Stop confusing me. You just don't want to lose your weapon."

A stern red glower bore deep, "Forget those silly words and become my lover."

"Lo—lover?" mouth drying.

"I shall show you what you missed." The hand on the wall lowered and snaked around my back. My stomach flipped somersaults, and legs numbed. One firm tug from him drew me tight against the monster. He thumbed my chin.

Over the noisy crows, "The spell, Sarah."

But I focused on scrumptious lips near mine, not his command.

"I'll try."

I hated to lose the sexy visual, but squinted eyes increased concentration because I needed every bit. I fixated on the building energies that swirled around us because, as a weak mage, I required as much power as possible. Lucky for me paranormal creatures exuded energy, rich enough to empower any unpracticed spell. "Abscomdam." I envisioned two human lovers wrapped in each other's arms, inside a magical cocoon.

My mother's nasal tone echoed through the depot, "Grab her but leave him to me." Even with shut eyes, I sensed her on the platform as she scanned the alley. I fisted his coat lapels as the spell neared collapse.

"Concentrate."

Closed eyelids prevented me from expecting the gap close between our lips. I jerked, but tender patience eased me into a breathtaking first kiss. While we kissed, he inhaled to savor a luxurious delicacy, and curled fingers clenched my skull's base. After I waited for what felt like centuries, my shaky hands wound in his brown wavy locks.

No woman should ever get her first kiss from a calculated monster while worse enemies chased but hiding in a dingy black alley I made out with the leader of all monsters. Would you blame me? Restrained passions from a closeted life untangled. And who cared if death circled as an undead thing kissed me? Lust, I never knew scrambled logic and hurtled common sense before another oncoming train.

"Priestess Wardwell, I think they're gone. He had a head start."

Feet scurried, and Mum's faded voice called out, "Impossible. Check the—"

After destructive energies and growls dissipated, he jerked away and craned his neck down the alley's exit. Weak knees slumped me against the depot and my chest. When I stepped from the building to speak, his rushing palms captured my flushed cheeks. Though the sun disappeared while we hid, I still saw his heated stare scour my face. I moved to return to his arms, but Vasile stiffened while he cradled my head. I placed hands on his hammering chest. Vibrant reds and silvers devoured my blue eyes and imagined similar denials and forbidden cravings.

"My ruse worked." He let go and then jumped away. Released, I stumbled forward.

"Ruse? I thought—" my fingers found my puffy lips.

The station lights caught his cheekbones as he searched the platform from our little corner. Long fingers by his side flexed and inched near my mine. When I touched him, he snatched up my forearm. "We must hurry." A hard wrench propelled my jog to keep pace with his tall legs. I whimpered when a cold-hearted prod swapped places with and a heated man, I wanted more than freedom. Inside the dark alley among blown pieces of litter and dust, I met a different sexual predator. Bitter bile stung my throat. If only I jumped in front of the train, I missed thanks to him.

"You're hurting me!" yanks powerless against the vice-grip on my bicep. I locked my legs and fought the drag through an empty car lot. On the hundredth try to free a sore arm, he halted mid-step, then slammed into his back. He turned to face me, seized my other limb then shook my shoulders. I had no choice but to stare at the terrible rage and snarl brandished fangs, but I refused to back down. He rocked me once before we started yelling into each other's faces.

"Not once but twice we risked our lives—"

"Don't flatter—"

"—to save you. And I—"

"—yourself because—"

"—knew better than to keep you alive. If you bewitched me—"

"I didn't bewitch—"

"Silence!"

"You shut up—you, you egomaniac!"

A converse sneaker stomped an Oxford loafer. What eighteen-year-old wore those kinds of shoes anyway? Before anymore name-calling, a careening SUV sped sideways into the parking lot on squealed tires. The expensive black auto screeched to a stop a billowed dust cloud hid the car for a second. I choked on the acrid rubber and burnt engine oil as the passenger door sprung open. Dmitri leaned over a seat and ordered, "Get in!"

The count unlatched a rear door, nearly tearing it off the hinges before he flung me headfirst into the revved getaway vehicle. Like the evening he stole me, he tossed me inside headfirst while Dmitri yelled at him to hurry. My head banged on the vehicle's far side after a potato sack toss from a mood-swinging sexual predator, after my first romantic kiss. The night got better and better. I righted myself and rubbed my scalp.

"Jerk!"

The angry monster flattened a hand against the roof and grasped the middle armrest as the vehicle peeled out of the lot. "Perfect time, old chap."

I slammed the seatbelt buckle in place as the irate prince adjusted the rearview mirror to parade a scowl. As the driver once more, he stomped the luxury vehicle's gas pedal and tires squealed. He jammed the transmission through its gears, and we hurled through another moonless night, over an unlit wet road. Not using headlight, expert driving skills, and superior vision steered the car."

I muttered, "Deja vous."

"Milord, the plane is on standby." The abnormal formal address affirmed Dmitri knew the difference between work and play.

I squeaked, "What Plane?"

The smug politician next to me touched a shirt's platinum cufflinks. "Brilliant. Most appreciated."

"A quiet three hundred years. We were long overdue, Sire."

I folded sore arms and huffed, "Take me back! I'm not flying anywhere."

"Please, Sire, shut her up?"

"Look D, I didn't mean to make you mad, I'm sorr—"

"Sire, if you don't shut that witch up, I will."

"Leave her be, my son."

"I'm sorry, D! Honest!"

Dmitri swatted the air, and the auto swerved on a flat road. The jerk nearly catapulted me into Vasile.

"Is there a problem?"

Dmitri waved at a buzzing housefly. "Fly keeps—" as he batted the air again. "—landing on me."

A wrinkled brow count batted away a fly as another pest landed on my nose.

"Sire, what the—" A mass of humming flies instantly filled the cabin, then dived into our faces and shut windows. Tires squealed as the car bobbed and fishtailed over the road.

"Dmitri, the vents!"

The prince growled while he flipped closed front air vents and lowered all windows.

"Um guys, I'm kinda sensing alota magic here."

"Sire, make that blight speak English."

"Kindly drive a bit faster, old chap?"

Silver disks glinted when Dmitri shot me hate through the rearview mirror. "Trying. The road is very wet, milord. They must have been nearby when she ran off."

"And judging by the flies, closing in fast."

Dmitri's arm slapped a chrome gear shift, and heads fixed to headrests. "Our little dinner party drew attention."

"Never underestimate mages, m'boy. We expected them but not her running."

"I'm in the car, ya know."

"Very fortunate Sire because you only just located someone to assist her ritual."

"Assist my ritual?"

"I quite agree—"

"So, you guys are gonna ignore me all—"

Vasile's stare whipped to my side of the auto. "Silence when your betters speak."

"Betters?! Betters!"

"If the twat runs from all her problems, she'll never amount to anything."

"How dare you—" My words died when Head Monster turned towards me, inch by painful slow inch. In the muggy darkness, wild red hair lashing my face from lowered windows, I sensed his lasered anger. I gulped a frustrated sob when animal eyes leaned closer. Again, I ruined everything to include a friendship.

Accepting my forever-pitiful existence and the recent sexual manipulation, rained hopelessness over any desire to complete the rite. I wanted to wither and die, not get stronger for someone else.

CHAPTER 10

Social distancing

WE SWAYED ALONG A DIM curvy road for twenty minutes when the street changed, and the prince broke the bone-crushed silence. "We're here, Sire." A neck jerk stop screeched the tires when one fly landed on my knee. Dmitri flicked on the headlights. I poked around his seat as tall pines parted to reveal a remote airstrip. A shocked mouth dropped at the chromed Gulfstream V that waited on the narrow tarmac. The jet sparkled glamor as high-pitched engines whined, and a starched uniformed crew reported for duty near polished metal stairs.

The less than dynamic duo jumped from the SUV, and Dmitri's snap sprung employees into action. But the count's demands met resistance. Vasile labored to yank me from the auto while two crewmen dashed for the car's boot. Orders barked, and luggage flung while my antagonist battled kicking feet. No way in hell was I getting on that contraption with them. I twice kicked Vasile square in the forehead.

As I dodged another grab, Mother Nature started a hidden Halloween smoke machine. Dense clouds clumped and snaked along the ground, choked the headlight beams, and fashioned small blinking wing lights into large yellow balls. The breeze dropped and familiar rot assaulted our noses. Precious minutes trickled away if we wished to escape. The chancellor stopped a renewed grab for a thrashing leg and shot Dmitri a worried look as chaotic rushing ceased.

"Smell that?" A cawing crow cloud blocked the moon, and electric lights dimmed.

I screamed, "They're here!" I nearly knocked Vasile over when I blasted from the car, and converse sneakers sprinted towards doubtful safety, the plane. The prince barked more orders while our shoes crunched gravel in time. We pounded up the chrome stairs then scrambled across the aisle as Dmitri boomed, "Get this thing in the air. Bangor, Maine. Now."

A collective, "Yes, sir!"

A man banged a Louis Vuitton suitcase under the jet. The prods stored luggage for ill-timed ventures, and over the years, each fashion trend changed the contents. Based on the thinned lipped man who tossed bags under the craft, he too sensed the lethal danger. "Forget the bag, man!"

"Yes, sir!"

Dmitri pushed me into a cream-colored leather seat to storm passed me.

"Rude much? Social distancing not in your vocabulary?" After no response, my voice rose higher, "I'm scared, too, ya know."

The prince thrust a thin brown briefcase at the stern count. "Sire, new passports, money, and requested papers." Dmitri tightened his jaw, stuck fingers into a coat pocket, then plucked out a sleek cellphone. A clenched fist pulverized the smartphone into a million black fragments. Plastic crumbles dropped into a seat's cup holder, and then he briefed the unimpressed leader while I puzzled at the seatbelt. I ignored their exchanges. When a steward buzzed past to secure the overhead bins, I moaned. In moments, they forced me to take my first flight.

The satisfied attendant buckled into his crew seat as the jet screamed. Seconds later, the aircraft devoured a pitch-black runway and pasted its passengers against their seats. The reckless pilots flew the airplane the same way Dmitri drove when they pushed the craft's engine RPMs to a level, aeronautical engineers never intended. The walls, cabinets, and china rattled while the plane forced into thick air. "Oh God, we're gonna die!" When we hurtled into the cursed fog, the cool steward examined his nails. Yet I clasped the armrests with a death grip.

Skilled pilots defied physics when the craft ate the sky from a scientifically impossible climb. But despite our hurried efforts, smelly rot clogged my nose. Both worried prods scoured the blank windows like they expected to see witches on brooms keeping pace as flies dive-bombed our heads. Then, tiny pings peppered the hull's outside. Dmitri skittered away from a window when a few thuds turned into an avalanche of bangs from birds hitting speeding metal. The mages used every trick to pluck us out of the air.

"If they hit the engines, we're done." The sick bangs clenched fists and curled toes.

The flashing overhead seatbelt sign clanged, and when plastic air masks dropped, I whimpered. Alarm sounds blared beyond the closed cockpit doors. The shuttered craft bumped but continued an ear-piercing climb. After ten tense minutes, the last suicidal bird hit metal. A minute later, the floor's incline leveled a bit, and alarm buzzers silenced. The bar's champagne flutes stopped rattling, bins popped open, and cashmere blankets spilled to the mocha carpet.

"We are okay, Sire."

Dmitri unbuckled, passed a wide-eyed steward, and knocked on the cockpit. When a white shirt pilot opened the door while seated, the prince asked, "Everything okay?"

"Yes, Your Royal Highness."

"Excellent work, chaps."

"Thank you, Your Royal Highness."

Dmitri returned to his seat and scowled as he waved off the last fly. To avoid thinking about the near plane crash, I reviewed the known facts. I evaded an insane mother and her merry band of twats, but I flew God-knows-where with monsters who blamed me for their misfortunes. I shrugged off the hurtful attitudes, and a terrible temper replaced remorse for running.

I rudely pointed at the sulking prods. "Don't blame me. I didn't make you chase me." Neither acknowledged me. I yelled louder. "Not my fault, so stop glaring." But like last week's newspaper, he ignored me, and my head threatened to pop off shoulders. I shouted so loud my torso bit into the seatbelt. "And for the record, it's your war, not mine!" The wing's flashing blue exterior lights trained their stony expressions. "Look at me, damn it!" The brooded pair made reluctant eye contact. They never saw a woman kick-off. "Destroy me already! I'm living in purgatory!"

The golden immortal's head shook from my undignified rant. "Bloody hell, witch."

"Sod off you, you—bloody—"

Dmitri bent forward. "Bugger—"

"—jerk face!" Vasile unbuckled and slinked to my seat and interrupted my tirade. "About time! Get it over with and crack some bones—"

Strong hands rested on my armrests, and the passive-faced count loomed above me and cast a shadow over my flushed body. I felt raw anger, not natural terror. Death ranked the worst fear, but I craved its release. A puffy-eyed frown deepened, as I itched to slap his smooth expression.

"Anna."

"Sarah!"

"Sarah." His liquid timbre calmed erupted resentments. Seconds froze like when we stood in the alley because somehow, the creature rolled over stubborn time to expose a submissive belly. An urge to claw his perfect face dissipated.

"Jog on!" I jammed shaky hands under my armpits. From his Burberry wool coat, the stalwart monster pulled out a fancy silk handkerchief and then passed it to me. I blew snot onto the slick cloth then barked, "What do you want, more bloody threats? Bugger off you, you—"

"Sarah"

130

"What?" my sulk more even-toned.

A thousand-year-old leader kneeled before the likes of me and then spoke. "An advisor will meet us."

"Huh?"

"I hired a lady to guide your ritual, and everything will be okay."

Dmitri inhaled, "Sire."

"Leave her be," he nipped at the crossed armed prince.

"You got someone to make sure you get your damn weapon."

He purred, "Sarah."

"Let's see, a second murder attempt, running to a foreign country, predators vowing to keep me safe. So, don't Sarah me. Just kill me and get it over with because I'm done helping you."

"Sarah." Fresh tears leaked at each time he kindly spoke my name.

"Stop saying my name!" A careful touch neared wet, red skin, but I flinched. The gentle fingertip touched a teary cheekbone, and an angry slap matched my hearty yell. "Don't touch me, you filthy prod. I'm not your pawn."

"You are nobody's pawn, and you determine who your future powers benefit."

"Sire."

"Excuse me? More mind games or another mood flip?"

Vasile's kind voice pressed to smooth anger, but Dmitri's heavy-lidded eyes rolled. "Until you decide, we promise to protect you." He stood to return to his seat.

"We'll see. I don't trust you two."

Left with exaction after no more adrenaline-soaked my veins, I closed tired eyelids and curled weak legs into my chest. While I slept for hours, a kind person draped a green cashmere blanket around my huddled body. But Dmitri's griped complaints wormed into a weary brain and half-woke me. I buried deeper in the throw and strained to block his annoying voice. But everyone struggled to ignore the insufferable blond.

"You saw how badly they want her. Evil coated everything and can't get it from my bones."

"I know."

"We only survived these long years because we stayed hidden and now—"

"I know."

"Yet, you tempt our fate?"

Newspaper crinkled. "I prefer to clean my messes, m'boy."

"No, you hide something." Fists tightened. Dmitri's bold tone pushed the count's limits, and the prince chanced another one of Vasile's nasty moods.

"Only because I risked your life will I explain."

"Thank you, Sire."

"Though born to the occult, she has a pure heart."

"And worth the danger?" Curiosity, not malice, motivated the question.

"Yes."

"Any ideas why she is uncorrupted?"

"Besides not instructing magic, they forgot to teach her hate."

"No offense, Sire, but you are the one teaching the hate."

"I know. If I abandon her—Sarah never—"

"—asked for this?" They hit the nail right on the mage forehead. The golden monster's sympathetic understanding extended a glimmer of hope.

132

"She did not. Without us, they kill her."

"She's innocent." Dmitri's sounded less angry.

"Sarah faces a worse fate than Anna. If they take her—"

"They will doom our entire species and what's left of your human heart. Admit it."

"Admit what pray tell?"

"You fell for her." The blunt and unexpected claim crouched me deeper in my seat.

"Hold your tongue, boy. Such insolence I inexcusable."

"You chased her because you love Sarah, not Anna." If eyes opened, I might see Dmitri's point at me.

"I bore of this conversation."

"Admit love, and I will endure the remaining flight silent." Ready legs coiled, ready to race and hug the brusque prince. But I feigned sleep.

"When we land, fly to Romania and debrief the council as demanded."

Mentally I screamed, 'Who cares? Do you love me?'

Dmitri growled, "As you command Sire, but if you need—"

"I know, my son."

I cracked an eyelid when he touched the prince's cheek. Dmitri's clenched fists released. Newspaper crinkled. The count went back to his paper. Nonexistent nerves from many turbulent lifetimes permitted the leader to read while he discussed other people's fates. Since our complicated kiss, the monster showed passion, weariness, concern, and love. The recent crush mixed with the onetime kiss made me forget about his poor treatment. I also forgot his true nature and started to see him as a man. Such forgetfulness risked my life and future independence.

But if we stuck together, I had a chance to gain the prophesied title and its promised powers. Once I owned the mysterious abilities, I planned to take control and my freedom. After the train station, I didn't plan to capture prisoners. As the strongest mage in the world, I no longer filled the role of someone else's pawn ended. But someday, the stiff prig might become mine. However, I had to wait another thirty days for the right moon to earn what was rightfully mine, but a lot can happen. The engines' mellow white noise and gentle sway lulled my tired senses. I yawned.

* * *

The planes decent changed the floor's pitch and lifted my puffy eyes. Both monsters huddled over probable survival plan documents. I guessed a hasty dash across an ocean of time zones while they avoided the sun, required careful contingency plans. But I hoped they got painful paper cuts. The bright aircraft monitor on the wall reported the flight lasted nearly six hours. Vasile's attention flicked from the papers on his lap to me, and an eyebrow raised to discover me awake. A single finger commanded Dmitri's silence mid-sentence. When I blinked twice, he swapped seats with the chair opposite me, and I growled through a groggy haze, "What?"

"Time is brief. Please listen."

"Huh?"

"We land soon. We must go below."

"Why?"

"It is the afternoon—"

"Oh, yeah—the sun." I offered a rebellious shrug then rubbed my face.

"It's imperative you carry out a few arrangements."

"Sod off."

The patient immortal ignored the petulance and shoved a small maroon passport into the limp hand. I remembered the desk's booklet stack. When I opened it, I saw next to my photo an alias. "Jacqueline Hutchings. Treated me like crap, and now you want help. Bloody brilliant."

"Sarah—"

"Go fry in the sun."

"This beneath you."

"By God, Poppet meant it!"

"Shut up Dim—"

A bellowing count pinched his nose, "Silence!"

I jumped. Jaws snapped shut. A frustrated chancellor hurtled his instructions while I struggled to absorb the details.

"Here, Sire." A contrite Dmitri passed him a stack of papers.

Vasile stood and stretched over me to grab the various documents. Body heat and a rich male scent tingled my skin, as the closeness jumped my slow pulse. He gripped my headrest while he balanced on an agile foot. Random turbulence lurched. The graceful leader lost his balance.

Vasile hopped on one leg, slightly staggering. The note clutching hand slammed on my armrest to prevent a crash into the glossy wall. Someone with more agility than a cat invaded my personal space when the other grip on my seatback collapsed against my upper thigh. Long dexterous fingers curled around my leg muscle and flexed. Wide-eyed gawk flew to my leg. Even if I formed coherent sentences, a dry mouth prevented audible words.

Wispy dark hair tickled an ear. "My apologies, Miss Wardwell."

I gulped when he took the seat across mine. A month before the ill-fated flight, he pulled my hair. A week previous to running through his fields, he touched my finger. Hours before he touched a leg near my groin, he kissed me. Where did the next weeks take us? If a fortune teller and not a future queen, I would have jumped without a parachute.

While he inspected his watch, "Shall we continue?"

After the count re-crossed his legs, he settled a crooked finger between his lower lip and chin. Gold onyx cufflinks caught the overhead LED lights. He stabilized the papers across his knee. My gaped mouth snapped shut. Did he purposely cause that scene to change my anger, or was there more to it? Anyone who underestimated the sly master's did so at their peril.

He rattled off the last instructions. "—understand?"

"Huh?"

"Did you hear me? You must understand the details."

"Oh, yeah. Open the airplane in sunlight. Fly to Tahiti. Got it." I shoved wavy red hair into a wrist's elastic band. When Dmitri sighed, I thought someone punctured a tire. Vasile straightened the offending papers with a withered expression.

"Now, your chance to ask questions."

The mood changes and time zone swaps clanged already pained temples, and the laundry list made my head worse. "Got it."

The plane's noises altered when the crew readied for landing. I stretched to free the sealed window. A fast hand covered mine.

"The sun. Crud, I forgot." Dimitri glared when he smushed papers into the briefcase.

Mechanical engine buzzing diminished when the flight speeds reduced. Noises whirred on both sides when wing flaps lowered. A dull thud below vibrated our feet when the landing gear extended. The unfamiliar experience petrified me. I again clawed my armrests. More than moody undead leeches, I hated flying. The bored steward bustled around the cabin to collect blankets and drinkware.

An overhead speaker crackled. "Chancellor and Your Royal Highness, we are arriving at Bangor International Airport. Local time is one o'clock in the afternoon. Temperatures are a comfortable twenty-four degrees. On behalf of the entire crew, enjoy your holiday. Cheers." The pilot's cheery announcement pointed to an undiagnosed mental condition. After almost crashing, while flying supernatural creatures, the composed crewmember sounded professional.

"Some holiday. Wait, the pilots—"

"Well compensated for their discretion. Please remember the details. Failure costs the lives of those able to protect you." I gaped a fish mouth.

"Don't forget, Poppet."

CHAPTER 11

Cheeseburgers and broken dreams

BOTH MEN STOOD, THEN marched the incline to the rear. Near the lavatories, Dmitri pulled on a brown carpet to reveal a hidden cargo hatch. After they shot me one more glance, their heads disappeared underneath the floor. A mechanism clicked in place. Moments later, tires squealed when the flying bullet kissed the tarmac. The jet shimmied across a bumpy runway while engines roared, and when the pilot applied the brakes, I yelped. No sun-sensitive marrow-suckers occupied the cabin, so I flung open the plastic window shade.

Unfamiliar sunlight threw a forehead salute. Once the slower plane smoothed around a corner and my vision adjusted, I saw an old beige 70s airport. Different modern planes shimmered in the blazing afternoon heat. I tossed the secret door a quick shrug and thought they should rot for a couple of days, but the dangerous mess required supernatural help.

"Crap the carpet!"

After the plane parked and an official stamped out passports, we watched the plane placed in the rented hangar. Enormous metal doors banged shut after the tug pushed the jet inside an old metal building. Flecks of orange rust floated to the cracked concrete. I checked off a mental list, Homeland Security checkpoint, and plane storage. A pilot with big white teeth asked a cordial airport attendant to call me a taxi and take the crew to the main terminal. The team booked commercial flights home until their phony employers again needed their services. Two pilots, like programmed footmen, performed well-oiled duties, and the steward pretended he served immortal requests since birth.

A dirty yellow cab that stunk like old cheeseburgers and broken welfare dreams idled outside the private airport. The dated car and insignificant town looked dingy. Locked up my entire life in a London flat, I ogled potholed streets and salt-crusted cars, puzzling how overweight Americans wore unsightly trainers. An equally shabby motel ended the silent six-minute ride.

How exactly did one check into a motel? I tried to recall a movie where an actor played someone checks into a hotel, but Pretty Woman would not work. And though I spoke the same language, I banged on like a daft idiot. "Right then. I have a reservation."

"Name?"

"Right. Um, Sarah Wardwell."

"Nothing under that name." The employee picked her pierced eyebrow, and a scab fleck floated to the faded laminate countertop.

I fumbled the backpack. "Oh, um—bugger, yes! Try—" Out of view, I opened my stiff passport and said, "Try Jacqueline Hutchings?"

The clerked checked a computer under the counter. "Yep."

"Brilliant. How much?"

"It's paid." The bored clerk slid papers, a pen, and square paper. My lip jammed between teeth. "Sign?"

"Right." Shaking hands signed the first letter of my actual name before remembered the false alias. One fast motion swapped the signature card for the electronic keys, scared she might change her mind about letting the room.

Bags piled high on the squeaky luggage dolly, I bumped and pulled along the musty hallway. The teal carpet's spotted gold diamonds indicated the owners last renovated the motel in the early 90s. But the considerate proprietor updated the locks to frustrating cards because, after five groaning minutes and a wiggled pee dance, the smudged door clicked open. Stale cigarettes and crusty mold drifted into the airless hall.

After I used the toilet, I slumped on the brownish-orange duvet and touched cigarette burn holes. The telly offered something to do until the next set of instructions, but I watched the filthy window and listened to the air conditioning hum. The drab brown drapes with yellow squiggles billowed from the pushed cold mold. I shook off my daze. Soon the dreary landscape devoured the sun and called for my readiness.

Moments before twilight, the blank employee hailed another cab. Five minutes and five dollars later, I again entered the private airport. The small terminal laid out several rows of connected blue chairs just as burned as the hotel blanket and dated vending machines. Dirty windows overlooked a deserted tarmac. A different clerk, dressed like a gas station attendant, sat high at a tell laminate countertop. He stopped filling out a form to shot me a quizzical look.

"Hi. Um, I flew in this afternoon and need to get something off the jet?" The affable guy jumped off his stool into action, relieved to have tedious boredom ended.

"Always happy to help! Never seen you before. We see a lot of A-listers through here, ya know." The man beamed while he batted his eyes. "Just yesterday, David Bobrik flew in."

"Um, lovely."

"You're British!"

"Other than the accent, how'd you know?"

"You said lovely and not cool."

"Right."

"See, there ya go again." He flirtatiously grinned, but the smile quickly faded. "I say something wrong?"

"It's just, I know someone who always picks on the way I speak."

"Sounds like a real jerk."

"If you only knew."

"Come on. I'll shoot you over to the hangar." He swiped a walkie-talkie near his elbow and rounded the counter.

"Thanks." I laid a jacket across some blue seats.

"By yourself?"

"Yep."

"Look, if you're not doing anything later..."

"I wish I wasn't honestly."

"It's cool. Maybe next time you're in town."

I squirmed under the attention. "Yeah, sure."

Inside the dim metal building, broken bird nests and fallen rust sheets littered the concrete floor. The chilly shadows tucked the sleek white jet to one corner, and another smaller prop plane huddled on the other side.

"John Travolta comes here a lot."

I boosted my voice over humming fluorescent lights. "Damn, it's cold! Bullocks, I forgot my jacket in the lobby," when I took my turn to bat big blue eyes.

"I'll go grab it and be right back! Snag your stuff." Bob, per the red name tag, puffed his chest.

"Brilliant, thanks!"

"Can you get inside?"

"No problemo, mate. Done it tons of times." I thought, 'Problemo? Really Sarah?'

When the cute guy sped away in the dirty decade's old van, I searched for something to bang the plane's side. I spotted a shovel against the rusted corrugated wall, but the random garden tool might damage the expensive getaway vehicle. "Never easy." As hard as possible, my fist's meaty part hit cold white metal and hoped supersonic ears heard the dull thud. Seconds later, the exterior handle tilted, the oval portal popped open, and chrome stairs unfolded. When bulky shadows darkened the half-lit hole, and animal eyes blinked, I breathed more natural, not screamed. Dmitri and Vasile jumped out, shoved the hatchback, and then twisted the latch.

Vas flicked his head to returning headlights that bounced closer. "Do you recall passing a chain-linked fence separating the road and runway?"

"Oh, yeah. I do."

"Fantastic. Pick us up there."

"Um, okay!"

Time apart to cool tempers eased Dmitri's anger because he winked then tugged my blowing hair. The pair bolted into the vast darkness, again one with the night. But for a mighty warrior, Dmitri had a goofy run.

"Got your jacket!"

In minutes I said goodbye to the helpful attendant and promised to stay in touch. Lucky for me, the idling nicotine cab waited. "Thanks for staying!"

"Sure. You Brits always so polite?"

"I guess. Hey, my two friends broke down nearby. Can you take a right and pick them up?"

"Your dime."

The twenty-year-old Oldsmobile chugged into action. Rusty struts squeaked along a bumpy road as I scanned the gloom for monsters. A few minutes, the headlights appeared tall shadows that walked beside the runway's chain-link fence. My white-knuckled grip on the seat relaxed. When bright lights shone on their downcast faces, they looked at the car. The pair avoided looking at the artificial light to hide creepy reflective eyes. If the driver noticed an abnormal silver animal stare, he might freak out and take off with me. The first monster ever created swore the entire species to secrecy, and prodigia lacked compulsion powers to force amnesia. So, a runaway cabbie became a dead guy with a missing spine.

Once we crammed into the rear, Dmitri commanded, "The main terminal."

I asked, "The airport?" One deadly look from my friend silenced me. D just finished being all pissy with me, so for a change, I shut my mouth.

After the rusted guzzler chugged us to the airport's drop off lane, Vasile ordered the man to wait.

"Your dime." As we climbed out, the wheezing driver's greasy fingers punched at a digital red meter.

Outside the car, pungent jet-fumes whipped through our hair, and Dmitri informed his flight to Romania boarded soon. The detailed plans made during such a brief time left me gobsmacked.

"Thank you, Poppet."

"For?"

"Vasile got me here, but you kept us safe." He pinched my nose.

"Not pissed anymore?"

The stylish creature shrugged his black bomber jacket, and then checked his watch. "Never with you, Poppet."

"Since we're best friends again, did ya sleep with the steward? He kinda had the hots for you."

He reared his chin and stepped away. "Sex with a marrow donor? Are you bloody mad?" The word 'mad' in true English fashion elevated an octave higher.

"Just asking."

"Silly witch, oh how I shall miss you." He kissed my hands one at a time. I giggled.

"I already miss our fun. Sorry for the trouble. Honest."

He tugged a strand of hair. "Tis nothing to fret over, Poppet. Warriors go soft without a spot o' danger. Especially that politician." An amused grin flicked to the tall, silent prod behind me. "Take care of him?" A brief flash of concern eased his playfulness.

"Leaving him with a mage, so what could happen?"

"My sentiments exactly," he smoothed when a black Tumi duffle bag lifted at his feet.

"You suck. Don't go." After the chancellor's snicker, I threw myself into Dmitri's arms.

"Hey, now, what's this?"

"—don't leave me with him!" I giggled while pointing at Vasile, who patiently waited for goodbyes to finish.

The pantomimed distress erupted three gut laughs. After escaping certain death, we needed the comic relief. A palm flattened across my hair. "He'll fend off the monsters under your bed."

"He is the monster, remember?" I twisted a snarl at my nemesis. Notwithstanding the garish airport lights, a cut figure reined larger-than-life.

"Come, he must leave."

Dmitri kissed a cheek before he turned to his brother. For a long minute, the two grieved immortals, locked by lengthy history, conversed without one vocal word. "Right." The prince reached inside his jacket and produced a cellphone and then passed it to the sad-faced chancellor. "We knew the stakes, Sire."

Vasile shoved the phone in his coat pocket. "Indeed, we did and drew our private battle lines."

Dmitri bowed. Uncharacteristic humble respect thumped a fist to his chest, "Fidelitate, Sire."

The count gripped the shoulder of a friend, not a subject as he knotted over his old heart. "Fidelitate. And lest your troubled heart bend from worry, fear not you trained me well." Vasile attempted a joke, but amusement unshifted his solemn expression.

The somber banter warmed lodged dread as profound respect and love between the pair emptied my gut. If only I had a similar relationship. The godlike Dmitri waggled jeweled fingers goodbye before he disappeared past automatic double doors. The old airport swallowed the magnificent creature and left behind a resonant void. A bleary horn beeped.

I hovered near the handle as Vasile considered his polished shoes. Yellow fluorescent lights made him look forlorn. For centuries, he relied on one faithful companion. But the chancellor sent the keeper to a legal assembly who wanted us all dead. Dmitri's departure exposed Vasile's lost, vulnerable humanity. When did he swap roles as a manipulative killer to a man?

Back in the cab, Vasile faced a cloudy window. Squawked struts and radio filled uncomfortable silence. The force of nature's rare vulnerability and reaction rattled me. I counted vinyl seat repair patches to distract my mind from an inevitable spiral. In the dark car, two odd teammates shared bone-crushing loneliness. The starkness hurt more than a cold family's treatment. He heard my involuntary sniffle, and for a brief second, and his hand hovered inches above mine before he shoved it into a jacket pocket.

My voice cracked. "Small town."

"Yes." An exhale signaled his relief for the light chatter.

He ordered the driver, "Through downtown, please."

The cabbie punched a chubby finger at the blinking screen and stated, "Highway 95 is faster."

"I wish to see your historic area. I like old things."

"I don't."

"Your dime, chummy."

The taxi bumbled past granite buildings against narrow one-way streets, and after several traffic lights, the gray offices swapped for once-stately homes. While we idled an intersection, a white clapboard house growled my stomach. The sign said, 'Tri-City Pizza.' After the shop, grungy strip malls replaced the dilapidated Victorian dwellings.

"The houses are falling apart."

"Politics drove away most modern industries and impoverished this place. The Bangor city council allowed slumlords to chop up the stately buildings into tiny apartments."

"Nothing stands against time."

"Sometimes, not even an immortal." Vasile no longer looked like a teenager, but a tired man who carried centuries of weight.

For twenty minutes, the cab headed northbound along a double lane highway before the driver chose a numbered exit and departed the road. Compared to London, we took a turn onto 'Nowhere and Lost.' Before the car crossed a long bridge, I read a faded sign. "Welcome to Indian Island, Penobscot Reservation."

Past the bridge, many bumps and dips almost crashed me into my new partner. When righted, a smattering of widespread porch lights glimmered through dark clustered trees, suggested great distances between house. Tires crunched a secret drive's pea gravel winded us through pines to a small ranch-style home, well off the street. The box-like structure's vinyl siding contrasted his English grand estate.

Vasile interrupted the cabbie pulling bags from the boot and tendered crisp bills. The driver nodded before he tucked the money into his plaid shirt. Without a thank you, the creaky auto left us in the dark, alone with singing crickets. After the headlights disappeared, a discrete security panel next to the front entrance received Vasile's finger jabs. A high-pitched beep released the solid white door, and then he stepped inside and flipped a light switch. I followed him as he slid the briefcase across a laminate kitchen countertop. "It will have to do."

"The Brady bunch heard we were coming and left. You picked a dated house, not the Four Seasons?" I grew up closed off from the world, but a wealthy family afforded me the best of what they allowed.

"The best on brief notice. Your bedroom is down the hall. Before you go—"

"Hmm?" Monumental effort blinked dry eyes.

"My accommodations are downstairs." A messy-haired monster pointed at a sealed door near the compact kitchen. "Stay out." Clipped words marked matching tiredness.

Any prod's caution unpacked intense dread into the bravest of souls, but I only cared about a bed. "Yeah, whatevs."

"Bulletproof windows and doors block the sun and any determined mages."

I yawned and decided later to explain how no Earthly materials blocked magic. "Yeah, sure. I keep undead hours anyway."

"I repeat. No venturing past that door. Whilst sleeping, I cannot control certain tendencies."

The creepy threat envisioned hot fangs buried gum deep in a shoulder. "Right. And on that note."

CHAPTER 12

No more eating grapes poolside

FOR THE FIRST TIME SINCE escaping from my
London flat, my family's magical searches unbothered my peaceful
sleep. Before we ran from home, if Anna's memories did not wake
me up, hummed magic currents from their probes did the trick.
Three things caused me to slumber like the undead: sleep, jet lag,
strange peace, and a month of keeping prodigium hours. My pasty
mouth crackled when I rolled under smooth cotton sheets. I
slapped the clock to move it into view. Sunset an hour ago. I
groaned.

"Better get up before he thinks I died." I sat up.

My pale feet struck cool gray carpet to investigate the room. I moaned to myself, "But Sarah, he hears hearts. He knows when you are sleeping; he knows when you're awake, so be a good mage for goodness' sake." I sighed, "Sarah. You lost your mind."

The closet accordion-style doors whooshed open to clothing with price tags. What creepy American minion stocked the house so fast? A tiny attached bathroom supplied fragrant soap bottles, and plush towels itched my greasy scalp. In minutes, a gushing hot shower soaked off the time zones and dried tears. Based on previous encounters, I poured the extra vanilla liquid onto my palm because if I dove headlong Lord Jerk, I wanted to smell good.

I slipped on sweats, and a blue University of Maine tee-shirt then ventured into the modest living area. Vasile, who finally looked his human years, lounged at a cramped square kitchenette. The stuffy politician traded a jacket for worn jeans and a black turtleneck. A dark hair swatch on his bare feet peeked from under his jean's faded hem. He perched a newspaper high in the air. "You don't wear a suit when you sleep in your coffin?"

He laid the paper on the clean table. Amusement twinkled wine-colored eyes like I just asked him if he was a boxer or brief kinda monster. "Good evening, Miss Wardwell. Sleep well, I presume?"

"Hi. Yeah. I did. Not a morning person or a night person. Whatever time it is." I yanked open the refrigerator door and grabbed an orange plastic bottle. I hoped Tropicana was decent juice.

"We will soon entertain."

"Entertain what? Whatevs. Can I go outside?"

A sleepy fog made the hunt for drinkware too tricky, so I swigged from the jug. I waited for Mister Control's outrage about not drinking from a glass. When a prod ate normal food, they became violently ill, so if he one snotty word, I promised to squeeze more than juice from his neck. Snapped crisp newsprint interrupted the heavenly fantasy. Like I said, not a morning person.

"Very well. The security code is the four-digit year."

"Do you even know the year?" Still bitter from his sexual manipulation, I wasted no time flinging attitude in his direction and took my juice outdoors. Little twilight remained, and I wanted to see, not smell the gorgeous land.

Outback and above tall grasses, a small wooden deck jutted off the one-story dwelling. A weak light cast my shadow on the whispering field. A meadow's dry whispers heralded a warm Indian summer. Craggy blue-green spruces, leafy maples, and shimmered ash guarded the remote acre. Across the grass, a pine-scented breeze coaxed a distant deer from the darker forest. A tan head dipped to graze when a grasshopper landed near my foot. I placed the bottle on the porch while my bare toes wiggled deeper into nature's perfect stage. The dirt texture soothed clashed irritability that rivaled Vasile's worst mood.

As I relaxed, I noticed energy churned all around me. Every living and dead organism produces vibrations, even an untrained occultist can detect. Like many food flavors, mystical trembles present various uncommon sensations. Area energies come from emotional and physical pain, embedded in bedrock and buildings. The ability to sense and manipulate vibrations separates real mages from fake human witches. But Maine's vibration felt distinct.

Unlike the U.K., purity vibrated the soil. England's countless wars, death, and sickness tainted the ground and dirtied natural pulses.

Lost in my musings, I never heard the back door slide open or his footsteps in the grass. A long shadow and familiar male scent betrayed his quiet presence. Not wanting our typical verbal sparring to shatter the newly discovered tranquility, I ignored him. But thankfully, the egomaniac allowed peace to continue and swapped tension for silence.

I think he also appreciated the stolen moment and beautiful landscape, but his sexy voice ripped the calm. "You never smile, yet now you do so?" I felt his eyes on my neck.

"Do you blame me?"

"A logical question."

"I'm the happiest when around my element."

"Your element?" The wind whispered through the sticky pine boughs, and hair brushed my cheek.

"You know, Earth, water, fire, and air."

"Those things are not human lore?"

"Hardly. When we are born, some God assigns us an element. Our leaders get two."

"Might I ask about the importance?"

I perked up, happy to talk as his equal. "It's how we fuel spells. We use elements the same way a hydro dam creates electricity from water."

"Ah, yes, I see. And yours?"

"Earth."

"Earth?"

"Yeah."

I finally looked at him and expected him to correct my language, but he teased, "Not fire?"

I chuckled, "Hair color and magic are unrelated." I stretched a hand towards the field. "See watch." Scattered leaves rose from the fragrant grasses and suspend a few feet above the meadow. When I raised my palm, the colorful foliage swirled into a spun twister. I crooked a finger, and the orangish-yellow tornado meandered closer to our long shadows. "I once tried this spell with Grandfather's important papers. I got in serious trouble."

"Amusing parlor trick, but you will encounter stronger magic."

Leaves collapsed when I dropped an arm. "Okay, Count Buzzkill."

"I mean no offense, Sarah."

"Right."

"The deer." He used his head to motion towards the grazing doe across the meadow, arms almost touching.

"What about it?"

"I admire her ignorance, oblivious to our nature—mage and immortal."

"Yep, we don't exactly get along."

"But for now, we stand together."

A long index finger straightened closer to mine. I flexed my pinky response, "Please excuse me. Our guest arrived."

"How did you, oh yeah—superhuman hearing."

Over a shoulder, I watched lengthy legs skip both porch steps. He moved like James Bond, fists positioned at his waist, shoulders squared, and a bouncy stride. The dwelling swallowed his remarkable dynamism. I equate immortal energy to electric subway tracks, invisible to the naked eye, but strong enough to kill when touched. I poised a foot off the dangerous platform named Vasile.

I chewed my lip as I considered the mystery guest and grumbled, "Hope they're not human." On cue, the backdoor slid open, and a stubby older lady marched onto the rear deck. Fresh fall wind blew an orange leaf into a long gray braid. Nondescript clothes and a thrift store purse suggested the woman had little money or use for worldly things. When she stood beside the tall prod, she reached his chest's middle.

"Sarah, may I introduce Mrs. Margaret Davidson from the local Penobscot Indian tribe."

"How do you do?" A posh mother trained me never to say, 'nice to meet you.'

"And Mrs. Davidson, may I present the person we spoke of, Sarah Wardwell. A stroke of luck when Mrs. Davison so graciously agreed to prepare you for the rite."

We traveled so far not only because of danger, but the non-affiliated lady knew everything occult. "A human? Really?"

"Mrs. Davids—"

The scowled woman threw one palm at us. her ability to silence the control master gained instant admiration. "No more talk, Thing. Call me, Maggie."

I laughed at the brave nickname. "Good one."

"You ain't no bettah," she growled and tossed a thumb his way, a harsh Maine accent grating my British ears.

"Excuse me?"

"Sarah, let her—"

"You must be a big deal if he just let you live."

"Let's put the kibosh to this garbage and talk about the elephant tha room. You both claim to be higher beings above humans yet throw off nature's balance."

"I hardly—"

"Let me finish." Her bite snapped shut my mouth. "One greedy species uses energy to manipulate everything to get what they want. The group's existence alone imbalances nature. Either greed or not havin' the balls to roll over and die throws off the universe. No wondah the world falls apart." The harsh statement gutted me, but the prod comparison tickled me.

"Trust me. I learned a lot about my people, and things need to change."

"Trust you? Ayuh, and I wanna a million dollahs. Talk inside. I'm cold." She curled her upper lip when she walked past Vasile's blinked eyes. Score a point for catching Control Master off guard. Sycophants surrounded him for too long, so he needed the reality check.

His puzzled expression suggested, 'What did I do?'

I shrugged.

Two bewildered supernatural creatures followed the bossy human into the warmer home. She plopped on an overstuffed chair with judgy eyes, ready to discuss our unholy union. Vasile perched on a matched blue couch, and a million unasked questions formed jaw-gritting suspense. I picked jagged nails and waited for her to start.

Never one to leave silences alone, "As I said, I want to lead peaceful negotiations—"

"Lemme stop you there. Lead your people?" A hearty cackle shifted me in my seat.

"Yes, through dialogue and diplomacy, I can end the war and restore the craft's honor."

"The craft never had any honor, kid."

"One must admire her optimism, Mrs. Davidson."

"Ain't you stupid for something so old."

She called the most powerful immortal in the world, stupid, and I about fell out of my chair. Crimson eyes slashed at his hired meal, not my tutor. "I'll go get a mop bucket and cleaner."

"If the kid knew how everything started, she would be so perky." When her words returned him to his seat, Maggie scored my undivided imagination.

"I fail to see how a history lesson is necessary, Madame."

"If you're gonna make a kid fight a war, she needs to know."

"I'm not a kid." When they both glared at me, I huffed back in my chair.

"It started when the Romans occupied the Carpathian Basin. The land birthed a supernatural catastrophe."

Surrounding iron mountains and dense forests pooled metaphysical energies in the farming valley. The mages of the area's forgotten race, the Dacians, often used the mystic stirring to fuel magic. But how much confused the world because Slavic invaders absorbed the Dacian language, customs, and records. Eventually, the Dacian's sun god religion melded with other pagan cultures. When societies combined, a perfect storm brewed. The denominations birthed a supernatural cauldron large enough to mix a massive paranormal disaster.

"What disaster?" The older woman sparkled as she waggled a yellow, nicotine-stained finger. She knew how to tell a story.

After Dacian mysticism mixed with the Thracians and Celts, local wild superstitions multiplied. Tales of monsters living in the foreboding landscape entrenched daily lives. Nobody ventured in or out of the valley until the Romans marched over the mountains.

"Today, some country folk still cut the heads of the dead."

"But how do you know what happened if records never survived?"

Vasile half-smiled and said, "Scientists unearthed a few artifacts, but I can confirm the details."

"Oh. Yeah, you're old. I forgot."

The mystic woodland affected both invaders and locals. Only brave souls ventured past the dense mossy wood and kept to the fields. The Carpathian dread even infected the Roman military psyche and colored their Britannic invasions.

"How?"

"They killed all the Druids."

"Wow!"

During that period, a Dacian warlock rose to power, but the intense craving for more magic and wealth blinded him against his backstabbing friends. Unexpected rivals became jealous of the warlock's prosperous business dealings with the Romans and increased occult abilities.

"Infighting and squabbling? Shocker?" as I rolled my eyes.

Before the greedy warlock grew too magically and politically powerful, his coven crafted the perfect plan. The conspirators needed to act on the one thing capable of crippling him the fastest, the warlock's beloved human partner. The priest never expected the murder plot.

I wrinkled my nose. "Human?"

After the warlock took over the area coven, his enemies acted before he completed a rite that granted more elemental magic. So, the schemers promptly hosted a celebration banquet. Upon a perfect killing stage, secret haters positioned his lover. The backstabbers counted on a grieved warlock's suicide or too devastated to seek more power and revenge.

"Hello, Shakespeare."

After the main course, the mage's beautiful lover convulsed and fell to the mosaic floor, a twisted mouth seeped foamy bile. The crowd scattered and pretended to find help while the high-priest tried every known spell to save his true love. Nothing worked. As his lover's body cooled in his desperate arms, the warlock remembered an ancient blood enchantment.

"He created a prodigium?"

"Bingo."

"A sun-worshiping pagan made a night-dwelling prodigia."

"No irony there, kiddo."

Life again filled his dead boyfriend, but the creature required something, during new immortality's early moments, to complete the transfer. The requirement cost the young prodigium, the warlock, and the world.

"Let me guess, the mage's blood?"

The woman smirked when she received our polite host's coffee cup. "We're talking prods, not vamps."

The new immortal cared less about blood, and only wanted to chew through flesh until he hit bone. When his head cleared, the resurrected lover clutched the priest's detached head in his lap. Heartbreak ruled the monster's actions for a millennium. Like the Dacian people, history forgot the lover's names, and the epoch buried their story. Like Christ and Alexander the Great, faith, not facts, declared their existence.

"The prods call him, The Father." The statuesque count shifted her attention.

"Um. Maggie, they consider that word a slur."

She tossed a wrinkled waved. "Anyways, onto the war."

The Father knew nothing about his lover's murder or his. For the longest time, he blamed himself. After he read the spellbook and understood his new nature, a wild-eyed monster stormed from the banquet hall. He intended to grill those who attended the feast. When the long dark-haired immortal whipped open the door, the glaring afternoon sun splashed his body. He screamed when charred flesh curled blue smoke.

"No more afternoons at the pool, eating grapes." I scored Maggie's smile.

A surprised coven hastily planned how to control what they saw their dangerous property, an unknown life unworthy of nurture. When night fell, the sobbing thing burst into the temple and demanded answers. Lies spun about the party to conscript the grieved creature. The spin-doctors explained servitude to mages injected sense to his lover's awful death. A life of service erased his murderous sin, and the warlock's death mean something. The new creation loathed the wicked lot but wanted to honor his partner.

"You're quiet, Vas—Chancellor."

A regal wave followed, "I shall correct the messy bits."

"If The Father guessed the truth that night—"

"You got it, kid. World order might be different."

My pointy elbows riveted to knobby knees. "Tricked into slavery."

"Grief causes thoughtless deeds." Vasile's flattened words carried deep meaning.

"Ayuh! And boy did it."

"The war started?"

"Almost."

Once he learned how to create more immortals, mages enslaved the entire breed to do their night work. Still ignorant, he agreed. For several hundred years, the creatures conducted the darkest whims and deeds of their masters. Eventually, the uncharred painful truth wiggled into truth's light. After he put pieces together, the first creature hid a vindictive rage while he planned an epic retaliation. "But I only know the legend."

I shook my head. "How did he stay calm for so long? Why not rush in and rip everyone's heads off?"

Vasile raised a finger.

"Go ahead, Marrow-suckah, it's your story."

"Natural and magical UV rays hobbled him and endangered the well-being of his children. Any plan had to be perfect."

Quiet centuries passed. Mortal players changed. Memories shortened. But the game stayed the same, and mages worldwide took the docile creatures for granted. The master waited for the ideal moment to sever ties with his slavers and commemorate his creator the right way. To break a mage deal is to break a bargain with the devil. The act carried heavy consequences. While he whittled away time, the prod's humanistic traits and the recollections of the occult warped. Outlandish diligence, patience, and prudence replaced human compassion. Such honed characteristics still serve the prodigia like splendid weapons.

"Explains a lot," I recalled his den when he played roulette with Smith's life.

Under the entire world's nose, the spider's strategy worked. The new immortal traits increased his people's autonomy, sovereignty, and power. Cracks webbed through the slavery agreement into fate's mystical fabric. Occultists, busy with the witch persecutions, became complacent about quiet immortals no who no longer conducted their dirty night work. The Father knew that to fight both mage and human, endangered their small numbers. So, he forever swore his children to keep their existence a secret. Anyone who broke the law died.

"And if he woke up to lab-created marrow and defeated mages, goodbye humans." Vasile waved me off.

Maggie chimed in, "You're not telling her about the thing you guys used to destroy the pact."

"What, their fangs?"

"Very astute, Mrs. Davison. We employed an asset only we owned. Time." Nobody interrupted. "Immortals internalize time as a curse, a blessing, and a resource." The Father took three hundred years to create an undetectable fissure between prodigia and mage. He bore the long period like personal dark ages and secretly formed a government and a skilled army. "But one glorious night, our Father stepped into the light of a magnificent renaissance."

When occult leaders could no longer ignore the disobedience, a priestess traveled to the new immortal headquarters. She demanded he ceased creating new monsters. The master monster's answer? He created his carbon copy and quintessential son. Once a prodigium, a dedicated man-child threw himself into his creator's agendas and trained an undead legion. But twenty years after the son's creation, another delegate beat on the master's door.

Maggie banged her mug on the coffee table, "Yep! Tried to put their dog back in the yahd." I winced, but prodistic patience calmed Vasile.

She recounted how a mage ordered a species-wide return to full conscription. The enchantress presented an impossible condition to forgive to prove her point. For a sign of compliance, she demanded to return the perfect son's head inside a gold chest. She threw the gilded box at The Father's feet.

"Wait!" Both Maggie and Vasile snapped their heads in my direction. "You were the perfect son!"

"I am the perfect son." A whistle sailed, as the plot thickened.

Maggie pressed. The Father loved one other person besides the warlock, his protege. The ultimatum and the devotion disintegrated the spider's calculated patience. "He stepped from his throne and strolled to a casino's all-you-can-eat buffet." The enraged creature stood before the haughty priestess, and one blurred movement ripped a beating heart from her chest. When the gory mass slopped to the floor, he plucked the mage's head off her body and shoved it in the golden box meant for his son. The spider got his insect. An immortal guard delivered her rotten skull inside a chest intended for an undead.

"You guys made the first strike."

Though the chancellor lost many citizens during his term, a strong military prevented a full attack. "And the witch trials kept your kind quite busy. We probed homes for weak defense spells because they weaken with time."

"And you guys have nothing but time."

"Exceedingly so. Our death squads murdered many sleeping magic dealers. Other pests perished throughout the trials."

"Marrow-suckah is right. A people divided had no chance to come together and fight as one. Human governments use that same tactic today. Just look at that social media thing."

"So, why me? Aren't you handing your enemy a loaded gun?"

"In a manner—"

My brain fired at an incredible pace and jumped up. "You risk empowering me just to end small skirmishes. What are you not telling me? Do you need me for something else?"

Vasile wandered to the black reflective French doors that overlooked the meadow and admired a world hidden from mortals. "The acting chancellor relies on soft power to maintain peace. My people are dying. Last year, they killed one of my remaining children. Only the prince lives because he stayed with me these long years. Next time—"

"It could be Dmitri." The reason sounded logical, but I sensed more hidden motivations.

"One by one, they eradicate my chosen. I doubt it is—"

We both said in unison, "—a coincidence."

The older adult snorted. "So, maybe your idiot leader plots with mages."

"Victor has faults but would never do such a thing. No immortal would."

Maggie supplied a random thought. "Your maker's love for you started the war."

"A statement or question, Madame?" Icy energy crackled the air.

She had no clue about his black moods and how easily they flipped. Though prodigia lived inside a human shell, they twisted up normal emotions. "Um, yeah, Maggie—I—"

"Self-blame for a war that killed your wife is dang stupid."

Did the mouthy bold woman carry a death wish and a safeguarding charm? The sullen creature, who breathed infrequently, froze his chest. I gulped and braced for impact. Where did the house owners store the mop bucket? I needed to deviate the topic to save Maggie's life.

"I can help! As the leader, I'll broker peace or just surrender the covens to you guys!"

"Naïve, kid."

"Mrs. Davidson, I grow weary of the name-calling."

"And your egotistical stupidity wears me out."

"Maggie! Keep it up, and I'm cleaning blood off the walls, not you."

She tossed up her palms. "My death will not expose the actual truth."

"What pray tell is that, human?"

I shuddered and shrank in my chair because I recognized that look.

"Prods eat the bones grown by mortals. Occultists can curse more species. Humankind can create more slaves. Prods only make more undead."

Forget cutting the tension with a knife. I needed a chainsaw.

"If you have a point, Mrs. Davidson, I urge you to arrive at it."

"Getting' there, don't get your shorts in a wad." She had the nerve. "After the ritual, she needs to convince more than just mages that your kind deserves to exist."

"And precisely who does she need to persuade, Mrs. Davidson?" When agitated, Vasile resorted to proper names.

"Mother Nature. Humans teeter the planet near destruction, so how close will your stupid war push her into action?"

"It was a mistake inviting—"

"But what you sensed is correct, Marrow-suckah. The kid offers the entire world hope."

"I do?"

She pointed the finger at his chest. "But if she dies in the process, you risk all life. You then chance her next reincarnation comes with an evil heart."

"I'm still here, ya know."

"Therefore, if we do not proceed strategically, all species perish."

"Not as dumb as you look, Marrow-suckah."

"No wonder everyone wants to control me." Maggie gathered her worn purse to her chest as Vasile swallowed a frog. "If she teaches magic, will you teach me how to lead?"

He blinked, then crossed the floor to me. "First, the ritual." A thrill about the willingness to learn earned a cheek stroke.

Pleasure hummed as I rounded on the old woman. "But why help us? I don't mean to sound selfish, but you're justa human."

"Just hedgin' my bets, Toots. Besides, that one sent our school lots of money. Don't go expectin' a building named after ya."

"Would never dream of it."

"Last advice, kid?"

"Sure."

"Get yer powers. Save the world. Stay independent. Don't become someone's puppet."

"I'm trying." Words trailed into a whisper, "I'm trying."

"Magic crash courses start tomorrow morning."

"I bid you good evening, Mrs. Davison."

"Fine. Learn fast. We ain't got much time." The gruff woman dropped a mint's crumpled cellophane wrapper on the coffee table before she waddled to the front door. When Vasile showed her out, he palmed offensive trash. Deft young fingers poked the door's datapad, and the beeped metal clicked its release.

"But you aren't a mage. How can you?"

"Thank God for large miracles! I'm what my tribe calls a Motewolin. It's like a shaman. Penobscot Indians are children of the light and predate every civilization. We define the epoch when we count Earth's very grains. We know." She left without a goodbye, and a sputtered old car crunched gray gravel.

Heavy steps walked to the kitchenette, and then slumped to a kitchen chair, palm on the table, and his other hand pocketed. When Vasile's history laid bare, the weighted noose of centuries clenched his spirit. I witnessed the effects wandering lost for so long, absent a kingdom.

"Do you miss him?"

"Hmm?" as he tore a dazed gaze from the barren table to me.

"The Father? Do you miss him?"

He drummed his manicure. "Yes."

CHAPTER 13

Crop circles and a Creature Double Feature

NOBODY EXASPERATED ME LIKE those two, including Mother. Every night Maggie hauled me outside among the crisp pines and yellow grasses to practice energy control. Each lesson I created air pressure to crush various symbols in the grass. First, I made simple shapes, but the lessons got harder, and the designs more intricate. Yes, I created crop circles. After we played in the field for a week, my irritation neared an all-time high.

"I did this a thousand times already! And why don't you ever answer questions about my ritual?"

"Because you gotta learn how to crawl before you—"

"A cliché? Really?"

"Kid, you got no clue about your future abilities—"

"Because you don't tell—"

"—do you?"

"Well—I—"

"Do you?"

"No. I don't know. Maybe."

"Those idiots growing up taught you nothing." When she recognized my crappy family life, my defiance smoothed a tad. She touched an elbow, and warm energy flowed up an arm. "Someone needs to rip up your mother's occult card—"

"Tell me about it."

"Okay, listen." She sighed pity. "The test will send you into a remote dimension. If not trained properly, you'll never make it out alive."

After a collective sigh, we looked at the spun satellites and faraway stars that decorated a black canvas. Everywhere, cosmic bodies blinked cryptic SOS messages into a vast emptiness that cared less about universal woes. Like Heaven housed trillions of forgotten souls, the universe collected billions of unnamed planets. While exploring another plane, I risked the detachment from reality's anchor. Inside the dimension, I faced the proper chance of untethering and floating away, forever adrift beyond the observable universe. Not even Vasile's inescapable black hole-gravity would pull me back.

"I'll trust you, Mags."

"Think of it this way. What do your people harness for spell power?"

"Um, elemental energy and the black mages use demons."

"Go deeper."

I pursed my lips and flicked eyes side to side. "I don't know—
they tap into some hidden place or something?"

"Bingo!"

I jerked. "Wait. What?"

"So, where does elemental magic come from?"

"The other dimension!" I leaped to my feet.

"You got it, Toots. Witches, I mean Mages, try tapping into
it—"

"—for more incantation power!"

"Yep! And don't forget dream manipulation."

"Kinda forgot about those. I hate thinking about things I
hate."

"Bad sleeper, huh?"

"You could say that."

"It's like this. Dreams serve as doors to mystical goodies."

"So, if I could access the dimension anytime—"

"Control the dimension's portal—"

"—I control magic. Holy—"

"Kid, you ain't gonna waste time chanting and stirring
cauldrons. You'll be the only one on the planet who just turns on
an enchanted faucet."

A whistle sailed. "And make anyone my minion!" I glowered
at the dark dwelling which housed my first victim.

"Survive the test first, kiddo."

"Always a catch." I kicked a pebble.

"Hard enough for a seasoned mage, and near impossible for—
"

"—me."

"Don't get discouraged. How can you use a fire hose if you can't turn on a garden spigot?"

"I guess."

She slapped her knees before she stood. "One more try. Then, we'll call it a night. Deal?"

"Okay!"

She whistled into the evening's light fog that coated the quiet field. A hundred feet away, a twig snapped near the furry pines. The usual doe tiptoed into view and poked along her territory's grasses.

"The deer?"

"With only thoughts and no magic, make the Earth absorb her life force."

"Wait, you want me to kill a defenseless animal? No way. Can't we—"

The jaw clenched woman turned and then walked towards the house. "Always with the lip. Go—"

"I—"

"—home. Go home, kid."

My voice raised. "Fine!"

Maggie yelled while she marched away, "Marrow-suckah warned you—"

"It's always him!" The Earth trembled under our feet, and the docile doe's whitetail jerked before she bounced into the swallowing trees.

"If you're sick of this, go home."

"Stop telling me to go home!"

"Why?!"

"I don't have one!"

"Do everyone a favor, call Mommy, and go—home."

I chased after her. "I can't."

She rounded on hiccupped sobs. "Stupid kid. Love makes you stay, not homelessness or a terrible family life."

"Excuse me?" arms clenched around my chest.

"You heard me. Love clouds yer noggin."

"Dumbest thing—"

I flinched after her hard breastbone jab. "Run from that creature. Stop running towards him. Run far away."

"I don't—"

She the finger on my chest thrust at my angry face. "They are master manipulators and do the worst imaginable things. And that damn creature," howling as she pointed at the ranch. "—is their leader, who you love!" Maggie's chest heaved. She cared enough about a near stranger to succumb to anger.

My words danced absent conviction. "I don't love that thing." In case Vasile's supersonic ears picked up our argument, I yelled at the house, "I hate him!"

"So, you said." She lifted my downcast chin when I scrutinized her scuffed black hospital sneakers.

A bully switched to a gentle grandmother. "Want some advice your mother should've given you?"

"I guess," sniffing my response.

"Women can't value themselves or their lives centered on relationships or partners. People do not give us strength because we make our own."

"I get it. But maybe Anna's memories make me love him? No way I fell in love on my own."

"Does it matter?"

"I mean, you met him! He's moody, calculating—moody—manipulating and moody."

She patted a tense arm before the backdoor slid open. The barefooted master stepped onto the porch. Angst bubbled boiled blood. I shot Maggie one more glance then stomped past the blinking monster. A poor attitude always angered Vasile, like how his sullen moods infuriated me. I counted on a quick reprimand.

"She ain't ready. Misdirected her passion into loving your dumb butt, not training—"

"Mrs. Davi—"

"If you are sleeping with that kid—"

"Mrs. Davidson! I find your accusation—" Too exhausted to listen; I went to bed.

Still wearing dirty clothes, I flopped under the covers. The mattress granted little comfort after the hard lessons and runaway emotions. An already messed-up circadian rhythm, constant bickering, and energy-draining instructions sapped my residual strength. I tugged puffy blankets over my head and welcomed any dream. Just not the one I got.

The backyard shimmered under a gorgeous fall moon. The Maine fall's chill trembled pale skin, and the fresh air slicked down my nasal passage. Clean air filled my lungs. Hands drifted over dried grass tops as I wandered to the secretive trees, never explored. The dense pine boughs released the familiar doe, and she picked her lopping way towards me. When she reached me, I slid a line across her supple brown back. The brown hide smoothed like real fur and rippled unaccustomed to touch. Intense liquid eyes looked past a muscular shoulder.

Suddenly, a spoiled garbage odor twitched our faces. The same aroma the night the count stole me, and before we jumped on the plane, gagged me. The dream shifted into nightmare status. How did they find me in my sleep? Before another concern crossed my mind, the deer tensed and convulsed underneath the gentle touch. Stiff legs toppled her to the cold ground while she gasped for air. To avoid sharp thrashed hooves, I dove sideways. When I searched the field for the cause, I spotted nothing out of the ordinary. The animal bleated one last rasp.

The trees whispered, "Sarah."

I plummeted to weak knees. "No!" I touched a death frozen rib cage. A leg nerve fired a last signal and twitched. "Justa dream. Justa dream."

"Sarah." The increased wind murmured near a shoulder.

When I lifted my head off the dead beast, a dark heap heaved across the field. "What the—" When the mass drew closer, I noticed a crawling collection of spiders, roaches, and worms. I jumped to ready feet, and seconds later, the corpse became a pulsating bug pile. Millions of crunching insects slapped ringing ears. I dreamed something from the old Saturday Creature Double Features.

I cried, "Wake up. Wake up."

Sticky laughter filled the backyard. "Sarah. Sarah."

When a wild whiplash searched for the source, a fuzzy spider crawled up my ankle. As I swatted the gross bug, more disjointed chuckles erupted near my back. "S—ar—ah."

"Wake up! Wake up!"

A waspy voice whirled around me. "No, daughter." When I spun, my parent hovered right behind me, toes inches above the ground. Under a dark hooded robe, she oozed dread, Chanel perfume, and perfect makeup.

"Mother." She floated closer. "Why are you doing this?"

The dead deer moaned, "Sarah."

"To strip you to nothing."

I pinched an arm over and over. "But I'm your daughter."

"Daughters are a dime a dozen, but not your powers."

"Just take them."

The black robe's fabric whooshed when she glided dizzy circles around my shrunk shoulders. "You already agreed to give them to me and then broke it. Once I drive you to murder the chancellor, I'll kill you for the betrayal."

Demented laughter bounced around the field and inside my skull. A pounded head dug fingers at each temple. Heavy French perfume and a rotten flesh closed my throat. Mother pulled her red lip and sneered inches near my wet face. Hood folds touched my forehead. Long-legged spiders crawled from her twisted mouth and ran up her rouged cheeks. "I'm your child!"

She hauled up a long pink fingernail, a spell ready to end me. Incessant crunching stopped. Gross bugs abandoned the carcass and slithered a crooked line towards us. I had to reach the house. But glued feet glued to the ground. Mother's cackle at the struggled efforts downed a guttural whimper. Greenish-black beetles fell from her flared nostrils.

"Run, you prod slag!"

The nightmare's quicksand faltered each cumbersome step, and countless red-eyed hairy bugs scuttled up my strained legs.

The futile screams burned as I fought to run while slapping insects. If I died in a dream, my sleeping body perished. I strained to manipulate the terrible nightmare when I imagined an angry Vasile rushing outside the home to save me.

Her shrill voice drilled inside my skull. I stopped hitting bugs to slap my head. "Call your worst nightmare. He'll be your worst dreams come true."

"Sarah, wake up. Wake up!"

Drenched in sweat, I bolted in bed. I clawed awareness to discover he clasped my shoulders. Hysterical shrieked sobs racked my body. I hurled into Vasile's stiff arms, but his strong limbs never raised.

"Just an awful dream," rumbled beside my ear.

"No! No, it's not! Mother found us!"

Hard fingers separated me from his chest as I recalled the first nightmare under his roof. A caring young face stared into mine. "Do explain."

"In my dreams. She found us in my dreams."

Vasile laid me down and tucked covers around my quaked body. The sudden news didn't repel him far from the bedside to pace the room. Then again, he considered pacing wasted energy. "Are you certain?"

I sat right back up. "Yes! And she's right."

"Right about what?"

"I'll fail. I always fail. And this time, everyone I love dies. Everyone!"

"—ah yes, well."

Again, I smashed my head into his fragrant chest. "Who are we kidding? I'm no Queen Regent material."

"Well, now—"

I sobbed. "I'm an idiot."

"Perhaps I should call Maggie." Awkward hands, unaccustomed to panic-stricken women, patted me.

"She'll only make it worse."

Again, I collapsed against his broad chest, and firm arms wound their way around my torso. Tense muscles relaxed, my breaths sounded less hitched, and a palm smoothed sweaty, matted hair. After I limped against his warm body, he again lowered me to the sheets. Red pupils invited me deeper into his radiated enigma, but inside their liquid appeal, my identity risked drowning. Maggie was right. A lovesick mage harbored feelings for an enemy who sat on her bed.

"Mum said she'd make me destroy you."

His right brow lifted, "She—"

A hand shot from the plush comforter. "But—I'd never hurt you! Please believe me! I lo—"

A rare gut laugh reared his regal head. "The first time an enchantress ever swore to protect me. If you only knew me better, you would run back to your mother and plot my demise."

"That's what Maggie said."

"Smart woman."

"If you called her smart, I'm still dreaming."

Vas winked as he smoothed a wrinkle on the bed. "And who is exactly safe in whose hands?"

I noticed the digital clock. "It's the afternoon! I thought you guys were in comas during the day?"

"Your pounding heart and screams again woke the dead, milady."

"Mad jokes."

"Sleep. You're safe." He pushed on sluggish legs and jiggled the bed, but before he stumbled from reach, I tugged on a fist. He regarded our joined fingers, and seconds ticked like hours when his handsome head lowered inch by slow inch to mine. Heated gazes locked and communicated what fate and lips refused.

"Put away foolish desires. I'm much too tired." Warm breath circled my mouth expectantly. My heart jackhammered as plush lips hovered centimeters near mine.

"Stay."

"Sleep."

"Wait," I called to a man, not an aberration.

"I wait for no mage."

"Was the kiss an act?"

"Yes and no. Sleep."

After the door closed, mucky joints turned to curdled goop. The memory of his arms around me, near lips, and half-confession curled toes. Eyes closed, I rolled over and strove to find sleep. But the bugs on Mum's face, and an unnamed longing, prevented any peace. I jumped from the bed and didn't stop moving until I reached the forbidden basement door.

I lingered at the locked doorknob. I played out how wrong the next moments could go. Clanged alarm bells refused to silence, yet I still waved my hand across the knob. The latch on the other side clinked. "Thanks, Maggie. Not what your lesson intended." I screwed up my life, so what was one more bad mistake?

A tiny light orb lit the pitch-black stairwell, and slumbered shadows stirred. Musty dampness erased Mother's rot from memory as I gripped a rough wood railing, fingertips hovered a small sphere. When a toe touched the frozen basement floor, I saw him. On the far side of the cellar, against unfinished drywall, a long shape lumped on a flat surface. The dream's terror and replay of his half-confession moved hesitant feet forward. As I crossed the cold concrete, I swallowed bitter concern, not the yearning for death's harbinger.

My soft blue orb shuffled the room's gloom, shadows, but not the hulked mass laid motionless. Despite the severe threat about disturbing his sleep, I crept on the balls of cold feet. A sweaty palm closed and extinguished the soft magical light when I neared the bed. Not one breath expanded my ribs.

Compared to suffering another nightmare alone, I preferred a wild monster ripping at flesh. I took the most significant risk. I climbed me into a prod's bed. Later, after the emotional duress passed, I distinguished a pattern of dangerous decisions. Thanks to a sheltered upbringing, I never slipped in bed with a man or supernatural killer. After the floor's cold traveled up my legs, teeth chattered. I released a bitten lower lip and pulled the dark comforter. The mass inhaled but stayed still.

When I tucked under the covers, the bed dipped me into his firm back. He growled ash he flopped over. I stifled a squeak. A considerable arm tossed across my torso, and one tug crushed me tighter to his chest. I tried to breathe while mentally chanting, 'Please don't eat me.' After a minute, convinced he slept and not about to tear my neck open, I released a paralyzed breath. Blood rivers raged in fired veins. An excited heart struggled to keep pace from soaked adrenaline.

He shifted, and fingertips brushed against my abdomen. I tensed. Vasile again snatched me against him, like afraid I might flee. The unrealized strength whooshed out air from my chest, and for a few seconds, I couldn't breathe. He nuzzled my skull's base, where he once pulled my hair and inhaled deeply. Did he sniff food or my needs?

A groggy growl stirred my delicate neck hairs. "Bad enough sharing share my bed with a witch. Slow your heart so that I might sleep."

Why did he warn me about not going downstairs? What exactly was he trying to resist? Maybe he forgot he resisted eating Anna when married to her. Based on my dream, I knew they shared the same bed. Under his polished surface, emotions raged higher than his genuine nature allowed visible. I didn't give him credit for more feelings than grief and rage. Did he show me the real Vasile, or use meticulous seduction for immoral gains? Time told all. Underneath a heavy arm tucked against life and death, I concluded something new. A man lurked inside the monster who needed me in one form or another. I soften his horrific edges like how authors wrongly humanized fictional vampires. I sunk into a tranquil slumber filled with soft green hills and a dark-haired guy with glowing red eyes.

CHAPTER 14

Count Chocula ain't talking

WHEN I WOKE ALONE, I slapped my forehead. I played the part of a desperate woman and snuck under the covers with a prod. A prod! I wagered the night would be awkward as heck, a barely manageable relationship lashed by more sexual tension. Worse, I guaranteed Maggie would figure out what I did. Upstairs, the floor creaked. I groaned because Vasile waited while he clutched his precious newspaper. But the call of bacon and coffee propelled me red-faced up the stairs. Wait, he cooked?

The basement door squeaked open into a small kitchen. Faded laminate countertops, white tiled backsplash, and chipped oak cabinets fashioned a narrow place to cook. Wes Montgomery smoothed his jazz guitar through a Bluetooth speaker beside a plastic mixing bowl. An exciting décor piece transformed the bland room. The rumpled chancellor wore faded jeans, a Cambridge tee-shirt, and stood at the counter in his bare feet. He scratched two-day-old scruff. The absurd chef who acted like he cooked every day, cracked an egg into a Teflon pan. The food and black coffee maker spat and gurgled. A pleasant man coiled inside fangs of an unpredictable monster made me breakfast.

"Nice music." I wanted to groan. Lame Sarah, lame.

"I thought Billie Eilish might wake you. This is softer."

"Billy—" Of all mornings—I mean nights, he looked and acted his human age. "What's your name, and what did you do with Vasile?" The mood guaranteed to flip quicker than the popping eggs.

He twisted a heart-stopping smile across a shoulder, and a hot blush defiled my freckled cheeks. When I parked at the table, he turned to talk and waved a plastic spatula like a royal scepter. "Slept better?"

"Yeah. I did. Hey look, I'm sorry—"

"Fortunate, your throat's intact." Did he use a contraction in his sentence? So, getting in bed with an undead ghoul froze Hell over. Got it.

"Yeah, thanks." I held my breath and waited for him to correct my vocabulary.

"Very Good. Henceforth, we shall share the same accommodations." A lack of coffee forbade coherent sentences, so my chin perched on the heel of a hand as scrutinized him in silence.

After he heard no reply from me, "Whilst the sun shines, tis folly to venture upstairs. I required my entire strength to reach you."

"Thanks. Um, about that—"

Glossy eggs slipped onto a thin white Corelle plate. After he added buttered wheat toast, Vasile slid the food across the wobbly table. "Bob's your uncle." Our sheepish gazes met.

"Bob's my—okay, what's your name, alien. And can you stay? The other guy was an ass."

"Eat."

Vasile pulled a chair and dragged his customary paper closer. I bit the golden toast as he touched his expensive timepiece. He abandoned rigid mannerisms and placed his elbows on the table, index fingers meeting under his nose while he watched me eat.

"Not eating?"

"I dined already."

"On what? I mean—never mind." I shoved delicious bacon in my gob.

"Precisely."

On purpose, I spoke, mouth full of food. "It's good."

"Glad—"

"I'm not into you or anything."

"Pardon?"

"Just putting it out there."

"Into—" as he wrinkled his forehead.

"God, you're old. What I'm saying is that I didn't try to seduce you. I don't like you like that."

"And there we are, a young lady discussing intimate affairs over breakfast? My, my." The cool admonishment and smirk clattered a fork against the half-eaten plate. Enjoyment tapped the goon's fingers under his chin. Whoever broke his nose when he was a man, I applauded their ghost. Again, a source for entertainment, I stabbed an egg's warm yellow blob, and food magma spread over the dish.

"I'm not an expert or anything," I moaned while hid behind a curtain of red hair. When the edible lava touched the last piece of toast, I stole a glance.

The pompous ass smirked, and a palm flattened the folded newspaper. "Surely, you jest."

"I jest?"

"And here I believed all modern women possessed a certain knowledge of those delicate areas."

"Remember? Locked up my entire life?"

"So, my kiss—" as his smile deepened. I choked on the egg and covered my mouth to prevent spitting food. As usual, the jerk positioned me right where he wanted me.

"Yep, first kiss." While I held arms wide, "Newsflash, I'm a virgin!" I hoped the blunt talk miffed him into silence. Vasile cleared his throat and re-crossed his legs. I clanked the breakfast plate into the shiny stainless-steel sink, and behind me, his paper snapped. "And Vas?" When I whirled around, he perked a brow past a drooping corner of The Bangor Daily News.

"You may call me Vasile, Count, Count Simeon, Chancellor, Chancellor Simeon, Champion of Bulgaria, or my favorite—"

"Oh, God—"

"Close, but not quite. *Lord*." A debonair wink flourished the word 'lord.'

I groaned. "You're too much."

"You were saying, Sarah?"

"Tell me about your world before you know—"

"An immortal?"

"Yeah. Maggie's taking the night off and thought we might kill some time."

"You refer to my human life?" He perused the paper with slight chin movements and then directed a palm to the empty chair next to him. "Grab a cuppa. Tis a lengthy tale."

"Really? Thanks!"

"Did your parents locked you up too?"

"Hardly." He grinned and launched into his story.

As the third son to Tsar Simeon the First, Vasile would never see the Bulgarian title. Thirsty to lead, he commanded his father's vast armies, and his young military career began at the early age of fourteen. He became the continent's youngest general by eighteen and prepared Bulgaria for the inevitable war with their Byzantines neighbors. To quiet a grumbling battle, the Tsarina arranged a political marriage between her son and a Byzantine princess. But the idea repulsed Vasile, who only cared about warcraft. So, he sidestepped the union when he crafted a story about distant territory strife needing his attention.

All Romanians knew about constant dangers valley farmers faced. Various countries landlocked Transylvania and the forest walls no longer terrified raiding Slavic gangs. Vasile announced his plans and accompanied by four officers. The military delegation traveled many miles northwest.

"Wait, Mister I'm-Not-Scared-of-Anything, ran away?"

He echoed my grin. "Quite."

Far into the Carpathian Basin, a dense haze rose above distant hills and grabbed the warriors' attention. Worried men spurred

horses onward and clopped into a ransacked village. Acrid smoke
from charred huts choked the mounted soldiers, and scarves soon
covered dirty faces. Faint orange embers matched the sunset as
straight-backed officer swiveled necks to survey the mayhem.
Whispered concerns circled about absent bodies or survivors.

The young silent general pointed two fingers at his watchful
eyes, then swept them across the smoldered village. Men touched
sword hilts. "How my fine soldiers lived for such adrenaline-soaked
moments. So long ago, yet the dust still lingers in my nose." When
the guarded soldiers reached the encampment's edge, the wind
changed. Pungent burned flesh replaced dusky wood smoke.
Horses pawed and snorted. Warriors shifted in their saddles. When
the cautious five rounded a corner, a disgusting sight filled their
vision.

I leaned on elbows, coffee mug halfway to my lips, and asked,
"What did you see?"

"Half-charred cadavers of all ages piled at least fifteen feet
high."

I wrinkled my nose. "Was that typical?"

"No."

Cloudy fear-filled eyes on gray faces with frozen screams
watched the military procession. Flies darted between the silent
mouths. A soldier pointed out the many mangled throats and
decapitated bodies. Everything about the dead village felt, looked,
and smelled wrong. Trained soldiers tugged on reins hold back
white-eyed warhorses. Sleepy swords sang when men woke them
from scabbard beds. Polished metal glittered in the smokey sunset.
Everyone lowered foreheads, sharp weapons ready to maim.

"How scary! And so far from help."

Vasile shrugged. "Such was basin life and the reason for our visit."

"Who killed them?"

"One cannot simply rush such a glorious story and endanger the ending."

"And I thought Maggie was an excellent storyteller."

I earned his wink.

"Based on body conditions, the attack happened twelve hours before we arrived. We knew a possible ambush lingered in the dark, so I ordered my spooked men to retreat." Vasile paused the narrative, looked at the ceiling, and pulled the tale from hazy memories. We spun horses in the dry dust as the sun sunk behind an ice-covered mountain. A yellow-robed man, caked with blood, stood on the cart path. "Nobody was there one moment, and the next..." The hair rose on everyone's necks, worried the unholy smoke birthed another horror yet to unfold.

The passive survivor returned the jittery stares. Men half-watched the robbed individual while they scanned the landscape for an assault. The Egyptian-looking man in his thirties wore bloody silk robes, dusty gold jewels, and watched us with kohl smeared eyes. He lacked muscles, a weapon, or guards, but the harmless person wasted precious time. Vasile questioned the lord while wary officers faced the dusky hills and guarded hidden enemies. The heightened senses fed snorting steeds more anxiety, and the animals pawed the dust. Vasile asked what traveled him so far from home. Vasile's looming warhorse unchanged the calm stranger, and after several languages received the same odd silence, he tried another approach.

"A guy appears out of nowhere, surrounded by bad-asses, and just stands there? Creepy."

"So, we thought."

Nervous mounted officers glanced across shoulders, then at each other. The arrogant lord survived the assault without a weapon or entourage, and his behavior suggested he played a part in the village attack. Frustrated and wishing to avoid a surprise attack, Vasile rode away. "I intended to question him later." The general flicked a low signal off his saddle. After two men reached the man to take him, prisoner, the oddity sprang to life. Speedy jeweled hands shot from sullied robes, and in seconds he clutched both warriors' bulged necks. The weak-looking Egyptian lifted flailing soldiers off the ground. Swords clattered to the parched dust as faces turned purple. "His red stare never left mine when he snapped my men's spines."

"Wait, was he—"

"I never grasped why I failed to notice the odd eyes before that moment. Alas, none of that matters now."

"Who was he?"

"You will find out, milady."

When the limp bodies hit the wagon road, he yelled. The two remaining officers attacked. Vasile switched his ornate sword, then swung off his horse. Heavy leather boots landed and fashioned a dust cloud, ready for anything. Before he took one step, the other warriors met the same fate. The robed man sneered before he tossed muscular men like dolls. Rage, not common sense, inflamed Vasile's mind. Careful cross-steps circled the inhuman foe. The battle-hardened young general watched his new nemesis for a telltale shoulder drop before a potential strike. After long toying minutes, patience ended, he abandoned prudence. He advanced.

"It was the fight of my life. I never saw such startling speed. The enigma dodged every attack and parried every swing. Twas not the stranger's brute strength that finished me but my own weakness. I could not take in enough air, and tired muscled failed. After four years in service, I finally met my match."

"What did you do? What happened?"

"I stared death in the face. Literally. But determined to die a good death."

"A good death?"

"A religious distinction if you will. People obsessed with earning a quick ticket into heaven and the lessening of time in Purgatory. Wealthy individuals purchased masses for future funerals, and warriors died for the faith."

"So, a good death meant less time in Purgatory."

"Precisely. Christians believed one's sins and spiritual life dictated time spent in the Godless space."

"Like life in general because I see no God down here." I waved a hand. "Then what happened?"

"The *correct* question is what did not happen."

Vasile gripped his sword's jeweled hilt until white knuckles almost popped. Smooth lunges and perfect parries lessened to imbalanced jerks. However, between tired swings, he admired the unusual man's fighting style. As he sunk to his knees before the father of all monsters, a random wish fluttered through his muddy brain. If only he could one day train under such a skilled master, even if the teacher was strigoi.

"Strigoi?"

"Unaware of the truth, we believed in Vampires."

Underneath a lowered head, he tracked the monster's shadow from twilight's weaker glow. A long shade seeped across the gritty dust and fell over his bowed body. The nemesis loomed, blocked Vasile's last warm kiss from the sun, and pitched Vasile to the darkness. The young man accepted his fate and prepared for something else to kiss him. Death. Tears trickled clean streams over his grime crusted face as he committed the ultimate warrior sin. A prized sword clattered to the cart path, and a jeweled finger raised Vasile's chin. "He forced me to stare into those terrible eyes. Then the oddest thing happened. He stepped away and then beckoned me to follow him across the hills."

"What did you do?"

"The only thing possible. I gave my dead comrades one last glance and obeyed."

After one silent mile, the young general calculated running from someone so fast only got him killed. Vasile kicked himself for ignoring local superstitions. He followed the odd lord into a tent filled with furs and silks. After the creature washed and laid against supple pillows, the lounging Egyptian confessed his identity as the oldest creature in existence. The strange pair talked for hours. Vasile swore the bizarre man only spared him to chase away a lonely night. Little did he know, the undead lord fancied Vasile's company longer than one evening but an eternity. "Before dawn, he changed from monster to paragon. He laughed when I inquired if he was strigoi and provided a glimpse of a true immortal." When he sensed Vasile's eagerness, the lord offered to mold him into a great prodigium, but at a cost.

"Someone better pay me to become a prod, I mean, immortal." Vasile's nose wrinkled, so I urged, "So what was the price?"

"One I would gladly tender thousand times over. The Father shared his vision for our kind and required me to build him a permanent empire."

"Wait, that guy was The Father?"

Vasile beamed. "None other, milady. He warned me, not every human survives the attempt to shed mortality."

"You mean people die when they try to become one of you?"

"Yes."

"That'd suck."

"I could not turn my mind from endless fantasies our one commonality."

"What?!"

"An insatiable hunger for great destinies men killed and toppled countries to obtain. We understood the fragility of man's existence and societies. Tucked among silk pillows, insistence, and fur blankets, we dreamed up an empire as immortal as our people."

"An immortal society?"

A fingertip fidgeted the paper's serrated corner. "Human civilizations fade when close to three-hundred-years old, and the oldest lasted only a thousand."

"It'd suck to live forever and go through major upheavals."

Λ hypnotic stare glimmered as he twisted his official ring. "You think like an immortal. After a lifetime of night work for the occult, we deserved better."

"I understand, or I will try to at least."

He softly smiled. "Tis all I can ask for from the queen of enemies."

"So, what's his actual name?"

His chin reared. "Why would one know such a thing?" Based on the count's face, I posed the most bizarre question ever.

I changed the subject. "Did it hurt?"

When his head tilted, hair caught the kitchen's harsh yellow. "Did what hurt, Sarah?"

I tucked poised legs under the chair and leaned forward, my spoken name hummed excitement higher. "You know—the change."

A cheerfulness from long-lost glory days sobered. "Death is the most excruciating pain I ever endured and will ever endure."

I winced. "I had no clue. I figured lights out, and that's it."

"During the transition, one keeps complete awareness while dying, forced to experience death's extreme mental and physical agony."

"We are alive when we die? Isn't that an oxymor—mor— something?"

"For a rebirth, a person must succumb because one is born with a death debt, quite impossible to cheat. Thus, a person dies to live as another, free of debt."

"But how does it work?"

"A man or woman digests a maker's blood before the heart stops. If death does not reject the final payment and clears the obligation, immortal cells take root and replicate. The maker's DNA strengthens mortal cells."

"A cure and virus all rolled in one."

"Clever little mind. Do we have a remedy for being a Lower? Yes."

I squinted. "I hate it when you talk like that."

"Like what pray tell, Sarah?"

"Like an elitist. So, what takes place after the cells take over?"

"Very simple. The first immortal breath happens before flesh rots. A successful transformation clears any death debt and permits eternal life."

"Neat loophole. You guys are alive and not, in fact, undead, just re-dead."

"Thus, why we are mammals and the third Homo species. We require nutrition, warm-blooded, and able to reproduce."

"Wait. What?"

"Tis rare but has happened."

"Did you and Anna—"

"Regrettably, no."

"Any mage immortals?"

"I do believe that is where nature drew a line in the proverbial sand. A man may elevate from a Lower to a Higher, but no mage ever survived a lateral transfer."

"I can see that. The person would become a demigod. Can I ask something else?"

He extended a palm.

"If UV rays and beheading kill an immortal, what happens if someone rips out your heart?"

He answered matter-of-factly, "One, but shoves it back inside to heal."

"And if it's destroyed?"

He leaned against his chair, hands in his pockets. "Another grows in a week." When his long legs stretched under the table, his knee touched mine.

"Shenanigans."

He did his famous one-eyebrow-raise. "Shenanigans?"

"Yeah. Some rich guy decimates some remote village for no reason. I call shenanigans."

He clapped once. "Outstanding, Miss Wardwell!"

That night my forehead wrinkled so much I need Botox by twenty-five. "Huh?"

"You spotted the clue. Well done, you." Rare praise and excitement squirmed excited hips. "As the continent's youngest general, I controlled vast armies, and attracted his attention all the way from Egypt." Pride puffed his chest as he bragged, "He relinquished a Pharaoh's bed just to journey to Bulgaria. Father watched me from the shadows and then followed me to Transylvania."

"And in the village?"

"An ultimate test if you will. Much like your rite."

"He would only adopt you after stalking you for years, and after killing an entire town and your best mates? How are you not creeped out?"

"A fair question. But all things Father did had reasons."

"Sounds like someone I know."

He chuckled. "We conduct various trials to assess a human's fitness and qualities as a future immortal."

"Like a fraternity hazing?"

194

"Not so low born. The council assesses one's bravery when a mortal experiences death's futility. One's true quality and mettle bloom as one dies."

I crept closer to answers every mage fancied. "Gross. But why does it matter what they are like?"

His tee-shirt wrinkled when he shrugged. "We abhor spending eternity with inferior immortals. Humans chose not to exterminate their dregs, but we refuse such burdens caused by unsuitable mentors and mentees."

I gave him a hearty eye-roll. "Talk about red tape immigration policies."

"Our laws govern makers, their candidates, and a lengthy application period."

"Even If I survived the change—"

He waggled a finger. "Even with me listed as your creator, they would deny you."

"Not that I wanted to—"

"Mhm, I see."

"No, really!"

When he grinned, I smiled. "Too bad Vlad the Impaler inspired Bram Stoker's book. He should have picked you like the vampire poster boy."

He lifted the newspaper, and flatly said, "I see."

"What'd I miss?"

From behind the gray newsprint, "Vlad was an immortal, you see."

"Shut the front door!"

"Shut the—"

I peeled back the corner of the paper to see his amused face. "Never mind that. Another shenanigan!"

"You are on quite the roll, Miss Wardwell."

"You used his first name in the present tense."

He flicked at an invisible fly. "Because I ordered his second death."

"Hello, bombshell."

"I possess no bombs—"

I rushed, "It's an expression. Like, shut the front door. Tell me! What happened to Vlad?"

"The imp refused to discreetly live as our laws dictated."

"Who was his creator, I bet they got in trouble."

"Victor."

"Shocker. But why fight a forever and an improved condition?"

"Vlad embraced immortal life but not the council controlling his region."

"Sheesh. Vampires are weak imitations."

"One may always find a grain of truth in every legend. One must sift through the sands to discover the speck before it scratches reality's eye."

"Pretty deep there, Vas."

"I try."

I fired another question. "When did you become the chancellor?"

"In 1152, my creator ordained me as a lifetime chancellor, and our young government progressed nicely until the early 1800s."

"Anna's murder?"

He nodded. "I found it hard to forgive or understand when Father claimed tiredness and required a deep sleep."

After a long life, the immortal architect passed the kingdom keys to Vasile, entombed himself, and hibernated. Nobody challenged the lengthy slumber because none neared his age. Unable to cope and tired, he left the place that housed his wife and creator's memories.

"What if he's dead?" Another creature, more horrific than the count and a thing that taught everything Vasile knew, trembled my core. I hoped never to meet him and stayed entombed or starved to death.

"Once a month, I feel his heart pump at least once."

"You do?"

"Maker and child are forever connected across significant distances and sleeps."

"No shi—"

"Language, Sarah."

"Sorry."

"He vowed to awaken if a terrible wrong befell the nation or me, but my exit undisturbed him. So—"

"Taking off was not bad."

"In a manner."

"Do you hate him for abandoning you?"

"Sometimes."

I touched his massive ring. "Do you miss home?"

Stiff lips pursed. "Course."

"So, go back!"

"I will not be received unless I bring a gift no other can—"

"You're not taking a hosted wine for a dinner party. You're the perfect son! Just walk in and take over."

He ran a hand through his hair. "After branded me a traitor, the council banned me from the court." A grimace tugged at his pinched face. "To ignore the decree is to confront execution," through a clenched his jaw.

"Yeah, but—"

"Fear not. All is not lost. No soul is brave nor strong enough to kill me. My maker would have to awaken to serve as my executioner. And because he is gone, they would imprison—"

"Bring a gift, *wait* you mean *I'm* the gift?"

He sighed and took his sweet time to answer. "Yes. As you sit here with me now, you award me hope." Three weighty, simple letters wounded me deeper than my family ever managed.

"After I control the mages, you're gonna gift wrap me, march me in a clout parade, and hand me over to those monsters?"

"Sarah, when you phrase it—"

"Gamble my life with uncontrolled things who want us both dead, just to get your throne back?"

"Sarah—"

"No matter what happens between us, I'm *still* a means to an end. This is all one big manipulation to you." The sexy prodigium skipped gooey heartbeats one minute, only to break them the next.

"Not all of them are monsters. Dmitri will be there." A soft, seductive smile further tensed my spine.

"My life is not a joke. And we had a deal!"

The contrite monster showed both palms. "When we return to Romania, I promise to protect you with my very life."

"Liar!"

"Sarah—"

"You said *I decided* who got my powers. But you planned to seduce me first." Hysteria climbed, "That kiss was a damn act."

He hissed a sigh. "Sarah, such foolhardy sentiments from your lonely existence and my wife's memories, cloud—"

"I'm just some practical thing to you. Admit it, coward!"

He reared his chin when my icy words cut him deep. "I survived a thousand years, and one could not fault me for practicality, or accuse me of cowardice. Love is impractical, and I refuse to suffer from it." In seconds, a hot man changed back into a brutal monster.

My shaking legs pushed against the kitchen chair. The table wobbled. Lukewarm coffee splashed over the rim. Weird political aspirations only left room for unrequited love. My throat closed. I choked back tears. Air refused to rush into my lungs. "You're not human. And I need to stop making you into one. Highers can't regress to Lowers, ya know."

"A sensible conclusion, I must agree."

When I hurtled more insults, we clutched our noses and paled. Hostile scowls flickered to lifted eyebrows and wide eyes. Rotten meat overwhelmed the small house. But I ignored the telltale sign and raised my voice higher. "So says nature's intended subservient creature. You sacrifice the truth for self-gratification. You unsafeguarded your precious wife, yet vow to defend a sworn mortal enemy? Dare I presume you grew tired of Anna and I stare at a thing complicit with her demise? Culpability and guilt drove you from Romania, and greed runs you home."

"Sarah."

"These childish emotions debilitated my agenda. I shan't pursue you or the matter further." I gasped for breath after my long-winded tirade.

Through gritted teeth, "Sarah."

I muttered through fingers, "Oh my God, those were not my words! I swear!" As fast as the foul aroma smudged the kitchen, the air cleared.

"In your—"

"I didn't say that!"

"I am aware. I think we—"

"How'd that happen—"

"Sarah. Calm. Please. In your dream, your mother linked minds with you." Despite the blameless truth, our mutual fists remained clenched, eyes flashed, and jaws tense.

"I sounded like my grandfather." Though I detested his motivations, I would never hit below the belt and aim for his wife's memory.

"I am sure you are." The apology unaffected his ridged posture and cold tone.

"How'd you know?"

"You did not stutter and spoke proper English."

"I deserved that. But—"

"Sarah, the timing troubles me."

Like a true tactician, he zeroed in on the actual problem. "They're closer."

The spell's pressure eased, but emotional tightness cranked a few notches. When he didn't apologize for his manipulative actions, a worse mood festered. "I need air."

I jammed fingers at the beeping black datapad, then wrenched on the sliding door. When the glass stayed in place, I squealed and fumbled the lock. I slammed the handle behind me so hard. The door bounced inches off the frame. Inside, wall decor rattled. I pounded the wooden porch steps. Dim interior lights strained to illuminate the backfield. I clenched fists near my sides and screamed into the hollow night, "I hate him!" Past a palm fastened to my mouth, I mumbled sobs any superhuman ears could hear.

One moment we snuggled in bed, and the next, we resumed mutual hatred. I wept until gentle skin touched a chilled hand. Vasile had warm fingers, and the ones that touched me radiated ice. "What Maggie." Hyperventilating hiccups paused then spun to Maggie's worried face.

"You got a dead deer over there."

"Yeah, in a dream."

"Your dream? What in the—Count Chocula ain't speaking? Let me in then stormed downstairs. You're out here cryin' yer eyes out."

The soulful concern stopped the teary torrent. Over noisy sniffles, I confessed an unconditional stupid love and our row's details. "I need to sit." She eased into a plastic lawn chair, still drained from our sessions. She patted an empty seat. I brushed away yellowed maple leaves then slumped beside her. When I rested against her shoulder, she slipped her arm around me. My mother or aunts would have recoiled.

"Why do we fight so badly? Hot one minute, cold the next."

"Think about why you fought."

"Mags, it's all I've done."

"Since your kind created his, the two species battle—opposites in every way."

"Don't tell me opposites attract."

"Afraid so, kid. Magnets push each other around. But sometimes the right ends flip and stick.

"I guess." I used a shirt's long sleeve to swipe a nose drip.

"Family troubles make up half the danger you're in."

"What do you mean?"

"His political enemies for one. They will go after his weak spots."

I sniffed. "And I'm the spot."

"Afraid so. You got a target on your back from both species. And God forbid if my kind ever learned about you."

"Jesus."

"Besides, I don't blame him."

"Maggie!"

"Another heartbreak might kill him."

"And he sees me as the next source of death's pain."

"Bingo."

"So, my broken heart protects him and everyone else? He thinks his actions make me concentrate on the ritual saves everybody."

"You're on a roll, Toots."

I looked up at her. "But did he have to make me hate him?"

"Count Chocula acts like a prod leader, not some lovesick teenager."

I winced, then returned to her shoulder. "What are you not telling me?"

"The other chancellor destroys a culture designed to protect humans and world order. If The Father sleeps and this other guy sets those monsters free—"

"—humankind ends."

"Yes."

"The entire world needs Vas more than I do—"

"Ayuh. Now you're a leader, kiddo. Go easy on him, would ya?"

"What did you do with Maggie?" I sniffled a grin.

She tapped a knee. "He's doing' the best he can."

"Men suck Maggie." Heavy lead words clanged around a deflated mind.

"So, do prods, kid. So do prods." The pun and won a teary smile.

"If I become potent enough, he doesn't have to protect me." An alternative path presented a pinpointed goal to focus on improved efforts.

"Pretty much. What you do afterward is your choice."

I peered at the house. "I said some nasty things."

She chuckled. "He's heard worse and deserved it."

"I'll never find normal love."

"Ain't nothin' normal about it, Toots. You're a pedigreed hottie. If he can't see that, he's more damaged than I thought."

I wanted to squeeze the snot from her. "Plenty of fish in the sea?" She tightened her meaty arm around a sagged torso.

When the doe visited for a nightly forage, I stood. A cool breeze rushed around me and replaced the senior woman's warmth. I squared determined shoulders, raised a defiant chin, and spread feet apart. I outstretched at the animal and her two new fawns.

Eyelids closed and fists clenched, I sucked crisp air into fired lungs. I spooled raw spinning forces that hurtled Earth through nothingness into my chest. I imagined the wildlife's force blink its last in the black onyx vacuum. Only I registered Earth's tiniest tremble. The grasses loudly whispered. When eyes opened, three animals laid motionless, and my head hung.

"You're ready. Grab Marrow-suckah."

"Can't you?"

CHAPTER 15

Don't kill each other

THE MOTEWOLIN SAT TWO sulking adults at the four-person kitchen table. "Research took time, but I have an idea of what we can expect." Vasile thought it safer to brood at the wall clock and not directly at me. She ignored the high tension between us. Hard to believe, but the egomaniac sat silently through the entire briefing.

When she finished, "How may I serve, Mrs. Davidson?"

Maggie thumbed at his sullen face. "Can't."

"Mrs. Davidson—"

"Oh God, here we go."

"Nothing you can do. Up to the kid."

He growled, "Why did I hire a bobolyne?"

"In English, yer high and mightyship."

"I think he called you a lazy fool, Mags."

"Alright, Creature Double Feature—"

"I shan't—"

The wrong night spiraled uncontrollably. The snarky tone sprang a vision of me melting his skin off old bones. "Shut up for God's sake and just listen to her!" Vasile snapped his mouth shut as he stood. He glared from the black kitchen window at a mysterious world known only to his kind.

After he remained silent for thirty seconds, Maggie explained the ritual's many steps. If I wanted to claim anything, save the world, and live, I needed to memorize every intricate detail. The dimension made me vulnerable to other dream-walking mages and wandering demons. The one thing I could take to help me survive was newly developed magic. Once on the other side, Maggie predicted a trial before someone granted me the title and new powers.

"Who is the proctor, Mrs. Davidson?"

"I don't know."

"If I passed a test, I come back with secret magical capabilities and the queen title. But if I fail, I die?"

"Yep. Afraid so."

"Always a catch to magic. Did you figure out the issue?"

"You learn fast, kiddo."

"At the moon's highest apex, we need a sign that you passed the test and have the crown."

Vasile watched from a window. His shirt's fabric strained under crossed arms. "Sounds quite impossible."

I chirped, "I'll just wake up. Girl rules the world, full stop."

"Slow down, Toots. Nobody can instantly awaken from a multi-layered trance on command."

Vasile looked up from a nail inspection. "What do you suggest, human?" How he enunciated 'human' again proved how lowly he regarded her species.

Maggie ignored the slight. "We need a dreamwalker."

"Sound complicated."

"It is. You have to cross over with you, an observer. Once you got the crown, a dreamwalker will wake up, and then we wake you up when the moon apexes."

"Who's—"

Vasile interrupted the critical question. "You propose we stand around, watch and do nothing?" The control freak got under my freckled skin.

"But who's—"

"No standing about. Witches are near. You pull security."

"Damn it. I have a question!" Both faces snapped to mine, and mouths closed. "Thank you. And its mages, not witches."

"What?"

"They are nearby based on dreams." The pair awarded me a sympathetic nod. "Maggie, where do we find a dreamwalker?"

Vasile's emphatic tone cut, "I shall do it." Unsurprised disgust prevented eye contact with the jerk.

"Leave occult business to the professionals. You'll have your weapon."

"Slow down, peeps. You can't, Bone-breaker. Prods sleep in coma states and don't dream."

Her new nickname scored a chuckle. "Not just heavy sleepers, Mags. They screwed over death, so they get comas." She directed a pitiful glance at the snarled Vasile. My attitude sucked if the devil got her sympathy.

He spat a snotty British inflection, "Madame, I refuse to sit idly by."

"You avoided the question. What do we do about a dreamwalker?"

"I have some ideas. Let me worry about that."

I picked a hangnail. "So much to remember. Will it work?"

"We'll see." Maggie gathered her worn purse before she hobbled to the door. "Tomorrow night, rain, or moonshine. Now let me out."

I pointed at the table. "Here at the house?"

"No kid, on tribal grounds."

"Woah."

"I'll pick you guys up. Until then—don't friggin' kill each other."

Vasile let her out the front entrance. The old rust bucket chugged Maggie away, and deafening silence soured air dense from bad attitudes.

A white-faced analog clock said the sun rose in thirty minutes—time for bed. Sleeping arrangements, not the close ritual, thickened my throat. Did I sleep alone and face dreams on my own or go with—him? The living room brass lamp clicked off, but I fixed on a blackened ceiling. I perceived his anxious stare.

"Please set aside your anger and come with me. You are safer when with me." Yet his sexy tone mollified a darker temper.

"A matter of opinion, liar. You have yet to me angr—"

"Sarah."

I soon became the Queen Regent, so I had better act like one. "No." I marched past him, head high.

With sighed frustration, "Suit yourself."

I slammed the door. "Jerk." Rude hatred towards him might prevent more rejection agony. I counted on insolence to revert the sexy guy to a hated monster.

* * *

A female chuckle near an ear. "Sarah. Sarrrraahhhh."

"Huh?"

"Sarraahhh." Soft steps pattered.

"Go away."

Someone giggled. "Sarah. Wake up. It's time."

"I'm up!" My heart pounded then groggily bolted in bed. To adjust dull senses to the quiet room's darkness, I rubbed eyes. God, I hated dreams. Primary function as a powerful queen? Cast a spell and never dream again.

The kitchen's soft yellow light tumbled under the closed door. The fated night arrived. And not a moment too soon, given the house climate. I jerked the covers above my head when nerves tightened temples. Why suffer from loving a despot and not performance anxiety? I wanted to conquer the impossible rite for his benefit, not mine. A success shifted cemented destinies, warring species, and warmed his unpliable heart. As the Queen Regent, if he still refused me, I owned the powers to make Vasile regret his choices.

I drew a slow breath while I monitored the light under the door. Emotions should never motivate a leader and exemplified the outstanding quality I lacked. An unselfish ruler puts their people's wishes above their own. But I cared less about my people who never loved me. As a queen, who soon oversaw an entire species at war, I needed to emulate Vasile's restraint and calculated actions. It clicked.

I tossed the covers off and bolted from bed, hands perched on hips. I understood the guy. Why he believed human sentiments foolish made sense. Who had time for that crap? When I put heart above head, I diminished any chance to break the trajectory of an evil people. My evil people. If I distracted Vasile, he became blind to his political adversaries' next moves, and like Anna, never keeping me safe. I needed to squash feelings for him before we died.

I jammed on white ankle socks. "Time to put on big girl panties."

A familiar male's voice drifted along the hall and landed at my closed door. "—said what? Did you mean it? I can't leave you guys for two—"

A girlish squealed erupted then wrenched open the bedroom door. The glorious golden Adonis immortal stood propped against the kitchen counter with crossed arms and legs. He wore dark skinny jeans and a gray skin-tight athletic shirt. The synthetic fabric accentuated ripped muscles. Shiny flaxen hair fell across his broad shoulders and touched a well-defined chest muscle. When he turned to me with a wrinkled, his nose. "Do I sniff a stinky witch?"

I launched down the hall, right into his muscular arms. A feet-dangling bear hug rewarded the adoration. I breathed in his cheerful citrus and lemongrass scent.

"Miss me, ma chérie?"

"You're here!"

"Good evening, Sarah."

"He's an asshole."

Dmitri tugged messy hair and whispered back, "I know."

Vasile kept his sullen mouth shut while he touched his expensive timepiece.

"Can't believe you made it! We didn't hear from you and—"

"Miss your big day? Besides, you two needed a referee."

"No, he needs his keeper."

"Yes, thank you for returning old friend."

"Thanks for being a proper friend, D." I shot my one-time crush eye daggers.

"I had to come, Poppet. Maine is a cultural mecca." The prince circled a finger in the air and eyes rolling.

"Did the council visit go, okay? Are they pissed?" I whipped frizzed hair into a knot as I waited for news.

Vasile answered for my friend. "Let us talk discuss such dull matters later, shall we?"

A somber Dmitri swatted blond locks behind his back and darted my worst enemy a severe look. In a flash, he brightened. "I agree, let's not bore Witchy-poo."

"Yeah, sure." I sensed trouble but had more important things to worry about. "Glad you came. We need as much help as possible." I hugged his waist.

His arm flopped over the top of my head and dangled his fingers in my face. "My fearless leader is useless without me. His mouth can get the better of him."

I giggled and pushed his hand to clear the view of the chancellor who long lost control of the house.

"Quite enough, both of you." He admonished to re-establish the pecking order, but the anger checked his ego.

The pair chitchatted about the local weather and Romanian current events. I ignored their catch-up and shoved the pitiful nail remains between teeth. At the quiet worry, Dmitri tapped a finger from my mouth. He tossed a heavy arm around my shoulders and looked down at me.

"Fret not, little mage. We have your back. Right, Vas?"

"Thanks, D."

"Think nothing of it."

"Well, Count Butthurt said—" Doorbell chimes interrupted the insult as Vasile pushed a kitchen chair.

"Sheesh Vas, she's truly gutted." He caught Vasile's pitiful sheepish look as he strode to the door.

"Do I smell human?"

Vasile opened the metal door. Maggie and a bunch of fall leaves blew in the house.

"Let's get a move on."

"Hello to you too, Magg—"

"Jesus Christ in a breadbasket. Another frigging marrow-sucker!" She threw hands, spun on hospital sneakers, and then marched back outside.

"That went well."

"Who in God's name was that?"

"That's my trainer."

Over her shoulder, "Hurry, we burn moonlight."

Vasile grabbed his jacket from a wall peg. "Shall we?"

Maggie called from the drive, "New one rides in the damn trunk."

Dmitri snarled a lip, "Is she quite serious that one? I will crack—"

I pinched his triceps. "Be nice. I like her."

"You would, Poppet."

"Well, I like you guys."

After we piled out into the dark fall air, the count popped around me and reached for the car. When the door opened, he stood to one side, "No toss headfirst?"

"A Buick Skylark? Egads!" Dmitri frowned as he gripped the chrome handle with two fingers. Over the rusted muffler roar, Maggie unheard the diva immortal.

"Just get in, D."

After we piled in, the corroded auto jostled the passengers across a pine, surrounded the bumpy road. Weak headlights bounced over rough, dusty gravel. Each quietly sunk to personal musings. The shadowed creatures rode in the back and took up comedic sketch roles. I sat up front and gazed at the Motewolin's sage profile.

"Thank you, Maggie—for everything. I want to make you proud."

She cracked a tired smile and tapped my leg. "I hope you do. Besides, who would miss a chance to drive around some horror novel characters." A finger shoved eyeglasses up her bumpy nose. Then she glanced in the rearview mirror at the sullen pair.

"Maggie, I gotta joke. Two prods rode in a car, one prod said to the other prod—"

She jerked the steering wheel on a straight road. She hit a deep pothole. The butt of our jokes banged their heads on the car roof. Maggie launched toothy giggles but sobered when the rusted Buick slowed. To avoid someone striking the Buick on the narrow country lane, she parked half slopped in a steep ditch.

"On foot from here, folks."

"Where's exactly is here, old woman?" Dmitri sounded snotty while he unbuckled.

"Sacred ground, Marrow-suckah Two." She closed the squeaking driver's door and pulled a flashlight from her fuzzy fleece. Weak light flicked over the muddy ditch.

After Dmitri climbed from the car and pranced around the mud, his lean body stretched. "This island—"

"Yeah, yeah. Indians slapped on a big 'ol island in the middle of a river. You comin' or gonna ask questions all night long?" Not waiting for a snarky reply, she eased down the steep grassy embankment to a dark timber wall. The moonlit woods devoured her lumpy form and the cheap flashlight's yellow glow.

When an invisible twig snapped, her gruff voice called beyond the trees. "Stand around, and mages are gonna get ya."

That speed our feet after exchanged looks, then we shrugged. Dmitri cleared the gully with one mighty leap. Vasile stepped into mud, turned to face me, then extended his hand. Anger aside, love and habit slipped our flesh together. I let him guide me across the muddy, branch laden ditch. The four of us picked through sticky pine trees. The heady fall leaves, dense pine, and caked mud infused each careful step. Thorny bushes tore at our clothes and skin as barbed tree branches whipped our stung faces more than once. Maggie and I strained not to trip on fallen logs and hidden rocks, but supernatural night vision benefited the pair. The immortals strolled while we mortals stumbled. In between multiple tripping and the occasional overhead branch dodge, I guarded the aged woman. But she traversed through the forest better than I, the lands deep in her DNA.

Before I could question how much further the trek, tangled pointy pines unwrapped their grabby arms. The trees revealed a circular meadow large enough for a small shack. Trees swayed and tinkled musical windchimes while gnarled sticky branches dangled ornamental shapes crafted from feathers and twigs. "We're here." The secret place buzzed mystical energy into dry bones. Such high-frequency pulsations irritated humans sensitive to spiritual vibration, but the waves calmed any anxiousness.

"Amazing!" Even the grouchy immortals stayed respectful and quiet.

Seven mini campfires formed a fifteen-foot-wide and danced the clearing's shadows. The sacred place would inspire ancient dead druids. Trees communicated with each other through tinkling wind chimes, but no breeze stirred a blade of grass or flame. When I arrived, the thick guardian pines and crisp night refused to breathe. A man moved in the circle's perimeter. A human male carried a smoking sage bundle, and a waved long black and white feather through the herb's smoke. Our ears picked up his mumbled chants.

"Gang—Thomas. Thomas—the gang. Our dreamwalker," barked Maggie's three-pack-a-day habit. The man paused his smudge work to walk towards our motley crew. Thomas rested the charred sage bundle on a rock moved closer. The moonlight sharpened his high cheekbones. Long black braids hung over a flannel shirt, and his worn jeans completed a Maine resident appearance. Behind thick-rimmed glasses, a few wrinkled marked his period on Earth. Thomas had a strong familial resemblance to Maggie. The Native American wafted the ceremonial smoke around our shoulders and heads.

"You carried extra sage? These two carry a lot of baggage." A bitten lip suppressed nervous laughter.

When I strode beyond the tree line, wired nerves dissipated, and windless chimes quieted. Absolute confidence filled my heart where once timid self-doubt hammered. Previous to protecting the world and its inhabitants, I stared at the starry night sky and inhaled deeply. The time arrived. *My time.* While I admired the celestial heavens, blood-crusted clouds seeped around a pregnant moon. An ominous red fog hazed the lunar orb. She gasped behind me.

We both uttered, "Blood on the moon."

The dreamwalker stopped smoking the meadow and glanced at the questionable night sky. "Grim omen. Someone dies tonight."

Maggie nudged my lower back. "They might be close. You'd better hurry."

CHAPTER 16

The center of a mage pop

MAGGIE SHOVED A BULKY glass bottle in my hand. "Remember our lessons. You're a novice, but you got raw potential I ain't ever seen before." I raised the cool container to the moon and spotted a dark, granular substance. "Liked we talked about, ceremonial black salt made from a common condiment and consecrated graveyard soil." I shot her a worried glance from the side of my face. "Always does the trick."

After I uncorked the top, I strolled around campfires and poured the dusky grains into the shape of a circle. The occult material disappeared in the grass and formed a protection ring that sheltered people inside from harmful magic or evil entices. Any person or thing that crossed who wished me harm, in seconds pulverized into dust. I murmured a sealing spell on the defensive border.

"Done." I walked back to the expectant four.

Maggie touched Thomas's arm, and a typical stern face softened. "Ready?"

The kind-faced man kissed her wrinkled cheek and nodded. I liked quiet humans.

Dmitri crooned, "You will be brilliant, Poppet."

My hand became warm and weightless. "The first of many wonderful things soon to accomplish, Sarah Wardwell. That I am most certain." Vasile pecked the top of my hand as both sets of expressive eyes radiated unspoken apologies.

"Break a leg, kid!" Maggie's extended arm invited me to take my mystical stage.

I kissed her cheek. "Thank, Mags."

The dreamwalker and I strode into the fire ring. I stepped over the salt and then observed the quiet Thomas's powerful aura swirled greens and yellows high above his head. As I concentrated on my new peaceful partner, the spectators melted into forgotten shadows.

"With blessed heart and an open mind, do you Thomas cast yourself unto this circle of perfect peace?" My laser-focus pierced his liquid eyes. Maggie might trust the guy, but he had my life in his hands, not just smoking herbs.

"I do."

"May a pure heart enter lest turned to ash."

A confident grasp guided him across the protective barrier. Then we offered a sign of vulnerability awaken and appeal to the Gods' interest. We stripped naked. I groaned when Maggie first told me about that uncomfortable part, but the hard concentration limited attention on the chilly air or Vasile seeing me nude. A luxurious breeze caressed my fired senses and bare skin, while nameless dangers no longer trembled my mortal bones.

We again clasped hands, and our joined life-force hummed along with every nerve fiber. If a person heard the pulsed energy, they might think a buzzing fluorescent lightbulb went on the blink. Our arms raised high as we soaked up the vibe from the pure consecrated ground. The clean soil under my bare feet reminded me of drinking the clearest spring water.

"I call to thee Cerridwen, Goddess of Prophecy, take this rite as proof of the will and might into your divine eye. I call upon thee to open your gates and receive my soul."

I drew whirled force fields and Thomas's aura into my chest. Unseen Native American ancestors mumbled ancient chants around the clearing. The mini fires simultaneously flared, and floating orange embers resembled a lightning bug dance from a different life. A red cherry landed on a ceremonial dagger stuck into a log. As instructed, I grabbed the hilt crafted from a carved deer antler. I sliced a six-inch cut along my outer thigh, air hissed through clenched teeth, and fresh blood trickled down my leg.

When I walked around the dreamwalker, my blood formed a second circle. Once finished, I faced naked Thomas, heaved arms upward, then pointed the bloodied dagger at bright stars behind red moonlit clouds. Wind chimes tinkled the sign to call to the guardians of the four watchtowers. Once I channeled the last element, the high energy concentration would launch a magical Batman signal into the inky sky. When the unstoppable egg timer flipped, I stood the chance of the dimension or nearby mages killing me.

"Hail to the Guardians of the East, I summon powers of the air. Windswept meadow, breath of life, torrent removing strife, I invoke thee!" A breeze lifted the hair from across the dark field and disturbed the meager fire blazes.

"Hail to the Guardians of the South, I summon powers of fire. Flames from crackling blazes quickened heat of heart's cravings. I invoke thee!" The element guardian heeded the summons. Fires flared high before returning to small burnings.

"Hail to the Guardians of the West, I ask for—for—" faltering for a second. "Hail to the Guardians of the West, I summon powers of water. Rushing streams of rain, churning oceans, I invoke thee!" I expected drizzle to dampen the fires, but tears wet my cheeks.

"Hail North Guardians—I mean, hail to the Guardians of the North. I summon the powers of Earth. Cave of darkness, mountains of stone, hard flesh, and bone, I invoke thee!" Miles away, I detected rocks worn thinner from relentless waves.

Blue, green, orange, red, and white all churned in a vibration whirlpool above our heads. Over the louder crickets, "I ask thee, Goddess Cerridwen, for permission to take this mana." The spun wizardry stretched down towards the energy stored in my chest until they joined. My back arched then I groaned as the two powers sink into my torso. The chimes silenced. Bugs quieted. No fires snapped. No words described the sensation of having so much force housed inside me, but I understood why power addicted to fellow magic dealers. Because no mage in history ever took in that much-conjured force, but I got the nod from some mystical force.

I circled Thomas then saw my reflections echoed in his thick eyeglasses, my azure blue eyes completely white. We held hands and laid our naked bodies in trampled grass to begin the ancient chant taught the previous week. Thomas's voice joined mine as his calloused hand tightened around my fingers. While still conscious, I whispered a shackling spell to connect his life-force to mine. I pulled us down.

A female chuckled near my ear. "Sarah. Sarrrraahhh."
"Huh?"
"Sarraahhh." Soft steps pattered close to my head.
"Go away."
Someone giggled. "Sarah. Wake up. It's time."
"Wake up, Sarah!"
"I'm up!" I sat up in bed, groggily, but I saw no little bedroom.

The tiny clearing shimmered vibrant mismatched colors. Birds warbled tunelessly. Friendly trees used fragrant branches to whisper to relatives and friends across the field. Unmoved air smelled like static electricity on an old television screen. The fire rings disappeared as if never there. A red smog hazed the crystal-green sky. A giant moon, not a sun, squinted my eyes. I sat up in the tickling pink grass.

Thomas laid awake but motionless beside me. I did it. The successful trip emboldened timid bravery, so I pumped my fists and squared for the next task. Why did he not move and track my every movement with a wide-eyed gape? I wanted to figure out what was wrong with the guy, but a strange enemy entered the field. Time.

I stood. "Guess you can't do anything here, but I can. I'll hurry and find the crown. You just be ready."

A twig snapped. I spun. Across the grass, the waving trees ejected my twin into the odd colored moonlight. No rotten odor or threatening vibe announced a potential foe, so her welcoming smile eased my taunt shoulders a millimeter. The doppelganger floated towards me while she peeked at the paralyzed dreamwalker over my shoulder. The way she held her hands behind her back suggested she concealed something. I craned my neck, but she grinned and twisted her torso.

A crystalline voice echoed inside my thundering head, "Not yet, child."

"Who are you?"

"The sacrificed druidess who birthed your kind. We long-awaited your births."

"We?"

"The original sisters."

She shifted to the motionless Thomas as his frightened eyes tracked our every move.

"A dreamwalker. Brilliant. The sisters chose well."

"Um, is he okay? He's not moving or anything.

"Humans can only enter a mage's dream halfway."

"That's a relief."

"Human sympathizer?"

"Why does everyone keep saying that?"

The druidess television body flickered. "Do you understand why we picked you?"

"Care to tell me while you hand over the crown?" I wanted to ask who shot President Kennedy, but the moon neared its apex.

"After we talk a spell. Let us begin with your second ritual attempt, Duchess Annalyse Simeon."

"I thought this was my second. What was my first?"

She ignored the question. "Your ancestors believed they knew better and wrongly stated the rite forbade marriage between the Queen Regent and the king of beasts. Our plan required a grand union and the intended groom no longer lived—"

"Who!?"

"Tis of no import. Future powers great enough to govern every species does not originate solely from magic, so we needed a replacement. Their inability to read the runes and ignorant actions cost your second life and delayed our progress." She drifted closer as the confession and nearness shivered spooked skin.

"You fated her or me to marry someone?" How many deception licks did it take to reach the center of a mage pop? She mirrored my movement when I scratched my neck.

"Someday, you will understand, but for now, we require you fastened to your destiny to rule both species. However, for one to toiling at fate's requirements and survive, requires the entire truth."

She singsonged the worst secret I ever heard. A month before Anna's rite, The Father and a coven plotted her murder. Neither party wanted Anna and Vasile to marry, but they eloped. When the father of all night's terrible creatures crafted a lapse in her security, mages executed the deed. But the original repeated a mistake. He struck a deal with diabolical occult leaders. The occultists agreed to hide his betrayal and never harm his treasured son if The Father slept for one hundred years.

"But it's been three."

"So, it has. They tricked him as good mages should. They left never attacked the chancellor because his death would counteract the sleep spell."

"If he wakes up, he's gonna be mad as hell."

"We entrust you will use the chancellor's anger when he hears the truth and convince him to make The Father's ailment permanent. Better yet, kill The Father while he hibernates. Magic, even your extra powers, could never terminate the first atrocity."

The red haze deepened, and from behind her back, she extracted a petite gold crown. Centimeter-thick metal shaped a snake's body, and its fangs bit a half-eaten apple carved from a ruby. The warm alloy runes inscribed on the sides glittered in her pale hand. Iconography professors would sell their souls to study the headdress. When the gilded snake blinked a jet-black eye, I forgot all further questions.

"Crafted from Roman coins forged in every raped Britannic kingdom. The red stone belonged to our druid brethren."

With little ancient British history at my disposal, "Um, okay."

"Doth I displease thee? Shall I unleash The Father then start the prophesy anew?"

"So, you are gonna release the Kraken while you gods played with living dolls?"

Her slow chuckle affirmed Maggie's statement. I might not make it out alive.

"It's not the crown. The secret will crush him."

Her echoed words touched me behind my forehead, "If you wish him ignorant, dispatch the dreamwalker."

"Do what?"

"How wise to use the enigma as you see fit. We picked well."

"You mean you want me to kill him?" The Native American man blinked his wide eyes.

"Power controls information and information controls power. Will you give that human the influence to shape our destinies?"

"I don't know." I traded family control for a prod's, then pushed my gambling markers toward a dead druidess. It got old because a dark direction enslaved me once the ritual concluded. I could always convince my friends to go on the run with me. I backed away from my flickered twin. "I changed my mind."

"No, my child, I refuse to cut destiny's yarn. We shall wait for your next birth."

"Fine." Damned if I did and dammed if I didn't. I resolved to live past the dangerous moment to plan the next. "The test."

"Already started. Queen Regent Sarah Elizabeth Constance Wardwell, I bind thy life and eternal fate to transport death's burden until thy coronet becometh dust. Thy hand orders death's hardships."

"Wait!"

"I bind thee, Queen Regent Sarah Elizabeth Constance Wardwell, to live until we breathe once more. I bind thee to our true sufferance until the stripping of mankind." As the metal snake hissed, she shoved the icy gold in my grasp. Goosebumps peppered my skin.

"Now what?"

"You must face your darkest fear, dear chosen child. Pass the test happening right now. Be worthy of the mages that came before you and the ones thereafter."

"Which one? I kinda got a lot of them!"

Fingers tightened around the crown that tingled like a low voltage electric fence. A telltale foul odor charged the strengthened breeze as dusky mold darkened the pink grass. I screamed my next question, but she disappeared, and a carnival mirror, not the field warped as a burst of haunted laughter echoed. I spun in each direction as a dark hole melted through the trees.

Through the reality portal, I saw Maggie and Dmitri's tortured screams. I raced towards the inky void and then banged on the onyx glass. They didn't hear me, too busy with their horror. I screamed at the slick glass, "Wake me up." I twirled to the useless dreamwalker as smelly black mold grew on my feet. "Dude! Wake me up already!" When I received flicked wild eyes, I hit harder on the wormhole. One more second of watching what happened to my friends, I might lose my cool. On their own volition, my shoulders shook, and my neck wobbled. Someone struggled to awaken me. "Harder!"

"Owww—" Vasile rattled me until my neck threatened to let go of my head. Screams reverberated through the dark meadow and worked to clear a foggy mind. After he wrenched me to unsteady feet, I leaned over and vomited on the grass. An arm whipped across my mouth as a full coven. What I saw while on the other side was no trick.

Dressed in long black ceremonial robes, thirteen shadowed faces under drooped hoods surrounded my protection circle. Chants rose, palms exposed at their sides. Figures kneeled, two hard-won prisoners, a hand on each of my friend's heads. Magic immobilized and contorted my writhing friends. Their blood-curdled screams knotted their taunt expressions. Froth and saliva dripped from gnarled mouths.

I stepped away from the sleeping Thomas towards my helpless mates, but Vasile snatched an arm to shoved me behind his shielding body. I grabbed the back of his sweaty barn jacket as I stumbled to steady myself. When he turned to look at me, his long, exposed fangs reflected the red hazed moon and smoky firelight. Silver disks searched my face as dark capillary veins transformed his elegant refinement into something monstrous. The dreamwalker correctly predicted death, but whose was anyone's guess.

Shrieks and chants nearly drowned my words. "You got inside!"

"Barely." When I stepped beside him, his arm straightened to block a further advance.

"This is part of it. The test is to face my worst fear."

"Whatever the trial, we must free him!"

"Both of them, Vas."

"Think again, beast." When my mother's threat leaned Vasile forward as he hissed at the circle's edge, hands curled to claws, and muscles tensed into hard iron.

"Cross the circle, creature, and the sun comes early for your friend." A cousin spoke from under a hood.

"It takes a second to rip half of you apart before you can kill both of us." Vasile poised to strike as I wiggled against his steely grasp.

I yelled above the screams. "And then I annihilate the rest!" I elbowed his hip. "Let me go. This is my fight and my trial."

"Hope you have a plan, Sarah."

"Working on it."

A different black-figure laughed. "A contest to see who moves faster?"

He released me and spoke and an inch from my ear, "An opening—make one. I need an opening. Just one opening."

"Karen, look at Sarah's energy. It's stronger."

"Not now, Father."

Vasile's heated words inflamed my deepest willpower. The small half-dead fires flared higher while a thousand cawing crows cracked the night. "If I choose your victim, will you let the other three live?"

Vasile gritted. "What are you doing?"

"Shut up. I know what I'm doing." Did I?

The woman's voice in the other dimension invaded my mind, 'Choosing who lives is your worst fear. Chose.' Teeth gnashed, and stiff fingers flexed around the crown hid behind my back.

A cousin waggled a finger. "Stupid Queen of Nothing. We agree. Choose who dies, and you keep three."

The druidess's curse to levy death made sense. If only I knew how deep the hex would take me until my last breath. I tallied a mental scorecard. Vasile only loved Dmitri and just wanted me as his weapon. But regardless, I loved them all. The logical sacrificial lamb churned my stomach. Some dumb fated omen forever suffered the grim reaper role. There had to be an alternative way. If I crowned myself to kill my enemies, everyone but me died. If I sacrificed a makeshift family for benefit and survival, I became another corrupt mage.

The druidess's voice echoed again. 'Choose, Queen Regent, or we pick for you.'

I clutched the signet that warmed like a muscle car engine.

"Cousin, feel that?" More murmurs broke from the coven.

Supernova colors beamed the clenched device to life as I shoved it in the air for all to see and wanton stares transfixed on the raised crown. I decided between loved ones that craved my entire existence and dumb future powers. I hoped my hasty plan unfolded better than the last one.

Spittle flew around his gritted fangs. "Sarah." Vasile glared straight ahead. "Enough deliberating. Leaders choose. We scatter our chosen sacrifices across our reigns for the greater good of our people. Pick an opening, or I make one."

"I know. Everyone lives, or I die saving everyone." I calmed as I pooled elemental magic into my chest. Gritted teeth groaned when the crown's rainbow aura pulsed and grew larger.

"If I perish, promise me you will awaken The Father and rid us of Victor."

When I assembled as much power as possible, "Only people dying today happens to be them."

"Tick-Tock, Sarah." Mother's voice elevated above anguished screams.

The vibrating snake demanded to slither on top of my head. So, I focused on the crown's palatable forces that slid across arm nerves. My disabled friends' skin grayed. Their shrieks died as two cousins sucked at Dmitri and Maggie's remaining life-force and my opportunity to act. I needed more energy and a good stall.

"Wait!" My yell circled the clearing, and in unison, ominous hooded figures twisted heads from the writhing pair to me. Their gray pallor pinked a few shades.

"Time, you waste, their life we taste." This time, they didn't toy with a desperate woman who crawled on hands and knees through a rainy London night.

After my calculated stall, I accumulated almost enough power for a huge spell, but the seasoned mages, blinded by greed, never noticed the piling mana. "Look, make me a puppet leader, and again enslave prods. Just let the two humans go." Each second, Maggie's muddied aura flicked fainter.

Vasile bristled. "How dare—"

I hissed under my breath, "Take my lead."

"Truly daughter? Is there a mage in there yet?"

For supernatural ears, "When I signal, I get the six on the left, and you take the next seven. Start in the middle. Move your foot if you hear me." His hiking boot swished dead grass.

"No more resisting?"

"They mean nothing to me. I'm your kid and just want to go home. Here, take the damn thing!" As I predicted, the stunned crowd gasped, crippled by greed for unattainable legendary magic. I immobilized the gathering.

"Why—why now? Gran—Granddaughter?"

"Take me home. I hate them. You have no idea the things they did to me." When I shoved circlet higher, the darkened figures groaned. Black fabric billowed, but their mesmerizing state froze solid, so I wiggled the spellbinding object for effect. The jet and ruby stone caught the moonlight. I killed no one before, so I fought to hold back stinging tears. Whoever thought I could murder people before having sex? "Now!"

As speed blurred Vasile's rigid body, I clutched the gold conduit in both hands. The liquid gold's warmth slicked into my soul's core. When they raised their arms to cast a retaliatory daylight spell, I bore the full weight of the curse. "Wither and die! Into the sky, your dust flies high!"

The crown's mana streamed pinpointed white light into my six victims' chests. Have you ever stared at the sun with your eyes closed and saw nothing but pink? That same flesh tone showed past my clenched eyelids. When shrieks died and the vivid glare diminished, my eyes opened one at a time. Cousins, uncles, and aunts clawed their chests. Massive hoods fell from panicked faces. Bodies writhed as papery skin sucked inward. In seconds they turned to dried husked mummies while my stomach stayed strong against rank burnt meat. A sucking sound imploded collapsing bones, suspended spheres of ash hovered in still air as I returned accumulated power back to the Earth, gray dust scattered into the wind. Empty robes fluttered to the ground.

We left my coven no chance to react because while I cast the fatal spell, Vasile ripped out five out of seven throats. While I crafted soot piles, he fashioned corpses. Like The Father did a thousand years ago, he clasped the last two living necks. Previous to any excited about my plan's success, my cousin and hated mother needed to stop wasting oxygen.

My Mum wailed. "Sar—ah!" If she caught her breath, she could cast a spell and kill Vas.

"Everybody lives, or I die." Clear defiance perched the crown on my head. The snake shivered as it uncoiled and slithered through red curly hair. Its buzzing force-field, endorphins, and dopamine addictingly trickled along with each nerve fiber.

She gasped sick praise. "Baby girl, all grown—"

"Had to kill to earn your love?"

Wine-colored lipstick whispered more unintelligible words.

"She's casting, run!"

Before he released the death grasp on my mother's neck, an empty black robe floated to the dirt when the air mage manipulated the wind to escape annihilation. Vas sneered at his tight fist as I fastened a palm to a pounding heart. But a whimper drew our attention, my cousin's neck still in a vise grip.

"Please—beg you sorry—don't—I beg—" I crossed my arms at her frightened eyes flashed begged remorse.

"May I, Queen Regent?" He requested a queen's permission to dispatch one of my subjects. I experienced pure exhilaration from magical forces, but the greatest thrill came from that moment. The start of me controlling both species began.

I shrugged, "By all means."

"Dmitri?" Vasile's deep tenor boomed to his brother-in-law slumped against a tree.

"Here—Sire." Dmitri's elbows found purchase in the grass to help him sit.

"You need to feed, and tonight I am serving witch."

Awful dark veins webbed across Dmitri's porcelain skin while he lumbered towards prey and predator. Peeled lips revealed long, glorious fangs as breathtaking as his maker's. Perverse pride raised my chin high. A tongue flicked between piercing tusks and circled hungry lips. The golden prodigia's stagger narrowed the distance between mouth and living bone.

"It's the law—can't break it."

Maggie's unconscious body rushed, "Work it out later. She might cast a spell, and Mags is still down. I can't watch everyone."

Vasile yanked raven hair from my cousin's clutched neck to expose more pulsing arteries. "This night, I grant thee permission to break sacred laws, hereby assuming all responsibility."

In seconds, Dmitri tore and slurped through ripped flesh to reach precious vertebrae. Distressed shrieks became familiar garbled gore bubbles while Anthony's ghost watched over my shoulder. When Dmitri popped the first bone, his mouth trickled coppery blood, and Vasile swiped a finger over the crimson river. Identical to the night Antony died, I enjoyed watching. Deep in my mind's cavernous spaces, I belonged to my species.

Vasile squeezed a fisted and hovered it two feet from her surging chest. Dmitri raised a hungry stare, not drilling fangs. Vasile's white-knuckled fist buried his arm in her crunching breastbone. The horrific splinter intensified my cousin's garbled screams. A twist of the wrist, a yank, then a sucking sound, produced a softball-sized bloody mass. Her quivered heart spasmed its last before her petrified eyes as they clouded.

Vasile lisped, "Your miserable brain remains active seven seconds after your heart stops beating." He shoved her convulsing organ into an anguished face. When Dmitri separated a grin from her neck, the lifeless body and ticker slopped to the blood-soaked grass.

An unseen hand cued the mystical golden reptile. The warm gold slithered from my hair and across a bare shoulder. As it traveled down my arm, I held my limb level to the ground, eyes painfully wide. "What's happening?" witching it coil around a wrist. Three shocked stares watched the circle burst into a brilliant yellow flash and forced us to shield our foreheads. The snake blinked its black eye at me as I showed the stars my underarm, then sunk into my pale skin. An exquisite euphoria elicited a soft moan when my limb flashed too bright to observe. When the blinding light and seductive tingles faded, I opened my eyes to see a brown henna tattoo marking my arm. The serpent curled into an "S" and its fangs plunged into a whole apple, not a half-eaten piece of fruit.

Vasile's long strides reached my side, and his gentle cold fingers capture my forearm. Transfixion from the novel mark ended when Dmitri groaned. When Vasile tended to his weak companion, I scrambled to grab my clothes. As I dressed, like the evil never existed, the dooming red haze and putrid smells dissipated. After the tremendous natural magic disintegrated, the field became a simple break in the pines. Once clothed, I raced to Maggie then dropped to my knees. While my companions murmured about the evening, I closed my eyes to direct Earth's healing energies into her frail body. A faint flush bloomed weathered cheeks and breaths less labored.

"Maggie? Maggie, wake up. She's not waking guys! Come on, Mags—" My unlimited powers had restrictions. "If you wake up, I'll treat you to a Bingo game." I clutched her wrinkled fist because legendary abilities unworthy of her death.

Dmitri tossed an arm behind him to slump on the dewy grass. "Feel like hell, Vas."

"Bi-bingo? You're—on, Toots."

"Maggie!"

What's Marrow-suckah Two whining about?" She squeezed my hand with little strength.

"You're alive!"

She rasped as a sun spotted touch rested on my cheek, "You did it." She half-smiled at the snake tattoo.

"No, *we* did it."

"Proud of ya, girl."

Dmitri struggled to rise and mumbled, "Let me assist."

"Paws off!" The snarled command erupted small laugher and long exhaled breaths.

"Yes, ma'am." Too feeble for a verbal war, he laid beside the old human.

"And my Thomas?"

"Dear God, we forgot about the dreamwalker!"

Vasile and I spun to face the sleeping Thomas still inside the salted circle.

Vasile offered, "I shall retrieve the man."

I tucked Maggie's coat around her slumped shoulders. "Vasile's checking now."

"Sun rises soon, Poppet—must leave."

"Sarah—" Vasile's stern concern rang across the glade.

"Damn it." I knew that tone. I jumped to my feet and jogged to where a kneeling Vasile blocked most of Thomas's body.

"Sarah, what is this—" He pointed at the Dreamwalker.

I stepped around his back. Thomas's stubbled gray skin smoothed from chin to nose as if born without a mouth. I took a step backward and whipped my head to Maggie. "Jesus Christ—"

"What happened while you were in there? Seen nothing like it."

Maggie called out, "Thomas?"

Vasile stood, and we parted from the corpse. The older woman slapped her lips.

Near an ear, he asked again, "What happened?"

"I—I—don't know—I don't think I know."

"No time. Sun rises soon."

When Maggie tried to stand, she fell back and moaned, "My grandson?"

"Grandson? Damn it, Vas!"

Through her fingers, "Oh God, what'd I do? What did I do?"

No way I took the druidess up on her idea to silence him. Or did I? The details grew more blurred as seconds piled into minutes. I prayed my celestial twin did the terrible deed not me, because I had enough murder for one night. But I tucked the dilemma away because the everlasting sun soon claimed the sky, and Maggie needed a doctor. Besides, Mother still lurked in the shadows.

CHAPTER 17

Kill three birds with one sabotage

THE NEXT EVENING, EXTREME tiredness from the trial slowed minds and bodies. We recovered enough strength to check on Maggie before we headed to the airport. The grieved grandmother won a week's bed rest in her mobile home, so I placed any needed necessities of her fingertips. From the plastic bags Dmitri carried inside, I scattered magazines, drinks, and snacks around her bed. My best friend even bought treats for a small dog zoo. I angled the TV remotes and double-checked ample blankets.

Fingers smoothed over her crepe hand. The ordeal of getting her life-force nearly sucked out aged Maggie another twenty years.

Vasile's cleared throat reminds everyone the sun enforced a tight schedule. We said goodbye to the infuriating woman who niggled into our hearts.

"If ever in the United Kingdom, you will be my honored guest."

She gave him a thumbs up.

Dmitri tendered his farewell version. "Had doubts, old human." Before she stung back, "But my sword is forever yours." He clicked his heels. Then his head snapped down at his feet.

A dog yapped over her sniff. "Out. Both of ya, before you catch the sun."

I picked my head off her malleable shoulder as Thomas's death made her kind regard impossible to return while a feeble hand caressed my teary face. I patted her hand.

"Go. Marrow-suckers are waiting."

"I'll miss you."

"I have a feelin' you'll be back."

I promised her to be greater than the sum of my people's crimes after again tucking covers around her frail body. "Right. Get cracking."

"Bye, Toots."

"Yep! Cheers!"

She never saw my tears.

* * *

The early fall welcomed two warring supernatural creatures, but a frosty Maine tarmac said goodbye to a cohesive family. The familiar shiny white tube with whinny engines perched ready to spirit us home. I brightened to see the same smiling crew waited beside the chrome railings. Their continued presence cemented a vital idea; they valued human life or considered usefulness beyond elitist notions.

We thumped aboard the opulent Gulfstream, and as we buckled, I hoped for a less eventful flight. Pilots worked an unrushed preflight checklist as James, the same cheerful steward, bustled about the cabin. The glowing attendant passed the bleary-eyed lord his treasured London Times and delivered a hot cup of tea into my eager hand. James loitered over Dmitri's uncharacteristic dark circles and showered him with blankets. I reached up to shutoff an overhead light and rested against supple cream leather.

When the high-pitched jet engines roared, and the door thumped shut, my stomach somersaulted because soon I hurtled across a darkened runway to the scene of other crimes. Mentally, the buzzing mopeds delivered take away, and old church bells clang, but London had to wait because Heathrow obeyed local noise ordinances. No aircraft took off or landed during the night until early morning hours. Before we left Maine, the pilots filed a plan to Gatwick so the immortals could hide until sunset. Something tickled my fingers. I blinked hard to sharpen blurry vision when Vasile pressed a small, maroon-colored book into a limp hand. I crammed the official booklet in my duffle bag next to the fake. The temporary passport and tattoo served as the only

State of Maine souvenirs. Thoughts drifted to the unavoidable and less pleasant things that awaited in London.

An occult cabal waited to hear about the ritual. If my mother raced her return to peddle vicious lies, I faced an uphill fight to win over coven label me a traitor. Unlike the prod council, our covens never banished traitors but executed defectors. The future political battle required strategic planning, but lucky for me, an expert strategist and spin doctor across the aisle. I yawned, resolved to comb a million ideas when better recovered.

The runway's miniature blue lights fought a smidgeon of night gloom as the plane bumped along the cracked taxiway. I closed my eyes. When the metal beast ate black tarmac to unshackle its passengers from their Earthly confines, I longed for regular hours and a warm tan.

Vasile closed his eyes while dim LED lights glinted against his enormous crested ring, and smooth cheeks looked darker as the unshaved skin detracted Vasile's youthful vigor. Sheer fatigue and unguarded trust, even around an old enemy, lowered his defenses enough for rare rest. Vasile's tired peace comforted me, and when my defense slipped, my mind slid towards an avoided memory. Did Dmitri know The Father's betrayal? Such earth-shattering disloyalty might cost my best friend's life and me the chance to win his heart, but for some ghastly reason, the God's wanted the secret used. A truth and an odd commonality joined us as we played innocent pawns in an underhanded game, but unlike me, the others hid his stooged role. I doubted he would endure the unfamiliar part.

I filed the mental burdens in an internal filing cabinet of loathsome thoughts. Instead, my murder victims' death faces popped to mind. Thomas's confused, scared expression wilted me, and a loud sigh broke the engine hum. Guilt loomed next to apprehension. Did I betray Maggie and subconsciously chose to forget? I came from a supernatural world where people instinctually deceived as natural as breathing. I combed through my memories to search for the dreamwalker's file while fixing a distracted, deadpanned gaze on Vas. But what was new? I always stared at him.

An impolite stare long pulled the vigilant creature's notice. When my meditation snapped, Vasile's lips shifted a tired smile, then craned his neck at sleeping Dmitri, who never slept at night. After a few days, supernatural-healing capabilities would restore the glorious pain in the ass. Vasile's arms uncrossed, then two outstretched fingers beckoned me to him. The intimate summons skipped jaw-dropping heartbeats, and the icy resolve to resume hatred for Vasile melted in boiling needs.

I crawled into his lap, my slight frame cradled against his broad chest, and I curled tired legs into a ball. Strong arms encircled me inside a much-needed cocoon, and I rested against his chiseled torso. The reasons for our horrible row became distant excuses as tense muscles seeped away. To avoid another fallout or a legendary mood swing from a poor word choice, I remained quiet.

"It may never come easy." Warm breath cascaded around an ear.

I fixed nervous eyes on white dress shirt buttons. "What won't?"

"Taking a life." I smoothed a long hair strand off a cheek. Solid arms tightened around my shoulders and knees.

"You knew?"

242

"Years on battlefields, so I recognize ghosts returned to haunt their killer."

Sad facial muscles squeezed as I willed away tears. "I hated doing it."

Vasile set his chin on my head while a finger-tapped my knee, and we fell into strange silent ease. We abandoned heated words and talked like friends, not about the latest movie, but murder. "Does it get easier?"

"Yes. For you? Maybe not." The act of killing and ordering death for a thousand years flattened his tone. Death no longer excited.

After a few quiet minutes, "Vasile?" Eyes opened halfway while I breathed in his chest's spiced scent.

"Hmmm?"

"What about you and me? Do you still feel the same?"

"About?"

"Our future?"

I endured a long pregnant pause. "Yes and no."

"Oh," I lacked the bravery to ask what he meant. One wrong word might toss me off his lap and launch him into a terrible mood.

"Sarah, nobody dismantled unending grief but you."

Rejection circled the misery drain, so I changed the subject. "Dmitri avoided talking about his Romanian trip."

"Yes." Jesus, he evaded answers better than a tax criminal.

Vas traced a line across my kneecap to an upper thigh. An electrical current shivered muscle as new dread re-knotted my stomach. When I peeped at his melancholic face, "When do they want us there?"

A corner of his mouth lifted a centimeter. "We?"

"Yes, *we.*"

"And you still agree to the original plan?"

"I'm invested—and in exchange, you help me figure out how to win over the leaders."

He teased, "So a deal amendment. I see."

"Kinda."

"Of course, I will help you. Succeed or fail with the covens, we must return to Romania, or if not, they come for us all."

"*They?*"

"The council uses only the best assassination squad in the world, ma chérie."

"No pressure."

When his tone changed, I sensed he hated his next words, so I avoided eye contact. "The councilmen ordered Dmitri to execute you if you cannot control the covens or refuse to return with us."

"That's dumb. Why?"

"Unattended, your species may corrupt you or your powers."

"I barely understand the new capabilities, forget letting someone else manipulate them."

"The reasoning goes much deeper. If Mrs. Davidson is correct when she said you create spells, not just cast them."

"Basically, your council worries I might undo immortality?"

"Very astute. Yes."

One word became a death sentence. I peeked at the prince as James tucked a blanket around the immortal's slumped. "Could Dmitri—"

"—kill you? Yes, and I shan't intervene because disobedience orders his execution, and if they try, I will be forced to exterminate my kind." matter-of-factly concluding.

"You'd finish your society to save him?

"As you can see, I am glad you agree to visit Romania."

"But you didn't answer the other question."

In an instant, a threatening monster became a playful human. Hot breath and a liquid voice rippled my neck's flesh. "Remind me?" The rapid mood swings and role swaps tumbled my thoughts.

"Do we have a future together?"

"Not until you—"

"—can ensure my immortality."

"Precisely."

"Like, become a prod?" An unenthusiastic tone sailed the slur as I found the undead elephant in the room or airplane.

He ignored the ugly name and pressed, "Your potent magic might assist you to survive the change. As an immortal, you are no longer a danger. If you become one of us and help restore my chancellorship, you lose your people. However, at my side, you gain a different empire lasting forever."

"What about the application process? Can pedigrees bypass the laws?"

Vasile's arms snaked around me. "No, but I am already an outlaw."

"Again, risking my life?"

"Our lives."

"No matter the course, we chance death, and because you transcended as Queen Regent, new pitfalls opened for you."

"We never really thought beyond the rite, so what's the unknown danger?"

"Failure to rule the covens while a mortal, you become the most hunted woman in history. Villains from powerful species will spare no morality nor expense to eliminate your threatening liability."

I snuggled in his arms and listened to Vasile's heartbeat once every ten minutes. "I see."

"And nobody can leave a loaded weapon lying around."

He nodded, and stubble lifted glossy red hair. "I am afraid so, and the protection lasts only so long."

"No matter what I decide—I—I—"

"Sarah please—"

"I have to."

"No, please—"

"I lo—" While the jet descended into Gatwick, the smell cut off the ill-timed affirmation. A mage worked magic as rot plugged our noses, and Dmitri's eyes snapped open like a creepy vampire inside a coffin. "What the hell—Vas!" We jumped to our feet.

"I know, Dmitri." I bet he felt relieved for another supernatural battle rather than echo those damming words. Perfect timing.

Concentration, not smell, pinched my nose. I stood in the aisle, winced, and gripped a seatback as the two peered from black windows.

"We are flying, not sitting ducks, Sire." I sensed the pair spin to me.

"If the fight exhausted Mother with the entire coven is dead—"

246

"And only the council knew our plans."

Dmitri gritted, "We'll later crop the cross—if we live." Dmitri's Victorian meant they would soon find the guilty party. If we lived.

After a deafening bang shook our feet, the aircraft pitched. As we flung to one side, the captain rushed an announcement about a Heathrow emergency landing. Lucky for us, the world's busiest airport opened runway for emergencies. But if we landed without a prepared ground crew to secret the immortals, the rising sun endangered my friends. Someone doubled down and wanted to kill three birds with one sabotage. An oval window glowed orange when an engine shot out yellowish-blue flames and lit worried faces. The plane jerked downward as we dropped an alarming rate, and frantic grasps searched for seatbelts.

"Sire, the council does not conspire with witches. This is magic."

"Call someone at Heathrow and inform—"

"Shut up!" Rattles, small bangs, and shudders replaced their excited voices. I slammed hands on the cabin wall when the steward yelped. The snake tattoo itched. Mentally, the serpent design slithered along an arm and lifted off the flesh. I screamed when natural instincts ignited. I spoke an unknown ancient language capable of casting more than bugs flung at windows or freezing tea.

The plane's catapulted interior and panicked passengers melted together. I no longer flew on a crashing high-priced jet but stood on gray city sidewalks. Early crowds bustled around Piccadilly Circus. From the arriving trains, I watched a fireball in the sky. A woman walked through me. I ignored the tickling sensation as long ethereal arms stretched into wintry dawn air. I closed one eye, then two fingers pinched the tiny plane. I whispered, "Mar eun." The Gaelic words meant, 'like a bird.' As red buses and morning commuters crushed through my frozen body, a determined pinch lowered the airplane to the ground. "Mar eun." The gray sky faded to black.

* * *

"Sarah—wake up! Poppet!" Dmitri's clasped cold cheeks while Vasile covered his chest. I laid in the aisle's middle. I turned to see the steward's sagged head bob. The aircraft's tires bumped along a solid surface. Overhead LED lights burned. At least a rotten meat odor left my gut alone.

"Right o. Bully for you! There's our girl."

"Wha—what happened?"

"What happened? You bloody well saved us—you did!"

Nausea and skull-crushing pain promised to eject my skull's eyeballs. "I'm gonna be sick."

Chapter 18

Coffins and silk pyjamas

AFTER A MECHANIC CHECKED the Range Rover for tampering, the journey to Vasile's manor differed than other car rides. We again escaped death, so we took our time to smooth along with a pitch-black road because Vasile's human chauffeur used headlights. No longer the driver, Dmitri watched for an unknown saboteur as I returned to a former prison. I dreaded going back to the infected horror estate because its immortal warden once used and abused me. I nagged myself of the ways I irrevocably changed both place and master. A chewed nail shoved into my gob, but the prince tapped my hand. I scowled.

A still pounding head sagged sideways to gaze from an inky frosted window, showing nothing but the night's stark void. Life became a series of thin black windows, and the glass separated me from its lonely nothingness. But that night, the hollowness ate through the fingerprints as the estate lights grew larger.

Centuries-old protocol greeted the car's arrival when the SUV crunched the long driveway. A full staff complement waited at the ready in the cold on both sides of the sculpted Georgian entry and formed two neat servant lines. Both undead and human servants remained fastened to aged standards, so the uninformed employees received my hearty eye roll, not a welcome smile.

After Vasile greeted the pert staff, he bounded up the entrance steps and popped his usual James Bond stride. As he passed a stone lion guarding the entry, he fist-bumped its nose. Dmitri high-fived a blinking footman, unaccustomed to direct contact, and the abnormal exuberance cleared the butler's throat. Both companions relaxed the moment they crossed the gravel drive. After a scenery swap after centuries cooped up in the manor, escaping death, and return home, the odd couple acted reinvigorated.

Dutiful servants bustled past Smith as they hefted suitcases from the auto. She pushed a dawdled footman struggling under a bulky trunk across a bent back, and the butler bossed the others. Once the work's intensity satisfied her, and she received a perky nod from the senior man, her determined strides beelined towards Vas. The former leader of deadly creatures blinked, then took a few steps backward. The mean-looking housekeeper stood before her master with hands on her hips while she glared at his wrinkled forehead.

"Done, for now, old chap."

When Dmitri and I looked at each other, our silent words and grins spoke, 'Avoided death but murdered by a human maid.'

She flung her arms around Vasile and hugged his waist because the maid's white bun only reached his breastbone. The stiff chancellor half-smiled while he patted her shoulder. After she released him from a shocking display of affection, Smith searched for her composure inside an empty apron pocket. I guess she found it because she spun lasered concern on poor Dmitri.

She lowered her forehead and marched to the blinking Adonis. He fluttered a limp hand at his chest before he crept back a step. "A little assistance here, old boy?"

"On your own. You know how much she terrifies me." Vasile shuffled through the envelopes he took from the butler's small silver tray.

She swatted at the prince's arm and ordered, "Shut your wicked mouth and give us a hug."

Dmitri scooped her off kicking feet. "Give me a kiss first, you dishy treat."

"Put me down! Me old bones are too chewy to eat!"

"Spoiled sport."

Smith smoothed her bun once the affable prince set her back on her down. Then a fresh victim fell into her crosshairs, the instigator of her domain's chaos, me. I whipped my head left and right as my friends chuckled. The human turned bone-eating monsters into playful lads and the most powerful mage into a simpering child.

"Saved me, boys, you did!"

"I did?"

"No time fer modesty. Mind helping me with dinner?" The gruff forgiveness signaled an acceptance me into her strange fold, her concealed concern reminding me of Maggie.

"I would like that." A minty-mothballed cheek earned a quick peck.

Plump shoulders squared, she bellowed, "Bags you, daft idiots! Bags!"

Vasile passed the various envelopes to the butler posted at his elbow, then gestured at me. "Come."

I shrugged as we walked single file along a narrow corridor, hidden by a giant pastoral tapestry. The windowless hallway sloped a few degrees downward. Too knackered to question the odd passageway and where he took me, I silently marched behind General Vasile. A male servant hefted two bags and my backpack while he brought up the rear. My room was in the manor's south wing, so why carry both suitcases?

After fifty feet, a solid black door ended our silent stroll. The smooth metal entry rose a foot taller than Vasile and lacked a doorknob. A sleek datapad like the one at the Maine house positioned to the left of the sealed entrance. The crisp male servant set the luggage near the mysterious safe after he passed me my backpack.

"Do you require anything further, milord?"

"No, thank you, Stephen. You may go."

The striking boyish man spun on a heel, and in seconds the unlit corridor swallowed his back. Assured we stood alone, Vasile touched the black panel and digital buttons illuminated. After he fingered several beeping numbers, his head lowered inches from the glowing pad, and a mechanical woman smoothed, "Scanning, please remain still. Scanning, please remain still." Blue numbers vanished, and a bright bar traversed his passive face. "Good evening, Chancellor. Please enjoy your rest." The hissing door clicked, then inches at a time, a foot-thick metal tucked into wood-paneled concrete. The lord coveted unbelievable wealth if he required a biometric vault that size. But why lockup our suitcases? Vasile stepped into total darkness. When he snapped on a light, my question disappeared.

Two fingers curled as he smoothed. "Come."

Vasile waited for me while standing in a beautiful room with modern accommodations. Several David Hockney paintings created a fresh change from the manor's oppressive art. A black leather sofa positioned in front of the most shocking piece of furniture, a giant flat screen, and DVD filled shelves. Across the bedroom, wine-colored bedding heaped atop an enormous bed and contradicted the meticulous owner's personality. The living space looked more age-appropriate for his human years.

"Um—your bedroom. We're in your room?"

He noticed my fixed stare. "Please excuse the condition because I deny Mrs. Smith access when not at home. After you concluded your stay with us, I had insufficient opportunity to make my bed."

"Oh? Oh! You're serious." Annoying butterflies fluttered in my stomach before they turned into somersaulting gremlins when I understood a marrow-sucker confined me inside his Fort Knox panic room.

Electricity shot up an arm when he traced a touch up my skin. "Sarah?"

"So, no—cof—coffin?"

"Coffin?" he perched hands on his hips. "I only require coffins when traveling aboard ships."

"Like Dracula—oh—OH! You're joking."

"Not quite. He lacked any taste—"

"Coffins. Right. And why exactly am I here?"

His face lowered as he glanced sidelong at me. "Here," while he pointed at the floor. "In my lair?"

I pursed my lips and puffed hair from my face. "You must love escaping certain doom because you have mad jokes. I'm serious."

"You are here," Again, he pointed to the cream-colored carpet. "Because you belong here." He tossed in, "And I demand your presence." Sexual tension sprang from the declaration and dropped my jaw.

"I—I—"

"I see this displeases you. Shall I ring for my man to escort you to your old rooms?" Vasile's head tilted towards the sealed door as the ancient creature enjoyed outsmarting me.

I bit a jagged nail and refused to give in to the pressure. "Why live in a vault?"

Vasile removed his jacket and shoulder muscles strain against his wrinkled dress shirt. He tossed the expensive fabric across a leather chair, then fingered a platinum cufflink as he considered a witty response. I gulped. He smoldered while lifting our suitcases to a lengthy dresser's top. "Down here, the sun is no threat, and I am unreachable if someone penetrates security."

"Oh. I see."

He winked and unzipped luggage as he growled a toe-curling Eastern European accent. "Not all penetration bores the mind, Sarah. Then again, we—"

"Okay! Right then." He chuckled when I asked, "And if that happens and you get trapped in here?"

"This is a fifteenth-century house and has many hidden corridors and tunnels."

"Like ones Smith used to spy on me?"

He wrinkled his nose for a second before continuing, "There is such a tunnel connection this room to secret caves. Nobles once utilized to hide debaucheries and society parties while—"

"Like the Hellfire Club?"

"Not as vulgar." He flipped a palm, "I the last fête and won the property at cards. Georgiana Cavendish never expected my winning play and left her husband very distressed."

"Not to so sound morbid or anything, but what happens if someone casts a daylight spell when you're asleep?"

Graceful movements traversed closed the space between us, and the purposeful steps slammed a pounding heart faster. "Quite dead, Sarah."

"Brilliant. Locked in a—lair—with a prodigium and cue creepy music."

A dark renegade curl fell across his forehead. "A conundrum."

"Conundr—Wait—you plotted to bring me down here during our flight home?"

"No."

I but my lower lip to freeze a sneaky grin. "Liar."

"I can assure you the exact opposite is true."

"And my people are just misunderstood, and I've gots ocean property in the Sahara Desert to sell you."

"Tis no lie, sweet Sarah. I planned to secret you away in my lair not hours ago, but the minute I tossed you in my auto."

"The first or second toss? Wait—what?"

"Sarah, I may be an immortal, but I still suffer a man's needs."

"You do?"

"Yes, but at a distinct intensity. Emotions require time to notice, but when permitted to wander freely, sentiment can take root and grow wild." He tucked a stray curl behind an ear as he studied my limp arms. "The truth displeases you."

"Vas, you are always cold, and you manipulate every situation and person. How is this any different?"

"Because I am doing what you asked."

"What I asked?"

"Me letting you in, and I do not mean in the figurative sense."

"I see."

"I hoped you would be pleased."

"I'm your weapon one minute and a woman the next, only after you told me to sod off. Me and your bloody mood swings are a damn Yo-Yo."

"Sarah—"

I stepped back. "If I stay here with you, I'll just get hurt when you tire of your paltry toy weapon and return me in your control box."

Vasile's forearms crossed, and a finger wedged under his chin. "I concede your point. But consider this, few know about this room where I am at my most vulnerable, the one you now stand inside."

He patted arms and said, "This is me registering emotions and doing as you asked."

"But—you—you never brought other—other—" How did a girl ask a monster about their sex life?

"Women?"

I nodded.

"After Anna, I extinguished all need for carnal pleasures."

"You switched them off?" I snapped my fingers, "Like that?"

"Endless time from immortality distorts an emotion's potency and urgency."

"English?"

He traced an elbow, and a sweet smile radiated at my lippy pout. "The ol' engine takes a while to restart."

I bit my lip and asked, "And your—engine?"

"The moment I plucked you from London, it purred as an exotic race car."

I leaned on the balls of my feet, moments from throwing myself into his arms. "Then why always a jerk?"

"Anger? Denial? Both? Yet, I do not expect you to sympathize."

"But why now? I resemble her, and all, but—"

"Sarah, the rising sun exhausts me, and I require a shower." The expert steered our delicate chat because the creatures never changed. But to love someone meant embracing every personality trait, no matter how insane they acted.

He disappeared into a bathroom and left my mouth agape. Muffled water spray unfroze my rooted feet and a gulp. I calculated how he intended the night to go. But I lacked any sexy lingerie, so I raced to a small suitcase to find something decent to wear.

I muttered, "It's what you get for imagining sex."

"You said?" he called past the closed door.

I hated his unnatural hearing. "Nope!"

After I dress in one of his white undershirts and clean panties, I dashed a panicked gaze towards the bed. What would it be like to lose my virginity to an immortal I loved? Puffy blankets and piles of pillows swallowed my tired body. A goose-down pillow's familiar masculine smell pulled at my toes. Vasile's trademark unpredictability and moodiness implied a hellish ride while locked in his lair, but something besides a shocking personality reversal promised a good Hell. Because our time freed from ritual preparations and avoiding dodgy antagonists, I guessed how Count Simeon intended to fill our moments.

My head lifted when the bathroom door's quiet creak jolted swollen eyes open, and a jumpy heart whooshed blood. The most exquisite male ever created stood in a triangle of yellow light, and his long shadow stretched towards me. A delicious man clutched a towel around chiseled hips, low enough to reveal deep cut muscles and an ebony hair trail from groin to navel. A water droplet off his ear and more from his damp locks fell and bejeweled the warrior's ripped muscles. I prayed to whatever cruel God, playing with living dolls, who placed me in the vault. They ensured he slept naked.

Playful curiosity arched his brow. "Something amiss?"

"Bloody hell—" I needed a filter.

Deliberate slow paces creaked the floor as he roamed, and when he sat next to me, the mattress bowed under my stiff muscles. A soft bedside lamp illuminated a shoulder's jagged silver scar. I dared to smooth a careful thumb along the raised mark, but

a woman shoved her entire hand into a piranha tank. "Did you get this when a human?" Other scars in various lengths and shapes marked his entire torso. He lifted his arm to squint at the long-forgotten injury as goosebumps decorated his olive skin.

"Yes. We do not scar. Sarah, the sun rises. I demand slumber."

"Um, okay."

When he stood, the mattress sprang up and released my breath. Vasile pulled silk pajama bottoms from a dresser, and I flopped on the fluffy comforter, wild hair fanned around me. I afforded him privacy and angled away from my transfixed stare, but I still heard the towel plop to the floor.

"Your heart, Sarah."

"It's not nice to eavesdrop."

"So, I was once told."

When his watch dropped to a table, I turned my head. Thin green silk bottoms tied low about his waist and revealed more eye-popping male shapes the towel concealed. Oblivious to my staring or friendly for a change, he ignored the impolite attention and slid under the covers. When his torso stretched to turn off the bedside lamp, sculpted abs and faded scars rippled. I chewed my lip and clutched the duvet to my chin as the first night at the manor. Drenched in utter darkness, I jerked when his touch covered my shoulder.

An exhaustion fog lumped his words. "The sun saps all strength. Because I could not stop for death."

"Emily Dickinson? Now I know you're tired. Sleep."

"You know, Em—"

Lengthy breaths sounded every ten seconds, and a heavy hand slumped between us. While I laid in the pitch-black room, I relied on my ears to paint a picture of the strange surroundings, but the only sound came from a comatose monster. I saw ample terrible things birthed by death and night, enough to make any sane person terrified of the dark. But cuddled under warm blankets while blind, I knew rare peace. An entrapped sigh hissed when I rolled on my side and groped for his hairless chest. I swallowed disappointment from another night of unexplored physical attraction. I slid into a dreamless sleep next to my gentleman killer.

Unsure how long I slept, my tickled nose swam me from a blissfully blank slumber, and a groggy swat hit nothing. The tickle slunk to my chin while faint breaths trickled along my neck radiated heat, and a sweet spiced male sent painted the picture my eyes denied. The dip suggested the day reprieved Vasile, and the night freed him from his daily coma. When I touched smooth skin stretched over hard muscles, his slow exhale erupted while he watched me sleep infected goosebumps. A shiver raked my spine because the world's most dangerous hunter stalked me in the dark. A casual touch sneaked across a cheekbone.

I groaned, "Aren't you supposed to be in some undead coma?" Another tickle to my nose dislodged a giggle, so I batted black air but hit nothing. "Let me sleep."

"Entertain me."

"Haven't I been doing so since we met?"

"Quite."

"Well, at least I'm not your meal. What's the time?"

"The sunset an hour ago."

"You're joking."

"Quiet."

"Excuse me?"

"Stop breaking my concentration." I felt, not saw, his seductive grin.

"Someone woke up in a pleasant mood."

"Mhm."

"Can it last more than an hour?"

A slow-paced thumb trailed across my breastbone as he drew an unhurried circle down my flesh. "Perhaps." Heartbeats slowed from sleep jumped into high gear.

"Prodigium vision. Lovely."

"You wish to talk abilities?" I fisted the silky sheets when the mattress jiggled again. A deepened Romanian accent spoke above me. I pictured him elevated on an elbow as he leaned above my flat body.

"Um—I—"

A thumb rested on my lips while another hand inched along my curves but avoided the indecent parts. Bottled longing and timid hope tingled every nerve. When tender lips grazed under my ear, I flinched. I forgot how, at any moment, sharp teeth might sink into my neck because I replaced such life-saving terror for total trust. I relaxed and shoulders pressed into the mattress while he kissed a pulsing neck artery. A nervous hand snaked through the black and searched for the night's master, but fingers clasped my wrist and returned my arm to the sheets.

I never heard him whisper until then. "Be still."

The husky command domineered any whipped-up whim he desired. I gulped around a fresh fear, Vasile never doing more than kissing me because for an immortal, foreplay might last decades, but I lived mortal years. My tilted head touched a bare shoulder, then my back arched.

He half growled, "We proceed on one condition."

"Huh?" when unnamed urges prevented a coherent question.

"Before our joining, you must belong to me." A fang's point grazed my sensitive neck and expected to touch blood but felt nothing wet.

"I—I—will? I mean, I sorta already do."

"I command it." The rumbled, stern tone left no room for willful disobedience.

I whimpered, "Command what?" I imagined two-inch-long fangs a fraction from heightened flesh when the terrible sharp things trailed my pimpled flesh to a clavicle. Then the mattress sagged. Vasile returned to my head and skimmed my needy lips for a moment, so I kissed empty air. When a searching touch rose, he again pinned the wandered touch. "Wha-what do you mean?" Whatever he required to end the torture, I gave without reservation.

A heavy exhale tickled hair against my skin. "Here and now, we consume each other. I shall hold your hand as I walk you to death's door."

"Become one of you?"

"Yes."

"How?"

Warm lips grazed the top of a breast. "How what, my Queen?"

"How will you kill me? How will I die?"

"Painlessly. I shall slit your throat, and the blood-soaked sheets will last, unlike Jesus's shroud. As mine and—of—mine, we will spend eternity making love I now deny you."

"I don't go under—"

"I to use a modern colloquialism, how bad do you want me? As your precious magic, are you ready to pay the price death and I demand?"

"Pr—price?" The reply he sought lay between my trembled thighs. He just needed to explore my body to find my eagerness.

Vasile licked a lip, "Oh yes."

Mister Sexy issued no warning before he reached to turn on the lamp. Blinded eyes blinked. But before I begged my answer, Vas kneed my legs painfully wide, and Death's messenger crouched between shaken knees, hands beside my shoulders. Plump lips pulled a dreadful snarl, and meandered dark capillaries distorted his youthful face. But the fanged demon that knelt to claim a unique brand of a victim no longer scared me. Hundreds of years of pent-up desires, not a hungry glare, drilled into my skull. Neither of us breathed.

"I'm not sure what to say."

"Swear allegiance and pledge your immortality to me alone, then complete your obedience by—"

A tiny voice tore at me. 'The world-class seducer trapped you and your people. Poor Sarah failed another escape.' A brilliant light flashed, and an awful migraine seared my forehead, and the crouched naked immortal morphed into an unwanted person.

I again stood at the fantastical meadow before the druidess. 'Send me back!' I yelled inside my head, paralyzed like dead Thomas.

'The master knows you won't endure the change and knows he violates his own laws. He remembers you said no and sacrifices you and your people to survive. You are not a weapon but a tool.'

'He is not like that!'

'He is that. One species rules Earth, and your commonplace desires alter everything and spoil everyone's destinies if this night you become a beast.

'Lies!'

'This is not your destiny, child of ours.'

When he explored my body, and I looked down, I laid on pink grass, not blankets.

'Feel that?'

'Yes. Take me back.'

'The chancellor will change more than your body. Open your minds to the selfish manipulation and see him.'

'Send me back!'

'See him!'

'I'm trying!'

'Not those eyes. These eyes.' Either she or Vasile touched my forehead. Then the vision's paint smeared as reality bled through the hallucination.

Her last words broke through denied thoughts. 'Poor little Sarah, forever a tool.'

I reared back on the pillow as firm hands clutched my flushed cheeks. A horrific prodigium about to create another monster and have sex, disappeared, and transformed into a worried man. "Sarah! Wake up, my darling!"

"Huh?"

"Sarah, what happened? Your pupils turned white as they did during the ritual!"

I crawled out from underneath his massive body while gasping for air, then leaped off the colossal bed. I almost tripped when a sheet wound around a leg. We rasped ragged breaths while a monstrous stare reflected the lamp's soft glow.

"Slipped into—dimension. I—I—am sorry. The druidess— she—"

He wronged when a flicked gesture summoned me back to bed. "Come, Sarah."

"No!"

"Whatever is the matter?"

"You—you are the matter."

"Sarah—"

The tattooed snake itched. "You want to change me for selfish reasons."

"Sarah, I do not—"

"Admit it! I see it in your creepy stare!"

Heated expressions drilled into each other's souls for long, quiet minutes.

"Yes." Vasile's tender admission threatened almost forever lassoed my emotions to his prodistic whims.

"Again, you use sex to get your way and increase your success odds in Romania." I shrieked, glad for thick concrete walls. "I thought you were a different kind of leader, but you'll stop at nothing!"

"I would never—"

"I said no, and you know why." A nervous hand swiped at a lone tear.

"I am not manipulating you." He jumped up, then tossed on a plush robe at the foot of the bed.

"Rubbish."

He dashed around the furniture to capture my limp hands. "I need you as an immortal to protect my life and my people. No more, no less. I require you an immortal to conserve whatever remains of this black heart." He shoved my palm against his breastbone. "Can you not feel the green now growing where only dust and famine ruled?"

I wrenched away an angry hand. "Do you love me? Or can you tell the difference between an agenda and genuine feelings?"

Anguished turmoil radiated across his guarded face and told me everything I needed to know. In my head, I thanked the guardian druidess for preventing such a terrible mistake.

"I cannot give you the answer you seek."

"Vas, we go from hot to cold, then back to scalding each other. We are opposite breeds from opposite forces. Even if I do not become a prodigium, we will someday kill each other." He opened his mouth to interrupt, but I threw a hand inches from his face and screamed, "I cannot demand my people's fidelity in the body of a mortal enemy. You'd risk your life for your people. Respect I must try the same."

A thumb wiped a solitary tear from my chin, bereft of sage words or apologies. Then he nodded.

"The druidess was right. If you loved me, you'd never put me in that position."

"I erred, Sarah. You sacrificed your desires and future immortality for your people, and each night I admire you more. I celebrate the mature woman and leader inside you." If his arms opened, I change my mind and chance eternity while inside them. How ironic, my people would never know nor appreciated the sacrifice I made for them.

"Never again. Promise."

"I won't, Sarah."

"No." I clenched fists and gritted, "Promise."

When he crushed me against his chest, breaths required a supreme effort. A possessive touch shoved deep into my hair, and cradled my head tucked against his hammered chest. "I promise thee, ma chérie. I will never disrespect you again." If I only know how soon he broke that vow.

CHAPTER 19

You should see her broom

UNDER THE LONG TABLE'S ornate chandelier, we sulked like a contentious married couple. An English breakfast and a plate of synthetic marrow claimed little table space. A regal Vasile scoured through his usual London Times, legs crossed, and posture rigid. A servant pulled back a blood bag clasp and poured fresh blood into a delicate teacup. I read, 'A Positive.' The indifferent male footman conducted the grisly duty as he had done so his entire life.

Gloomy Vasile flipped a page, then flicked at the servant at his side. The holiday relaxed man reverted to the usual stuffy starched lord. True to his nature, Vasile switched personalities and detested moods at a moment's notice because earlier, an all-consumed passion entangled us. As he skimmed the news, Vasile detected the onerous gaze and produced a gentle smile. I resumed eating, self-assured the man I loved still lurked inside the monster's depths. If Anna broke through his defensive wall made of calculative maneuvering, so could I.

My best friend breezed onto a live sitcom stage, not the opulent dining room. "Slept in late too?" When he remained fixed on a plate or newspaper, "Well, hello tension!"

"Hey, D."

He flopped into a chair.

"Poor old chap sucked in bed, didn't he?"

"Boy, mind your—"

"Spill sister—"

Vasile and I groaned in unison, "Dmitri."

He touched his messy hair then my ponytail. "Because we are longer in danger, it is high time for your makeover."

"I see—you—feel better."

The humiliating banter unaffected the paper-scanning Vasile while Dmitri linked playful eye contact with me. A ringed finger dangled over his shoulder, a delicate teacup, and a dutiful servant left his buffet post to take the cup.

"When are we going, Sire?"

"Going where, D?"

Dmitri reached past me to grab Vasile's half-eaten synthetic bone marrow while Vasile remained fixed on the news. Not tearing his eyes away, he slapped the insufferable prince's hand away.

"Romania, Poppet. So, when are we going, Vas?" The bored servant brought back Dmitri's red brimming teacup.

Vas's meticulous fingers reduced the paper to half its original size, then tucked it beside a saucer before he pinched a dainty cup. "I will advise when. I have much to contemplate." A single blood drop glistened across his upper lip when he returned it to the tiny plate and took his sweet time to lick the drop away. Nothing wasted.

The petulant gentleman groaned, then flung himself into a seat. "What might be left to consider, Vas? We scored our weapon."

"I'm here, ya know."

Vasile lifted a casual hand while he re-crossed his legs. "You know very well before we can return, we need her people controlled."

"My control or your control?" Okay, so my attitude reeked of bitterness.

Dmitri perked a brow as he sipped his fresh bio-waste. "Testy, testy. I shall endeavor to ask later." He turned full attention to the master who orchestrated the lives of those breathing the same air. "When does she reign in the witches?" while he plucked a piece of lint off my green sweater.

"Prince Dmitri, I tire of—"

A studious examination raked along with my clothing. "I only enquire because if the big event doesn't happen for quite some time, I'm taking this creature to Harrod's." The hovered servant removed my plate after I shoved away from the half-filled china. As I fingered the table's HP sauce, I mentally screamed at Dmitri to shut the hell up.

Dmitri winced and touched his right temple. "Ouch, girl! So, mean!"

"Sorry—extra powers, ya know."

"When I deem the proper opportunity, I shall inform you posthaste."

"So dramatic! How I detest theatrics, not of my creation."

Vas and I said, "We know—"

"Such utter tosh, waiting—"

"D!"

"Don't you agree, Poppet. The entire—"

"Dah-mee-tree!"

"Poppet!"

"His fingers are tapping. Shut up!" My best friend snapped his mouth shut and grimaced.

Vasile glowered past me at his maddening brother-in-law. "I agree. Do reacquaint yourself with proper behavior whilst in my presence and exhibit princely manners by removing elbows from the table."

The prince's eyebrows hoisted when he showed us his white palms.

"Don't look so worried, D. If I fail, I'll burn alive every coven leader."

"Poppet!"

"And if that fails, I'll try to become a prodigium."

If a pin fell, more than immortals would hear it hit the floor.

The prince's back straightened, and he whipped his hair into a hasty ponytail. "Bloody brilliant. Right then, what's the plan?"

"I go to London. You wait here." A servant's squeaking leather shoes and Dmitri's teacup clank broke the tense silence. Vasile's fingers tapped louder.

"Are you bloody mad?" The word 'mad' pitched as high as his brows.

Vasile slid a pinky across a news article title, then placed cup his on a gold-rimmed plate. "Occult business, m'boy, and we shant interfere."

"But we can at least—" Mrs. Smith shuffled through the servant's door.

"Sorry, Your Lordships, urgent message for milady."

"Can I just start the last twenty-four hours over?" I took the extended cream-colored envelope, and then across the linen front, I read my name written in a familiar elegant scrawl. My mouth dried.

"Sarah? You look distressed."

I chose a silver letter opener off Smith's balanced tray then ripped open the silky stationery. "Damn it. It's from Mother."

"Well? What does she write, Poppet?"

"I'm summoned."

They said, "Summoned?"

"The leaders want to see me."

Deep male voices again in unison, "When?"

"Tomorrow night. I better figure out a plan because if they will accept me as their Queen and put on a power show."

Vasile placed his elbows on the table. "This time frame leaves little chance to sort a strategy."

"So, begins the Rubicon, and Vas' chances to—"

"Enough, insolence for an evening! Dmitri. Leave this instant."

"He's sorry—aren't you, D?" I elbowed his ribs when I suggested, "Say you're sorry."

When a scowling Smith returned but avoided the servant's door, Dmitri muttered, "Not the only one who forgot their place."

"Milord! Sorry to interrupt."

Vasile sighed away, anger as he responded, "Yes?"

"Man at the door."

"My brief holiday clearly crumbled an entire house. Very well, Smith, show him to the parlor."

"But milord!"

"For God's sake, woman, out with it!" His hand tapped the table as the quiet servant, and I scoured the area for a cleaning bucket.

"He didn't ask for Count Meroeur."

"And who exactly did he ask for, Smith?" Vasile expression narrowed, and lips thinned.

"Chancellor Simeon—"

"Bloody hell, Vas!"

"I told him, this here property belongs to Count Meroeur."

"No visitors from the capital in over 300 years. News traveled fast."

"I thought the council forbade guests?"

"They did."

"Very well." As Vasile stood, "Seems I shant finish my paper today. Show my guest to the drawing-room, please."

"Milord—" she moaned while she wrung arthritic hands.

"Yes, Mrs. Smith?" A hand rested on the table, but I bet he wanted to rest it around her throat.

"Red eyes, Your Lordship! He had yer eyes!" Smith's forehead creased into a million wrinkles when she swayed on her feet.

He adjusted his platinum cufflinks and lowered his brow. "For the love of all things holy—please show the visitor in, and then seek a medicament to calm your nerves." Between our recent fight, Dmitri's childish behavior, and the mysterious guest, Vasile neared an epic meltdown.

"Ye—yes, milord."

She half-spun to go when Dmitri asked, "Did he provide a name or a card?"

"Nikola, Your Highness."

Both jaw clenched immortals whipped their heads and gaped at each other as slack shoulders and backs straightened. Dmitri's fists opened and closed several times while Vasile's tapped his thigh.

I went for it. "Who's Nikola?"

"Bloody hell, Vas. They sent Nik."

Vasile raised his chin to peer past his nose. "Why is Nikola here? Was something amiss during your Romanian holiday?"

The sobered, carefree immortal memorized the carpet as eyes flicked back and forth. "No, Sire."

"Think, lad."

"I cannot fathom why they sent him."

My voice tenser after they ignored me for t5he millionth time, "And who's this guy?"

"He came for Sarah or brought a council message."

"Then, Sire, why bring any word when we have telephones."

Vasile sighed, "Right then."

"Wait, he came for me?!"

Vasile paced with a hand on his hip and one finger under his chin before he twirled on a heel to rounded on distressed Smith. Whatever or whoever disturbed the strongest immortal chilled my core. "Show Nikola to the drawing-room. Return and escort her Ladyship to my quarters."

After the nervous housekeeper darted away, I touched Vasile's tense forearm. "Hate to ask again, but who is he?"

When icy regard raked over me, I went down my removed and stepped away.

Vas closed the distance between us and captured my hands. "Apologies Sarah, I am not angry with your questions. My visitor is a council diplomat."

"I gathered, but why so afraid of him?"

"Poppet, he is not afraid of Nikola, only the message he carries."

He kissed the top of my head. "I will come to you later."

"But—"

Smith again huffed through the formal entry. "Milord, I did as you requested but—"

"Very good please—"

"Milord, I—"

"—show Sarah to—"

"—milord! I beg yer pardon, yer Lordship! He demanded to see—" A blaming digit pointed square at my chest, "—her!" Fewer than twenty-four hours after I returned to her graces, I regressed into a detested enchantress.

Vasile's thick wood chair creaked under his strained hand while he pinched his nose, twirling to Dmitri.

"When we go inside, both of you are to remain utterly silent. Understood?"

"Okay."

"As you command, Sire."

Vasile looked at me while he scratched the back of his neck. "If the council sent Nikola to—"

As our mutually clammy fingers entwined, "I know."

"Shall we?"

I towed behind two tense immortals locked in separate thoughts as my wobbled mind dizzied. One conclusion I made while legs ate the long hall, I vowed not to force the pair to make any hard choices. Thrust into another random situation with little facts, and I again trusted prods with my valuable life. Unsure if my new powers would keep me safe, I followed their lead, but missed Maggie. She would know the right thing to say around an unwanted guest.

The doors swung open wide and revealed a large parlor designed to impress the wealthiest person. I recognized the space from that memorable dinner. The same brocade chairs and couches scattered under intricate ceiling moldings and painted scenes of cloud bound angles high above the velvety furniture. Oil painted judgmental nobles hung on every sky-blue wall and watched from monocles or horses. In the parlor's far back shadows, a short bald male prodigium stood beside a chase. I whispered an invisibility chant, so only my friends could see me.

The unexpected visitor removed a thick hand from the chair-back and trekked closer. Once in the room's middle, standing in a better light, the stranger planted polished shoes shoulder-width apart. The glinted bald undead wore a black turtleneck, dark gray slacks, and a brown Hermes belt. The stubby supernatural creature resembled a famous actor named Jason Statham but in short bulldog form.

Vasile claimed a spot ten feet inside the room, while Dmitri and I hung back at the open doors. My tense companions mimicked the bulldog's posture, closed fists at the waist while not breathing. Vasile and sobered Dmitri waited for the stranger to speak first, but the stranger's head shook once, and hands unclasped. When purposeful strides took him straight towards Vasile, I stepped away and wished I was in Vasile's lair.

A thin translucent pink coating swept over the odd prod's blinking eyes when he arrived feet before Vasile and a clenched fist thumped his chest. A knee dropped to the green oriental rug, and the repentant head caught chandelier light. The crisp salute differed from Dmitri's often casual gesture. Something or somebody dumped a deadly predator to a submissive knee.

The visitor fixed his chin to his chest, "Chancellor."

Dmitri winked at my marveled face when I got my first glimpse of the lording chancellor as he worked his role. Dmitri was right because the new prodigium still feared Chancellor Simeon, their onetime hero.

"Nikola." The stiff immortal stood over his former subject as the bald prod seized the chancellor's ring held out towards him. He placed Vasile's official seal to his forehead, rose to his feet, then released Vasile's hand. The bulldog lowered his brow a few inches and avoided direct eye contact with the love of my life. Vasile eased into the pomp and circumstance like no time passed since he reigned supreme, motivated by a power play or just missing the royal attention. He would have to give me lessons later.

"Lovely to see you, Chancellor. Just lovely." The pale monotone niceties lacked excitement.

"Be at ease, and sit with me, Nikola." Vas adjusted a cufflink before he motioned to a red furniture cluster.

"Thank you, Your Imperial Highness."

"Shall I ring for refreshments?"

The visiting prod's shoulders relaxed as his inaudible steps followed his old master. Jesus, they all walked like panthers. Before the pair sat, they stood toe to toe and eye to eye. Nobody breathed. A grandfather clock's tick boomed. A hidden pipe dripped. The chancellor and former subject blinked once as I bit my lip. Dmitri unclasped hands behind his back to inspect his nails. But my hand found wallpaper. When the bulldog broke a toothy smile, the room inhaled. Nikola smothered the pinched chancellor in a great bear hug, then Vasile and Dmitri peered at each other from across the tense space.

"Blimey! Three hundred years since I saw you last!" Any moment, Mrs. Smith might push past Dmitri to demand who invited the mafia dirtying her rugs.

"The idiot can count." Relaxed postures and Dmitri's sarcasm eased me off the wall.

Grateful for my cloaking spell, my best friend's snarky voice turned the rough monster's close attention as he peered around the chancellor's shoulder. "You old bloody dog, you!" thundering across the room's polished expanse.

Dmitri flashed a boyish smile and two upright fingers. "Someone missed me."

Vasile waved once at the chairs. "Come—sit—everyone." A wrist flick released his jacket's top button before he chose a chair.

Dmitri punched the bulldog as he walked past, and the visitor's meaty paw slapped my friend's shoulder. Dmitri sat on Vasile's right. "Sorry I missed last week's visit."

I shifted weight between my feet, and after dangerous tension lifted, my figure uncloaked. The calmer energy lasted a few quick seconds until a shiny bald stare cracked in my direction, and his frigid glower analyzed me from head to toe. Humans suffered blissful ignorance of our existence, but prods and mages spotted each other miles away. Court etiquette prevented him from asking about my identity, so a regal Queen Regent bore the drilled inspection while the creature marched right for me. The old Sarah might have cowered and run, but I swallowed burning stomach acid and raised my chin at the tight jawed monster. Vasile and Dmitri murmured something about ringing for a servant to mask the same watchful stance that monitored poor dead Anthony. A hex perched on my ready tongue.

Five feet from me, the scary stranger's head sank as he thumped to one knee. Riddled shock unhinged a dry mouth while the sitting prodigia mashed brows and exchanged a puzzled glance. Dmitri shrugged then tossed palms into the air.

"Grand Duchess."

"I—" as my eyes flew to my smirking friends.

He stood, backed away ten steps still facing me, then spun to my friends. "How, my Chancellor? She's—we all believed— She's—alive—? Bloody hell, Sire!"

Vasile's fingers curled twice at the immortal bulldog and me to beck an approach to the impromptu throne. "She is not the Duchess, Nikola. Though she bears a strong resemblance."

How dare he summon me like some pliant subject around his guest? But I brandished hearty scowl while the newcomer again examined me and obeyed another hand flick to stand beside him. Based on my own impeccable manners and no permission for disobedience, I played his game. Vasile directed Nikola to an opposite seat, and the baffled beast perched on the chair's edge, still gawking at me.

"Uncanny, Sire."

Dmitri's petulant flopped against his chair, spread his legs wide, then pointed a rude finger my chest. "Let us rip the bandage off—that—shall we?" You better believe my jaw fell. "You traveled all this way without ringing just to see—her—I mean really—storm the chancellor's home—demanding—"

Vasile interrupted before Dmitri lost his mind. "Yes, well, I am sure you recall how propriety bores Dmitri."

"She's the mage, Sire?"

Uncomfortable, I wiggled.

"By all accounts."

"By Constantine's sainted mother—"

"Not the woman I met." Vasile aimed glance at a chaise ordered me to sit.

I jolted a buzzing energy current through an arm, along the floor, and into his foot to signal my evident disgust at his chauvinistic rudeness. Vas reached out and squeezed my hand as a silent apology, but I returned hot daggers into his skull. Two fingers rubbed his right temple for three seconds. I thought, 'Take that.'

"Beyond the obvious, what brings you, General? Quite a while since we saw you last." I listed to men, not prods, who measured lost time in years, not insignificant centuries.

"Alas, I find myself in a tough position, Chancellor." Nikola removed his glacial stare and rubbed his bare head while I sat back on the gold leaf chaise.

Chancellor Simeon lorded while he sat on a Chippendale chair, hands alighted on armrests, feet flat on the floor. "Speak freely. I am no longer the chancellor. Therefore, there is little I help with." His ringed index finger tapped once every ten seconds. If I closed my eyes, I pictured Vasile perched on a golden throne, noisy politicians surrounding him. Though a different era and seat, he reigned supreme.

"Sire, you—are—the chancellor. Victor might have rammed your exodus down our throats, and claimed the advantage, but you are still the rightful ruler."

"Thought lovely to hear your words, I am sure the nation does not share the sentiment."

"Please forgive me, but you are wrong, Sire."

Dmitri snarled, "Watch yourself—"

Vasile raised a finger. "Let our friend continue. He did, after all, travel all this way."

"Thank you, Chancellor. Your subjects honored your wishes and allowed you space and time to grieve a woman we all adore. We put up with Victor and his merry gang of sycophants while we await your return."

"Nikola it is foolish to—"

Each passing second, Nikola grew more impassioned. "I won't hear of it, Sire. I just won't." Dmitri's face palmed, and my boggled stare popped wide as Baldy's Manchurian's accent deepened. "The Father was sleeping when that twat stole your office, and no royal decree appointed—"

"Now, now Nikola—"

"Sire. Please hear me out. I beg you." Nikola took a huge risk when he interrupted Vasile.

"Father, please listen to Nik." Dmitri never called Vasile that. Nikola danced around vital information that my friend waited long years to tell Vasile. Prince Dmitri poised to tune the violin to play a powerful tune.

Vasile uncurled a finger perched under a lower lip and motioned the brave prod to continue.

"Chancellor, your leaving never woke The Father, and legally—" Nikola leaned forward, almost off his chair. "—you remain chancellor."

Vasile's pointed a wondrous expression at the ceiling as he absorbed much-needed words. "A time to pine over a broken leader, my old friend."

Nikola bolted off the chair then slammed a fist to his heart. "Bullocks, Sire!" Dmitri blinked, and I flinched. He raised a fist high into the air and exclaimed, "We'll hold fast the nation for another hundred thousand days until Bulgaria's Champion returns. That pansy and his fake ring can sod off!" Nikola panted as he sat again. "My apologies—my Chancellor."

I breached the stern command to stay silent. "Champion of Bulgaria? And he made a ring?"

From the side of Vasile's chair, I spotted a discrete finger signal my silence. What a bigot.

Dmitri cleared his throat. "Sire, legions of people await your return and Victor's overthrow. Legions, Sire.'"

I muttered, "Sparta, and the three hundred?"

"Why not tell me this sooner? How long have you known?"

Dmitri plunked elbows on his knees and leaned forward, gold hair swished over a shoulder. "You were not ready to hear it and showed little interest in life itself until you met—"

Vasile perked his chin. "Let me stop you right there, m'boy."

I whispered, "Here it comes."

A disobedient Dmitri pressed while he adoringly gazed at me. "She woke you up. Hell, woke us all up!"

Nikola jumped in, "Some even claim you planned this extended holiday to weed out wicked politicians and planned to capture and tamed that one," Evil Bald pointed at me. "Only the Champion of Bulgaria's could ever do such a—"

"Enough." Vasile stood and buttoned his suit jacket to pace the room's perimeter, leather oxfords squeaking. Three sets of eyes analyzed every second of his melancholy demeanor. The chancellor turned to the fireplace, his back to us while he spoke low. "What is your true business here, General?" I recognized the tone, so my nervous fingers played with dusty pillow tassels, and Dmitri's back whipped straight.

Nikola's ring, similar to Dmitri's, flashed under the artificial lights. "The cabinet demands her immediate delivery— Chancellor."

Vasile half-turned, the well-cut jacket flared at the waist. "Impossible. She has yet to perform the rite." The unexpected lie cast my attention to the faded carpet.

"Sire, if you fail to—" while Nikola's hands wrung.

"To what? And if I refuse? Are you still the state executor?" Shrewd consideration drilled into the marrow-sucker, unpracticed at dealing with his old leader. I watched Nikola walk right into a well-laid trap and dangle from an all too familiar ledge. Better him than me.

"Careful Nik, he's been in a foul mood this evening." How Vasile even tolerated D, I never knew.

"Are you still the executioner?"

"Yes, Chancellor."

Vasile's thundered gut roar gutted the expansive the parlor and rattled its occupants. "Over my dead body!" Startled schoolchildren jumped, and winced, then the count's voice elevated another shattered octave as he annunciated each word. "Do—you—hear—me—Nikola?" Vasile's rare anger display raged my pulse. The statement lashed at any logic because Vasile backtracked on the thing he prohibited when he choose me over his people.

The offender gawked at his laces then swallowed. "Yes, Chancellor."

Vasile growled past gritted teeth, "Take a long look at me, Nikola." As Vasile wielded manipulation and fear to rule the bald monster, I understood how he governed an entire dead society. General Bulldog upturned sheepish shoulders, and like us, he weathered the frightening mood. For a second, I felt terrible.

"Right then. Nobody will harm her until I present the order. Furthermore, only when I deem the journey appropriate, will we return. Do you understand, Executioner?" Nobody said a word, breathed, or nodded.

Nikola slid from his seat then sunk to his knees. "Yes, Sire." Vasile's solid performance dropped the monster. What could he accomplish if he wielded more than words?

"And Nik?"

"Ye—yes, Sire?"

"Resist spreading false hopes to tempt me into an illegal coup. Such treachery surely ends The Father's respite—and thereby ending you where you now sit." Vasile emphasized the word 'sit' when he clashed the 'T.' The natural-born leader glared daggers into Nikola's bowed, shiny head.

When Nikola jumped and violated Vasile's personal space, Dmitri sneered around exposed fangs, gripped his chair's armrests tight, and coiled legs ready to fight. I shrunk back into the chaise. First, I watched prods shred Anthony, my cousin, now that guy. Any minute hearts ripped from chests. But Nikola jammed a wrist under Vasile's nose, "Taste me blood, Chancellor!" Maggie explained how prods assessed another immortal's truth by sipping their blood. The act flooded someone's memories into the taster's mind.

Dmitri's hands flew up. "Jesus Christ and his theater of gay saints!"

Vasile grinned, chuckled, then dropped his shoulders. "Dmitri's right. Let us speak plainly."

Vasile reclaimed his seat, and not a trace of anger affected his visage. Every molecule in the room, including the painted lords and ladies, sighed intense relief. Like the time he kept me in the same bedroom for two weeks, the master pretended anger while she used another ruse to discover the truth and control events.

"Now, the true purpose in my home, yes?"

"Sire, I am here on official business—"

"But?"

"But—I use the opportunity to bring you word."

The chancellor fixed a crooked finger on his nose bridge, then motioned for the visitor to continue. "And that word being?"

Dmitri groaned, "For the love of all things holy man, spit it out!"

General Bald leaned forward and lowered his voice as eyes whipped side to side. "I've gots me this plan to bring you back."

Dmitri hated not being the center of attention. "And what idiotic plan is that pray tell? Laws state the council cannot remove a chancellor unless found guilty of murder or a unanimous vote of nonconfidence. Do you hold the votes?"

"I wish my prince. The weasel stacked half the council, but I gots enough dirt to blackmail the twat. And he'll murder me when I'm done wif him."

Vasile still silent, D chimed in, "Blimey mate! You want to frame Victor with your own murder? Are you daft?"

"With Victor deposed, voilà!"

Dmitri chuckled, "Rubbish plan. We could just obliterate half the council and be done with it."

"And which act awakens my creator first?" Vasile's finger tapped an outer thigh. "Who backs your plan?"

Nikola paused and weighed the next massive statement. "The Companion Guard, Sire."

My best friend leaped to his feet and, like a lost dog, circled his chair. "The Companion Guard?"

"Yes, my Prince."

"The entire guard?" loose hair flung from a puffed chest.

Nikola nodded, "Every one of us."

"I'm lost, fellas." But again, they acted like I ceased to exist.

Dmitri whistled low, "Do you know this means, Vas?"

Vasile pointed a proud grin at the ceiling. "My brothers in arms never leave a mate on the battlefield."

Dmitri and Nik both echoed, "Never."

For a long minute, Vasile digested the pivotal news while he scrutinized his polished leather shoes. On the one hand, he wielded mages, and on the other, he commanded a supernatural military. But the uprising endangered the Companion Guards and the entire society if the plan woke up the original prodigium. Vasile's maker would obliterate his willful children and start again. The saturated facts electrified the air. I hoped The Father slept forever, and we never met because the druidess was right, the original sounded dangerous.

"Can I just point out how you planned to off yourself, mate?"

"I quite agree. Find the numbers and not cost your life."

Nik seized the moment. "Part of my plan, if you will allow." Vasile motioned to the bulldog to continue. "The witch. The witch is my plan."

"Mages, not witches, General."

"Me?"

"Pardon, milord."

Dmitri flicked a hard stare then rested a finger on his lips. I scowled.

"You heard the earlier warning about not harming her, correct?"

Nikola's chin motioned towards me. "No harm should befall her. She performs the rite, gets all-powerful-like, and learns how to bring a dead immortal back to life."

"Undead an undead."

"Bloody hell, Nik!"

"Dmitri—another outburst, and I shall expel you to the kitchens." Stern words touched Dmitri's ass to a chair with a clamped mouth, then Vasile's palm opened, "Proceed, General."

"Right then. Once Victor kills me, put me body on ice. Prosecute him. Resume power and bring me back from the dead—again. How is this a dangerous thing?"

"You do remember death's pain, old friend?"

"Worth it. Besides, I will become the patron bald saint of the nation."

Dmitri's uncontrolled hysterical laughter caused Vasile's discrete cough. The prince gasped, "Immortal immortalized patron saint—of—of—a damn legend in your mind." A grin shifted my mouth when my best friend clutched his sides, and Vas chuckled, "Always the craziest buffoon—missed you—you stupid fool."

The whipped schoolboy's head picked up at the chancellor's low laughter. "Ya think me idea a good one, Sire?"

The question howled more laughter from the prince as he battled to breathe. General Baldy blinked. When Dmitri's giggle fit ceased, one look at counts bewildered expression belted more unhinged laughter.

"Glad to entertain ya, lads."

288

This erupted Vasile's constrained belly laugh, and even I giggled.

Dmitri gasped, "If Victor doesn't kill him, can I?"

Vasile fought to hide his merriment. "Now, now—this shan't turn into a terrible military prank because I shan't risk your life, General." The chancellor's voice rose over Dmitri's subsided laughter. "But buy me more time while I construct a better plan?"

"No, Vas! Executing the poor sod is bloody brilliant!"

Nikola rubbed his jaw, "Sire, I am dead serious."

The room silenced until Vas laughed, "Literally." Even Nikola joined the raucous laughter.

While the boys reacquainted and bantered, I narrowed my stare at the intricate tattoo under my arm. I was the Queen Regent, but they ignored me. So, I mimicked a regal stance when I said, "I can do it." Three heads in unison silenced then whipped in my direction because the three forgot an enemy queen listened to ill-laid plans and traitorous declarations. Vasile leveled a wintry glare from under a lowered brow. "After all, I am the queen of Mother Nature's favorite species."

"See, Sire! Not that I agree with her ludicrous claim. But even she thinks me idea a good one."

"Careful, Nik, she'll turn you to ash. That one has a temper meaner than the chancellor. I'm surprised Vas let her out of the cellar."

Vasile's entire palm tapped an armrest. Not a fantastic sign.

"Apologies your Queenship—yer majesty—yer—"

"We will take you to offer under advisement, Queen Regent. And Nik?"

The bulldog general fastened hard attention to my hands like any moment a daylight spell might radiate from them.

"Nikola?"

"Oh, yes, my Chancellor?"

When I twitched my fingers, he jerked—what fun.

"Do your best to stall the council, and Prince Dmitri, give him one of those stove telephones."

"A burner phone? Yes, at once, Sire!"

Dmitri nudged the frozen Nikola, "Are you okay, Chappie?" He followed the general's stare as Vasile stood then whispered, "Should see her broom." Nik paled.

"Jesus, D. I will not fry you, General. He is having a bit of sport with you." Nikola dry blinked.

"As you say yer—magest—yer high—"

I walked towards the fumbled immortal and extended, said deadly hand. "They never introduced us. Call me Sarah. Thank you for helping."

The bulldog's face softened, and my slim hand disappeared in two meaty hands. "Could not be more charmed, and the honor is mine, Miss Sarah."

"No, sir, the honor is mine to meet such an esteemed warrior." Best to get on his good side.

"Me likes her, Sire!"

"She is much like Anna, can charm the scales off a snake. Come then, gents!" Vasile motioned to his compatriots to gather around him. "The general has a long journey ahead and much to plan."

"If only I had me second in command," the general flashed the flamboyant Dmitri a wistful smile.

Nikola thumped a fist to his chest then bowed from his waist.

Military life and traditions called to deep to the instincts inside Vasile, and Dmitri. The males grinned while rough claps around each other's necks formed a group hug. While the three prodigia embraced, Vasile flashed me a scowl. A bloody nail neared my mouth, but I dropped it to my side. Screw him. I was a queen who answered to nobody. Even the high and mighty Vasile answered to The Father.

CHAPTER 20

Magical FastPass and Canasta

NIGHTS ALWAYS LENGTHENED during the fall and started the prod's favorite time of the year, yet they acted glum. The crisp darkness whisked away, swirled breath condensation, and sent the tiny clouds to the watching stars. House lights struggled to infiltrate the pregnant gloom and only illuminated a few feet of the arched driveway. A small shadow between two longer ones bumped over gray pea gravel as we lingered outside the manor's brick entrance. Together we watched for the black Range Rover, but silent concerns separated us. During the twenty-four hours General Nikola left, we waited and planned, then waited more.

Dmitri broke the troubling silence. "Rubbish sending her alone," he said as his arms crossed, and he kicked at stones. The greedy night also devoured the skittering rocks. "Need the marrow from three virgins to take this edge off." In true princely fashion, the world forever circled his brilliant orbit.

The tense kingly statue ignored my best friend's woes while troubled thoughts locked him inside a mental prison. I memorized the creature because if I lived my last hours, I took his memory to Purgatory. A foot shifted. I wanted to throw myself into his limp arms, but stubborn rage from our last row stopped me. An ankle straightened. I regretted not sleeping in his safe room. Endless questions churned and prevented any rest, even while I rested in my own bedroom. Who manipulated me the most Vasile or the dead druidess? A long exhale roiled vapors into black air. The constant survival fight and no sunlight dampened a worn spirit.

While I was in London, they prearranged to hide in the safe room in case mages stormed the manor. The jet, preloaded with luggage, idled on standby. If they received no call from me after midnight, the connected caves served as an escape route to the plane, then Romania. We gambled during a time of crisis that the council might protect them.

While I inventoried pebbled gravel and thought about the potential danger, Vasile's shadow joined mine, forming one long shape. He captured my chilled hands then pressed them to warm lips. Hesitant blue eyes met a shadowed face's intense silver stare. Both stomach and heart pitched when I fought the urge to lunge into his protective arms.

He whispered, "I know."

An arm encircled me, and Vas drew me under his armpit. Surrounded by comforting body heat, I rested against his ribcage and winced to avoid a teary flood. We suffered a painful and impossible commitment but preferred to conquer challenges at each other's side. No relationship joined us but an unwritten future's enormous responsibilities.

"If I fail, we still have option B and—" The SUV interrupted when it crunched gravel.

Dmitri grabbed a shoulder, and I spun from one monster to another. He scooped me off my feet in a bone-crushing hug. "Just come back." The prince set me down, turned around, and crossed his arms.

"Count on it." I pulled on his upper arm and kissed the tense warrior's cheek.

Vasile waved off the driver and opened the car door, and my thick tongue moved in a sticky mouth. "Thanks." After I climbed in, he grasped the door and the roof, dipping his head to peer inside the warmed car. Soft exterior lights exposed uncharacteristic worry. He cupped my chin. "I own two things, my heart, and my name. I give these to thee, Sarah Wardwell, queen of mages. You command my heart, soon to possess the other."

"I—"

Before I asked if Vasile meant he loved me and wanted to marry me, he shut the auto door. When his clunky ring banged the roof twice, the signal sped the car towards London. A small hand smeared the rear window as I clung to their images. Rigid postures walked up the portico stairs. Vas shuffled past Dmitri, who still palmed the cheek I kissed. When the backlights glowed the damp road and surrounding black trees red, I squared my shoulders and faced forward.

Then it happened. Strange confidence vibrated my entire body like some weird amphetamine sharpened my worried focus. Natural born instincts calmed me as I looked at Vasile's side of the SUV. "Time to make a plan."

"Sorry, Miss?" I shot the driver a withering stare. For better or worse, each day, I became more like the idolized chancellor.

The key to winning the leaders' respect and obedience rested with the origin of my species. What did I know about how we started? After Romans whipped out every druid, a secluded grove of female druids surfaced. No longer controlled by their brethren, the druidesses violated strict religious laws never to write magic. But the new era and freedom demanded they embrace the alternative world or perish. The conclave no longer a secret, the ladies devised curse tablets for purchase. On thin lead, they inscribed hexes, and exciting people traveled far to curse a criminal neighbor. The new visitors brought sex, ideas, and compelling needs for things denied by the druids. Women battled over the men and their plans. But the grove's high-priestess had enough of the infighting and announced the chance to solve all their problems. She invited nine robust and handsome men to their Imbolc feast.

But only nine of the ten women attended the highly anticipated banquet. Old paganism held sacred the number nine, and for the plot's success, the grove supported too many women. Lest the Gods discount them, success with the Gods relied on the ritual outshining their fallen Druid brethren. The group needed to cull a sister to obtain uncountable powers for later generations, so a weaker sister jumped to sacrifice herself and experience a glorious reincarnation.

Before the feast, the head-druidesses drenched her tears, and the sacrificed sister's blood over nine flat alters. Later, one drunk man laid on each of the nine prepared stones. Under the blood moon's eye, they harnessed tremendous mana through an intricate ritual only the dead druids ever tried. As nine forbidden pleasures climaxed, the women slit the men's throats. Pleased Gods separated the women's essence from the human spirit and granted future generations sacred elemental magic. But as we know, each spell comes at a cost or catch.

Every generation born from parents of mixed species, mage and human, bore magically weaker children. Fifty years after the sisters scattered across the globe, their occult abilities dwindled. Desperate to save their kind, they inbred. The ghastly practice worked but unchanged God's curse tablet to the sisters, and each generation found powers diluted at a slower rate. Time and mana ran in short supply. And that was the key. If I strengthened magic for future generations, and the leaders experienced such power, I stood a strong chance. But the prods might kill me if they discovered my idea.

I mulled the scheme for an hour when the car pulled up to my childhood townhome. The driver opened the door, and weak legs poked from the SUV. They refused to walk me to the dreaded white building because something felt off. Long afternoons at my bedroom window while dreaming about an unconventional life, I memorized the red telephone booths, sidewalk cracks, and whitewashed bricks behind black iron fences. So, I would sense anything amiss.

While I searched for the cause of my unease, an icy breeze tickled hair against my cool neck, I saw what was wrong. Nobody walked their dog or took out the rubbish. Even humans sensed the condensing static electricity around my old prison of horrors. I squeezed the driver's hand as a foot touched the sidewalk, and the wrought-iron gate clicked open. They knew I arrived.

When I looked down, my borrowed jeans and faded T-shirt scored a frown. Why didn't I get that makeover from Dmitri? I then knew why Vasile always dressed sharp. Before I gave my lacking wardrobe, another thought, the glossy black entrance opened, and a light blue Chanel suit waited. Mother never came to the door. But every occult leader never visited before either. I pictured her at the rug store, picking out red sidewalk carpets. Mum peeled back crimson lips and exposed her perfect white veneers. A slight breeze lifted platinum blond hair stayed when the coiffed lady motioned a jeweled hand. She faked excitement over a returning prodigal daughter.

When I reached the stoop, hands shoved deep inside pockets to prevent slapping her powdered face. I prayed the crackling energy leaders shortened her charade and lessened my time at home. That night I promised myself to someday nail Mother in a miserable box and bury her deep.

"Mother."

Red fingernails gripped both my shoulders to air-kissed my cheeks. "Lovely to see you."

"Liar."

"You look well since the last time I saw you." Expensive Dior perfume floated like poisonous Anthrax.

"Wish I could say the same, but at least you're dressed better," I snarled, wrenching from her steely grasp.

I stepped past the threshold, and paintings rattled against the wall when Mother flicked a long pink fingernail at the door, a thud sealing the point of no return. "Black—not my color, darling."

"Don't bother with a sealing spell to trap me here."

"Wouldn't dream of it."

"Why are you so nice?"

Heels stopped clacking the old wood floors. "Excuse me?"

"What's your angle, forgiveness, or a place at my side? Do you actually think I'd forgive you for locking me up to my entire life? Maybe you—"

My mother hissed, "Family drama later, darling." An arm swept towards a hallway. "They wait."

My voice rose, not lowered. "Why do you care? The aunts and Grandfather died, so the coven is yours." I blinked. "That's it! I know why you sent the entire coven to—"

Past gritted teeth, "Sarah—"

"And how's the coven membership drive going besides your split personalities joining?"

She tapped a pointed gold toe, then glanced again at the hall before a vice grip snatched my upper arm. She snarled inches near my face, "Like you or not, and you're my daughter. Am I unhappy you are screwing one of those foul creatures? Yes, but I'm still proud because you survived like a real Wardwell."

The unnatural praise wrenched my limb free, then a step back. "Sod off." Intense crackling energy nipped around her cheeks, and a hand rose to her overdone makeup.

I severed the unproductive exchange because the commanders waited. A heel spin and purposeful strides lead the charge as Mother in tow muttered something about buying me a suitable wardrobe after I returned home. I fired over a shoulder, "Fat chance. My first duty as queen will strip you and this house to nothing." I left her no opportunity to respond because I wrenched open a glossy white door.

Frumpy gray-haired men and women clustered around a garish rococo parlor. Old friends mingled at a book club meeting, not nine enemies ready to decide a throwaway teenager's fate. A zillion force-field pulses buzzed the room and betrayed the group's true identities as the most potent occultists on the planet. They converged to discuss policy and the species' fate, not play Canasta. Mother clacked heals across polished wood floors, murmurs stopped, and eyes pinned.

"May I present—my—daughter, Queen Regent Sarah Elizabeth Wardwell."

I studied the mingling crowd's faces. Despite a relaxed atmosphere, the broiled energies begged for caution. They counted on cardigan sweaters and frumpy dresses to put me at ease and show my cards early. Past passive visages and slumped shoulders, curious concern, and palatable distrust cluttered the air's vibe. Mother won annoyed glances from the cordial crowd as she paraded me around the room.

"Meet Senora Hrossdottir from Mexico and Russia's Priestess Rasputinov." I endured polite air kisses. "And this is Priestess Mirabelli from Brazil, African Priest Bondye—"

"Hi there. Bill Sutton. Massachusetts." A great bellied man in his sixties interrupted Mother when he stuck out a fat hand. I already liked the guy.

"Oh yeah, Sutton, the infertility curse. Cool trick." I offered a high five, and the cautious man softly returned the gesture.

"Sarah, let's not—"

The warlock's puffy face spread a cheeky smile when he chuckled, and then past a bulged sweater, he checked a Cartier tank watch. "Enough pleasantries, for now, let's get this show on the road. I'm not staying any longer than necessary." The blunt American shot Mother a withering frown, and the Brazilian snickered.

My flushed mother flustered, "Oh well—yes—Warlock Sutton. I—" But everyone walked off while she talked.

An amicable assembly chatted as they perched upon white seats set up in a U-shape while familiar servants freshened their drinks. The domestics, who practically raised me, refused eye contact, jumping threaded nerves against my pounding forehead, fists clenched inside my pockets. Alone, a dejected parolee before a prison board, not their queen. The group wanted an inexperienced eighteen-year-old intimidated, and their plan nearly worked. I resisted shoving a short nail between teeth.

When the door closed behind the last servant, I remained silent. Vasile warned me during negotiations, the first person who spoke lost all leverage. The oldest man wheezed through his bulbous nose, cleared his throat, and chubby arms crossed, legs spread wide. A passerby might mistake the most powerful warlock as a retired schoolteacher, but I knew better. Bill's dull, kind stare met mine.

"Your mother mentioned the rite's success and how you murdered your entire coven." Legs numbed when lifeless stares locked on mine because the word 'murder' explained how they considered my actions a crime, not self-defense. An effort to stay silent and not flinch required tremendous concentration. "I see two issues, the murder of fellow mages and the victims' extreme neglect inflicted the crime." Mother sunk in her chair. Score one for Potbelly.

Before I asked why such a big deal, the black-haired lady brandished a hard Russian accent. "Tha Wardwells hid sacred birth and future leader, da?"

A beautiful African man, skin violet as the night, scanned me from head to toe, and his liquid black eyes tugged at my powerful aura. "Let us not do the jump here. I need proof dis is thee girl." The sage warlock expressed friendly curiosity while others agreed.

"Si Senorita Wardwell. Show us de mana strong enough to throw de covens at yer feet." non-confrontational yellow energy encircled the Mexican high-priestess.

I stood straighter because the suggestion played right into my strategy. A chin lift returned each haughty stare, and the air cracked. They shivered. I pulled up a sleeve, twisted my arm, and reveal a sacred symbol written inside every historical grimoire. They sucked in air and filled lungs to max capacity.

As the night of the rite, I started a timer. "Where do we get our powers?"

"Tha girl confuse me, da?"

I pressed, "As our abilities fade, mages would sell their souls to possess what one thing?" A steady gaze traveled between each person.

The Spanish female sniffed, "Mana."

"Fine. But where do we find an unlimited supply?"

The Russian purred, "Poorly educated but not us, so we not need this lesson—"

A single step forward with my hands behind my back interrupted. I felt born for the moment. "I have the answer, but do you guys?" A gig as world leader might rock after all.

"By tapping into the other plane."

"Correct."

"Why to ask dis, senorita?"

Mother's painted lips parted, but a gesture from Potbelly muted the glaring group as they leaned away from my mother. Nobody breathed, and they forgot their expensive cocktails. "Correct, so would you say a mage who freely accesses the dimension's powers benefited future generations?" The crowd murmured their agreement. I had them. I raised a palm. "What if a person's magic strengthened when they traveled through the dimension any time the powerful person wanted?"

My mother adjusted her body in her seat. "Stop this silliness and do not let these fine people believe you can accomplish—"

"Yes, I can." The ceiling saw my chin, and the murmurs grew louder. "If the portal was Disney World, I have a magical FastPass. Queue up lines are short."

"Prove it."

"What is—FastPass?"

Bill suggested, "Do you mind doing as they suggest and prove it?" Predictable, greedy robots nodded in time.

"If you want. Sit and stow the tray tables and stuff."

I fixated on the tingling snake henna to pull Earth's energies through the floor and sucked them into my sucking core. Their colorful auras swirled while I tugged the force created underfoot. An excited heart raced intoxicating endorphins to tingled limbs. Liquid warmth unfolded in my body. A parlor's shiny black windows reflected my solid white eyes, devoid brown pupils, when the group gasped as outstretched palms beamed pure silver light.

The fat toads squatted as they stuck about for the freak show they traveled far to see. I had one shot not to disappoint my influential audience. If anyone died, so did a chance for a practical future. Besides, when I ruled the world, I had a hot monster to seduce. I enslaved then direct the mana mass. Across the expectant participant row, I waved, and the snake tattoo coiled around my entire forearm. Its teeth peeled the dimension's portal. Splayed fingers drew the colorful coalescing energies around poised legs. Each person's aura kissed the portal's vibrations, and then my digits discharged vivid glare. Nine white lasers formed individual pulsing spheres that made my little glowing orbs look like child's play. Unfettered magic containers floated closer to full shock. The reptile itched crawling skin when it slithered and contracted. Each bright light chose a forehead, and then the radiant balls hovered a few seconds before they sank into their skulls. The world's occult leaders dropped unconscious at the same time.

Some people fell off chairs, and some slumped awkward poses against their neighbors. Bill Sutton's large gut toppled him face-first on the floor, and Mother's drink shattered when she half-hung from her seat. While they lingered inside a place I barely understood, the group faced mysterious dangers, worst nightmares, and even pleasant fantasies. Importantly, the leaders experienced pure mana's ecstasy.

I concentrated on the link from my life threads to the souls I sent beyond the physical world. If the portal closed before I extracted them, everyone died. A murder charge already hung over my head, so another death sealed failure. Sure, during the car ride, I contemplated killing everyone, but become the very thing I detested. When the African's legs twitched and Bill's mouth twisted, I yanked out the unconscious group. Time to face their judgment.

The tongue-flicking snake eased pressure against my hot arm and cut the flowing energy that stretched between me and the others. The pictured snake sucked, humming white light into its arching fangs, the scorched arm nerves intensifying sharp pain. I whimpered, and the grounding Earth absorbed the power I directed through my feet. When the last white beam disappeared into my limb, the roaring wind tunnel noise muted. The reptile totem blinked at me once before it disappeared, returning to my arm. Blazing heat no longer coursed through my strained limbs, and a cold stiffened my muscles like for hours I laid on a frozen lake. Rotten meat and decaying mold closed my throat, and I gagged.

Like a hypnotist snapped their fingers, every eyelid opened. Warlock Sutton picked himself up off the hardwoods, meaty hands rubbing his face. Mum fluffed her skewed hair but too flustered to cross her legs, while others shook off faraway stares.

After several soundless minutes, "Unbelievable."

The Rasputinov priestess massaged her wrist and said, "Speak terms."

My back ramrod straight, I channeled my inner Chancellor Simeon. "As Queen Regent, the war ends today. Failure to comply will dissolve and strip an entire coven's abilities. If I can increase your powers, I can take them away." I paused at each startled face. Nobody responded, but a few looked amused. "If you obey these terms for a year, I'll designate a proxy queen or king to rule instead of me."

Bill replied, "Sarah, you absolve a sacred covenant and demand equal rights for those very unnatural creatures we cursed. It is because of them the Gods continue to strip us of our birthright."

"Yes. But I'm the workaround. If you want me to rebuild sorcery capabilities to first-generation levels, then accept my terms. Together we can help humans and the planet—"

"Are you mad, girl? You want us to help those who killed and tortured us in droves?"

"But they are killing the Earth. I can restore magic abilities, but not elemental magic itself."

"Then, use your great magic to curse humans into stupid primates."

Another priestess interrupted, "About the murders. Why did you kill your entire coven and not your mother? Are you a team?" I snorted. "Nobody trusts a Wardwell."

"My daughter and I are not a team." Mother's animated gestures detailed her version of the ritual, and the lies demanded diplomatic patience, an unsharpened virtue. Stares shifted between my parent and me as they waited for a teenage meltdown, but I channeled a master tactician, Vasile. I remained statuesque because one day, she would stand before me and the others.

A silver-haired priestess spoke severed mum's self-serving rant. "Do you know about the time when the druidesses left Britannia?"

"Um, not exactly."

"As you know, procreating with humans and the existence of prods dilutes our special magic. Because of this, we agreed to one strict rule. A mage who kills another is destroyed."

"But we always fight, so I don't see how—"

"Senorita, we use ruses, and de curses against others, not death. We are dee-ferant dan yer pet monsters."

My mother's face pinched. "My error keeping you ignorant."

"Karen, we'll get to your crime that led to this situation."

"Address me as High-Priestess Wardwell, thank you."

Windowpanes vibrated. "Later, Karen. We need to discuss sentencing."

"No! Can't you see she set me up? That woman wanted everyone dead just to take control."

"Daughter—"

I raised my tattooed arm to point at the woman who birthed me, and the group recoiled a few inches. "You brought them to Maine on purpose. Their blood is on my hands, not yours, just like you planned." Cue cheesy Telenovela music from a bad soap opera.

A nodding man whose name I forgot added, "We know what the Wardwell's are like, so how's is this one any better?" a foot kicking towards me.

"I am not—" Mother silenced mid-cry, but her mouth still moved, mumbled words garbled from straining against invisible bonds. Someone mentally cast an immobilization spell.

The Mexican priestess sighed, "Thank you—whoever."

306

Bill continued, "Between your upbringing and Karen's actions, made claiming the title impossible. A druid once envisioned the sisters united and strong, but your family thought they knew better and, for the last three hundred years, worked to undo the brother's prophecy. I speak for the others by commuting your execution."

The group murmured consent, and my nose exhaled minor relief. "Thank—"

"As a distrusted Wardwell, we must weigh the facts and your terms and—."

The Russian chimed in, "We debate how you choose prods, and let pets kill half tha others, da?"

"They are my friends, not pets—"

"Cannot blame dis girl for terrible choice in friends."

"If I can continue—they protected me when my family twice tried to kill me."

"Chancellor Simeon's manipulations are legendary, yet you believe he spared you out of compassion?"

"That's a tired narrative. He's different. Wait until you meet—"

Bill's lips thinned. "You lack any occult socialization, so no wonder you hold sympathies for the undead."

Karen mumbled against an invisible gag.

"But if you guys just—"

Bill's strained tone continued, "Sarah—"

I flashed back, "Queen Regent."

"Fine. Queen Regent, we will never agree to live with those aberrations but agree to spare your execution. We will debate your proposal."

"How American's say, we'll call you, don't call us, da?"

"Show your daughter out, Karen."

When Mother's magical bonds dissipated, "She knows how to leave."

Before I spun to go, mustered spite glowered at the heartless woman. "Magic laws state that only nine can rule, and I'm number nine. You still lose." I turned before tears crumbled the last specs of composure.

The old man called, "We'll be in touch, Sarah." Based on the tone, the chap disliked me living with immortals.

"And Sarah?" Mother's loathsome voice whipped my face over a shoulder. "Tell Simeon your little secret—before I do. If he discovers you kept the truth from him, you're good as dead." Her spat words chilled fiery blood.

CHAPTER 21

Is John MaClean an immortal?

GATHERED DEAD NIGHTS FORMED a week, then lumped another tense week. Nerve-racking silence teetered us on a thin, high-wire. Vasile stopped visiting the stables each night, and Dmitri's piano sulked quietly. After the second day of sitting around Vasile's den starring at each other, I broke the monotony. I suggested we pile into the safe room and watch the only telly on the property. Vasile looked away from a newspaper, and a typical hand flick dismissed the novel idea. But it was too late. Dmitri and I ganged up on the stuffy killjoy. One growl and a wrinkled paper later, we cuddled on the lair's leather sectional. Vas grumbled about our unabashed excitement as he thumbed through a dusty book. After several hilarious episodes of RuPaul's Drag Race, I regretted the suggestion. The boys exhausted me when they paused the television every five minutes to pepper me with questions about pop culture and slang.

"What is this ki-ki?"

"What is gaydar?"

"A gaydar is—"

Dmitri's diatribe interrupted my millionth explanation. "The art of cross-dressing is quite defunct compared to the Sun King's court."

"You knew King Louis?" What was he like?

Dmitri threw my popcorn at the screen.

"Not my popcorn."

"They disqualified Willam Belli! I shan't endure another moment of this show. Start the next episode."

"If you like Willam, watch his YouTube—"

"Yoo Boob?"

I extracted myself from under Vasile's warm arm. "Ya know—YouTube. Anybody can post videos."

"Anything?"

"I'll play a video from John Maclean, a makeup guru. He claims to be an immortal—"

Vasile grumbled, "An immortal would never break the law."

I rolled my eyes. "He said trends are for the anxious." Expert fingers queued up the video in record time as the safe room door beeped and rumbled open.

"Brilliant assumption. I must use—dear heaven. He is exquisite."

Mrs. Smith forewent a curtsy when she barged in front of us. Out of breath, "Your Lordship—"

"Is he an—"

"Lordship—"

Vasile flicked a palm, and a stare narrowed at the screen as he leaned closer. "A moment, Smith."

She jumped in Infront of the telly. "Your Lordship! A—a—"

I grabbed more popcorn. "Maid's stroking out, guys."

"Talking with your mouth full—"

I swatted D's wet finger from my earlobe.

"—a bloody witch at the door!"

"For the millionth time, mages not witches! Wait, what did you say?" The room heaved pure chaos as we vaulted to our feet.

"Did you show them in?"

She strangled, "Are ya daft, lad? Housekeepers take out the trash, not bring more in! Left her French smellin perfumed bum on the doorstep."

"Mother."

"Very well, escort our guest to the parlor."

I grabbed Vasile's hand. "Stay here."

The wilting grimace force-fed a hard gulp. "

"If he goes, I go!" Dmitri dropped the remote to the couch.

Vasile's long legs marched to the metal entrance while loyal soldiers nipped at his heels.

I whispered, "You've got this. You've got this."

Vasile jammed fingers at the datapad and reassured, "Yes, you do."

* * *

I flung open the parlor door and revealed my smug parent inspecting a porcelain vase. Wearing a subdued gray pantsuit and designer shoes, I spotted her forearm absent a dangling purse. Every time Mum left home unless standing a meadow in Maine, she always carried her six-figure, Birkin handbag. I resisted chewing my chapped lips. The well-dressed lady in her fifties set the delicate blue vase back on an elegant table. She measured a slow, flat gaze to the two cross-armed creatures behind me.

"Mother."

While I waited the last several weeks, I envisioned a groveling reply on bended knees, but the delegate the high-priests and priestesses chose obliterated the optimistic fantasy. The occult revered symbology, and my expendable parent played the perfect harbinger of refusal.

"Such refined tastes for your abominations. Your name, creature?" A snobbish tone raked across the chancellor while her chocolate stare scoured my face.

"Madame, I am Chancellor Simeon."

A red lacquered nail flicked towards Dmitri. "And that thing?"

"Your worst nightmare, but you may call me Prince Svetoslav."

Mother's spooky glare slowly veered to my snarling best friend. "Titled pets. How cute. Are you not ringing for tea, darling?"

"No. Spit it out."

"Such unbecoming rudeness."

I clenched my jaw tighter. "Mother."

"Right. I would not be doing my duty as your mother if I did not warn you. As Queen Regent, Bill Sutton will do everything to usurp your reign. I know these people's darkest secrets and weaknesses and suggest you make me your advisor."

"Bloody hell! You're off your trolley!"

"I was afraid of that."

Crimson pupils absorbed each movement, and supernatural ears soaked in every word.

"No, be afraid I might strip your magic."

"Very well, this brings me great pleasure."

Threadbare nerves and lost patience numbed my legs when electric currents condensed around the room. The snake tattoo itched, and my arm hairs stood.

Dmitri ignored a future reprimand from Vasile. "I'll pay out of my pocket to send the hag to etiquette class."

A scowling sneer whirled on a spiked heel, and Mother showed her trademark anger sign. Painted nails clicked a slow rhythm at her side, and sparkled diamond rings caught lamplight. "Silence around your betters."

Dmitri exposed razor-sharp fangs, and my stuttering heart leaped faster.

Vasile slapped my best friend's arm. "Control."

Garish maroon lipstick slicked a sickening smile. "Which one of you undead beasts is shagging my daughter?"

"Mother!" Fists tightened as rage loosened my thin composure. The energy swirling at our legs drew into Mum's feet.

Dmitri lisped, "I am, hag!"

"Enough!" My angry yell echoed the same room where I met Nikola and produced the desired outcome. Jaws snapped shut. "What's their answer?"

She fluffed hairspray crusted hair. "They considered your proposal."

I scratched the itching snake branding and ignored the throbbing forcefield around Mum. If I knew about magic what I know now, I would have ended her miserable life. "Well?"

As she clacked painted nails in a leisurely rhythm, "I deliberated on the best way to tell you, but the Russian had the greatest idea."

I stepped forward. "Mother." My shirt dropped a popcorn crumb.

"Maybe I should show your people's answer." She uncrossed her arms, feet shoulder-width apart.

Flesh tingled as mystical energy hummed even higher. The glowering monsters' heads turned at the changing atmosphere and rotten stench. Invisible currents popped eardrums. Mum tightened a glare and her fists. Someone then hit the slow-motion button on time's DVD player. Sound muted other than Mother's indistinguishable chant. Dark blue inky smoke snaked from her outstretched fingertips, and glowing mana traveled down her straightened arms. A brilliant laser beam shot from her hands, inching to its target.

"Nooooo." I intended to knock her back, but my feet through molasses. Dmitri became a side-diving soccer player, horizontally suspended in mid-air. When D dove in front of Vasile, the hot magic stream hit my best friend's rib cage. When time resumed its regular tick, D crashed to the floor with a grunt, and Vasile's shocked expression unhinged his jaw. My parent disappeared like never there. I understood the missing purse.

Panic grew the unshakable count's wide-eyed stare. In seconds, we went down to our knees around our friend, clutching his chest. My dry throat dislodged an anguished cry. I propped D's heavy head on my lap, and gold locks spanned across my thighs. Vasile removed Dmitri's hand and revealed a baseball-size burn hole in his designer tracksuit. Vas ripped open D's zipped jacket while his friend fought for air. The fresh wound oozed blueish-black bubbles every time he wheezed. Singed skin stung our noses.

"Why's he not healing?"

"Damn you, Dmitri!" Vas roared as he palmed the scorched skin.

The blond rasped, "Sorry."

"Why always so rash, boy?" Black goo trickled from the corner of Dmitri's mouth and dripped into his ear. Vas clasped D's ashen cheeks and smeared the foul sludge as he scoured the immortal son's clouding eyes. "Why?" Everyone knew the answer.

When the injured creature coughed, the gaping wound bubbled more tar-like slime that percolated down his struggling ribs. We watched once bright red blood trickle to the rug.

I stroked his clammy forehead. "What was that spell?"

"She infected him with a UV light virus that spreads through his body." Vasile's white-knuckled grasp clung to Dmitri's hand. "Always center stage. When will you ever learn, m'boy?"

Dmitri gasped for more air while he stared into his loving leader's worried look. Wicked streaks snaked under alabaster skin as the UV ray sickness darkened veins, and death marched straight for Dmitri. Another muscle spasm thinned his lips and darted panic-stricken eyes before clawing fingers grappled across the soiled carpet. "Don't let me die again. The pain—"

"Conserve your energy so she can save you." Confidence crooned when daggers shot ice into frayed nerves. "Won't you— Sarah?"

I hovered shaking hands inches above the bubbling black hole, but no amount of Earth magic reversed Mother's spell. Frustrated, I angrily slashed at terrified tears. "I'm trying."

Vasile growled while he touched Dmitri's cheek, "Sarahhh— "

"I'm trying, I said! Give me time!"

"There is no time. We are losing him!"

"I'm sorry for—childish behavior and—"

I squeezed my eyelids shut. "Need *more* time!" The room's energy waned, and the snake tattoo refused to spring to life with promised powers.

D's facial muscles twisted as he sputtered through gritted teeth, "I—about—Anna."

Ominous blackish-blue streaks leaked death from the burn hole to his bulged neck, and once pink skin diminished to ash-gray. Before our disbelieving eyes, an immortal regressed to a mortal, a Higher to a Lower. As threadbare life pulsed towards extinction, the once bright aura no longer swirled high a cooler body stiffening across my lap.

"I could—I could send him into the dimension, stop the spread. No, it won't work. I should—"

Dmitri coughed and panted, "Need to tell—"

Vasile rested a finger over his friend's lips. "Save your strength."

Sparkling ruby pupils turned to clotted blood. Nasty black spittle seeped between clenched teeth as D struggled, "Careful of The Father."

"Pure madness."

Dmitri flexed fingers in Vasile's grip. "Annalyse—was a mage to rule every coven—moved to—to hide her from them." Hacked up, dark dots splattered across a white collared shirt.

"Rubbish. Let Sarah concentrate."

I mouthed, "I'm trying." I clenched and unclenched my hands over D's convulsing body.

"Your Father—hired mages to kill her—no marriage— between son and mage queen." A gasp severed shocking words while blood-colored tears dirtied two sets of cheeks.

"Brain is fevered."

"No—listen. He bargained with them."

A mage killed Dmitri, but the careless words ended Vasile's heart. Death's dense fog joined acrid burnt flesh as rattled, and irregular breaths became too shallow to support life. Vas gripped Dmitri's face but screamed into mine, "Save him, you worthless witch! Save him or so help you—"

Vasile's desperate rage and sobs shook all reason. "I tried! Please stop looking at me like that!"

Vasile touched foreheads with his longtime confidant and keeper. "Stay, I beg you to stay. You cannot leave me. I forbid this!" Someone who never pleaded once, beseech the impossible. The imploring still haunts me. He clutched D's icy hand to his heaving breastbone, like willing his heartbeat and immortality one more time.

After a weak gasp, blue lips stuttered an exhale, and the blond's chest sunk its last. Vibrant life, raucous fun, and incomparable wit dissipated, only held by memories. A best friend saw no more delights, deft fingers produced silence, not spirited music, and a willful tongue wagged no further insults.

Vasile's blood tears mingled with Dmitri's on his ashen face. Cloudy mud pupils stared into death's nothingness.

I slapped my inner arm's branding several times. "No, no, no!" The as my fists pounded D's shoulders, "Wake up!"

Reverent Vasile released the stiffening grasp and placed it on the prince's motionless chest. Warm living fingers smoothed eyelids over crossed eyes, but flesh refused to close.

I only saw CPR on the telly, but I had to try. "You're not dead. Not happening."

A weakened Vas stood. "He's gone. Give him a little dignity."

Confused sobs wracked the cavernous room while I eased Dmitri's heavy head on the carpet, neck already stiff. Determined death muttered a parting shot when rigor mortis froze the larger-than-life immortal. The condition intended the living to comprehend the finality fully, but I refused to accept his death and threw myself at Vasile. The tortured sculpture responded, but how I expected.

Vas ignored my pressing body, immovable like his dead friend. Bright tears wet his wrinkled white shirt spotted from black droplets and blood tears. After a few uncomforted minutes, a deep voice cut through my wailing. "Did you know?" I looked up to see a stony face trained straight ahead at the bookcase as my jaw hinged open. "I repeat. Did you *know*? Did you know?"

"Yeah—yes. I found out when—"

Strong thumbs and fingers on my shoulders separated me from his hard body. "You, traitorous—"

In a flick of a second, I returned to diseased trash status. "Let me explain the night of the rite, I—"

"Nobody thought it wise to share?" Like the night of my first nightmare, I rushed to crush against his chest and avoid loveless eyes. But when my breastbone met a steely palm, air knocked from my lungs.

"It's not like that." I cried, straining against his arms.

"It *is* like that! Did you two little girls giggle behind my back while braiding each other's hair?"

"No, we—"

"Therefore, you coddled me?" Pure hatred bore into my teary flush as Vasile unleashed dammed pain and blamed me for many lost centuries.

"But—" My sobs changed into hyperventilated gasps.

"I loved you and my creator. Both love and your kind curse this world."

"No, stop it."

"I misspoke. I never loved you, only enjoyed working you." He slashed a damning finger from collarbone to floor. "Who could ever love someone like—"

"Stop saying that! You love me."

"Me love a witch?" He cackled, "I could never love something so vile as you."

"Please, Vas!" A shaking hand covered his hard fingers on my chest.

He yanked back and hissed, "Get away from—"

"I love you!"

"You left him to die!"

"Oh, God, I tried! Why are you like—"

The enraged immortal snarled a lip, "I chose you above my people. I wasted time and resources on your so-called limitless powers. Powers that let my beloved son die. I am not wasting another minute on a broken weapon."

"I don't know why it fail—"

"You want to lead when all you touch dies or fails. Failures that cost me everything."

Unabated anger sliced deep, so I hung my hair and absorbed each hate-filled truth. I whispered, "Please."

"Please, what? Forgive you? My humanity's last link lies cold on the rug, and I find myself quite incapable of forgiveness."

Bleary eyes lifted from floor to enraged demon. "I can be your anchor now."

White knuckles fisted and relaxed. A claw raised above my head as Vasile wrestled with reasons to let me live. Vas flinched his hand back towards his shoulder, and I cringed. After a tense moment of held breath, he dropped the poised strike, "I never want to hear your traitorous mouth again. Here, a trophy for your failures. Keep him."

"Vas—"

"Do yourself, and the entire world a favor by digging him a grave and tossing yourself inside."

It took years to cauterize the slice to my soul from the monster's crippling contempt. The lasting image of the seething creature standing over me still influences my decisions. Vasile straightened his belt, adjusted his shirt, and regained regal composure. But I knew he faked the serenity, as Dmitri's loss and the revealed secret ranked the lowest point in his thousand-year existence.

I raced towards him before he stormed from the death saturated room. "Don't go!" When my thin arms wrapped around his lower back, he half-turned and looked over a shoulder. One rough shove to my heart tossed me backward twelve feet. I landed on my rear. No vindictive mages sent me crawling from desperation, but a prodigium. When I peered through stringy hair, something deep inside ruptured. "I'll become one of you!" And those words ranked my lowest point.

An eyebrow rose into his hairline, and a gleeful smile twisted his knife deeper. As he flourished his heavy ring, he replied, "One of us? Your delusions of adequacy are quite breathtaking, Miss Wardwell." The doorknob rattled. "Next time you touch me, I will rip out every bone in your miserable body."

He walked out, and my ears rang loudly. Vasile abandoned the house. The creature left with his remaining dignity and the manor's spirit, but no physical possessions. Old masonry and wood became a lifeless shell, discarded by another broken lord.

After a wild gaze shot from the empty door to Dmitri's still body, I crawled towards him while fresh sobs tore at my sore throat. Tears blinded me, but I knew the way. As hands scraped against the carpet, I remembered the nights at the piano, whispering inappropriate jokes at Vasile's expense. I failed a genuine friend, and because of me, he died. I settled across a cool chest and clutched a stiff hand. Between the two deaths in recent months, I discovered how heavy dead bodies felt. Just like Maggie warned, blind love ruined everything, and Vasile's hateful accusations bulls-eyed my heart. So, I laid beside the gold-gray corpse, racked by pitiful wails.

I hoisted to an arm and glared at the tattoo. "Why did you not give me the powers to save him? I passed the test, but no powers, no people, and no love." I shrieked, "You tricked me!"

I clawed at the apple-biting snake and whimpered. I wanted the pain-producing mark off. Angry nails tore at pale flesh, but my mental anguish prevented feeling physical agony. Delicate underarm skin mangled into ripped strips of meat. Gelatinous blood rivers ran along a trembled arm while I gleefully cackled at bubbled, yellowish globules of fat. An idea tickled my brain through a strange crack in my psychosis.

I scrambled to my knees and leaned over Dmitri. "Work—work, please work." I smashed the bloody gash to blueish-gray lips, but the calm face remained motionless under the fresh copper blood. I shrieked, "Drink!" Ghoulish drops splashed on his ashen face when my determined nails clawed deeper. "You have to live and help me get him back!" Mage blood and immortal red tears dirtied the golden God's death mask. Weak elbows collapsed my body, so I laid upon a deathly quiet chest. Death's perfume wrapped sick tentacles around my dull senses. When I accepted tragic defeat and adrenaline faded, the mauled arm's pain seeped into my muddled brain. "Don't leave us, D."

322

The loneliness inflicted by a loveless family nowhere related to the new sentiment constricting my head. True isolation tasted way bitter. No loving relative, coven, or friend rescued me from the night. The covens knew one particular death crippled Vasile and me. I had no choice, so I pictured digging Dmitri's grave and heaving inside inconsequential trash. My knees hitched to my chest, and hands dropped from my ringing ears. I let Earth's spinning clutches weigh down my lifeforce, and under reality's gravity, I resigned myself to the universe's chaos. The ringing stopped.

CHAPTER 22

Leavin' on a jet plane

WHEN MY TIRED EYES fluttered open, I still laid on the same rug but alone. I raised a healed arm. How long did I sleep, and who took Dmitri's body? As I breathed in odorless dust, I noticed how weightless I felt. When the oil-painted nobles fixed their judgment upon me, the art hologram flickered. Instead of death, I smelled familiar static electricity off an old television screen. I groaned. How did I slip back into the dimension without a ritual? My dull heart refused to feel my confusing question. I sat up.

The Grandfather clock no longer ticked, now a gagged prisoner. My fingers snapped, but no sound met my ears. Careless curiosity replaced heartbreaking despair. Pink Floyd sang it best, 'I have become comfortably numb.' When I stood, I marveled at how hyperventilating gasps stopped, and I felt no urge to breathe. Out of habit, I wandered towards the music room.

When soundless steps came to the solarium, I yanked on closed doors, always open. I shielded my forehead when a thousand sunrises blasted through the tall windows. But the tranquil room's warmth never reached my anesthetized soul as I crossed silenced squeaky floors. After I slumped on the black bench, I clinked a muted key, but the emptied stillness orchestrated silence. Fresh hurt squeezed through the odd detachment, and my mouth twisted. A tear fell. The droplet vanished before the glittering liquid touched the ivory keys.

Lost in no thoughts, hair moved against my neck, and a flower arrangement stirred. Someone sat with me, but before I looked, the room's volume cranked from mute to full blast as air rushed around me. Noisy birds chirped, piano ivories clanked, floorboards creaked, and my pitiful sobs clasped hands to my ears.

"Sara." More tears from a familiar voice bejeweled shiny white keys, and the air tinkled when each drop splashed. A teary gaze turned towards Maggie's wrinkled face.

"You're dead too?"

"Not really."

"Maggie, I screwed up."

Her body and voice rippled, but an unseen hand tuned the reception in better. "I told ya to be careful of him. What's the plan, Toots?"

"Don't have one," I replied as my limp limbs shrugged.

"You'll die if you stay here."

"How d'you get in here?"

After a darted a sideways glance, the senior changed form. Her grayish hair turned platinum-white, and in seconds grew until the strange locks grazed the floor. Crinkled pale skin smoothed to delicious warm peach tones. Maggie became a remarkable Latin woman or man, wearing a lengthy, cream-colored robe. Maggie's soft brown eyes altered to shimmering fire opals that beamed patient acceptance.

"Where's Maggie?" But concern never inflected my tone.

"The costume comforted you."

"Are you Death?"

"No child, I am the start and the ending."

"Oh. Is this the dimension?"

"A place where departed souls face their memories."

I hung my head so low my neck hurt. "Not Heaven or Hell, huh?"

"This is Purgatory, absent God's presence."

"The dimension is purgatory?"

"Very smart child."

My gaze returned to the piano. "That's what the druidess said."

"Why do the dead remember their lives?"

"Souls are called for judgment when one atones for their sins through remembrance." Each word flickered the shimmery body. "The departed sort through a lifetime of sin, so imagine how long it takes when a prodigium dies. Immortals rarely see judgment day."

"I don't want to talk about them."

"As I explained, you must dwell on your sins, child."

"So, hanging out with prods was a sin?" I questioned with high irritability.

"Not staying true to your heart was your sin."

"Bible says nothing about that. I think."

"Something written by power-hungry men affected by their times."

That got a smile. "Who cares for those trapped in here?"

"Lucifer Morningstar."

"THE Lucifer?"

"He uses The Between's tired souls to grow an army."

"Ya lost me."

"Souls tire during their stay, and dark angles offer relief and a way out if they join Lucifer's legions. When they agree, suffering painful memories stops and—"

"But where are the angels? Can't they help?"

"Angles only come here to retrieve those summoned for judgment."

"They don't fight off the demons?"

"God's rules prevent divine intervention because one must prove worthiness through living or atonement after death."

I leaned closer. "What happens if God summons a soul is before they make peace with their past?"

"Lucifer wins another soldier," she replied, smiling at inconsequential words.

I reared back. "So purgatory is a big fraternity hazing."

"In a sense. Heaven is no place for embroiled souls."

"How does the devil convince the immortals? They're pretty strong, ya know."

"Because of their many lifetimes of recollections and sins, here they are feebler than others."

"No irony there."

"Souls become weaker the longer one stays, and a beacon for demons. Alive or dead, a soul keeps their freewill. If one agrees to leave painful memories and forsake entering heaven, anyone can escape with the demons."

"Are there many prods here, now?"

"A few. But the immortals always agree. Some souls—"

"Pretty dodgy, God sets everyone up for failure while Satan has unrestricted access."

Eyes crinkled from her warm smile. "I invariably enjoyed our spirited talks."

"I reincarnated more than once?"

"You must go back one last time."

"Can I get a different mother?"

"Time is too precious, so I grant you the same body."

My weary head lowered to my palms. "No." My elbows on the piano keys clanged harsh chords, and a chirping clamor erupted outside the glittering windows. "I can get past this place."

"Do not be so sure. Like them, you lived several lives and are immortal in your own way."

"Shocker."

"My sweetest child, I need you to rescue the immortals and prevent a battle capable of deluging Purgatory."

"Not my problem."

"As we speak, mages across the world prepare for war."

"They'll handle themselves."

"You can save the souls they will doom if sent to this place."

"But they never joined forces before."

"Dmitri's murder united the emboldened covens, and they believe mana weakens because their ancestor made the prodigia."

"So, what's the real deal?"

"I did not create your people, but powerful druid magic. The existence of both mage and prodigia imbalances nature, so magical powers reduce each generation. Soon, the magic disappears from my world."

I pitched facial muscles at the ceiling and gave a little head shake. "And that's a bad thing?"

"Yes, if you want to stop human's planetary destruction. As you can see, we enter dangerous times, my child."

"Still not my problem."

"The mages plan to kill Maggie for her association with you, and Vasile's people plot to execute him when he returns."

"Who cares." But my voice weakened.

"Vasile and Dmitri will become the easiest prey for Lucifer, and Morningstar carved a special place in Hell reserved for them."

Emotion electrodes flickered across my numb heart. "Everything I touch fails or dies, despite these dumb superpowers. You got the wrong girl."

"Would you sacrifice your life's happiness for the mutant king's wellbeing?"

"What kinda hypothetical is that? Even after how he treated me, I would. Are you gonna quote the Bible and ask me to cut a baby in half to prove it?"

"Brava child. You just conquered your worst fear and passed the ultimate test."

"I passed my rite in Maine."

She beamed, "On a smaller scale."

"Son of a—that's why I couldn't save him!"

"Only I can grant your full potential and a gift to win the war."

"Don't need—" Something whooshed air. I cringed, worried a demon entered the solarium. When I winced past a shoulder, a limp armed Dmitri stood in the room's corner. A confused expression returned to a glorious golden complexion. "D!" I flew from the slippery bench to launch into his arms but slammed against the wall behind him. I picked myself up and waved in front of his face.

"He doesn't see you because he's working through hard memories."

I fluttered a hand through his healed chest. "D!"

"He'll surrender. They always do."

"Just call him to judgment before they get him!"

"I'm afraid not. The chancellor's sins are too great. Only you can save them."

"Nothing ever changes. New game but same pawn."

"As a token of my appreciation, he may return with you."

"And the real reason?"

"Very well. When Vasile sees Dmitri alive, he will receive my gift to prevent mass extinction."

My best friend cringed and winced as he stared at something only he saw. "Right. What's the plan?"

"Excellent. Go back carrying the sun."

"Ya know the sun kills them."

A thin palm opened, and a shiny jewel sparkled against a flat hand. Some craftsman circled warm gold around a dazzling fire opal. The mesmerizing stone's cosmic fires sparked colorful dots over our faces. The gem resembled the Goddesses' expressive eyes.

"I picked the best stone for a worthy soul."

"He has a ring."

"But not this day ring," she said matter-of-factly. "Any immortal wearing it may walk in the sun unharmed or withstand daylight spells."

"Whoa!"

From beneath her gauzy robes, she pulled out the cursed snake crown.

I backed away. "No." I pointed at the dreadful circlet that only brought pain, "Not that thing."

"You will need the crown to craft more rings." The snake blinked its empty black eye at me.

"More?" When Dmitri flinched again, I rushed, "Look, cut to the chase."

"Vasile's Companion Guards needs to wear them to stop the battle ahead."

A finger jammed hair behind an ear. "So why you care?"

"Because the war will strain the balance between Heaven and Hell."

"Again, not my problem. Do it yourself. You seem pretty powerful."

"If I directly interfere, I negate my allowance of freewill. Therefore, I bequeath a gift to prevent what I cannot."

"Gift of freewill? What are you not saying?"

"A warlock fashioned the first immortal and Purgatory's only loophole. I designed purgatory to house dead mortals. Satan uses lacking preparation to shape the greatest demon army. Imagine humankind's fate."

"So, you worried about the devil getting control of undead super demons?"

"In a manner, yes. When I created—"

"Hey, wait a minute! You talk like you are God or something. But you're a woman, and God's a guy."

"The bible correctly wrote how I crafted humankind from my image. Like me, some humans are both men and women. Those are my special chosen children." Love flooded her expression.

"Holy shi—So what are your pronouns and are you a God or a Goddess?"

"I am Creator. Decide. I cannot tarry here. This place must stay absent My grace, or it crumbles." The kind face wavered like a hot road underneath a desert sun. "Do you want the world saturated with confused ghosts?"

"I get why the prophecy demanded one born from Satan. I'm kinda neutral."

"You figured out that same detail the last time you were here."

"Right then. So, go clean up your mess or deal with a worse battle between Heaven and Hell—"

"—a war that forced the second coming and end times."

"*Fine.*" A million whispers chanted my name. The lady's image wavered.

A raspy wheeze inhaled painful, life-sustaining air and seared my lungs. When a woman's shrill scream ripped the darkness, a wince sharpened my blurry vision. A weird cloudy gel-coated my pupils and several rapid blinks helped. Chattering teeth neared chipping as I laid prone on wintry grass in a dark corner of the garden. Another strangled scream cleared the remaining eye goo, and five dull moons melded into one bright crescent. Grave urgency, panic, and the cry clanged my temples when I bolted upright. Why lay outside in the cold?

A shrieking Mrs. Smith and a trembling male servant clutched shovels beside a large dirt mound. Incessant shrieks from a shocked younger guy sliced more icicles into my skull. I prayed she stuffed a rag in the guy's gob. "Why are you yelling?" I flipped on hands and knees, cold dew eating through denim. No waiting for an answer or silence, finding Dmitri became paramount. Five feet away, stretched on the grass, death's ravages still darkened his slack face.

"She's breathing, Mrs. Smith!"

"Dmitri!"

Pungent rot forced mouth breathing while I clasped Dmitri's stone visage. After a dull thud, I snatched my head at the sniveling pair. The housekeeper laid horizontal on her back.

"You killed her!" The footman's shrill scream jerked my shoulders.

"Jesus! Is that necessary?"

"Two corpses! Saw it with me own eyes, I tell ya!"

"I'm alive, you daft idiot."

"Dead fer days, ya was! Waited forever for His Lordship but, but—"

"Where is he?" Smith's simmered moans stifled the terrified man's words. "Speak up!"

"I—I—"

"Don't make me come across this garden. Talk. Now."

The employee gripped the shovel like a makeshift weapon. "After two days of waiting, yer bodies stunk!"

"Two entire days?" I groaned.

Mrs. Smith moaned and draped an arm over her forehead. I split my attention between the servant, maid, Dmitri, and an itching forearm begging for renewed fingernails as the maid struggled onto elbows. Despite the distractions, the significance of last month's events blared into understanding.

To physically carry divine gifts from the dimension, one must enter their entire spirit into Purgatory. I never died during the rite and used a trance to get into the dimension, or should I say Purgatory. So, I brought back a fake crown. When I remembered my more recent mystical trip, I dug inside a jean pocket. Icy fingers touched warm round metal, and my shoulders relaxed. But the reprieve lasted a second.

"Two blimey days!" The petrified servant backed up several steps, near running away.

"So, you said, mate."

"Evil creature, just like them!"

The kid needed to calm before he attracted more trouble. "Don't catch me out. I get working for them wears on the mind, so seeing a zombie isn't so bad." When he shrieked again, I muttered, "Bad joke?"

The grunting, overweight housekeeper hefted up on wobbling legs. Smith turned her plump body towards her mental helper as she wiped her hands on a mud-stained apron.

"Unnatural, Mrs. Smith! Tis bad enough serving those devils," he cried, creeping away on hesitant steps.

Collected, Mrs. Smith reached into a pocket. "Now, now, lass. Steady on with ya. If his Lordship were here, he'd tell ya to take a medicament."

"But ma'am!"

"Had a wee fright, 'tis all."

When he coiled to sprint, a compact revolver materialized in Smith's plump hand. The shiny black weapon aimed at the blubbering servant, fastened on Dmitri and me. He missed the surprise gun.

"Um, Mrs. Smith." Brief attention flicked over the silver landscape, worried about the impending bang attracting trouble.

"It's wrong!" Another stumbled step moved the hysterical lad further from the hasty grave. The trigger snicked back. At such close range, his neck cracked sideways before I heard the gun. The poor guy's left side of his head sprayed a cone of silver and pink mist. Pale brain matter and skull fragments rained into the dark hole. The gunshot reverberated around the garden long after the skinny body collapsed into the hole meant for a mage and prod.

Acrid gunpowder replaced the dead flesh aroma. "There was no need for that!" While I stared into the half-filled space, energies shifted. An alarm tingled my mind's eye as goosebumps erupted. When I whisked around, Smith's shiny revolver found a new target. Me.

"Filthy devil's hag! Running off His Lordship like that."

"I don't have time for this." I Sighed, "Put the gun away." I glanced back at Dmitri's corpse, not breathing as promised. I came too far to fail, and I required him alive for more than only friendship.

"I'll kill—"

I rounded on her and ordered, "I said, drop the damn thing."

"Both of yas were dead. Dead, I tell ya!"

A calm tone masked my hard annoyance while her shaking hand rattled the gun. "I brought the prince back. Honest. I need to finish—"

The grimacing housekeeper's thumb cocked the clacking hammer. "Nothing good ever comes from living dead things." Spittle and breath condensation sailed through the moonlight.

"I don't have time for this!" The rebranding itched incredibly, and in my mind's eye, the henna snake coiled and constricted around Mrs. Smith's neck creases. A dull clang opened my eyes to see sun spotted hands clawing at an invisible object, squeezing her throat. The gun lay harmless on a dark foot track on the dew. A terrified simper and thrashing legs offered a clue to the maid's condition. A flushed grimace changed dusky, then violet.

In the event Vasile listened from the garden's murk, I called into the nothingness, "You're right, Vas, murder gets easier." Smith toppled to her knees, then landed flat on her face, stone dead. I shrugged, harboring no desire to entertain foolish mortal sentiments such as care. That frosty night bore the Queen Regent.

Not a further thought was given, I kicked her body into the same grave as the young servant. A bullying housekeeper and her browbeaten footman entangled limbs in death's last embrace. The diplomatic fairytale of peacefully ending the war and naïve romanticism died when Vasile tossed me aside like garbage. The monster I humanized shattered every peaceful idealism and remaining innocence. If paranormal DNA prohibited decency, then the prods deserved the despot. A new resolve pulsed brighter focus and the perfect strategy sprang in mind. Forget typically running from danger. I prepared to run into it. First, I required Dmitri alive as the Creator promised.

I scampered to Dmitri's corpse. "D wake up. Wake up. My voice *follow* my voice." Nothing. A hard cheek slap produced the same result. "Dah—*mee*—tree!" A stiff neck offered no pulse, and he stunk worse. "I know what'll work!"

I got right in his face and sang a song we played nightly at the piano. I used the lyrics, and Earth's energy threads to bathe the mortal with immortality. "Bags are packed. I'm ready to go. I'm standin' here outside your door. Hate to wake you to say goodbye—" My limbs shook, and voice cracked as I pressed icy hands against colder cheeks, my song climbing louder. "But dawn's breaking. It's early morn—taxi's waiting—" Panicked tears splashed the ashy-gray skin, and thundered, "Leavin—on a jet plane—I don't know if—"

I jumped up and pointed my teary, red face at the pitiless black sky. "Damn you!" Clenched fists shook at the lonely empty while I screamed, "We struck a deal! Bring him back, or I fill up your place myself!"

I slapped hot tears when a weak cough sputtered, so I glared at the stars one more time before rushing to his side. Across the lawn like a baseball player stealing home, fresh grass stains darkened my knees. Pummeling fists met D's hard chest. Muddy, dead eyes tore open.

I screamed into his shocked face as he fought shallow breaths, "Live damn it! Don't stare at the memories! Close your eyes."

A welcome wheeze reverberated through the tall cedars. I whisked hair over my shoulder and fisted his stained shirt.

"That's it!"

The fangs released from destruction remained exposed because he straddled two worlds. Life's fleshy peaches replaced corpse-grays. Brown blood clot pupils sparked bright red flecks. But relief lasted seconds. The pink flush on the Adonis features reversed to grayish-blue, and Dmitri's panic darted side to side as gasps lessened to uneven death rattles. What did he search for, and why die again?

But I knew. Dmitri craved the one ingredient supernatural healing required. If I wanted to make a mortal immortal live forever, I needed to act fast. If I emulated the Dacian warlock and supplied fresh marrow, he might heal. Trust me, and it too gave me a headache. But If I lost consciousness while he fed, nothing prevented bone-lust from reaching prized marrow in my spine. Vasile mentioned spinal fluid marinates uncommonly sweet-tasting bone.

I shivered so much from my frost-soaked clothes and the actions required to save him, and I struggled to control the teeth chipping shudders. "Dmitri. Dmitri look at me." I slapped a stony, hard cheek. "Look at me!" But a bleak stare gazed into death's desolate vacuum. Another slap stung my icy fingers before he violently ripped clouding eyes from an overhanging tree branch to me. "Feed. Just—leave my spine alone."

I swished, matted red hair aside, and lifted my snake branding to his dark blue lips. Cold, shallow breaths cascaded around my sensitive skin, and my free hand fisted slick wet grass. Air dammed inside my lungs while I waited for incoming agony and another death. Instinct took over, and Dmitri's teeth slid deep into my forearm. The hard ulna provided little opposition for jaws designed to crack bones. An electric shock jolted when a popping crunch rang my ears. The stars spun. I let go of the lawn and drooped across his torso while a violent scream broke tiny capillary veins underneath my eyes. A sticky sweet copper perfume prevented breathing from my nose.

I collapsed onto my best friend's chest as his lips moved against my numb skin. As I turned against his chest, I focused darkening vision on his normalizing pallor. It worked. A childlike a hug around my back tightened into a predator's embrace. Dmitri's lips shifted against my goosebumps, and mind-scrambling pain waned useless consciousness. Before I surrendered to blank nothingness, a tight embrace relaxed around my back. Hot fangs scraped against bone when they retracted and then left my flesh. Under my cheek, I felt the wound my mother inflicted bubble and close. Weak limbs throbbed with fire. The garden spun wildly.

Dmitri struggled to sit while his weak arms cradled my limp body. He frowned at the punctured arm clasped to my chest, then studied the creepy grave intended for us. Fresh blood on Dmitri's chin mingled with the dried blood I force-fed him two days prior. Wordless minutes clung two reunited friends before we helped each other stand to face a changed reality. We looked past the expansive gardens echoing with spooky peacocks calls towards the empty house.

"He's gone?" Dmitri's heavyweight wobbled my legs. While I held my throbbing arm to my chest, I hoisted the heavy male's armpit under a shoulder.

"Yeah. I guess."

When pointed with his raised chin at the dirt mound and asked, "What happened there?"

"Nothing."

Dmitri left my side and stumbled to the musty earth, then peered over the edge. "Um, Poppet?"

"Yeah, I killed her. But she killed him. And I kinda got tired of her calling me a hag."

Dmitri sailed a whistle. "Never like her anyhow."

"We need to get you inside before sunrise."

We shuffled the long, wet distance to a manor reduced to a lonely shell. "I died?"

I sighed before I recounted the Purgatory details, and the bargain I made to restore his life.

"I'll take your word about an afterlife because I saw no white light—both times."

"I don't think life and death are what we wanted it to be and even meant to understand any of it."

"We need to hide, Poppet. He'll come for us when he learns we are alive." He shuddered.

When we shuffled to the rear servant's entrance, I shouldered the building and opened a palm. The moving muscles over punctured bone renewed zapping agony while the shimmering opal ring teetered hot in my hand.

"What's this?"

"I have a plan."

340

After I outlined my plan, I shoved the precious jewel back into my pocket. Again, I shifted the not-so-dead weight over my shoulder.

"What's wrong, D? I don't recognize this expression."

"It had better work, and we'd better find him first."

"Any ideas?"

"Only one place he might be."

"He's that pissed, huh?"

"Let's hope I don't die for the third occasion."

"You tell him about the plan. Vas threatened to kill me the next chance he saw me." My voice cracked, "I'd let the entire world burn before listening to top that crap again."

"I know, Poppet. He'll see me alive and will listen."

"Say that again, but with more conviction? Just—just be careful. You kept the secret longer than me."

We inspected the black tomb devoid of Vasile's happiness before we entered.

"That I did. But you're telling him about his precious housekeeper."

"Crap."

"And Sarah?"

I winced when I banged my arm across D's bony hip. "Huh?"

"When you sang?"

"Um, yeah?"

"Don't quit your day job." I fought a grin because only Dmitri made me smile during the worst times.

"Jerk."

Dmitri tugged a curl. "No, seriously. Your singing wakes damn dead."

I groaned, "Well, quit diving in front of day spells and won't have to. It sucks losing your best friend."

"I'm your—?" Pride brightened a tired face when his pinky touched my nose tip. "I'll do my level best. And thank you, Sarah."

"Now, I know you're serious." I twisted the doorknob.

"How so?"

"You called me Sarah."

CHAPTER 23

Your heart, Miss Wardwell

THE EMPTY CAR LOT overlooked Anna's painting of rugged the ocean splendor cloaked by night's mysteries. When we alighted from the rented Jaguar, a fragrant sea breeze whipped through our hair, embedding crystalline salt and sand in our clothes. A dazzling full moon lit the silver skittering clouds as they churned through the embroiled night sky. Through the dimness, anyone could appreciate the oceans raging anger. The crashing waves thundered their might against packed wet sand, and a full tide belched gray foam onto the dark beach. Ocean, sand, and sky all rhythmically danced, ignorant, or not caring about the trouble between the species. Nature and her mystical forces sung a tune, only the most potent occultist grasped. Though the waters hummed for me, a wrecked spirit deafened my mystical ears.

"He's here."

"Poppet?"

"I feel his vibration."

Dmitri touched my chin and winked. "Cheer up, old girl. If he's in a mood, I'll stall the chap while you run."

I gulped. "Yeah, okay, sure."

We picked along calf-burning dunes to avoid the unpredictable waves, and when dried seaweed caught between my legs, Dmitri clasped an elbow. He let go of my arm and pointed at a lone shadow cloaked in the murky distance, captivated by the roiling waters. When I tensed, and half-sobbed, Dmitri's hand tightened around mine.

For a second, I considered abandoning what was clearly another foolish plan by yours truly, run for the car and never look back. Reasons to rescue an entire species fought against hurtful memories inflicted by the still shadow. Though weeks passed since Vasile wished me dead, his unique vibrations through the stormy darkness renewed emotional scars.

"You have to. What if God changes their mind about me being alive?"

Lips pursed as I listed reasons Vasile, as violent as the water, surveyed a storm blowing out to sea. The growing profile fixated at the thundering and hissing water. Despite supernatural hearing, he ignored our nearing footsteps until sand crunched fifty feet away. Slight pressure against my arm paused my steps.

"Stay."

I shuffled about on white windblown dunes while Dmitri neared painful judgment. When Dmitri stood two feet before his forlorn leader, Vas snapped to awareness, backed up, and almost stumbled. An expanded chest held precious breath. Painful tears welled, and an exploring caress touched a dead son's chest. Two hands patted Dmitri's sweatshirt as the wind wheeled 'not real' to my strained ears. Dmitri's clasped his master's shoulders, and then Vas gripped Dimitri behind his head. The slap from Vasile crushing his immortal son to his chest thumped louder than the angry waves. I lowered my face as their foreheads touched, and shoulders heaved.

Dmitri took Vasile's arm and guided him further down the beach and never once looked at me. The pair clenched hands behind backs as they wandered the biting winter shore. Darkness enfolded the couple in a mysterious embrace, and the figures became dots of nothing. Only fools prayed, so I begged God to bless Vasile with the ability to forgive. While thoughts lingered with the dune crossing immortals, I clutched the velvet pouch. The weightless bag held a substantial peace, thirty-nine daylight rings promised.

But the future demanded a heftier price. When I first tried to match the Count's devious wit, I falsely promised to become his living weapon. After mentally invested, I committed to ending the Species War. Destiny and a deity enjoyed the irony because regardless of mental anguish, they demanded I keep the foolish promise. But feelings and factors changed. I no longer suffered puppy love, and a fervent wish to save lives replaced blind devotion to an unfeeling creature. I also started living during the day and slept at night. Each sunrise I replayed the truthful and hateful words, 'Me love a witch? I could love nothing so vile.'

As I waited, more salty air crusted my clothes and weighed down my stringy hair. Teeth chattered near chipping when the cold wet reached the bone. When faint moonlight cast long shadows approaching across a dune, I released my coat wrapped around shaking knees and jumped to my feet. Teeth gnashed, ready for more rejection or another death. No matter, because once I handed over the rings and explained the plan, I left for good. I plotted to cast an amnesia spell to forget everything.

Dmitri nodded then executed a tired half salute because, after several weeks of new life, D still suffered death's effects. My best friend walked past me and squeezed my clammy hand, leaving me and Vasile wrapped in comfortless anxiety. The Neptune statue, wearing an older naval peacoat flapping at his knees, stood feet shoulder-width apart in the shifting sands. Strong hands that once shoved me down pushed deep into heavy wool pockets. Chocolate wavy hair lashed at a stern face's thick stubble. The coat and impressive wave crash cracked the crusty air, hopefully masking my thrashing heart. Engulfed by shameful failures, I failed to form wise words or a coy greeting and just stared at him.

Vasile's lips moved, but the gale deafened the graveled flat voice, so I cupped to an ear, "Sorry?"

He took several steps closer, and every nerve ending battled flight or fight instincts. "I said, you faced hell's bowels and risked yourself to return him to me."

I shook my head at the lonely ocean, and God powered to whittle the hardest mountains into grains of nothing. Time and water forged as complicit criminal partners to erase all traces of anything. "Not quite Hell, but close. Going there was an accident, but while there, I bumped into The Creator, and they agreed to help."

Though our bodies faced the stormy sea, not each other, I still heard his familiar haunted voice. Distrustful skepticism slowed his words. "He claims you bring me a proposal."

"Yep." Supernatural ears picked up my horse whisper across the noisy landscape.

"You owe me the facts, no matter the anguish."

I sighed, "That's where you are wrong. I don't owe you anything. I owe a God, who I made a deal with to save yours and Dmitri's life. God owns me now, not you."

"I see. Perhaps start at the beginning?"

While I listed the details about Purgatory and the facts I learned while there, windblown sands scraped stranded seaweed like our raw emotions. I kept the accounting factual because frivolity bored the emotionless monster. Only the gale shifted the flapping coat while I confessed the trickery surrounding Thomas's death and the belief that I committed murdered to control the truth. When I explain the details learned about The Father's betrayal, he never interrupted.

"I planned to tell you everything before we went to Romania because I didn't want anyone to use it against you."

Vasile flattened his response, "Is that so?"

I snapped, "Yes, that is so. If Dmitri knew anything, I didn't want him in more trouble. I had eighteen years, not centuries, to learn how to handle family drama."

"How kind of you." For days I prepared for an abusive onslaught, but it never came. A deep-drawn-out sigh hissed into the subsiding wind. The tidal breakers and shore exhibited the effects of our risky relationship. An unrelenting lunar tug stretched everything in opposite directions each time they met.

"Right then. As I said, God devised a bloodless arrangement and returned Dmitri and me."

"Why?"

"I don't get the question."

"Why return you with the Prince?"

"To save my life so that I could carry out their plan."

"Save your life?"

"Twice. First, I refused to return to a life taken by a broken heart." I darted my eyes to read his expression but saw nothing. "Second time was sending D back with me. If you noticed him first, you might not murder me, and besides, they wish you on their team."

"They? More than one God?"

"No, just one. Look, I don't have time to explain nonbinary identities."

"Sarah, I'm lost."

"I told them that you'd kill me if you saw me again."

"But—"

"Your words, not mine." Weeks of gut-wrenched emotions fashioned from lifeless words.

The disapproving wind howled and ripped at Vasile's voice. "I see."

"You see."

"Sarah, I said horrible things. I could never harm you, and you know that, right?"

The dance across slippery shards of a broken heart and bottled life-changing feelings left no energy for our typical row. My factual response burned my mouth. "Look, I get how your culture sees betrayal, so I kinda don't blame your reaction. But love, not prodistic manipulation, held my secret."

"You've changed."

"Yeah. I met you."

"Sarah, I of all people appreciate misplaced, noble motives because I made plenty of them. The inexcusable trust requires time to rebuild, and Dmitri and I need that time."

"Good. I guess."

"Ego aside, the real quarrel lies with my creator, not you."

I plucked the precious bag from my coat pocket and thrust the small bag towards him. Any more words would derail my plan to walk out of his life, so I concentrated on tinkling metal inside the green pouch. "Take it."

"I would love to see what you brought me, but the sun soon rises."

At his mention, I turned my head to observe whiter sea caps and a lighter night sky. Hints of an unstoppable sunrise obeyed the insistent universe's call. I thrust a hand into the velvet and extracted the God's golden ring. When I raised the jewel level to a worried stare, the opal cracked the moonlight into a million glittered sparks. "Stay. God's gotta plan."

A wrinkled, tilted forehead examined the unexpected jewelry, and a bright spark caught a glinted pupil, he blinked. "The ring is the plan? Sarah, I must go. Now." He shot the lightened sky, one more suspicious glance.

"A weapon."

"Weapon?"

"To you from God, and probably no love."

"Why me?" The creature of my heart transfixed on the gorgeous jewel tugging on frayed soul threads.

"The why comes later. Put it on. It protects an immortal from the sun—and daylight spells." I again shoved the warm jewel towards the slack-jawed monster.

"Are you telling me?"

"Yes, Vas. I'm telling you." I cloaked my anxiousness to leave with lacking patience to coddle. "Take it so I can explain the strategy, and I can get out of here. I've gotta human life I want to live."

Vasile's cold, chapped hand avoided my touch when he plucked the large ring from my blueish fingers. "Impossible."

"Try it. And hey—" I shrugged, "—if you die, I can bring you back."

"For a millennium while locked in night's tomb, I never glimpsed—"

The mournful cornflower sky looked pretty to me but meant dust to a prod. "Just put it on. I'd rather not perfect the new life-saving abilities."

I longed to watch the love of my life witness the first sunrise in a thousand years. How I lived a few months with no sun, and he tolerated no natural light for an eternity, boggled anyone's mind. When my conscience released minuscule sympathy, my jaw tightened because the more time I spent with him, the more he again risked my freewill.

Laser intensity searched me for truthful answers. "Truly?"

"It'll work."

"I—I trust you, Sarah." The weighted word 'trust' sunk into my thirsty heart.

While the perfectly fit opal jewel glided past a large knuckle, I blurted the plan's details. The way the fire gem glinted a million colors and replicated the morning's soft glow, I think God trapped a sun fragment in the gem. A lighter inky sky emptied its belly of violet storm clouds. A pale-yellow sliver eased over the ocean horizon, and diluted sunrays sparkled whitecaps and my lethargic face. White-gold tendrils raised across the water and up the wet sand. Inch by inch, the warmer rays illuminated his feet, then spotlighted a wondrous look. He splayed his fingers to examine his ash-free hands.

A gasp strangled his throat when he sunk to knees, stunned, arms limp, and palms faced a long-forgotten constant. Blood eyes riveted to the horizon as life-giving light warmed olive skin. Wavy hair glimmered orange highlights when a salty wind breeze tickled his head. When the entire yellow orb cleared the turmoiled rollers, he winced strained sensitive eyes. The star became his alchemist when its light changed a guarded monster to an enthralled child. Vasile sobbed, laughed, and dropped to a crouch, his head bowed. The emotionless control freak acted like a bloody lunatic released from a sanitorium.

After he rose to his feet much calmer, he twirled around to face me. The puzzled immortal scrutinized the dunes, and the parking lot behind me then spun towards the ocean. Vas, unable to absorb the forbidden pastel details, he turned in dizzying circles. While glancing from a new ring to fresh sun, he closed his eyes as a long-lost memory warmed his chapped face. Night's creature, birthed from black magic, walked in the light as the sun inched higher towards an unknown day and era. God knew best. I hoped.

When he recalled my shivering presence, a boyish face remembered from a distant dream or time, beamed me a brilliant smile. A hot eighteen-year-old guy, not a thousand-year-old monster, dashed straight for me. Before I took another step backward, he scooped up me and wrapped me inside strong arms. Wild red and chocolate hair entwined as we dizzily whirled on the sand. Like the night we met, my feet left the ground, and I don't think they ever touched Earth since that time. After a few seconds, he set me on wobbling legs and captured my hands. We studied our joined our hands before I pulled back. But he tightened his grasp, careful not to hurt me. An unhealthy love wielded too much power over both of us. "Looks like you decided not to tear out my throat."

"Sarah." Again, an emotional face pointed towards the sun, a reasonable distance above the sea.

"Not happening, Vas." I yanked my hands from his and stepped back. A great whoosh exhaled my breath at the same time a wave gobbled at packed sand. His face told me everything I needed to know. "Rejection hurts, so get used to it. I did."

I again shoved the small bag at him. "Take it. Inside is enough daylight rings for the entire Companion Guard guys, err people."

"Excuse me?" I presented a child a bag of forbidden candy because Vasile snatched the pouch to dig inside. Various rings tinkled deep in the unassuming pouch. "They look familiar."

"They're Dmitri's. I enchanted the lot. And he already wears his."

"He saw the sun!?"

"Yeah."

"How?"

"How did he see the sun?"

"No, how did you do this?" as he held up the pouch.

I grinned at his shock because, for once, I out smartened the chancellor. He removed an oversized, garish Victorian ring then shoved it at the sun. "Quite gaudy things for such a noble purpose. May I presume Dmitri chose these?"

"We are talking about D. He never asks for permission."

He grinned. "Quite."

"Dmitri planned to give Nikola that obnoxious thing."

We paused before we roared with comedic relief. The jewel dropped into the bag, then he inspected two more jewels, whispering conquest ideas into his fevered brain. "Again, how?"

I shrugged. "An entrusted spell. But God made your ring, not me, so try not to lose it."

He shot me a very 'Vasile' look. "Can you make more?"

"When I have your ring, but it's hard. I'd have come sooner, but it takes a ton of time and energy to craft those things."

"With these, we can—"

I read the military instincts claiming the childish exuberance. "That's the idea." I shoved whipping tangled strands of salted hair from my obscured my vision. When absent the bag's weighty responsibility, I craved the deadly trap of his spinning embrace. "Look, I gotta go."

"I have more—"

"Here's the plan," I warned the interested chancellor about the incoming assault and advised him to hand out the rings to the loyal soldiers. If a cohesive military unit wore the jewels, they stood a chance against a magic assault.

"Why attack us now?"

"My betrayal started it, and Dmitri's death only encouraged them. You need to take these to Romania now because they are on the move. I feel it."

"Every coven?" The immortal glanced past a shoulder, expecting to catch a stalking nemesis.

"Every coven."

"Can you not talk with them?"

"You saw how well it went last time." I studied my feet, fists clenched inside jacket pockets.

"Thank you. I—I—"

"See Vas; I brought the covens together after all." I turned, and as planned, I walked away.

When I grabbed my tattooed forearm from behind, my skin trembled, and the snake tattoo hissed in my mind. He released my arm like he touched a cobra. I faced away from him, towards an existence absent Vasile Simeon.

"Sarah." My floating name mingled with hungry seagull squawks.

I pulled towards the car lot as my resolve teetered. "Let me *go*." A crashing wave drowned out the word 'go.'

Vas smoothed husky and warm after he clasped my arm once more, "Sarah."

"Let *me* go." I sobbed, "Let me and my arm go. Don't do this to me anymore."

"Please," he implored after clasping my frigid hand.

Anger replaced heartbreaking despair and spun me wildly to face him. A gust ripped at the commanding God's thick wool coat, slapping at his locked legs. Trepidation, anger, and joy transformed into renewed purpose. The immortal politician knew an unassuming green velvet bag held more than his future, but his people's dreams and lives. The chancellor took charge once more.

"Vas, everything that was done and said cannot be changed no matter how hard you try to manipulate my heart. These extra powers can't turn clocks backward, but they can sure as hell make me forget about you. Don't make me hurt you to walk away."

"No, my love, you can turn back the clocks, but I created one you refuse to touch." He touched my cheekbone, "You don't have to do anything, let me adjust the time for you."

Before I roared a retort, one yank on my coat lapels pulled me into his arms. A single finger across my chin upturned my teary face. Pages from the countless emotional volumes written during Vasile's dutiful existence begged for my eyes. Though I irrevocably loved him, crossing that intimate bridge again risked more than my sanity. Besides, the Champion of Bulgaria had to save him, and I had a human life to go live. Neither of us needed a silly distraction. Everything he said to me in Maine made sense.

"What, Vas?"

"I cannot return to Romania alone. You heard my general."

"Oh. I see."

"The acting chancellor could try to seize the rings if we survive the attack."

"You never change, and I understand the actual reason you want me to stay."

"No. No, you possibly cannot, but I shall make you understand." He caught my pants belt loop and dragged me closer. Lips and willpower crashed while tedious strength and resolve dissolved into vague oblivion. The chilled touch traveled up my cheeks and ensnared in tangled my curls. The invading kiss branded my mouth as the warming ocean smells, and his neck's familiar aroma mingled into one seductive fragrance. Hot tears dripped along my salt-encrusted face, and tension released me into the recognizable tall frame. Across oceans of time and hard sentiments, I flew home.

The unexpected hungry passion itched my healed tattoo. Muddled visions of a hardened monster ripping me off him and the toss to the floor like unnecessary trash cleared most of the wrong desire. When I stiffened, he parted our swollen lips, clutched me tightly, and rested a worried forehead against mine. A long finger removed a stray curl plastered to my face.

"Words cannot express my sorrow for the hurt I caused."

I cleared away from the intoxicating embrace. "I get it. Besides blowing our chance, you've got a long road ahead. Just think you were right all along. Love for leaders should be about duty, not personal cares."

"I see."

"You always saw Vasile. I'll meet you in Romania."

Before I shifted a sneaker, he lifted my limp hand, bent at the waist, then planted his free hand behind his back. Vas upturned my hand to expose a wrist. When warm lips met my blue veins, keeping eye contact from under his lowered brow, my ears whooshed from a raging pulse.

"Your heart, Miss Wardwell."

"I know."

CHAPTER 24

The perfect monster buffet

THE DENSE CITY OF CLUJ clustered city lights, then spidered them into the vast darkness. The arriving private plane proved a view of a black winding river and its steep banks buttressed by crammed dwellings. Humans packed into the urban landscape surrounded by countryside. The headquarters of the terrifying creatures on Earth bottlenecked people behind walls, falsely believing proximity to others kept away fabled monsters. But little did the ignorant Lessers know, they created the perfect monster buffet.

"Ready?" Dmitri extended a wrist towards his eyes.

"I guess." I waved a hand in front of my flushed face, dreading the landing. "I hate flying."

"And I hate suits."

"But you look hot."

"Of course, I do. I am Prince Svetoslav, after all."

"Dear God. Why did I bring you back from the dead?"

"Because I am Prince Svetoslav."

I ignored a thump under the aircraft. "I swear—"

"You are cute when aggravated."

"I'll change my mind and blast you with the sun if you don't be quiet."

He raised his hand and waggled his fingers. "Can't."

"D, shut up!"

"Poppet."

"What!?"

"We landed. My little distraction worked."

I snapped shade shut. "Cheater."

"But you love me."

"I do." I unbuckled, then kissed his cheek. "Let's get this done."

Two silent women dressed in severe gray pantsuits met us at a small private airport. The security guards wore colored contacts, but an instinctual mother still arm yanked children to her side, away from the scary stern females. Once we sat in a limousine, a terse female shoved a wad of blue cloth in my direction. In broken English, she demanded I place it over my overhead. Tense words and icy stares suggested they detested my kind. Warned about the possible cool treatment, I showed no emotions.

The grumpy guards glared at Dmitri after he clasped my hand. Dmitri snarled, "You regard your Prince and the Queen Regent. Avert your eyes lest I remind you of your place."

In the chorus, they echoed, "Yes, Your Royal Highness." Score a point for D! I never witnessed my best friend chill others into silence, I covered my head with the sack while grinning.

The limo bumped and hummed along ancient cobblestone streets before the sleek car stopped for a few minutes.

Dmitri snapped, "I shall escort the Queen."

"Yes, Your Royal Highness."

Dmitri guided my elbows from the car to the road. When someone removed the ridiculous blindfold, blurred vision focused, I discovered we stood before a towering gothic cathedral that dissolved in the inky night sky. Under weak streetlamps clustered a few tourists staring up at the endless stone structure. Dmitri told me how seven hundred years ago, immortal workers tunneled under the architecture to construct hives of offices, courts, and chambers. Unlike the blindfold, the granite and marble mountain concealed a hidden government. Mages long perfected the art of intimidation illusions, so I eyerolled at their smoke and mirrors.

Past the thick front doors and the golden altar, limitless torches flickered along a dim walkway. From heavy stone, a sooty silence ladled secrets from an archaic age. Large rows of sandstone columns unraveled into the swallowing shadows. I recognized where masons once march inside to prevent the sun's deathly intrusion and walled off tall stained-glass windows. Breathing as Annalyse, I walked the church halls that knew no religion. Centuries later, under an alias, I again braced my soul deep in the Immortal Nation's belly.

Though I finally crafted and executed a flawless strategy, the next steps required a measure of their guarded trust. The unnatural players must believe me too meek to zap anyone with a fatal daylight spell. Failure to convince prod politicians and guards of good intensions prevented a deeper delve into the sacred hive. I needed to go further. So, the immortals only detected fear replaced by diplomatic confidence. A nugget of thought bore me strength. Prods lacked any capability to imprison or kill me because when not crafting daylight rings, I honed new magical skills. Besides, if events soured, I always had plan B. Break the Immortal Nation's succulent spine.

Though marching long, my young bones ached older than the confining halls, I emulated the confident leader, Count Simeon. At my sides, I smoothed my white gauzy dress, glad I swapped torn jeans and sloppy sneakers. A braid dangled down my back, and light makeup accented delicate facial features. An ethereal high-priestess breezed behind stiff guards, ignorant the mage in tow concealed a weapon capable of ending history's longest war.

The pouch, the size of a small hand, contained an immense responsibility and weighed each assured step. Thanks to my best friend's help, I strapped the unassuming velvet bag to an inner thigh before we landed, and thus hid hope for the fated world. I avoided thinking about the chaffing between my legs because if anyone discovered the divine rings, the game ended.

After a long echoing walk through thin incense clouds, Dmitri said, "This is where we must part, and I find the man of the hour."

"But—" Dmitri winked a goodbye before the murky shadows swallowed him whole. But thanks to his confession of his nerves while traveling to Romania, his reassuring wink missed the mark.

After my best friend left, my two glowering guards ordered to wait alone. Maybe they wanted the ominous ambiance to unwind my controlled nerves. Every creak and echo diluted by the damp gloom strained my senses until familiar murmurs behind a giant pillar caught my attention. Unwilling feet shifted me forward several inches, but the foreboding feeling that many watched me breath fastened me in place. So, I did what any magic dealer would do. I flexed my index finger and whispered, "Audite."

"She hides something. Tell me." Vasile's Eastern European accent sounded strained and pronounced.

Dmitri questioned, "Why do you say that?"

"She is not the same. She shifted."

Dmitri hissed, "After what she suffered? Your admonishment and a visit to Purgatory? I forgot my time there and cannot deal with the experience. She lives her memories."

"I concede to your anger, but alas I am worried—"

"You should have directed your temper tantrum at your creator and me, but not—"

Vasile cut his tirade off. "Betrayal weakens me."

"—not her. She deserved your last fleck of humanity."

"Son, I know—"

Dmitri hissed, "You realize nothing. The woman throws herself at a corrupt council for you—for all of us. You stole her spark and—"

"That is quite enough—"

"You changed too. Tore that girl to shreds then dared to convince her to come here? A selfish need to return to power." Dmitri summed up every grappled emotion concocted between England, Maine, and Romania.

Footsteps echoed and clipped their heated words clipped short. Two stern males, several feet taller than me, interrupted my eavesdropping and motioned me to follow. Inches from the floor, my cream-colored dress billowed behind me, and cool air whispered between my thighs. I folded my hands before my waist and pretended not to care where about the silent, endless corridors. A twinkle beckoned deep from the tunneled darkness. In moments, twenty feet high, ornate metal doors severed the hallway. Each strong sentinel strained against gold door handles until the groaning entry swung open. Beyond the sullen pair, a monstrous gray marbled room stretched wide stone jaws, eager to consume me.

Once in the space large enough to fit two small houses, I observed a gigantic table on a tall dais. I noticed no other furniture, only lit gas torches along the windowless walls. Slick gray-blue marble heaved and entwined white veins. Against the cold room's edges, formations of males wearing black suits and ornate red sashes across their chests waited for me. The stiff obedient soldiers stood not blinking or breathing. Behind the warrior, rows mingled well-dressed businesspeople, politicians, and dignitaries.

I grew glad for the hours I studied Vasile's regal mannerisms, and the falsified confidence breezing me into the arena. No curious or angry stares flicked my way but a collective consciousness of stony regard. Better set the tone and force their attention. Thirty gas-fed flickering torches around the auditorium diminished to cigarette lighter size when, in my mind, my tattooed snake bit down on its mouthed apple. Delicate skin itched, and for several seconds, flames scorched to life as mini flame throwers. I directed my feet at the stunned crowd and radiated invisible electric shards across the vast icy floor towards them. When the reptilian fangs sunk into the apple, the buzzing energy shot from the marble and drilled into stiff legs. Tingled shivers ran along stalwart spines. I unlocked their immobile dead stares. I snapped and dissipated the vibrations as I assumed the designated position pointed by a blinking guard, center on a polished football field. If only Maggie saw the powerful spectacle.

Standing to the raised dais's left side, Vasile and Dmitri wore matching black suits, but D sported a military sash. But even the common entry guards displayed official-looking ribbons across their chests. Vas looked out of place and ordinary, and the stark contrast thinned my lips. I wondered if he suffered humiliation from the lacking suit because he showed no emotion.

Seven males wearing silk judge's robes used a small side entrance to file in the courtroom and amputated my troubling observation. Each stern officiant took a seat on the raised table to conduct their perverse civic duty. At the center, a shorter individual sat a foot higher. The easily spotted fake politician sported the only black sash in the hall. Other sitting officiants, from various nationalities, wore light purple sashes. The elitist prods might act chauvinistic but not racists. Equal curious stares, teeming with eons of shared history, returned my firm stare.

The Immortal Nation's committee and false chancellor glared down at an underestimated wispy girl. The small-eyed pretender twisted his head sideways like a nostril flared raven. My skin crawled. He lacked every noble trait and dashing characteristic Vasile embodied. Rodent features and skinny body suggested someone cursed a ponytail-wearing weasel into a prod. So much for a perfect application process choosing quality humans. As a human, that guy got beaten up regularly at school.

A silver-haired prod at the end of the table banged a gavel. "Call to order."

When the weasel's falsetto voice opened the proceedings, hard judgments from both sides paused. For a change, my facial muscles obeyed my brain and froze. Accustomed to Dmitri's and Vasile's grumbled accents, the acting chancellor's lyrical Italian laced English sounded odd. "Before us stands self-professed queen, Sarah Wardwell." The councilmen's shrewd gaze and the gloating ringleader scanned the silent crowd and chilled more than bones. "I briefed the assembly on the dangers that woman poses. We appreciate her shocking willingness to appear, but must examine her motive, no? For those new to these proceedings—I ask the questions, then councils passa the judgment."

What trial? For a nanosecond, Dmitri's eyebrows furrowed. I walked into a first-class trap that lacked powers to hold me, but capable of ripping my loved ones to shreds.

"Fire away." The chamber absorbed my voice's timbre.

Stolen from Vasile's playbook, the weasel pretended I never spoke. "Did you complete tha Queen Regent Prophesy?"

"Yes. Therefore, the proper address is Queen, Your Majesty, or my favorite, Queen Regent Wardwell." A sneaky stare stole to Chancellor Simeon, who once said something similar. Score a point for Team Sarah.

Already thin lips disappeared. "You possess occult powers your peers do not, si?"

My slow, annunciated words tightened the proverbial noose around his skinny neck. "I have no peers. But yes, I have unmatched abilities." My chin raised before I poked the fanged bear.

"You only confirm what we know, but those attending should hear our offer—delicate arrangement," dramatically clearing his throat.

"Arrangement?" All eyebrows rose.

"I become your maker. As immortal, you notta threat but an asset, si?" Not a single jaw dropped, or hair moved, only the wind whistled through the catacomb. After the shocking proposal received no reaction, "If you survive, we welcome with rights befitting tha citizens." The stinky political power play stunk from evil reasons. The notion of drinking a rodent's blood almost curled my lip. 'Fat chance, Bucko.'

The council granted applications on rare occasions because prodigia revered the offer of change. A strict population control permitted new creatures when my kind killed them. The perverse laws, centered on long application traditions that formed an elitist immigration policy, concluded by death or immediate naturalization. Lucky for me, it's what and who you know.

After the smug ass-hat presented the perceived glorious opportunity, he paused. He blinked fast. Did he expect platitudes of gratitude? Let them stew in my silence. The weasel's features pinched while the other councilors froze passive expressions. One might have heard a fang drop on the frozen marble as my thighs flexed around the soft strapped bag.

366

"What say you, Sarah Wardwell?"

Everyone's breath held swirled supernatural energies through the tense chamber. Unbeknownst to them, a single finger snap powered by the multiplying force would kill the entire crowd. Tempting, right? From my peripheral vision, Vasile's fist clenched, and for a brief second, everything paused. I wanted him to experience a hurt greater than the one he inflicted the night he walked away from me. I contemplated backing the wrong chancellor and let him watch his entire species implode. Hello darkness, my old friend, it's me again.

"No." The control freaks' leaked gasp greatly rewarded me, but I stared straight ahead.

"I place Sarah Wardwell in custody pending sentencing. Next. Case 1974VN23, Immortal Nation versus Grand Duke Vasile Simeon. Pending charges include treason and absent without leave from military service." My wish to hurt Vas dissipated when the acting chancellor stood, and two guards approached me from both sides.

No way he expected a trial, so I had to take control. "No, he will not," I commanded the chamber's soul, and those standing inside the hollow marble. After I pictured my arm's snake coil tighter, every dead organism froze. The mystical branding- bit the apple hard, and bodies shivered.

A scowling Victor leaned against the glossy table. "How dare you—"

"No! How dare—you? I entertained your little Kangaroo Court long enough, so here are the Queen Regent's terms—Vic." Once haughty council members flushed furious beet-colors.

With one swift move and a rip of Velcro, I lifted the front of my dress and crushed the velvet bag in my hand. I hoisted the fabric above my head. A councilor's squeezed lips advertised displeasure over guards missing the hidden velvet.

"The impertinence—"

I raised my voice above an elevating clamor. "Listen! Mages are forming a massive attack while you waste time. I hold the only weapon able to stop them." I pushed forward, rippled energy waves, and crackled static electricity around everyone's heads. Victor returned to his chair and enthralled gazes locked on the lowering jewelry bag.

Victor's elevated pitch exclaimed, "Offer rescinded. Anything further before immediate sentencing?"

My chin poked towards the high table. "In this bag are magical rings that protect the wearer from sunlight and daylight spells." For effect, I jingled the pouch, and inaudible murmurs elevated to an echoing roar. Thunderstruck immortals and abandoned programmed discipline, and the slimy chancellor lost control of his play. Everyone continued with rowdy reactions while passive Vas stared at thin air. Dmitri girlishly giggled and nudged an elbow at his brother-in-law.

Victor stood then his flat hand banged the marble table. "Silence!" Military machines ignored the directive, opting to talk, point, and stare. After several nasal screams for silence, Vasile thrust a fist into the air. Everyone at once silenced. The white knuckles lowered when everyone regained composure. Contained pride burned my chest after he demonstrated who controlled the masses. One minute I strained to roast everything he ever loved, and the next, I wished him to again command my soul the same way.

"Impossible. A childish ploy to buy more time for tha fallen, Simeon. No?"

I lowered the soft bag, not my intense glare. "The proper address for your lord remains Chancellor Vasile Simeon, the Champion of Bulgaria, or a personal favorite of mine, Imperial Highness. The Father gave the leader rank to his chosen son. Victor, you are seven times removed from The Father, so give -a little respect."

Victor's head wiggled, ready to pop off his body. "Immediately—"

I was on a roll. "By the way, the legitimate leader already has a ring." More shock from the awe gathering spurred more courageous words. "I'm sure he'll testify to its authenticity." The tense conflict exploded, and raucous talks erupted. Poor Vasile, who valued exhausting preparation, did not understand what came next.

"What say you, Chancellor Simeon?"

The steely immortal slowly faced the preening weasel but stared at the air above the rat's head. "I received such a gift and since witnessed many sunrises."

A councilor elevated a shock question above the raucous din. "Will you subject to a Blood Calling, Chancellor Simeon?"

"Yes. I permit it."

I rose a hand to giggle at the word choice, but Dmitri beat me to it. "The sheriff is back in town, miboys!"

An African councilman signaled, "I motion for the Truth Scribe to administer the Blood Calling. Do I hear a second?"

"Motion seconded."

"Third."

"Objection, no set precedence compelling a chancellor to the summit to—"

"Overruled."

"Seconded."

Third."

"Very well, motion sustained. Approach, Simeon."

A renegade councilor muttered, "Such vile indignity—"

Vasile raised a hand and leveled a kind gaze at the upset officiant, then reported before the lifted table. He stood with exceptional military rigidity. A five-foot-tall female materialized from behind a row of virile males. The Egyptian-like goddess wore flowing robes with kohl-rimmed eyes, and white hair brushed polished marble when she shuffled to the front. When she quaked before her sire, she executed a curtsy capable of snapping a mortal's knees.

"Imperial Highness."

Vasile's nod released her from the deep greeting. He leveled an arm to the floor, pulled up a jacket sleeve, and exposed an olive-colored wrist. The priestess's trebling dress fabric and twisting lips suggested the rite fell outside her comfort zone.

"Do you, Chancellor Vasile Mihail Simeon, Grand Duke of the Simeon family, Champion of Bulgaria, Commander-in-Chief to The Companion Guards, and one true son to The Father, offer blood as proof of truth?" Vasile's eyes sparkled, and a culture's pride swelled everyone's chest except for the few loyal to Victor.

"You may begin, Truth Scribe."

The petite woman stood taller than Vasile's mid-chest. A palmed golden bowl hoisted under a stubby curved knife poised under his wrist. The blade trembled until Vasile softly nodded once and steadied her hand with his. The aged immortal returned the gesture and squared her shoulders. After a quick deep slice, an inky crimson stream splattered into the lifted dish. The hollow chamber amplified the splashing blood. Supernatural healing cauterized in seconds, and the wound and stopped the flow. He fixed his sleeve once he lowered his arm and resumed a far-off gaze. The ritual priestess peered inside the ceramic before she raised the red liquid to puckered lips. After a noisy slurp, a distant stare catapulted her into another dimension as small hands tightened around the ceremonial bowl. The officiant's face slacked. "It—it—" When the vessel shattered in her trembling fingers, shards and leftover life force dirtied the immaculate floor.

The murmurs again climbed. "Truth Scribe, what say you? Does such a ring exist?" Victor scanned the ancient woman's red watering eyes.

Lips moved, but it took seconds for sound to go with words. "I saw the sun! I saw the beautiful sun through his Imperial Highness." The Egyptian female smeared red across her weathered cheek before performing another deep curtsy for Vasile.

Above the shook chatter, my impassioned tone silenced the courtroom. "Here are my terms."

"Each member of The Companion Guards will get defeat the incoming attack as soon as the council at once reinstates Chancellor Simeon." Full chaos erupted. Males forgot military composure, and dignitaries their dignity as they shouted, laughed and cheered. Victor screamed for silence. Nobody obeyed. Dmitri's chest quaked while Vasile's ring index finger tapped a leg.

Long overdue for a domination demonstration, I brushed a hand past my breasts, "Silentium!" Magic transformed the rowdy crowd into excited, silent statues. "Better. As I was saying, when the true chancellor resumes power, you get the rings. Failure to comply, and I destroy the only thing that may save you." I held up the bag. "These jewels." Again, my arm swept across the room. The air roared.

I analyzed Vasile's closed expression and his two tapping fingers. To the untrained, Vasile acted unphased, but to me, he looked pissed as hell. As much as he hated uncontrolled situations, he detested secrets.

Dumbfounded, Victor behaved the opposite. When I saw the humanoid weasel bested, I internally cheered with the crowd. The fake politician brushed the air with his copycat chancellor ring. "Seize tha bag and execute tha witch."

I again waved, expecting the stupid move and chanted, "Rigescunt Indutae." Guards mid-run. Red-eyed shock devoured the pouch when they realized their plight. No jewel protected them from the undisputed Queen Regent. Time to twist the knife with a white lie. "Not so fast. If I'm murdered, the rings turn to dust. You have one hour to deliberate on my offer. Oh, and if Chancellor Simeon or Prince Svetoslav is killed? I will obliterate your chances to see the sun and The Father's tomb." Had I predicted The Father's future actions when he awoke from his three-century slumber, I would have honored the dramatic threat. But I'll tell you that story later. When I splayed fingers, guards stumbled, and the nervous crowd shifted.

"Call to motion. Those in favor of reviewing the matter say, aye." A smattering of 'ayes' echoed the chamber.

"Point of order, councilor!"

"Chancellor Victor, I recognize no point of order and commence the vote. Those opposed say nay."

An equal 'nays' trickled past the table.

The presiding chocolate-skinned counselor called "Division! Clear the bar!" Based on the witnessed proceedings, I knew what parliament inspired England's government. I shuddered to think who served as party whip and their tactics.

Red-faced, Victor stared down the steadfast councilors who hamstrung his orchestrated show. But the despot obeyed official procedures rooted in ancient traditions. Weasel Vic needed the chance provided by the recess to choose between weaponized rings capable of defeating enemies and his reign or face Vasile's loyal supporters. Whichever he decided, he had better decide wisely and leave my adopted family alone.

"Sarah Wardwell, we remand you into custody during deliberation."

I shot stoic Vas and worried D a ferocious look. The fight just began.

"Your hour started ten minutes ago, gentlemen. Lose the weasel and get the rings or die." A finger snap commenced a phantom clock tick.

I haughtily grinned and followed guards from the chamber. Behind me, I heard a councilman release, Vasile, into Dmitri's custody. When I passed the last immortal row of soldiers, I glimpsed Nikola's shiny bald head. He and three others lowered their gazes and hid fists placed over their hearts. A great general saluted an eighteen-year-old mage, and I hoped he never regretted the gesture. The rare respect, reserved for high-ranking officers and the chancellor, about chipped my polished veneer but added more confidence.

* * *

The jail inflicted a petulant attitude because of heated threats, and underground dungeons unserved their creators. After I visited with God and passed the actual test, I commanded not one but four natural elements. Better yet, I prepared. From the moment I resurrected my best friend until I walked in the immortal capital, for countless hours, I honed magical skills until my nose bled. In the past, my status quo as a constant victim prevented me from saving loved ones. However, the stronger magic granted invincibility against prods and new composure became a reliable trait. My previous trademark meltdowns solved nothing and only embroiled me in more trouble.

My self-satisfied reflection broke. A hundred insignificant whispers danced aloft in the stale air. "We come. We come. We come."

I groaned, "It's too soon."

Before I left the United Kingdom, I cast a heavy cloaking spell to hide my location. So, I knew fellow occultists amassed not to end me but finish the creatures they blamed for our magic's demise. Based on the growing smell of rot, I had an hour before the attack. I chewed my lip while staring at the holding cell's moldy wall. The plan failed if the prodigia believed they jailed a magical trojan horse.

I paced the room and relived every scene. The velvet bag crushed in my hand as I hoped the council soon accepted the presented terms. I prayed Vasile, and Dmitri stayed safe until the ridiculous session resumed. If something happened to them, I long resolved to start with the original sleeping prod then burn down his entire nation. I never met The Father, but his selfish decisions cost me everything.

A key rattled a locking mechanism while lost in miserable speculations, and the heavy metal entrance swung open. Guards snapped aside to permit someone to pass. Before I knitted my brows, Vasile, ignoring the crisp salutes, marched over the threshold. I jumped to my feet. The sentry's observation never strayed into the room as the door shut. A weak smile hid my urge to race into his capable arms. "How did you get in here?"

Silence fashioned a pregnant moment before he confessed, "You never told me about your strategic demands." Someone unfamiliar with Vasile might infer anger brewing under the surface. But not me. I watched a stunning male grapple for the right words to express foreign emotions.

"I didn't."

"Why?"

"Kinda a last-minute thing. You know me, always making things up."

"No, Sarah. You planned this night long before my first sunrise. Vas's face reddened, and his chest shook a bit.

"Don't be mad!"

"And you call me calculating." A playful wink released my hissing exhale.

"If you knew my plans, I would not be here now."

"Quite."

"Besides, it's a twofer."

"Twofer?"

"Two for the price of one. As your weapon to stop the war, your people get peace, and you return to the office."

"I see."

A persisting unreadable expression began my usual babbling. "Right then. A bit over the top when I threatened your maker."

"Twas bloody brilliant!"

The surprise praise showed my worthiness to play at the adult's table. I dropped my raised shoulders. "I got better at planning. At least I didn't lie about killing my Mum while jogging to the nearest station."

His grin matched mine. "There's that."

"So, where's D?"

"With Nikola, doing what they do the best—conspiring."

"That's not good."

"Never fear, the chaps might torch the capital if things go awry." An infectious smile dimpled his shaved cheeks.

"I can see Dmitri now, running down the halls lighting everything on fire while belting, 'I'm Henry VIII, I am.'" Bubbled titters unleashed his great belly laugh. We caught our breath after a minute. When our merry expressions sobered, Vas stepped a foot closer.

"You seem in good spirits despite that lame trial."

"One does what they must and carries on."

"Will Victor step down?"

"The crafty weasel will seek council with his uncouth allies and perverse your terms. Trust nobody."

I sat on the edge of the bed. "But you got in here somehow?"

He perched on a thin wooden chair as a wrist unbuttoned his tailored jacket. "The guards appreciate the old days. Since I returned, I listened to countless troubling stories about the goings-on."

"I can imagine."

"Sarah?"

"Yeah? I mean, yes?"

"Where will you go when freed? Tis not right of me to ask."

Chilled anger lowered my tone. "You're right. Not your problem."

He jumped from his seat and sat next to me. I jerked when the thin mattress bowed me into his hard body, and Vas collected my limp hands. I avoided eye contact and fought to keep my resolve to leave him forever in my past. My skin slithered free.

"Sarah."

I stood and snarled at his forlorn look. "Did you forget when Dmitri died? Do I need to tell you about what I faced when bringing him back?" Tight air crackled around the tiny room while I white-knuckled the ring bag.

"You changed."

"No limitless powers or leadership changed me, but you."

"Sarah, I erred, and will regret my actions for the next thousand years!"

"Right."

"Look at me."

"Sod off."

"Please?"

"Go wallow for the rest of my natural life."

"I deserved that." When he walked over to me to skid fingers across my flushed cheek, I wished to lose myself inside those strong arms. "I caused all this?"

I spun away when the gentle touch soothed buried pain. "What do you think?"

He grabbed my biceps- and spun me. "Forget my earlier conditions to become a couple. Join me now."

Eyes popped open. "Excuse me?"

"You may stay human."

"What are you saying?"

"You know, Sweet One."

"I can't." Catapulting emotions loaded into one inaudible whisper, ready to launch at his psyche.

"I refuse your refusal."

"You can't use ref—"

He clasped my cheeks to force eye contact. "We loved and hated each other across seas of time and water. I cannot wait another three hundred years to find you again." Vasile's complicated feelings penetrated my bones instead of his bone marrow sucking fangs.

"You're juggling a political and occult war, so there's no place—"

He cut my words when he softly shook me once. "Your place is at my side as my wife."

"Your—I can't—" I could not look at the assuming bastard.

"If you faced the council, surely you can face our destiny. You can."

My next breath hitched when his branding words ingrained in my mental tomb of memories. "Do you know what you are asking? I never lived life on my terms. Some bad playwright wrote my part in someone else's playbook, filled with awful plotlines and sucky dialogue." Utmost gentleness tucked me well inside protective but hurtful arms, and a shaky grasp cradled my skull. He stoked my smoldering worship brighter."

"Say yes, my darling."

"You don't go under—"

"Three simple letters. Say them."

"Wait—"

"That's four letters. Try again." He nuzzled my jawbone.

To sensitive paranormal ears, I crooned low, "I'll love you until the last and enough to let you go. Take the freedom I bring to lead and fix the dying Earth."

"Sarah—"

"I hate it when you are right. You fail if I'm around to cloud your judgment."

His trembling arms tightened. "I refuse to do this alone. We earned this moment."

"You will do this," I murmured confidence. "Your people and the damn world needs you more. Take the supernatural helm for all our sakes."

"I shall never give you up."

Through gooey tears, I smiled and crossed my hidden fingers under his scratchy lapels. "That's what I love and hate about you. I need time, so big decisions today."

"Will you give us one more morrow?"

"Let's just live. Then we can talk when we get out of here." Vasile's serene face told me he bought the lie.

The next growled proclamation near an ear shivered the room's energy. "Nothing to fear, Sweet One. You refuse marital vows, so these are mine. I will pluck apart anyone who stands between us then spend lifetimes searching for you." The firm arms around my torso stiffened, and Vasile's breathing paused.

"Something—"

"Someone comes. Promise me not to say or do anything foolish?"

* * *

My drained soul sunk to the narrow and uncomfortable bed, too fatigued to cry. A voice rumbled beyond the closed metal door before a poker-faced guard clanked the lock and entered. General Nikola shadowed behind a straight finger across his pursed lips.

"I am to escort her."

"As you command, General."

"Ensure sure the barristers are ready."

"Sir, yes, sir."

When the obedient sentry left, a hawkish Nikola rushed to my side. "Milady, cast a spell to clog stray ears."

"Oh, God, what now?" I waved my hand and muttered, "Silentium."

He hurried, "Something is amiss."

"Like what?"

"Victor summoned our full military force to the sentencing." Head tilt from me prompted, "The whole army never attends unless we are under a major attack or The Father awakened."

"I'm guessing he is still asleep?"

"Yes, milady."

"So, what's up? Did they take my warning seriously about the occult attack?"

Nikola rubbed his scalp. "Doubt it, milady. I think it ties to the weasel knowing how every Companion Guard remained loyal to Chancellor Simeon."

I gulped. "So, he gets the perceived traitors in one spot. Is it too late to frame him for your murder?"

"If only, milady. The only way Victor executes Chancellor Simeon is if my comrades—"

"—are killed beforehand."

"Precisely."

"No way he kills everyone unless—"

We both voiced, "The incoming attack—"

General Bulldog went corpse pale. "You don't suppose, milady?"

"Suppose he's in league with the attacking mages? If you only knew why I believed such. What if we are overreacting, and it's a show of force while the nation witnesses his fall?"

"Vasile?"

"Chancellor Simeon."

"Right then. Kill the whole council, then turn our cares to the incoming battle."

"Something always goes wrong with hasty plans. I know."

He gritted his teeth and slicked a hand over his shiny bald head. "Me thinks the sneaky weasel's in bed with the witches—no offense m'Queen."

"None took. Just watch your back, and I'll do my best out there."

"We'll try to protect you, but—"

A touch to his meaty forearm paused the head rubbing, and a worried glower met mine. "General, mages are a dime a dozen, but there is only one Chancellor Simeon. All species die if corrupted officials, immune to sunlight, govern your—"

"Yes, but milady—"

"I have no right to my next words, but I order his safety above mine. Are we clear, General?"

The emboldened General raised and squared his jaw. "The Grand Duchess once said the same thing once across a time."

"And did you listen?"

"She died, right?"

"And I shall again to protect your leader."

"The Nation and I thank you for your sacrifice and service."

"You bet. Hey, since we are friends, may I call you Nikola?"

He extended an elbow. "You would deeply hurt me if you didn't."

"Shall we, my Queen?"

"Oh, Nikola?"

"Yes, milady?"

"Check your pocket."

"My—"

"You will know what to do."

When a beefy hand rose towards his chest, I nudged Nik's ribs. "Not now."

"Already a legend among my people milady. Come now, lass."

CHAPTER 25

Her majesty's harbinger

I AGAIN ENTERED THE hallowed chamber, my head impossibly high. Unlike the last occasion, a more massive crowd piled in the cavernous courtroom, filling it to capacity. As top general, the councilors awarded Nikola the honor of parading the Queen Regent through a sea of parted silent immortals to the center. Countless hate-filled crimson pupils radiated disdain, confusion, and distrust at the council and me. Other suited males, missing uniform sashes, stood to the left of the aisle while neat rows of polished soldiers formed on the right.

The prestigious Companion Guards warriors, hands clasped behind backs, claimed the honorary first row. Their embellished fabric swatches across beautiful suits far out shown other military personnel. Each time a soldier killed a mage, the individual sewed a silver star. Officers represented battle success with a bright moon for each won skirmish. Sashes of the oldest immortals displayed brilliant threads, absent a hint of red silk. Dmitri's sash, like Nikola's, glittered pure gold.

Attention on the stunning uniforms turned when ten hard-eyed females marched into the courtroom and lurked at the end of the formation. They sported matching pixie haircuts and muted pantsuits. The female's energies swirled deadlier than their male counterparts as they locked eyes front, hands also behind their back. The surprising women and recalling how only the prominent gathered during extreme events, shattered my belief that Prod's suffered a patriarchal society. Unlike other curious foot soldiers, court guards, or spectators, not a single feminine warrior's attention strayed. Deep inside, a proud and star-struck little girl clamored to become one of them. But the teenager wanted to dash towards them and run high fives down their row. But something predictable tore my awe from the spectacle.

Left of the tall dais, Vasile stood isolated and removed from a loyal army once under his command. Like the steely females, he gazed into blank space but kept his hands clasped at the front because he never placed his hands behind his back for anyone. Poised, controlled, and regal to the core, he projected unending intestinal fortitude to the questioning masses. A proud lion missing his sash surveyed at a pride taken from him. When I considered the stripped regalia, long-drawn air burned when I prevented a gushing sigh. A part of me detested the monster, but my entire soul loved Vasile, the man. I pursed my lips and mentally demanded to become the catalyst to alter the undignified uniform. How times and motives changed. I no longer planned failed escapes from galas and estates but plotted to free a whole species from tyranny and catastrophe.

The nasal weasel assumed the monster circus' ringleader role. "Sarah Wardwell, as a self-professed queen, you promise invincibility from our sworn enemies and offer an end to da slavery to tha masters who enslaved this nation." I ached to correct the idiot's timeline and bad English because the nation formed after their mastered severed the covenant between prod and mage. I raised a wrist to glance at an invisible watch while rocking on my feet. "We reviewed tha terms and question da motives. I afford you five minutes to explain the reasoning for your proposal."

When the shifty chancellor glanced at the closed doors behind me, Nik and I stiffened. Nothing added up. Why the concern over well-guarded entrance, and why give me extra time? We smelled a weasel.

"Immortal Nation, for centuries, we kill each other off while a third species destroys our shared planet. The Earth and pretty much everyone dies if the Species War does not end. The occult leaders refused my reign, but for the first time gathered for your destruction." Victor's hard eyes again flicked at the sealed doors behind me. "These rings secure independence and stop the bloodshed, but I will not help you usher in a new era with the wrong chancellor. Would you choose a guy who would deny my gift and risk your lives just to sit at that table?" I scanned the silent crowd. "You know what's right."

The civilian side grumbled, and the din grew to a loud growl.

I spoke louder and drove a spike to the heart. "Your nation teeters on a cliff, so let your proud culture and noble laws pull you back from a precipice of extinction. Because any minute they show up." Collective gasps revealed another successful plan, an enraptured audience. "If you choose wrong and I destroy my gift, you all find another death or re-enslavement." Underfoot, rising murmurs vibrated the marble floor.

Victor's pointy facial features missed the predictable flush. "Sarah Wardwell, I pass da judgment and sentence—"

As Victor crooned, his voice dulled, and my neck hairs stood as invisible vibrations condensed. Energy balls rolled off supernatural bodies and rolled towards the door. Decay tickled my nose. My hands fisted, while countless blinked. Soon I witnessed a moment humankind could not appreciate. But I shall explain.

Brutal Lowers depend on magnificent weapons and vast armies to wage warfare more atrocious than every Species War battle combined. Unlike the wall crumpling cannons used to siege Constantinople or the atom bomb that ended the Pacific War, paranormal use a quiet yet effective strategy. Our DNA fine-tuned us to life's tiny details and the appreciation of minuscule moments and movements. Only desensitized humans draw inspiration from ferocious atrocities. I unfolded the greatest supernatural battle in history, capable of great suffering and human disappointment.

A rumbling blast rocked the underground architecture when a shock wave rippled past the impenetrable doors. Cracks along the marble floor spidered towards our feet. Mouths dropped. Heads cracked at the entrance. Door guards exchanged puzzled glances. Someone beyond the sealed doors radiated a forcefield that increased the air pressure and crawled our skins. The shimmering energy collection, invisible to the prods, wrinkled the crowd's flickering auras.

Someone questioned, "Gas leak?" But I knew better.

A second explosion splintered the giant ancient doors wide open., and floating debris from the entry slammed against stone walls. The yawning cathedral above groaned and trembled. I strained to see past billowing dust plumes. Such chaos might send screaming humans running, but we stood firm.

After the smoke cleared and chunks finished raining on the calm audience, fifty people, dressed in ordinary street clothes, lurked at the blown doors. Four diligent door guards sprinted towards the fisted intruders. The Rasputinov high-priestess and the Mexican leader centered hands at their chest and squinted to burst bright light into the advancing prods' chests. In a half-second, the rushing sentries turned into sprinkling gray ash. Like I sniffed the same acrid odor from the night, Dmitri again died. Burnt immortal flesh had a unique tinge.

Pandemonium erupted. As I rushed the entrance, screaming civilians broke decorum and fled away from the broken doors towards the side portal. Breaking through the scattering monsters, The Companion Guards neatly lined up to block any further advance. Victor and three council members slipped from the chamber while the remaining executives hid under their stone table. While bodies clamored for survival, a thought thundered. If another plan failed, everyone but three the people wearing rings died. Those who stayed to save their kingdom understood they won ash piles, not more bedazzling for their sashes.

Nikolas was right. Victor conspired with the enemy to create an occult army and planned to attack before Vasile's loyalists wore my protective jewelry. The vindictive twat sold out his nation to guarantee power from the deaths of Vasile, and faithful supporters.

Vasile marched to the formation's front. Warriors stood shoulder to shoulder. The military force lacked the numbers. They could only strike so many mages before someone towards the rear cast a Limit Motion spell. Tight fists and compressed jaw readied the Champion of Bulgaria to swim in another battle's ash river. When civilians formed a third line behind the suicidal warriors, my chest hitched. Chancellor Simeon nodded once to the brave people who deserved a peaceful existence. The civilians' unexpected willingness to fight and the knowledge that he sent subjects to dust, bobbed Vasile's throat. Around the room, chins and fear raised when the catcalling enemies lifted their hands in unison.

The General of Bulgaria roared across the expansive marble, "Militibus, formatio!" Male and female soldiers snapped heels together and straightened their lines. Blank expressions, throbbing neck veins, and clenched fists hinted at restrained anger. Anxious dread muddied rainbow auras but never infected their eyes. Resolute willpower to annihilate their former masters flashed blood-colored pupils.

An occultist who looked like a barista, shouted, "This attack is the first among many to correct our mistake. You are mistaken." Rehearsed heated words signaled outstretched palms to raise chest level and fingers form diamonds.

"Wait!" I jumped between the opposing mobs. My dress floated around my legs when I spun in sweeping circles, and arms extended wide. I refused to watch my precious friends lost more loved ones because of another one of my plans failed.

"We deal with you like tha mother, dah? We save you for de last."

"No! We can work this out!"

General Nikola called from the front row, "Queen Regent, we will handle such matters beneath your dignity."

Circumstances never permitted me to protest.

"Now!" Grinning mages radiated bright natural light through me and into the immortal mass behind me. The ultimate battle began. Unable to watch, I buried my forehead in hands. I think I cried something aloud. After the energy ripple passed, a collective gasp hissed my ears. "How can that be! She stopped our magic!" I smelled wall torches burning, not monster flesh. I lowered my hands, opened my eyelids, and hope spun me around.

Shadows from living bodies, not dark ash, darkened the glinting marble. I raised my attention to would-be victims sneering at shocked occultists. A spell guaranteed to kill any immortal failed. The diplomats and civilians who ducked behind warriors straightened and narrowed angry eyes at the flustered attackers. Vasile whipped a dropped jaw between an unsurprised Nikola and Dmitri, then to me. Another plan hidden from Vasile worked. The general successfully distributed the rings I magically transferred to his pocket when he entered my cell. Even cheap parlor tricks come in handy for powerful queens.

"Again!" Perspiring, mouth twisting occultists raised hands once more.

General Nikolas called "Block the civilians. Heads down in the rear!"

The bright white light blasting produced only a display, and a crouched crowd stepped down from the dais and grew the ranks. Muddy auras cleared. As bewildered attackers stumbled backward, they mumbled confusion. Angry courtroom guards who wore no rings, detached from the formation, and moved behind confused mages. They locked an enemy inside a den teaming with supernatural killers who wanted justice. Revenge churned roiled ancient minds.

I thundered, "Chancellor Simeon, As Queen Regent, I authorized my people's massacre. Please leave one alive. Screwing with my friends and me ends now."

"As you so command, Queen Regent." Vasile deafened, "General!"

"Sire!"

"Your new orders."

"Aye, Sire!"

"Warriors, kill all but one!"

The room roared from lifted chins, "Aye, sir, Aye!"

Vengeful monsters chewed on revenge, not bone. Unleashed fangs popped. I stepped sideways to no longer stand between my people and Vasile's. A reasonable distance away, I winced to harness the abundant power. The Earth magic I pulled up from bedrock slammed down attackers gathered elemental energy. I castrated their magic. My helpful snake tattoo sucked any reaming power from their trembling bodies through hollow teeth. I think they groaned. My arms stretched wide while men and women begged for mercy.

Vasile jabbed a fist in the air. "Ready on the lines?!"

"Yes, Chancellor!" The deafening roar coursed through fired nerves, and to his day, the rumble still tingles my bones. Vas's lifted chin, chest puffed, and teensy smirk overflowed my bursting heart. Through my help, I witnessed a proud moment in prodigium history when Chancellor Simeon returned to rightful power.

Vasile snapped his fingers, and everything happened so fast. Dmitri and Nik joined their commander-in-chief to survey blurred dark bodies catapult towards Victor's useless mercenaries. The undead crush blocked my view, but my people's hair-raising screams reached my ears. Shrieks, dull popping, and crunches echoed the cold marble. Torches flickered. A duty to oversee my ordered execution never flinched a single muscle or flicked my eyes, despite the terrible sounds. When shrieks dissipated and invisible energy unclogged, I knew. My people died. The war ended. Or so I hoped.

Vasile's fingers again snapped, and the Companion Guards froze mid-strike. The programmed elite tapped the shoulders of the courtroom guards pounding on motionless bodies. Everyone stepped away from a pile of contorted corpses. Not a speck of blood smeared the cold marble. Neat lines of polished professionals returned to Vasile, D, and the general. Vas raised a chin towards the fearless sentries and civilians who milled about, unsure where to stand during the monumental occasion.

"Tonight, you are Companion Guards. History will remember your brave contribution." The extended top honor and praise squared shoulders and puffed chests as the immortals formed one group. From the corner of my eye, I saw two careful males link pinky fingers. Dmitri slid me a customary, discreet wink. Through silent thoughts, only best friends share, we celebrated how nobody suffered the same death as D.

When a female straightened her sash, I noticed everyone's cleanliness, and a stare dashed to an odd carnage. The fresh corpses lay strewn, limbs and necks twisted at painful angles. The warriors used hands, not fangs, to end the battle, suggesting uncracked occult bones disgusted the heartiest warrior. My people ranked beneath the 'Lowers.' Lost in revelations, a pair of standing legs across the death pile caught my attention.

Nikola wrenched the only survivor's arm as the three remaining councilmen materialized from under the dais. As the cowardly officiants stood next to the army, the general propelled the frenzied woman across the floor. Each immortal she flailed past snarled. Nik threw her to my sandaled feet, and the sniveling female landed on her hands and knees, prostrated for a proper grovel.

"Queen Regent, your survivor as ordered."

A switch flipped when the quaked mage clawed my toes. Near incoherent words pleaded for her life. A panicked expression shifted between Vasile and me as her lying lips spewed apologies. The chancellor's passive visage looked at me through a different sparkling stare. He was right. I changed. An undereducated, immature blight no longer crawled across his floor or broken pavement, but an upright woman who deserved his chest-bursting pride. But it was the weighted stares that demanded strength that stiffened me.

"Look at me." She kept her sniveling head pointed to a tear smeared floor. "I ordered you to acknowledge your queen." She wanted to harm those who were my real people, and I preferred to strangle her for it, but I needed to finish my plan.

"Ye—yes?"

"Your name."

"Reb—Rebecca Sutton."

"Of course, you are a Sutton. Rebecca, you can go—"

"Oh thank, thank you—thank—"

"—to serve me."

"Thank God! Thank you, Queen—"

"Silence!" Tight air crackled when my hard anger snapped, and breaths held fast. "Henceforth, you are my harbinger—"

"No!"

Dmitri kicked at the overwrought woman. "Quiet, hag."

"Not the harbinger curse—I beg—"

Dmitri raised a brow at a shrugging Nik.

All words ceased when I waved fingers before the begging woman's face. Her shaking hand flew to her lips. A purple muffled scream through bulged neck tendons sealed the courtroom silence. I restarted the hex. "Henceforth, you live as my harbinger. I curse thee for reporting my message to every living and dead mage. Harbinger, report the gift I gave the Nation, and if anyone harms one immortal or me, I'll unleash the undead into the day." Spectators gasped. "Do you serve me, harbinger?" I twirled a hand across her strained mouth.

"I do—I'll tell them. I'll tell everyone."

"You will?"

The young short-haired occultist near my age supplicated. "Yes!"

I displayed dominance for an appreciative crowd. "Yes, what?"

Dmitri kicked her foot once more.

"Yes—Queen Regent."

A tiny show of weakness around a cavern stuffed with prods promised future troubles, so I mixed Vasile's hard style to my flare. "Look at me." I crouched to her level. "No, I don't believe you."

"I do—I—"

"Harbinger, I curse thee with blindness."

"Please—"

My voice rose, "I curse thee, Harbinger Rebecca Sutton, until the last mage hears my declaration." Chamber lights flickered when I stood a foot back to admire my handiwork. Total power wielded some pretty cool moments. Too bad I planned the position to last only for a bit.

She screamed and clawed at her twisted face. "I can't see! Can't see!" I smirked when her hands swept hands across the floor, searching for my feet or a lifeline.

"General Nikola?"

"Yes, milady?"

"Would remove my servant? Have her dropped off at any coven house?" My callous actions and cold words won a careful glance from Vasile. The bitter side of my burnt heart wanted to give him a show to remember.

"At once, milady." Nikola motioned towards an immobile female warrior standing in the first row. The nameless soldier clicked heels together, stepped forward, then wrenched the hysterical woman from the chamber. The monster touched the screaming mage's arm as least as possible when she drug the flailing woman through the doors that she helped splinter. Before disappearing from the room, the grimacing warrior settled for an old-fashioned hair drag. The tense room relaxed when the panic-stricken echoes and kicking shoes vanished.

Vasile's loving stare of admiration tickled my skin. Like the night I won my mother's love by killed my entire coven, my hard response won Vasile's respect. I thought, 'Too late.'

"May I approach, Chancellor?" Dmitri sounded weirdly professional.

A finger flicked. Soft lights glowed a solemn boyish grin.

A sideways glance watched the imagined results born from weeks of tedious planning. My best friend took something from a councilor then walked towards Vasile. The immortal Adonis draped cloth across his stiff horizontal arms. The night-black silk, eight inches wide, glistened from swirling red, gold, and silver embroidery. Unique symbols, rich unknown significance, embellished the historic fabric. When D stood three feet before his leader, he sunk to both knees. The wild prince's head bowed as he extended the silk perfectly perpendicular to the floor. The entire structure around us and its enraptured occupants shivered. An exceptional moment of history unfolded before an honored few.

A councilman stepped from their small side cluster to stand between Vas and Dmitri. "Sire, I shall repeat the same oath you swore to The Father."

Vasile nodded once. "As you will."

"Does the Grand Duke Vasile Mihail Simeon of the Simeon family, Champion of Bulgaria, and one true son to The Father swear to uphold all sacred laws and defend the Immortal Nation against all enemies?"

"I do."

"Do you Vasile Mihail Simeon swear to keep the anonymity of this nation and citizens, lest your destruction?"

"I do."

"By the proxy power invested in me by The Great Father, eternal creator of the Immortal Nation, and its children, I pronounce you Chancellor Vasile Mihail—" The smiling white-haired councilman rose his voice higher than the erupting cheers."—Simeon, Champion of Bulgaria, and Commander-in-Chief to The Companion Guards." He took a grinning breath. "And I hope I got your favorite titles, Sire." I giggled at the ribbing.

A proud man beamed, and above raucous cheering, "The important bits, old friend."

The restored chancellor's slow hands reached for the silk still held by his son. Dmitri blinked back pink tears as Chancellor Simeon passed the delicate cloth over his perfect hair. The famous sash survived Victor's dictatorship like the British civil war, royal regalia. He adjusted the unwrinkled shiny black silk until it lay equidistant across his broad chest. A stripped-down suit transformed into the markings of an influential leader.

The prince's head lifted, and a firm fist thumped his breastbone. The entire formation and clustered civilians, who steadily filtered back inside after the battle, dropped to their knees and lowered revenant heads. Council members stood standing but worshipfully bowed their heads. When every prodigia slammed fists to proud chests, the loud thud echoed more than the ruined room. The headquarters again rang from honor, pride, and hard-won glory. As the salutes remained steadfast, hands sparkled from military insignias and daylight rings. The jewels represented me and him, forever joined but never together.

When Vasile showed solidarity and covered his heart, I swallowed past a lumpy throat. Chancellor Simeon's ardent word rumbled undefinable emotions. "Fidelitate!"

Prideful faces pointed at the ceiling, and one voice boomed, "Fidelitate, Chancellor Simeon!"

Vas raised both palms at the monster assortment, and the permission to stand jumped up the boisterous lot. Everyone released bottled relief, cheers, and suppressed feelings as a crush noisily welcome home their cherished hero. Loud shoulder slaps showed off new magical rings, and Vasile greeted long-lost friends. Excited boyish council members patted each other's arms. I caught snatches of, 'she pulled it off,' and 'heart of an immortal.' Two councilmen noticed my glow and nodded. It was not thanks but close enough.

As he started his second term, a square jaw, sparked eyes, and upright posture paraded regal joy. He celebrated life and love in a safe place with those who needed him more than me. Into memory seared smelly gas lamps, shimmered marble, celebratory laughter, and the proud man I loved. I would forever remember Vasile inside the arms of his true love, his people.

As endorphins faded, a deep tiredness weighed my mind. The moment arrived. A battle's afterglow, excitement about seeing a sunrise, and Vasile's return, kept everyone occupied while I picked around the rubble. Unnoticed, I slipped outside the shattered doors but stole another glance. Dmitri's smug look when Nikola clapped his back, paled my flushed cheek. Across the lively gathering, Nik met my watering eyes. I gulped. His brow raised as he flicked a slight nod at me past the destroyed entrance. He knew what I had to do.

I mouthed, 'Thank you.'

He slowly blinked once. A soldier clasped the general's shoulder, and he turned away.

I dashed from the courtroom, and hurried strides billowed the gauzy dress behind quick legs. I resembled a witchy Stevie Nicks music video, commanding my unwilling feet to spread space between Vasile and me. The hearty celebratory cheers and claps faded to an insignificant racket. When I piled out of the grand cathedral onto cobblestone streets, sideways rain drenched me in seconds. A run slowed to a jog. I rubbed water and soaked hair from my face to search for the ride I hired earlier.

Again, I ran my escape through a rainy night, fleeing minutes even more precious. Any second, immortals burst onto the street to hunt for the other hero and their first sunrise. But hopefully, a muttered cloaking spell ensured my successful disappearance and the next series of events. Once I reunited with Maggie, an amnesia curse promised permanent relief from terrible memories and a broken heart.

The distance between Vasile and I that started the night Dmitri died, physically grew. Every gut-wrenched walk on the slippery stones created inevitable space between us. Inches changed to meters, soon to spread into heartbreaking miles. Each trip across wet cobblestones tore thoughts to my significant life's decision, memorializing each tortured step. Shiny onyx pavers became highway mile markers along a heart's desolate road. I whispered to the stones, "Please, never let him lose another century or country because I'm not coming back."

When he resumed official duties, Chancellor Vasile Simeon would be too busy to search for me. That was okay because I could never remember the pain of his absence or neglect. A part of me wailed at our unwritten ending as a specific purpose pointed me down the barrel of a miserable life absent the man and monster I loved. Throughout the months on the run, lessons learned, hard battles, and falling in love, and I never lost a desire greater than the love for certain immortals. I wanted independence from supernatural control, including interfering Gods.

You see, women can break from love's rule and influence. Taking Maggie's advice, I planned to join the third sapien group, the humans. The defiant act might free me at the cost of never knowing true love or one that survives oceans of the universe. I laid my anguished decision upon Romania's cobblestones, too late to turn back.

One thought as I searched the wet street, broke a soft smile. But before I started my journey towards freedom, I gave my destiny's pulling threads and the puppeteer, the middle finger. The druid priestess required me to ensure The Father never awoke. But why deny Vasile closure? When he visited my cell, inside his pocket, I secreted the details of his maker's indefinite sleep and how to wake him. I prayed the child-like writing on the plain paper became his match to burn The Father's world and kept our lives separate.

I gave the shrinking dark cathedral another look. When I dashed towards a waiting cab, I smacked into a trenched coat knight, an angry rail station passenger, and a comforting friend on my bed blocked my path. Inky hair matted in rivulets and down his smooth, chiseled features as silvery red-eyed searched mine. The hard-won precious silk sash puckered.

"Vas." Dismay, shock, and hope seeped into his hissed name.

"I knew you would leave."

I unnecessarily raised my voice over honking horns and spattering rain. "How?"

"Centuries of your running."

"I'll gonna miss my—"

A hand stretched towards me. "Please, Sarah."

"—flight."

"Stay. I need your help."

"You got your army back, so go fix the world."

"They cannot help me."

"The rings should—"

"Before the sentencing, I learned a terrible secret."

"Not my problem. Look, I need to leave—"

"Sarah, what I unearthed will cost your life."

"I can protect myself. Go worried about them." I flicked eyes to the black cathedral against a lighter sky.

Vasile's white-knuckled fist ripped the sash from his chest to hold it to the rain. "This is meaningless if you are not in my world. To prove it, I shall hand it over to Dmitri."

Salty tears and the chilly dawn drizzle blended as sincere sliver, reflecting pupils flashed. We stood locked in defiant poses, ready for another epic fight until an undignified giggle escaped my lips.

"I lack the purpose of your amusement."

I slapped my mouth as a wounded gaze slowly lowered the sash. "Imagine Dmitri's swearing-in and some mega coronation."

My words infected his slow grin. "Dear God."

"I didn't work so hard to expose the Immortal Nation to a male Marie Antoinette." Laughter bridged the slashing emotional gap, and Vas closed the space between us that never really existed.

The only thing that ever mentally or physically swayed the powerful creature rushed into his endless embrace. Sturdy arms encircled me, and an unbending neck lowered him to me. Chilled hands clinched his colder cheeks. Could I find my free life inside the very eyes I scoured? The torn chancellor's sash matted to my wet cheek. Then Vasile broke character. He asked. "Stay?"

"I put something in your pocket."

"I know. Your note is part of the danger you face."

"Your return woke The Father?"

"More terrible than my creator."

"Who—"

"Not who but what. I found—"

"Hey, you kids going to frolic in the rain all day? We have work to do."

We touched foreheads, and both called "Coming Dmitri."

My best friend tossed his arms around us, and we walked towards the cathedral. "Marie Antionette was a scandalous tramp. I am more of a—Louis the fourteenth. The offices need sprucing up, maybe turn it into a mini sun palace—"

Coming 2020!
the Species Series second installment!

Sign up for the latest release information at:

www.marosabooks.net

ABOUT THE AUTHOR

M. A. Rosa is an author and freelance editor living in the North Georgia mountains with her dedicated family. Read more about M. A. at:

www.marosabooks.net